JILL BARRY

LOVE AT WAR

In the quiet Welsh town of Barry, Anna has almost
completed her business training when two high ranking
military men vie for her attention at the height of WW2

Contents

First published by Romaunce Books in 2023
Suite 2, Top Floor, 7 Dyer Street, Cirencester, Gloucestershire, GL7 2PF

A catalogue record for this book is available from the British Library

LOVE AT WAR
ISBN 978-1-7391173-3-7

Cover design and content by Ray Lipscombe
Printed and bound in Great Britain

Romaunce Books™ is a registered trademark

JILL BARRY

LOVE AT WAR

In the quiet Welsh town of Barry, Anna has almost completed her business training when two high ranking military men vie for her attention at the height of WW2

CHAPTER 1

South Wales - July 1943

'Still no letter from Pappa, Mam?'

Ruby shook her head. 'Not even a postcard, love. But you know how things are. Nothing for ages then three or four cards and letters turn up at once.'

Ruby watched Anna peer into her soup and gave her a wry smile. 'Oh, for a meal like the one I made that time your pappa arrived home unexpectedly for Christmas. I remember he brought beefsteak and I fried onion rings with it, until they were caramelised. He opened a bottle of wine even though there were still a few days to go before Christmas.'

Anna did remember, even though she'd been a child. She and her mother had returned from a walk to find her father back from sea. She could still picture the way he pulled pins from her mother's glossy, dark hair so it tumbled around her face.

'Pappa always says they make much more of the festive season in Norway than we do here. He still calls it Jul, doesn't he?'

Ruby looked up as the doorbell split the silence. 'Who's that, I wonder?'

'You won't know unless you open the door, Mam. Shall I go?'

'No, it's all right.' Ruby laid down her spoon.

Anna noticed her mother swiftly check her appearance in the mirror hanging above the fireplace, patting her hair as she went. Left alone, Anna fleetingly wondered if her father had arrived, having mislaid his door key, but waited while Ruby opened the door.

Her mother's memories of that special welcome home meal for her seafaring husband, matched Anna's. That same night, as a nine-year-old listening outside her parents' bedroom door, she overheard Viktor telling her mother a baby sister or brother would be good for Anna, and though she waited for some sign of this new arrival, no new sibling ever arrived.

Now she heard the creak of the front door opening, and her mother responding to whoever had called. Then, startled out of her wits, Anna leaped from her seat as she heard her mother wailing as if someone was tearing out her heart.

'Mam? What is it?' Anna hurried into the passageway.

A telegraph boy stood on the front doorstep, looking as though this was the last place he wanted to be. Ruby, clutching a telegram, pushed past her daughter and rushed upstairs.

'I'm sorry, Miss,' said the lad, blushing beetroot red. 'I know the lady's had bad news. I ... I'm glad she's not alone.' He pulled off his hat, bowing his head before hurrying off.

Anna closed the door, ran up the stairs and into her mother's bedroom where dust motes danced in a ray of sunshine beaming through the window. Ruby sat in the dainty chintz-covered chair beside the big double bed. Eyes closed; she held a framed photograph of her seafaring husband close to her heart.

Anna dropped to her knees beside her. 'Come on, Mam. Talk to me. Tell me what's happened.' She couldn't bear to ask the dreaded question. Every family whose menfolk were away from home feared the knock announcing delivery of a telegram.

Her mother opened her eyes. 'I have to travel to Scotland. To a place called Invergordon. Your pappa ...' She swallowed. 'He's been taken to hospital there. He's not expected to pull through.' Ruby replaced the photograph on the small table nearby, so the handsome, golden-haired Norwegian smiled back at his wife and daughter.

Anna buried her face in her mother's lap. She felt Ruby's fingers smoothing her hair and wondered why neither of them was shedding tears. Might this be the effect shock produced?

'I'll need to set off as soon as possible,' Ruby said.

Anna raised her head. 'I'll come with you. I want to see Pappa.'

'No, lovey, I really think it's best you stay with Nana, unless you prefer to be here. It's a long way to travel and I have to think of the cost. Besides, I don't want you missing business school. I'll need to pack and, oh, goodness, I must tell Mr Mapstone I shan't be available for a while.'

Anna's thoughts were whirling. She so wanted to see her dad, but realised the sense in what her mother said. Ruby would require a taxi to the station and their landlord would probably be offended if he wasn't asked to help. She suspected Mr Mapstone had more than a soft spot for her mother, but this was no time for such thoughts. 'Shall I go and tell him? Write a note for me to take if you prefer.'

Ruby still seemed dazed. 'That'd be a great help.'

'I'd rather stay with Nana while you're away – if she'll have me.'

'Do you feel up to calling on her after you've seen Mr Mapstone?'

Anna nodded.

'Well, be sure and break the news gently, won't you? She'll probably say where there's life there's hope. And when you come back, you'll need to pack a suitcase too. Thank you, love.'

Anna made her way to Frank Mapstone's house, where she used the big brass doorknocker her mother

4

kept gleaming. He didn't respond but after she knocked a second time, he appeared around the side of the house, wearing a green baize apron over his grey trousers and white shirt, and clutching a trowel in one hand.

'Anna, my dear girl, is everything all right? Is your mother ...'

She shook her head. 'I'm sorry to disturb you, Mr Mapstone, but we've received bad news.' She held out the note. 'My mother has written to explain.'

He dropped his trowel with a clang and took the envelope, ripping it open and scanning it in moments.

'I'm so very sorry.' He met Anna's gaze. 'Where there's life, there's hope, so don't despair, my dear.'

'Thank you. We – that is I – wondered if you'd like me to do some housework for you, while my mother's away. I wouldn't be as efficient as she is, of course, but I could come after I finish my college sessions.' Anna stood, watching the landlord's solemn face and wondered if he'd heard one word of what she said.

'Um, yes, of course, you're at business school, aren't you? Well actually, I'm wondering whether your mother would allow me to drive her to Scotland. What do you think?'

Anna had often read of fictional jaws dropping when fictional people received a shock, but this was her first experience of the real-life phenomenon. 'I'm sure my mother wouldn't expect you to drive her all that distance. Not that it isn't very kind of you, of course.'

'Anna, your mother has become more to me than merely my tenant and housekeeper. Do you understand what I'm saying?'

Although Anna disliked what he was implying, she met his gaze. 'My mother's devastated by this news, Mr Mapstone.'

'I know ... I know. I should say that I count both your parents among my friends, and please trust me when I say that as a friend, I shall take the utmost care of your mother. We'll break the journey and stay in a hotel en route so Ruby doesn't arrive exhausted as well as concerned for Viktor. I'd set off this evening were it not for the damned blackout, but will you tell her I shall collect her tomorrow morning at six o'clock, ready to start the journey? And don't worry about the housekeeping. Your mother makes sure the place is immaculate and it won't hurt if it's left for a few days.'

Anna hurried to her grandmother's and pushed open the back door, not looking forward to giving her news.

'Nana,' she called. 'It's only me.'

Her grandmother emerged from the pantry, brandishing a bunch of carrots, still earthy from the allotment. 'Anna! What's up, hen?'

Anna knew better than to rush into her arms. Her Scottish-born nana shied away from displays of affection and Anna still stood, wondering how best to begin, until her grandmother shook her head.

'Come on then, my girl. Out with it.'

'Could we sit down, please, Nana? I need to tell you something important.'

Her grandmother pursed her lips but nodded. 'What a palaver! Well, I could do with taking the weight off my feet.' She dumped the carrots on the draining board and led the way up the two steps into the living room to take her usual seat beside the kitchen range, black-leaded and shiny, only left unlit in the unlikely event of a Mediterranean summer.

Anna sat opposite on the ancient maroon chesterfield, ankles crossed and hands clasped in her lap. She focused on the vase of bright orange marigolds on the table.

'Well? It's no good you waiting for your granddad. He's gone back to the allotment.'

'It's not good news, I'm afraid, but it's not the worst,' she said before explaining about her father.

Her nana listened in silence, her back ramrod straight. 'Will you go with your mother?'

Anna shook her head. 'I wanted to, but Mam says I mustn't miss my lessons.'

'She's right. You'd be foolish to waste money now that course is paid for. Will you manage in the house on your own, or would you rather come here?'

Anna felt relieved. 'I'd rather come here, Nana, if you're sure you don't mind.'

'Wouldn't have asked if I didn't want you here, my girl! You can earn your keep by helping with the hens and you'll need to make up the bed in the spare bedroom.'

'I'll do that tomorrow, then.' Anna got to her feet. 'I must go home now. I'll put some things in a suitcase ready for the morning as Mam's leaving first thing.'

'Don't pack too much if you're carrying your case on your own and make sure your mother gives you a house key in case you've forgotten something.' She paused. 'She'll need a taxi to the station. I wonder if she could drop you off first. I'm always up with the lark.'

Anna nodded, deciding not to confide their landlord's offer. 'Maybe she will. If not, I'm sure I'll manage.'

'Tell your mother I'm sorry to hear things aren't good for Viktor and that I'll be praying for him.'

'I will.' On an impulse, Anna darted across and dared to kiss her grandmother's wrinkled cheek. Aware how the old lady scorned sentiment, she felt a pang to see tears welling before Nana hauled up her apron and scrubbed it over her face.

'Away with you now. We'll see you tomorrow.'

CHAPTER 2

'Anna? Wake up, love. It's just turned five o'clock.' Ruby perched on the bed while Anna sat up, rubbing her eyes. 'I know it's early, but I don't want us to keep Mr Mapstone waiting and I'll be happier if we can drop you off first.'

Anna nodded. 'Did you get much sleep?'

Ruby shrugged. 'I drifted in and out, thinking of your father all those miles away, up there in hospital.'

Anna had no idea what was wrong with her father, nor did she think her mother would know until she could speak to whoever was looking after him.

'You didn't want to talk about it yesterday,' she said, 'but I'm pleased Mr Mapstone's driving you. He must think a lot of you.'

'I think he's a lonely man.' Ruby stroked a lock of Anna's blonde hair back from her face.

'Mr Mapstone has just the one son and I've never heard him mention any brothers or sisters.' Ruby looked down at her hands. 'I – I think he's very kind-hearted, but I'd prefer you not to tell anyone he's driving me to

Scotland. I've been thinking about it and it's best if he drops you just around the corner rather than outside your grandparents' house.'

Anna saw the anxiety in her mother's eyes and nodded. Unless her nana was upstairs, curtain-twitching at the front bedroom window, she couldn't possibly see any comings and goings.

'If your grandmother asks whether you came by taxi, you won't mind telling a little white lie, will you? She's such a stickler for everything being right and proper. Not that I've anything to be ashamed of.'

'I can say you didn't want to come in and say goodbye because you were afraid it would be too upsetting. That won't be a lie, will it? And I'll ask Nana if I can take my things upstairs and make the bed up before I walk to the college.'

'That would do very well indeed.'

During her day at the business school, Anna's thoughts drifted to her mother, though she tried her best to concentrate on her studies. She had enjoyed learning to type and unravel the art of shorthand writing, a skill she found fascinating. Her tutor, Miss Ring, a woman whose fiancé had perished in the mud and mayhem of World War One, expected nothing but the best from her students, all of whom were progressing well. She seemed ancient to Anna, but according to Ruby, Miss Ring was in her forties. That still seemed old to a girl of seventeen.

Miss Ring called Anna to stay behind while her

classmates were leaving at the end of the afternoon session. A student who often walked part of the way home with Anna looked enquiringly at her, but seeing their tutor's expression, called a quick goodbye and left, closing the door behind her.

'Miss Christensen, forgive me, but is there something wrong? Your mind has not been totally focused today, has it?' Miss Ring sat down at her big desk. 'Take a seat in the front row, please.'

Anna did as she was bid. 'I'm very sorry, Miss Ring. I've tried my best to concentrate, but I keep thinking of my mother, travelling all the way to Scotland. I've no idea where she might be by now or where they ... where she'll be staying the night.'

'Is your mother visiting family? You wanted to go but couldn't, because of your studies?'

'I would like to have gone, but she didn't want me to miss my lessons. Even though my father's very ill in hospital.'

Miss Ring sucked in her breath. 'I'm so sorry, my dear. No wonder you're not your usual self. Is there someone at home with you?'

Anna thought how strange it was, hearing her tutor speak so informally. 'I'm staying with my grandparents until my mother returns. She said she'd ring my grandma's neighbour to let us know how things were. They have a telephone and they don't mind coming to fetch me.'

'I'll remember your father in my prayers, Anna.'

Miss Ring cleared her throat and pushed her spectacles back on. 'On another matter, I have here a letter from the Special Reconnaissance Department at the docks.' She looked up. 'The SRD is recruiting for a forthcoming vacancy in their offices. We have in the past sent girls who've graduated to be interviewed for positions there. If all goes well for you with your exams, I shall recommend you as my first choice. I hope this will provide some small comfort to you and your mother at this time.'

Anna swallowed hard. 'My goodness! Thank you very much, Miss Ring. I'll do my best to achieve good marks.'

'I know you will, my dear. And remember, while you're one of my best students, it is only you who can achieve the required standard allowing me to put your name forward for interview.'

Anna nodded. 'I understand.'

'If they offer you a position, you will start work in July. Now, you'd best get back to your grandmother.' Miss Ring hesitated. 'Despite the sadness behind your stay, she must be delighted to have her granddaughter with her.'

Anna noticed the wistful expression in her tutor's eyes and quietly left the room with only a whispered, 'Goodbye.'

CHAPTER 3

Next evening, Anna fed the hens their pungent mash of bran and scraps, and lingered outside, admiring the deep pink peonies her grandmother cultivated, despite most of the backyard being taken up with the chickens. She was bending to sniff one particularly beautiful bloom when she heard a voice call over the garden wall.

'Hey shrimp! Haven't seen you for a while.'

Startled, Anna straightened up and looked across at the boy next door, immediately noting his changed appearance. Davy wore a pair of dark blue overalls; his hair was cut neatly and he'd lost his gangly frame. The most important change was his voice. She remembered it as quite hoarse, sometimes even squeaky, but now when he spoke, she heard a deep, rich tone that touched something within her, creating a sensation she found pleasing as well as puzzling. Davy sounded like a man, no longer the cheeky lad she remembered.

'I notice you still can't remember my name.'

He grinned. 'I do so, Miss Anna Christensen. Where

have you been hiding yourself?'

'I've been working hard. I'm studying at Miss Ring's Business College.'

'There's posh! Keeps your nose to the grindstone, does she?'

'If I pass my exams, it'll be well worth it. I can't wait to get a job and start earning my own money.'

Davy gave her a long, hard look. 'Good for you. I don't earn much, but I'm apprenticed to a motor engineer and I want to own my own garage one day.'

'It sounds as if we're both ambitious, then.'

'Yes, even me with my valleys accent!' He looked anywhere but at her. 'I was wondering if you'd fancy a walk with me after tea? These fine evenings, see ... if we cut through the town, we can get down to the beach quicker.'

'I daren't go out in case my mother rings Nana's friend across the street. My dad's seriously ill in hospital and Mam's gone to him. I'm staying here while she's away.'

'My God,' Davy exclaimed in Welsh. 'I'd no idea. Where's he to, then?'

'At the hospital in Invergordon. It's a seaport on the west coast of Scotland.'

'That's a way to go.'

'Hundreds of miles,'

'I'll have to ask you again, then. I'm expecting my call up papers soon. Will you come out with me before I leave?'

She blinked hard, suddenly stricken with guilt. 'Um, I need to find out how my dad is. And my granddad's very strict.'

'He chats away when he sees me out here. It's not like I'm a stranger.'

Anna turned her head as she heard her grandmother calling. 'I must go. Enjoy your walk.'

'Will you come out with me if I'm still here when you're back with your ma? Please, say yes!'

She hesitated; conscious Davy was still watching. He wasn't her ideal choice for a boyfriend, but he was leaving home soon, and most importantly, she needed to practise her non-existent flirting skills on some unsuspecting male.

'I suppose it'll be all right.'

She stopped again as he called after her. 'I hope your dad gets better soon. Maybe see you tomorrow?'

'Maybe.'

The following day dawned grey and chilly for mid-June. After college, Anna went back to her own house, finishing a pile of ironing her mother hadn't had time to tackle.

Preparing to leave, she noticed a thick drizzle had set in so she took Ruby's big black umbrella and walked quickly to her nana's. She headed up the lane leading to the back door and, turning the corner, almost collided with a tall young man.

'There's a bit of luck,' Davy said, pulling off his cap. 'Can I shelter under your umbrella, Miss?'

'You should put your cap back on now it's raining heavier. My tea will be on the table soon.'

'I'm going down the road to get us fish and chips. Ma's round at my auntie's and I've no idea where my dad is.'

'Well, don't let me stop you.' Anna couldn't understand why Davy's mother wasn't at home cooking tea for her family. Ruby and Anna's grandmother would be scandalised at the idea.

But without checking if anyone was approaching, Davy wrapped his fingers round the hand clutching the umbrella handle. 'I dream about kissing you, Anna.' He was looking at her mouth. 'Will you let me? Please?'

Contrary to the story she'd fabricated to tell her friend Margaret, Anna didn't yet know how it felt to be kissed on the lips by a boy. But if anyone should come along and catch them canoodling, she knew she would die of shame.

He seemed to read her mind. 'Nobody wants to come out in this weather,' he murmured, pressing closer. 'Nobody will see.'

She felt his hand on her back and swayed towards him, her face almost touching his. Davy felt solid against her. Comforting. He bent his head and when their mouths met, the softness of his lips surprised her.

Moments later, he released her. 'I wish this war wasn't …'

Anna was struggling with her emotions. This boy her mother disapproved of, generated a sensation both

16

worrying and strangely wonderful. Unsure what came next, she wrenched the umbrella from Davy's hand. 'I must go now.'

'You're cross,' he said, jamming his cloth cap back on his head. 'I'm sorry, but if you only knew how often I've thought about you ...'

'Don't be daft,' she said. 'I'm not cross. Here, you'd better take my umbrella or you'll come back like a drowned rat. Leave it in the shed so I can collect it in the morning.'

She turned and ran the rest of the way. But that kiss stayed with her and her thoughts only turned to other matters later, after her mother's telephone call.

Anna followed her nana and the neighbour across the road after the knock on the door.

'I'll have a word first then hand you the phone,' Nana said as they went through the front door. The telephone sat on a small mahogany table with barley-sugar twist legs, its receiver lying on a crisp white lace doily.

'Are you there, Ruby?' Anna's grandma bellowed into the instrument, obliging Anna to stifle an inappropriate fit of the giggles.

The elderly woman frowned as she listened, while Anna waited impatiently for her turn. She watched her grandma's face, realised something was very wrong and, knowing the way her parents felt about each other, began praying in silence. Praying that all would be right and her mother would soon return home, leaving her father to recuperate and come back to them for a holiday before joining his next ship.

After what seemed an eternity, Nana handed over the telephone with a whispered, 'Now, my girl, for your mother's sake, try and be brave.'

Pappa's gone then. Oh, poor Mam. Anna grasped the receiver.

'Hello, darling girl.' Ruby's voice sounded husky. 'I wish I didn't have to give you bad news, but I imagine you've guessed by now. I'm afraid it's all over, lovey. We shall both need to be very brave.'

Anna closed her eyes. 'When did he ...was Pappa still ...'

'Your father knew I was there. He squeezed my hand and whispered to me.' Ruby gulped.

Anna knew her mother was struggling to keep her composure. 'I'm so sorry, Mam. But I'm pleased he managed to speak to you.'

'He told me he loved us both and he asked me to tell you he was sorry.'

'Sorry for what?'

'I don't know. There was no time to ask. The nurse was very fierce and shooed me out.'

'But that's terrible! After you travelled all that way?'

'I think she was trying to do her best for her patient, but whatever it was that affected your dad's system was too powerful in the end. There are formalities to deal with.' Ruby paused. 'Frank ... Mr Mapstone has kindly agreed to remain here with me until everything's dealt with. I'll ring and leave a message so you'll know when I'll be coming home.'

Anna heard her mother's shuddery intake of breath.

'I'm so sorry, my darling,' Ruby said. 'Is college going well?'

'Very well. You mustn't worry about me.'

'If you don't feel like going in tomorrow, I'm sure Miss Ring would understand.'

'I think Pappa would've wanted me to keep going, don't you?'

Silence. 'You're right, Anna. Yes, Vik would be proud of your courage and how well you're getting on. Now, I must go. Mr Mapstone insists I try and eat something ...' Her voice trailed off.

'That's wise. Will he bring you to Nana's or back home?'

'Straight home is best, I think.'

'I'll see you then, Mam. After ... when everything's been dealt with.' She gulped. 'Please give my regards to Mr Mapstone and – and thank him from me for looking after you.'

CHAPTER 4

Anna's routine helped the days pass.

Ruby returned and once mother and daughter were on their own, they fell into each other's arms, giving way to a deluge of tears. Ruby looked washed out, apparently not bothering with her usual face powder and rouge, and Anna knew her mother mut be finding difficulty in sleeping.

As she'd grown old enough to sense these things, Anna used to feel her father's energy and vibrant presence filling the house whenever he returned from a lengthy voyage. Her mind kept returning to the apology her mother mentioned and she wondered whether he regretted being unable to take a bigger part in her upbringing. Maybe he thought there might have been a sister or brother for her, if he'd been at home more.

But he'd made the sea his career and his unusual gifts and tales of faraway ports brought sunshine and magic into her childhood. It would be odd without the big blond man turning up every now and then, capsizing the dynamics of their quiet existence.

The morning of her interview for the typing pool, Anna washed in the scullery and put her dressing gown back on to run upstairs and get dressed in a smart blouse and two-piece costume. She left the house with plenty of time to spare and walked the mile or so to the supply depot; a large stone building overlooking the docks and whose entrance reminded her of a house illustration for a Charles Dickens novel, complete with ornate brass plate on the wall beside the door.

Inside, she was directed to a waiting room where she perched on a wooden bench, both hands gripping the leather strap of her handbag, her gas mask in its holder beside her. Inside her bag was a letter from Mr Williams of the corner shop, confirming her as a young lady of impeccable character and pleasant disposition. She knew Miss Ring had already provided details of Anna's examination results as well as a character reference.

A dark-haired girl entered the room shortly after Anna arrived. She caught a whiff of *Californian Poppy* as the newcomer sat down beside her, wasting no time in introducing herself.

'My name's Biddy O'Brien. Are we after getting the same job? Shorthand typist?'

Anna nodded. 'I imagine so. Pleased to meet you, Biddy. I'm Anna Christensen.'

'Not a Welsh name between the pair of us! Pleased to

meet you too, Anna, even if we are rivals.' Her brown eyes twinkled.

'Well, good luck anyway, Biddy. May the best girl win.'

'Tell you what, why don't you wait for me afterwards, then we can go for a cup of tea and compare notes? If you can spare time, of course.'

'Miss Christensen?'

Anna jumped to her feet. 'Yes, that's me.'

A thin brunette, dressed in a pale blue blouse and dark grey skirt, ticked off a name on her clipboard. 'Follow me, please.'

Anna turned towards Biddy. 'I'll wait for you outside,' she whispered.

'Lovely. Good luck to you too. Ooh, better take your gas mask.'

The brunette shooed Anna through the door to the interview room. In front of the window looking out over the dockyard two people sat, straight-backed, behind a dark wood table.

'Do sit down, Miss Christensen.' The woman wore her fair hair in a neat chignon. 'My name is Miss Napier and I'm the Office Supervisor. This gentleman is Mr Taylor.'

The man, consulting a sheet of paper on the table before him, glanced up and nodded.

'Can you tell us why you wish to work here?' Miss Napier removed her horn-rimmed spectacles.

'I'm anxious to gain experience of working in an office

and Miss Ring felt I was ready to apply for a job with you.'

'Your shorthand and typing skills more than meet the required standard and we hear you're a good timekeeper. Is that so, Miss Christensen?' Mr Taylor spoke this time and Anna, noticing how his scrubby, grey moustache quivered, tried not to let her lips quiver in sympathy.

'I've never once been late for college, sir.'

'Do you work well under pressure?'

Anna hesitated.

'If there were last minute changes required to a report, for example?' Miss Napier nodded at her, as if urging her on.

'I ... I'd do my best, just as I did when we were given speed tests in our lessons.'

She watched the two exchange glances.

'I'd like to dictate a letter,' said Mr Taylor. 'Then we'll ask you to go to the typing pool and transcribe your shorthand notes. If you should make an error whilst typing, please don't attempt to correct it.'

His colleague pushed a lined notepad across the table. 'Help yourself to a pen or pencil from the pot.'

Anna detected a slight smile of sympathy upon the supervisor's face.

'Honest to God, my teeth were chattering, but there was such a clatter from all the other typewriters, I don't think anyone noticed.'

Anna sat back in her chair and smiled at her new friend.

She'd never visited this café before and was enjoying the change of scenery.

Biddy was shaking her head. 'I don't think I stand a chance. When I went in, Mr Taylor asked me where my gas mask was. To think I'd reminded you just before! And my fingers turned into sausages as soon as I began typing. He must think I'm a numbskull. Anyway, I bet they offer you the job.'

'I wouldn't be too sure. I made two mistakes in that letter. The girl who arrived while you were still in the typing pool looked a right Miss Goody Two Shoes. They'll probably appoint her.'

'Let's hope there's more than one position available.' Biddy glanced towards the counter with its display of cakes beneath glass domes. 'I could fancy a slice of gingerbread, how about you?'

'Good idea. I reckon we deserve it after that ordeal.' Anna caught the waitress's attention and gave their order.

'While I think of it, Biddy, could we exchange addresses? It'd be nice to keep in touch, in case we don't make it to the typing pool.'

'I'd like that.'

Anna opened her handbag. 'I have a little notebook here.'

'You see!' Biddy laughed. 'Won't you make the perfect secretary one day?'

'That's what I'm aiming for. Do you realise, if we got jobs in the docks' office, we wouldn't be called up at eighteen because the work is of national importance? Although, that doesn't mean you couldn't volunteer for one of the women's services.'

'But why would anyone want to if they were working here? You might get sent anywhere.'

Anna looked Biddy in the eye. 'I wouldn't want to leave my mother on her own, but one day, who knows where I might go?' Briefly, she explained to her new friend the circumstances around her father.

'That's so sad.' Biddy shook her head. 'I can see why you want to stay with your ma. Are you courting? I bet you are.'

Anna hesitated.

'Is it a secret?'

'I suppose it must be, if even I don't know about it.'

Biddy laughed. 'I don't believe you.'

'Well, I've known Davy since I was fourteen and I suppose he's the nearest I've ever come to having a boyfriend, but I'm not going to tie myself to anyone. Not yet anyway.'

'I love reading romances,' Biddy gazed into the distance through the lace-curtained window and beyond the scattering of chattering customers. 'Imagine a handsome man falling for you, desperate to win your hand in marriage.' She smiled dreamily.

Anna sipped her tea. 'Well, if that led to washing his smelly socks and drawers and having his children, no, thank you very much!'

Biddy's eyebrows shot upwards. 'You're a cool customer. You're also far too pretty to be a spinster all your life, so put that in your pipe and smoke it.'

'You're very pretty yourself, even with that crumb on your lip.' Anna sat back, smiling at her new friend as Biddy dabbed at her mouth with a handkerchief. 'I bet you beat me to the altar, no trouble.'

'I thought you didn't fancy being married?'

'I suppose what I really mean is, I could never marry someone like Davy. I know he's sweet on me and I don't want to hurt his feelings, but that's as far as it goes.'

'Poor lad! So, what kind of man would you like to marry then, Lady Anna?'

'It wouldn't be for ages yet, but someone who has a really good job. A man who'd never treat me as though I was stupid. Someone who'd love me for ever and never treat me like a drudge. I sound like a snob, don't I?'

Biddy's expression changed. 'No. Some men do treat women badly, don't they? I hope your father didn't ...'

'No! Not at all. My father always treated my mother like a lady.'

It felt refreshing to exchange views with someone she'd never met before, but as she spoke, Anna felt a rippling sensation down her spine. When the time came, if the war was still on, how could she possibly hope to meet a man with class?

Some days later, Anna and her old friend Margaret left the cinema, chatting about *Penny Serenade*, the film they'd just watched.

'I'm so glad you wrote and suggested meeting up, Anna. You could have asked your new friend to go with you.'

'To be honest, I wish Mam could have joined us too, but she's not interested in anything these days and I didn't want to miss Cary Grant. I know you love him as much as I do.'

'He's super, but he's also ancient!' Her friend giggled.

'He's in his late thirties, Marg. A man of the world.'

'Come on, he's old enough to be your father.' Margaret clapped her hand over her mouth. 'Oh, I'm so sorry, Anna. I didn't mean to …'

'It's all right. It's far worse for Mam. They were married when she was eighteen and Pappa was twenty-two. He was only forty when he died in that hospital.'

'It was far too young to die. My father said it was extremely unlucky that Captain Christensen fell ill at sea. If he could have been taken to hospital sooner, he might well have been saved.'

'It was almost all over by the time Mam got to his bedside.' Anna hesitated. 'She told me he opened his eyes and looked at her when she took hold of his hand. It was as though he'd been waiting to say goodbye.'

Margaret bit her lip. 'I know I have to get used to people dying once I start nursing, but it must be so much more difficult when it's the person you love.'

'I suppose so.'

'Brrr, it's turning chilly.' Margaret looped her arm through her friend's. 'You must miss your father, even though he was away so much?'

'Of course. We got on really well. When I was little and stupid, I sometimes used to get cross about him coming home because he seemed to take all Mam's attention. I think I must've been very precocious back then.'

'What's changed?'

Anna chuckled. 'I refuse to comment.'

'Your father was very handsome, wasn't he? I couldn't help seeing his photograph when Ma brought me to your house after he … after your mother came back from Scotland. She noticed it as well, because later, I heard her telling my auntie that your father had film star good looks. You must have inherited the way you look from both of them – no wonder you get the boys after you. I should be jealous, really.'

'Whatever for? You're very pretty, Marg.'

'You're just saying that to please me!'

'I'm not. Really, I'm not. I remember that time you came to our house, you told Mam you still wanted to be a nurse. You've been saying that ever since we were playing with dolls.'

Margaret nodded. 'My father still isn't convinced I'll make a go of it, but I want to show him I can. Blood, bedpans and whatever else they throw at me!'

'Well let's hope they don't hit you.'

Margaret laughed. 'Anyway, how about you? Are you

enjoying your new job?'

'I've only been there a week. I like the work actually, but I can't say I enjoy being in the typing pool with all those other girls. Except for Biddy. You'd like her, Marg.'

'You never know – if you keep on doing good work, they might promote you one of these days.'

'I know I have to be patient.'

'Still, I'm glad you've found someone you get on with. I've palled up with a girl who's waiting to start her nurse training too. Her mother knows mine through the WVS.'

'That's good. Anyway, I may be only one of a dozen girls in the typing pool, but I'm determined to become secretary to someone important one day.'

'I'd just like to begin my nurse training,' Margaret said.

'When will you know if you're accepted?'

'Soon, I think. I'm eighteen just before you are and if I have a starting date, I can count the days down while I'm trotting round after Ma.' She squinted up at the big clock above the municipal building on the town square. 'My father's collecting me from your house at half seven.'

'We have plenty of time.' Anna gazed at the stars. 'You wouldn't think there was a war on, looking at that sky. Do you ever worry about being bombed?'

'Doesn't everyone? Especially after the awful attacks on London and other big cities.'

'I try not to think about it. We'd have to be really unlucky here, wouldn't we? They cop it in Cardiff much worse than we do.'

'We still never know what the enemy's up to though. My father says when the bombers come up the Channel, they usually go for Cardiff or on to Bristol.'

Anna shivered. 'We just have to keep hoping, don't we?'

'What about that boy you told me about? The one that's fallen for you?'

'Davy? What about him?'

'Has he joined up yet?'

'It won't be long.'

'Will you write to him once he's gone?'

'Of course not. It'd be cruel to get his hopes up.'

'You like him kissing you though, don't you?'

'It's good practice for the next one.'

'Anna – you bad girl! Surely you don't mean that?'

'But I do! When I meet someone really special, I want him to think I'm sophisticated, not scared to let him near me.'

Margaret stopped walking. They were almost at the bottom of the hill leading to Anna's house. 'But you wouldn't let a boy do the things married people do with each other, would you?'

Anna hesitated. 'It's wartime …'

CHAPTER 5

September 1943

Captain Charles Milburn drove his kingfisher-blue sportsman's coupé along the promenade and parked it at the end, opposite a small café. He sat for a while, watching the waves frothing over the sand, then took out a gold case and helped himself to a cigarette, which he lit with a slender gold lighter.

For a moment, he balanced the lighter in the palm of his hand, gazing at the words engraved upon it – *To my darling Charlie with love from Pearl* – before putting it away and winding down the window while he enjoyed his nicotine blast. Pearl had been an absolute delight until the silly girl pulled a fast one. He'd always made sure to take precautions, except for that one time when she'd turned up at his parents' house while they were away on holiday and he was caught out.

He'd been powerless to resist the little minx. Nor was

he convinced she'd done her sums right when, weeks later, she insisted he must be the father of the child she carried. He still believed she'd discovered she was in the family way and deliberately set him up.

Things had been sorted out, thanks to one of his many useful contacts. It had been a pity, but the more Pearl pleaded, the more he'd distanced himself. Even now, he still resented having had to fork out his cash to clear up some other chap's muddle.

Charles shrugged. Back home, he had a fiancée who worshipped him and, meanwhile, there were plenty of other willing fish in the sea. He got out of his car, locked the driver's door and strolled across to the café. The attractive brunette behind the counter glanced up from polishing cutlery as the jangling bell heralded his approach.

'Hello, Janice.' He walked up to the counter, giving her his David Niven smile.

'Captain Milburn, I do declare. Turning up like the proverbial bad penny. Your usual, sir?'

'Please. I'll take the window table.' He smiled to himself as he made for his favourite seat. He'd noticed Janice's hand trembling as she patted away a stray curl. She'd missed him all right. And if her old man was still sweating out the war in Burma, Charles might well be in for a cosy evening à deux once she locked the café door for the night. Life was good for a man like him, despite Hitler's machinations. He'd got himself a pretty cushy number and intended taking full advantage of it while he could.

The moment Janice arrived at his table bearing a pot of tea and two toasted teacakes, he caught a whiff of her perfume, floral yet spicy, and felt the familiar thrust of desire. She began arranging paraphernalia on the table. Pretty daisy-splashed cup and saucer, round white teapot and squat stainless-steel jug. No sugar lumps. She'd remembered.

'How was your trip?'

'Far too many meetings and tedious evening drinking sessions with fellow-officers who also drive desks. Did I mention the air raids? We don't know we're born, here.'

She frowned. 'We shouldn't get complacent and nor should you talk yourself down. The Army needs educated fellows like you to organise things.'

'You're a sweetheart,' Charles said. 'I've missed you, Jan. A lot.' He dropped his gaze so it rested on the swell of her breasts beneath the utilitarian apron bib. The tip of his tongue flicked the edge of his top lip. 'Any chance of you keeping a lonely soldier company later?'

She swallowed hard. 'I've missed you too, Charlie. Shall we say eight o'clock? Leave your car in the next street and come round to the back door. That time you forgot and parked out front, the old dear next door couldn't wait to shove her teeth back in and blab to the neighbours about my fancy man.'

He grinned. 'But telling her I was in the same unit as your husband was a good idea, darling. I need to return to base and sort out my accommodation so eight-ish will suit me fine. Go away for five minutes and they change things round. Even in a bloody tented camp.'

Janice stiffened. 'I hope you're not getting any ideas about staying overnight, Charlie – whether I say you're mate of my Ronald or not.'

He watched her shimmy back behind the counter as a couple of customers entered. He'd reassure her later, sweet talk her and reward her with a pair of nylon stockings from his secret stash. This clandestine relationship suited him well. A married woman was a far better bet than a girl with stars in her eyes because you were the first man wanting to pop her cherry. Janice was always clued up in one vital quarter. No fears of unwanted pregnancy when he was with the curvaceous café owner. And she enjoyed his visits as much as he enjoyed gracing her with his attentions. He'd wandered into the café soon after arriving at the camp two months before and, well, wasn't he keeping a fellow soldier's wife from becoming too forlorn in her husband's absence?

She didn't let him down. That evening, Janice answered his knock at the back door, wearing a frumpy dressing gown; in case it had been a neighbour calling, she explained. As soon as she bolted the door behind him, she shucked off her robe and stood there, wearing the black lace bra, French knickers, fishnet stockings and suspender belt he'd bought for her after they first began their meetings.

'Lord, but you smell good enough to eat.' He wound his arms around her and nuzzled the top of her head. She stood on tiptoe and whispered in his ear. He followed her upstairs to the spare room where she lay down on the ancient double bed, laughing up at him while he bent over her, feeling her expert fingers undoing his buttons.

'Your face! You look like an eager schoolboy about to get his sweetie ration!'

He was too much of a gentleman to remind her he was several years younger than she. He didn't ever experience a twinge of guilt at being between the sheets with a fellow soldier's wife. Janice could do that to him ... make him forget everything save her hungry mouth, those talented fingers and her husky voice driving him insane with provocative words.

They lay there afterwards, wet with sweat, recovering their breath enough for him to light a cigarette apiece. Charles hopped out of bed and fetched a half bottle of brandy he'd wrapped in a brown paper bag. They took turns to drink from it until he screwed the top back and put it on the rickety bedside table.

The rest of the evening was surreal. Janice had rolled away from his embrace eventually, picking up a black satin kimono to cover her lush contours.

'Your husband's a lucky son of a gun.' Charles gave her a lazy smile, propping himself up on one elbow.

He realised he'd said the wrong thing because she went downstairs at once, leaving him to get dressed.

When he joined her, Janice was sitting at the kitchen table, a glass of water before her.

'Night-night, sweetheart, I'll be off now.' Charles dropped a kiss on her forehead. 'I didn't mean to make you feel guilty and I humbly apologise if I upset you.' He cupped her face between his hands, watching her expression.

She blinked hard. 'I haven't heard from Ronald for ages. And here we are – you and I having it off in his bed while he's stuck in some godforsaken place. I hate this bloody war! It changes people, Charlie.'

He held her close, murmuring platitudes about mail taking ages and everything coming right in the end. She had a little weep and he dried her eyes with the pristine white linen handkerchief he always carried. One last kiss, then he beat it through the back door, negotiating the blackout like a wily fox returning to its lair.

On reaching his car, he noticed clouds no longer obscured the moon and contemplated taking a quick dip, but on a night like this, mightn't Jerry be on the prowl? Charles, not stopping to think further, grabbed a towel from his kitbag and jogged down the slope from the promenade. His feet slithering this way and that, he conquered the few yards of soft sand and reached the damp hard apron. At the nearest rocky outcrop, he removed his clothes and covered them with his towel. If anybody was daft enough to wander along the prom at two in the morning, more fool them.

Gasping as the water level hit his undercarriage, he waded out, feeling the ridged sand hard beneath the soles of his feet, confident there were no hidden dips and troughs to hinder him. He glided forward, then turned and swam his favourite backstroke towards the eastern headland, turning round after a few minutes, heading back to his starting point. After towelling himself dry, he scrambled into his clothes, ran back to his car and drove through the quiet streets and out of the town towards camp.

Charles awoke next morning to the sounds and smells and rhythms of the military day. Back from a fortnight of briefings and special training, he'd been gasping for an evening's relaxation with a woman and he entered the officers' mess tent with a smile upon his face. Despite sleep deprivation, he felt capable of triumphing over hell and all its minions. His aide, Captain Geoffrey Chandler, was ahead of him.

'Mornin' Geoff. Mind if I join you?' Without delaying, Charles pulled out a chair and sat down opposite the younger man.

'I was wondering when you'd surface.' Geoff grinned at his superior officer.

'Cheeky devil!' Charles thanked the orderly bringing his cup of tea. 'Yes, the usual, please, Corporal.'

The orderly hurried off while Charles looked around, acknowledging a couple of other officers.

'Anything exciting happen while I was away?' He turned back to his companion.

'We had one mildly lively air raid a few nights back.'

'How did that go?'

'It coincided with a couple of local lads, probably no more than fifteen, arriving at the gate, sozzled and desperate to serve their country.'

Charles laughed. 'Where did they find the money to get drunk, I wonder?'

'Raided the hooch from a stash belonging to the granddad of one of them, apparently. They were so inebriated they could barely string a sentence together, so the Private on duty locked them in the charge room in case they were foreign spies.'

'You couldn't damn well make it up.' Charles picked up his cup. 'Bet the blighters had sore heads next morning. What happened to them?'

'Someone gave them breakfast and kicked them out – not before telling them to pray the war would be over before they reached their eighteenth birthdays.'

'Hmm.' Charles picked up his knife and spread butter on a slice of toast. 'One can only hope.'

'You'll brief me later about your trip?'

'Affirmative. Sorry I didn't see you last night but I was visiting the wife of an old friend whose whereabouts I'd discovered. I called round to make sure she was OK. Nice woman. No kids to keep her company.' He began attacking the eggs and bacon the orderly placed before him.

Geoffrey leaned across the table. 'So, just how nice is

she, Captain Milburn? Did you perhaps receive a warm welcome?'

Charles cocked an eyebrow. 'You know me so well. To be honest, I've decided it's best to put the lady on hold for now. It wouldn't do to become too involved, if you understand my meaning.'

'I don't have any experience in that direction, but knowing you, there'll be another one along soon.'

Charles sighed. 'Believe it or not, I still have a fiancée so maybe it's time to stop playing and start writing love letters to Eleanor.' He reached across and tapped Geoff on the arm. 'I saw that smirk. You don't reckon I'm capable of fidelity, do you?'

'You're a man of many talents, Charlie. Who's to say being faithful isn't one of them?'

'How about you, old chap?' Charles sat back in his chair. 'You keep pretty quiet about your love life.'

'There's nothing to say.'

'Good-looking fellow like you ...' Charles stopped, suddenly embarrassed. 'Good lord, Geoffrey, I didn't mean to pry. I mean, if you're not interested in the fair sex, that's entirely your business.'

Geoffrey shook his head. 'I don't bat for the other side, if that's what you mean. I think you'd have known before now if that was the case.'

'Of course. Cripes, sorry and all that, old boy. But surely there must be some beauty pining for you back in ... where is it ... Hereford?'

'Right town. Wrong assumption.' Geoffrey leaned closer. 'However, there's a girl who works in the typing pool. We've barely passed the time of day, but I'd like to get to know her.'

'Pretty, ay? Then what's stopping you, my friend?' Charles felt for his cigarette case, flipped it open and offered it.

'Cheers. What's stopping me? She's out of my league.'

Charles lit his friend's cigarette then his own. 'Balderdash! You're a good-looking young officer. You could have your pick.'

'That I doubt. Anyway, this girl seems very young.'

Charles blew a smoke ring. He recognised the look in the other man's eyes. 'You're hardly ancient. How young is she, exactly, and what's her name?'

'I've no idea, but she's probably only seventeen or eighteen.'

Charles chortled. 'Bloody hell, Geoffrey, she's a virgin, I'll be bound. My advice is, don't touch her with a bargepole, my friend.'

'My mother was married at eighteen.'

Charles dabbed his mouth with his linen napkin. 'So? Are you seeking a bride, Geoffrey?'

'Good lord, no!' He hesitated. 'Though, I suppose if the right girl …'

CHAPTER 6

Anna was typing up a hand-written list of equipment and finding difficulty in deciphering its author's scrawl. Fortunately, there were only two pages, as stopping to peer and ponder caused her to progress more slowly than usual. At last, she completed the first page and cast her eye down the script, double-checking no errors had sneaked in.

While she sandwiched carbon paper in between typing paper, her mind drifted to the boy whose invitation to go for a walk she'd accepted the evening before. She still wasn't sure this was the right thing to do. But her life was so humdrum just now, her mother understandably still grieving for Viktor and horrified at the thought of setting foot in a cinema or café even. Ruby went out only to visit her parents, to keep Mr Mapstone's house shipshape, or walk to the corner shop, ration books in hand.

Anna had been racked with guilt when Davy proudly told her he was leaving for some unknown destination once he reported back to camp. That had finally decided her to go out with him. He'd talked too much about motor cars and football but Anna had felt relieved at not having to listen to his worries over his uncertain future. She'd succeeded in batting off his advances, while allowing a little of what she thought the other girls meant by "hanky-panky."

She jumped as her supervisor tapped her on the shoulder. 'When you've finished that, you may take your break, Miss Christensen. Then come and see me, please.'

'Yes, Miss Napier. Thank you.'

On arriving at the canteen Anna ordered two cups of tea, having been signalled by Biddy as she left the room, that she too was due a break. Anna had been delighted to find her new friend also turning up for work on Day One, protesting she'd no idea why on earth they gave her the job, after the typing errors she made in her test.

Now she carried the cups towards a window table where Biddy joined her.

'Thanks for this, Anna. My turn tomorrow?'

'Of course. How are you getting on?'

Biddy leaned across the table. 'I didn't tell you or anyone else actually, but that morning we both began working here, I made such a hash of my first letter, I thought Miss Napier would explode with horror and send me packing.'

'Well, she obviously didn't, so you must have been doing a good job ever since.'

'I took her for a right old battle-axe at first, but she

was so kind and understanding, I relaxed and now I'm actually enjoying the work.'

'Well done.' Anna sipped her tea. 'Some of it's interesting, but what I've just been typing was like wading through porridge.'

'To us, yes,' Biddy said. 'But it's bound to be useful to someone who understands what all that technical stuff's about, now, isn't it?'

Anna nodded, feeling ashamed. 'You're right and I know I shouldn't grumble. We're not badly paid compared to girls in other jobs. I should concentrate on today, not keep wondering what tomorrow has to offer – that's what Nana always says.'

Biddy put her head on one side. 'It makes sense. How's your ma then? She must be lonely, being on her own all day.'

'She's used to spending time alone, with my father being away at sea so much.' Anna hesitated. 'The gentleman whose house she looks after is very fond of her. I wouldn't be surprised if he asked her to marry him, after a suitable period of mourning, of course.'

'Is he a widower? I suppose he can't be married if he needs a housekeeper.'

'Yes, he's a widower. Marrying him would certainly save Mam from worrying about how to manage, even though my dad left savings and she has her job. A widow's pension doesn't go very far, or so I'm told.'

'Money's important but not a good reason to marry

someone, no matter how nice he is,' Biddy said. 'What do you think of this fellow?'

'I've known him for years and he's always been kind to us. His house is immaculate and not only because Mam looks after it so well. You can tell he's spent a fortune on furniture and décor, but to me it feels almost like being in a museum. Anyway, I'm usually home in the evenings, except for last night, that is.'

'Where did you go? Anywhere special?'

Anna knew she was blushing. 'Only for a walk. You remember I told you about that boy? About Davy?'

Biddy raised her eyes to the pea green ceiling. 'I do. Is your faithful swain back from doing his training then?'

'Yes, but only for a few days. We went for a walk last evening, down to the prom and along the beach. He's home on embarkation leave and goodness knows where he'll be posted after he reports back.'

'He'd not be allowed to tell you, even if he did know. Did you hold hands? Get a goodnight kiss?'

Anna laughed. 'Nosy baggage! If you must know, yes, we did hold hands, and, as for kissing and all that, I couldn't help but feel sorry for him.'

Biddy banged her cup down so violently, the remaining liquid almost surged over the side. 'You felt sorry for him? You surely don't mean the two of you went all the way? Come on, Anna! Tell me you didn't let that boy …'

Charles Milburn yawned and cast his eye down the equipment list Geoffrey had placed in a prominent position on his desk. While reading, he tapped his front teeth with the tip of the silver pen grasped in his left hand. The items were set out with precision – how did they do that, he wondered – and although he checked carefully, Charles couldn't find even one hint of a correction. He made a few notes on a big yellow pad, secured the typed pages with a paperclip and threw the list into a wire tray filled to overflowing with bumf, as he called the often highly-charged documentation. Captain Milburn was responsible for supplying military units with essential equipment, and keeping the Army on its feet was often challenging work. Despite his inherent love of alcohol and beautiful women, he prided himself on doing a good job.

His phone rang. He picked up the receiver and opened his mouth to speak. Something which proved impossible.

'Captain Milburn?'

He recognised his Commanding Officer's clipped tones and automatically straightened his spine. 'Good morning, sir. What may I do for you?'

'It's about time we organised a dance, Charlie. Public relations and all that – you know the score. Didn't you deal with that kind of codswallop in your last posting?'

Charles silently cursed his last commanding officer for dropping him in it. 'Affirmative, sir.' It was pointless protesting. 'Might I enquire when you wish this event to take place?'

'Sooner the better, don't you think? Talk to the padre about a suitable venue, church hall, whatever he thinks best. It has to be a Saturday night of course and preferably by the end of the month. Can we rustle up a band from our musicians?'

'I think so. A four piece would probably be enough.' Charles thought quickly. That torch singer he'd met in a nightclub soon after he was posted here but never got back to. With Janice blowing hot and cold, contacting glamorous Marcia might be to both his and her advantage. 'I'll see if I can find a vocalist. Someone a bit classy. And I'll liaise with Catering and get them to organise a modest buffet and soft drinks.'

'It all sounds excellent, Charlie. I know I can rely on you. By the by, I heard good things from Chubby Fortescue about the way you conducted yourself in London. Good show. Won't go unnoticed by the top brass. We'll have a chat soon, after you've briefed young Chandler, that is. It's more important the boy knows the score rather than I do.'

'Indeed. You have more than enough on your plate, sir. I'll keep you posted.'

The CO had put down his phone. Charles reached for another cigarette. Did his commanding officer really see Geoffrey bloody Chandler as young? Charles knew that, at thirty two years of age, he was only three years older than the second lieutenant. He smoothed the pencil-thin moustache women often told him made him look like David Niven. That always pleased Charles who thought the actor was a good bloke, having re-joined the Rifle

Brigade after the declaration of war. Stirling fellow.

Charles wished he too could have followed the Sandhurst path as Niven had, though he was several years younger than the film star, of course. He ran both hands through his mop of light brown hair and smoothed it back from his forehead. Last night, Janice had performed that same action on him. Amongst other delights. He'd turned up with flowers and apologies and offered to leave without delay. She'd pulled him inside the door.

Charles cleared his throat and shifted his position before remembering to light the cigarette still balanced between his fore and middle fingers. First things first. And that meant jumping to it when the CO cracked the whip. He reached for the phone.

Anna looked at her wristwatch. 'We must get back. I need to find out my next assignment.'

'Don't leave me in suspense! I promise not to tell anyone.'

Anna drained her cup and dabbed her mouth with a small pink handkerchief. 'A kiss or two ... there's nothing more to tell, honestly there's not. And if Davy ever writes to me, I'll have to tell him I've met someone else. He may think I'm his girlfriend, but it's not true and in some ways, I wish I'd never gone out with him.'

Biddy leaned forward again. 'What was it like, kissing him?'

Anna shrugged. She didn't want to admit Davy's embrace had aroused feelings within her. 'All right, I suppose. I don't have anyone else to compare him with.'

'Well, that does surprise me!'

Anna pushed her chair back and rose. 'Why? How many boys have you kissed?'

'None of course, but you're different from me. You look more worldly-wise somehow.'

Anna chuckled. 'I'm not sure if that's a compliment or not. What I do know is that in future, I intend being very choosy and make sure I never so much as kiss a boy on the cheek just because I think I should be nice to him.'

She began threading her way between rows of tables, Biddy following, and was about to push open the double doors when someone on the other side beat her to it. 'Whoops!' Anna froze.

Her face must have revealed her surprise over the near miss because the fair-haired man who looked familiar to her began apologising for his clumsiness and saying he hoped no damage had been done. But Anna's attention switched to his companion, also an officer, she noticed, though she wasn't sure which rank. The odd thing was the way the stranger affected her. Suddenly she felt her throat go dry. Her heart beat faster.

The officer who hadn't pushed open the door nudged the other one's elbow. 'Ladies, please come through. I'm sure you have better things to do than hang about listening to us apologising. No harm done I hope?'

'None at all, thank you.' Anna took Biddy by the arm and pushed her forward. She followed her friend and smiled at both men as she passed by. There was a definite frisson of something, she knew not what, between her and the man she'd never seen before. Her throat constricted, though she kept on walking, head held high. Hips maybe swinging a little more than usual.

She felt an extraordinary sensation of triumph on hearing the taller man's remark to the one she thought was a lieutenant and who she now remembered meeting before in the course of her duties.

'Hell's bells, Geoffrey. That delicious blonde bombshell you tried to mow down – who the devil is she?'

CHAPTER 7

She couldn't banish his face from her mind. There was time to visit the lavatory before collecting her next assignment, so she snatched the opportunity to smooth on more face powder and tidy her hair, worn in a French pleat for work. She'd have liked to pat some of her favourite perfume inside her wrists and on her throat but the supervisor disapproved of her girls smelling of anything sweeter than carbolic soap as long as they were in the office.

Anna realised her favourite perfume, *Evening in Paris*, wasn't up there with the designer fragrances, but she never tired of its rich mossy scent which made her think of carnations. When she wore it nowadays, it always succeeded in making her feel more mature. More like a woman than a girl as she'd confessed to her friend, Margaret.

She hurried back to the typing pool and tapped on the half-open door of the small office whose internal window enabled the supervisor to observe without leaving her desk. May woe betide any daydreaming typist whose gaze happened to meet that of the overseer.

'Come in.'

Anna walked inside. 'You wanted to see me, Miss Napier?'

'Please be seated, Miss Christensen. Yes, A situation has developed which I'm hoping you'll help me deal with.'

At once Anna racked her brain, trying to think what faux pas she must have made. Had one of the officers for whom she typed complained about her work? She was still relatively new, but fiercely determined to improve her chances of promotion. She couldn't decide what to say, so opted for a nod and a tiny smile.

'You've made a good start with us, Miss Christensen. Indeed, so good, I'm inclined to put you into a role that, even though temporary, is a very important one and which will prove challenging. What do you say to that?'

'Please … Miss Napier, am I allowed to ask what this role would involve?' Anna's pulse rate speeded up a tad.

The supervisor inclined her head. 'The Commanding Officer's secretary is indisposed and unlikely to return to work soon. I'm pleased to say that our Miss Morgan began in this very typing pool and has worked with the present CO since he was posted here at the beginning of the war. She's a highly competent young woman.'

Where might this be leading? Anna's tummy lurched at the thought of achieving anything like the efficiency of this shining example who she'd only glimpsed occasionally in the corridor or eating lunch with another senior secretary. She made no comment, hoping a pleasant expression upon her face and a gentle nod here and there was her safest reaction.

'It is therefore a compliment to your progress so far, Miss Christensen, that I'm prompted to recommend to our commanding officer that you take over Miss Morgan's position during her absence. You're very young for this role, but you have excellent shorthand and typing skills and this is a chance to experience secretarial duties in the field, if I may use that expression.'

She gave Anna a small smile. 'I could poach a secretary from the upper floor, but I'd sooner give you this chance. I shall be able to assist, should you find difficulty at first, but I see no reason why you shouldn't cope. You've been well-trained and Colonel Gresham's a very pleasant gentleman. You'd be required to report to him at eight-thirty sharp tomorrow morning.' She sat back in her chair, looking expectantly at her protégé. 'Well, what do you say?'

Charles sat at his desk, ticking off items on his list. Much of his day was spent in this fashion, convincing him that, if the Army was said to march on its stomach, then it must tick off items during intervals when it wasn't marching. However, he now had a venue for the dance, with Saturday, 19 September written in blood in his diary. He also had four bandsmen lined up.

Colonel Gresham had been adamant the dance shouldn't take place too close to the recent and tragic death of the Duke of Kent on active service. The poor fellow, Charles reflected, had celebrated the birth of his third child only seven weeks before.

For some reason, Charles had a crick in the neck. He probed the offending part of his anatomy where it met his right shoulder and wondered if the sensation related to his exertions of the night before. Or maybe he turned awkwardly after deciding he'd swum long enough and headed back to shore. Perhaps he shouldn't play tennis with Geoffrey that evening as planned. He'd need to think that one through.

Charles ceased feeling sorry for himself as an orderly tapped at his door and, without waiting for an invitation, entered, carrying a tray.

'Great stuff, Jackson,' he said. 'Now, tell me, how's our cricket team been doing in my absence?'

When the man left, Charles stood up and walked across the well-trodden patch of linoleum. His office, adjoining the one the CO occupied, meant he too enjoyed a delightful view of the dockyard.

Charles poured a cup of tea and sat down again, grimacing as he reached for his notepad. Now he'd sorted out the buffet arrangements with the catering bod, he could do with dictating all this information to a shorthand typist. That would save him having to rewrite his scattered notes. He clicked his tongue, recalling the willowy blonde encountered in the canteen doorway. According to Geoffrey, she worked in the typing pool, though he'd no idea of her name. His second-in-command had shuffled his feet when speaking about this young lady, causing Charles to wonder if she might be the same girl Geoffrey mentioned having his eye on. If so, he might deliberately have withheld her name.

Even so, despite Geoffrey's imaginary or otherwise affairs of the heart, Charles mused upon the delicious prospect of having the girl seated opposite him, her slim nylon-clad legs crossed, her attention totally on his voice as he dictated his memorandum.

He cleared his throat. Office protocol prevented him from requesting a particular employee when requiring secretarial assistance. He occupied the CO's good books at the moment and it suited him to remain there, despite his desire to take another look at the Snow Maiden, as he'd dubbed the girl. Something about her spoke of mountains and lakes. Frozen landscapes dotted with fir trees dripping with glittering icicles in the winter sunshine.

He was becoming ridiculous now. The girl was probably an Evans or a Jones and with those looks, she almost certainly had a young man, though it was to his advantage that so many women were currently missing boyfriends or husbands, dispatched like leaves scattered on the breeze, to so many godforsaken places.

Still, maybe the capricious Lady Luck would favour him once more, by propelling the blonde bombshell his way. He picked up his telephone and waited for the switchboard operator's response.

'Hello? David Niven here.'

He grinned as, on cue, the woman responded with a sultry purr. 'Hello, David. It's Lauren Bacall speaking.'

'Well, Miss Bacall, would you kindly put me through to the typing pool supervisor please?'

A few minutes later, hearing the tap at his door, he got to his feet, straightening his tie before calling, 'Come in.'

It required all his resolve not to reveal his disappointment when Miss O'Brien, who the office supervisor had assured him numbered amongst her best shorthand typists, turned out to be a dark-haired girl with a pretty enough face.

After he dictated his memo, he decided to quiz her. 'I believe we met earlier, Miss O'Brien?'

She nodded. 'Yes, sir, in a manner of speaking we did.'

'Your friend was first in the line of fire. I trust she suffered no ill effects? That applies to you too, of course,' he added quickly.

'Both Anna – I mean Miss Christensen – and me are fine, thanks, Captain.'

Bull's Eye! 'That's a relief. Well, I'd better let you get back to your desk. Thanks again, Miss O'Brien. If I could have that memo by end of play today, that would be absolutely topping.' He'd been told his Number One smile, the one kept for special occasions, possessed the power to turn most young women's innards to treacle.

The girl smiled at him before closing the door behind her. But Charles was already trying out the name she'd disclosed. Speaking it aloud … tasting it upon his tongue. He almost purred with satisfaction. Wasn't it the ultimate name for his snow maiden? He decided his neck wasn't too painful at that, and he'd absolutely no intention of postponing his game of tennis with young Geoffrey. Dammit, he wasn't that much older than Chandler!

Charles, with Geoffrey beside him in the passenger seat, drove his adored Vauxhall through the dockyard gates and towards the lawn tennis club he'd joined. Both men had changed into their whites before leaving and Charles had rolled down his window, his right arm resting on the ledge while the vehicle purred along.

'There are times, old boy, when you almost forget there's a war on.'

Geoffrey grunted. 'If you say so. I admit, we have it easier here than many do, but that could change at a moment's notice.'

'Glass half empty, old boy?'

'Maybe, but I see no point in becoming lulled into thinking we'll stay put for the rest of this damned war.'

'So, why not make the most of it while we can?'

'Follow in your footsteps, you mean?'

'Absolutely. Now, when we get to the club, we need to do a recce. We'll find a pair of likely ladies and suggest a game of mixed doubles. I'll even let you have first choice of partner.'

'I thought you were happy with the cosy arrangement between you and your, um, landlady?'

'Janice has a recurring condition of troubled conscience so I'm keeping out of the way for the time being. Just long enough for her to start missing me again.'

'I wondered why you'd returned to the lonely bachelors' hideaway.'

'Hmm … tents are all very well in the summer, but I shall do my darnedest to find another billet toot sweet. Wouldn't want to be under canvas once the cold and wet sets in.' He sucked in his breath. 'Sorry, Geoffrey, I'm a tactless sod. I know your brother's out in the desert, frying and freezing, poor devil. Like I was saying, we're amongst the lucky ones and we should appreciate it whilst we can.'

'In that case, I think I'll ask that blonde typist out, if I get the chance.'

'Which blonde would that be, old chap?'

'Her name's Miss Christensen. I found out that much. She's the one I nearly mowed down on the way into the canteen.'

Charles kept his eyes on the road. 'Ah, I remember now. Excellent idea. I have no doubt she'll agree to go out with a handsome chap like you. Let me know how you get on, won't you?'

'It may not happen for a while. It won't be easy, finding her on her own.'

'I wouldn't waste time if you're keen on the girl. You never know what dirty devil might have his greedy eyes on her, pretty little thing like that.'

Half an hour later, the two officers were running around a grass court at the clifftop club where Charles had taken out temporary membership and could therefore sign in his guest. With so few local men agile enough for tennis, Charles was soon partnering a long-legged brunette whose dark pansy eyes had taken his fancy. But he reckoned Geoffrey must have known something, as his partner, although shorter and plumper than her friend, possessed a cracking backhand. Charles liked to win but he didn't think it was going to happen that evening.

By mutual consent, the two couples decided to call it quits after winning one set apiece, as others were waiting to get a game.

'Fancy a beer, anyone? I'm in the chair. Ladies? Port and lemonade? Right, I'll leave you in the capable hands of Geoffrey here.' Charles headed for the clubhouse.

Geoffrey looked around him. 'These are excellent courts. How did you manage to persuade the powers that be not to dig them up and plant turnips?'

The brunette laughed. 'A couple of committee members are good at pulling strings. Fortunately, the beneficial effects of getting out in the fresh air and running about were a deciding factor. Particularly when it became known that the Army were setting up a tented camp just down the road. Sylvia and I were extremely pleased when we found that out.'

'Pleased about being able to go on playing tennis or pleased to have all those lonely soldiers arriving in your neck of the woods?'

The brunette gave him an appraising look.

Sylvia leaned forward, her expression earnest. 'Mary and I live in the same road and haven't far to come. We've been playing tennis here since we were schoolgirls so it would have been sad to give that up.'

'Happy days,' Mary said. 'Who'd have thought then, our parents would find themselves going through another war. Now we've had to say goodbye to our brothers and boyfriends and who knows when it'll all end.'

'It's a world gone topsy-turvy,' Geoffrey agreed. 'Charlie and I know how lucky we are, to have this posting.'

'I bet! Touch wood, so far there haven't been too many times when we've had to dive into the shelter. We're far enough away from Cardiff not to take the battering so many poor souls have to endure in the cities.'

Geoffrey rose. 'Excuse me, ladies, I'd better go and lend a hand with those drinks. Won't be long.'

Mary pushed her dark hair back from her face and leaned forward the moment he was beyond earshot. 'What do you think?'

Sylvia grinned. 'I don't think either of them would've given me a second glance if I hadn't been with you.'

'Nonsense, the stuck-up Walters twins were knocking up when the chaps arrived, yet they ignored them. Believe me, I notice things like that.'

'Maybe, but I'm afraid Charles makes me feel like a

pudding. I think Geoff's much nicer, but I wouldn't be surprised if they both had girlfriends back home – fiancées even, would you?'

'What's the old saying? All's fair in love and war.' Mary sat back in her wicker chair. 'They're not at home now though, are they?'

Sylvia pulled a face. 'D'you think either of them is married?'

'Not every man wears a wedding ring. I wouldn't put it past Charles to have a devoted little wife and kiddies tucked away somewhere in England.'

'My parents would never let me out again if they discovered I was spending the evening with married men.'

'An hour or so on court and a drink on the terrace. You won't come to any harm, Sylvia. All they want is some female company. Anything more and we won't want to know.' She lowered her voice. 'They're on their way back. Just enjoy yourself. I promise we won't get entangled in anything dodgy.'

'Here we are then, ladies. Geoffrey, you hop out so Sylvia and Mary can quit the back seat like the elegant young ladies they are.' Charles unfolded himself from behind the wheel and pulled the driver's seat forward, holding out his hand to help Mary step onto the running board.

Safely out, she let go of his hand and straightened the skirt of her white tennis dress. 'Thank you, Charles. That was a most enjoyable evening.'

'We must do it again.' He patted his pocket. 'I have your telephone number safely. If I don't see you before, you won't forget to round up some chums and come to the dance?'

'I'll see what I can do.'

He leaned forward and kissed her cheek, whispering something that made her laugh.

'I don't believe a word of it,' she said. 'Come on, Sylvia, we must let these two get back to camp.'

Geoffrey was shaking Sylvia's hand. 'Goodbye, partner. Next time, we'll beat 'em hollow, that's for sure.' He handed over her tennis racquet. 'That backhand of yours wouldn't disgrace Alice Marble.'

Sylvia blushed. 'Goodness me! Miss Marble wouldn't take half an hour to beat me in straight sets! She's such a brilliant player.'

'And a well-deserved Wimbledon winner. Mind how you go, ladies.' Charles gave a mock salute.

The two men watched the girls walk to the end of the leafy road and turn the corner without a backward glance.

Charles chuckled. 'Playing it cool! So, old chap, oh ye of the silver tongue – what else did you say to Sylvia? Did you ask her out?' He was taking his place in the driving seat once more.

Geoffrey climbed in beside him. 'Actually, I didn't. She's OK. More than OK on the tennis court, but I thought I'd wait and see how I get on with Miss Christensen.'

'Oh, I'm not sure that's such a good tactic, old chap.' Charles started the engine and put the car into first gear. 'Poor Sylvia was looking so very longingly at you.' He shot a mischievous sideways glance at his companion. 'She's bound to turn up at the dance, you heart-breaker!' He executed a neat three-point turn and began driving back the way they'd come.

His passenger kept his gaze on the road ahead. 'Are you seeing Mary again?'

'Probably not before the bun fight,' Charles said. 'She isn't really my type and, besides, I need a little breathing space after you know who.'

'Am I hearing right? Captain Milburn can't handle the pace.'

'Perhaps Captain Milburn has other fish to fry.'

Geoffrey sucked in his breath. 'I might've known.'

'Organising the dance takes up a lot of my time, Geoffrey, not to mention keeping all the plates in the air for the CO. You know that's true.'

'This is a side to you I don't recognise, is all.'

'Women have their place, old boy. I think our evening went very well. I have certain tasks to set in motion before I think about further dalliance with the fair sex. In any case, for me, the married ladies are always a better bet than the single ones, old chap.' He tapped the side of his nose with his left forefinger. 'As I've said before, they know the ropes.'

'What if I'm looking for something more than a quick

roll in the hay?'

'Then wartime isn't the right time to find it. Mark my words, you'd do well to remember that.'

CHAPTER 8

Anna, woke early, to the drone of aeroplanes, undoubtedly bombers, returning to their base just along the coast. Some nights she counted them off as they flew overhead, though dreaded counting them back in again in the mornings. Pushing dark notions away, she thought of the paddle steamers formerly bustling in and out of the docks, picking up passengers bound for one of the English seaside towns across the Bristol Channel. Her father had once taken her and her mother on one of these excursions during his leave when Anna must have been aged ten or eleven.

Her mother had teased Viktor about taking a busman's holiday, puzzling her daughter as to what that meant. She'd enjoyed walking down the gangway to board the steamer and was intrigued when her father had taken her below deck to visit the engine room, leaving Ruby leaning on the rail, in the sunshine. Anna could still picture the gleaming metal and hear the thump and swish of well-oiled machinery.

She sat up, shaking her head. The outbreak of hostilities had turned pleasure craft into war-horses and family outings were all in the past. Her pappa was no longer alive. Her mother appeared to be marking time. Anna didn't want Ruby to be alone and fretting over finances for the rest of her life and if marrying again could prevent that, she wondered if her mother was receptive towards the idea.

But she was forgetting what the supervisor mentioned to her the day before. Anna got out of bed, and standing on the multi-coloured rag rug, stretched her arms above her head. She'd decided the night before to wear the same lightweight navy-blue costume she wore for her job interview. The weather wasn't hot enough to warrant wearing a cotton dress. Today she wanted to make a good first impression by at least looking the part, even if she fell short of wearing the halo she imagined must adorn the CO's permanent secretary.

Her mother was calling. 'Anna? Are you awake? I've had my wash so it's all yours.'

'I'll be down in a minute. I'm just putting my clothes ready.'

'You'd better wear proper stockings if you're going to be working for the top brass.'

Anna smiled to herself. She sometimes used the gravy-browning trick but not today.

'Make sure you put on a pair with no ladders.'

Thanks to Mr Mapstone's valuable contacts, mother

and daughter each possessed a jealously guarded supply of nylon stockings. Anna finished her task and ran downstairs in her nightgown.

When she came downstairs again in stockinged feet, dressed in neat blouse and skirt, her mother already sat at the breakfast table.

'We're lucky your nana made a nice batch.' Ruby was spreading a thin layer of strawberry conserve on her slice of toast.

'And was lucky to find enough coupons for the sugar.'

'I don't think she used the quantity Mrs Beeton specified. I'm not complaining, but it seems to me there's more than a little imagination gone into this batch.'

Anna nodded. 'I wonder how much longer the war will last.'

'There are a lot of folk wondering the same, love. Now, I'll be out today, so be sure to take your door key, in case I'm late back. There's soup left from last night and cheese and salad stuff on the marble shelf in the pantry.'

Anna frowned. 'Thanks, Mam, but it's Tuesday. I was about to ask why you're wearing your best crepe dress. Has Mr Mapstone altered your days?'

Her mother blinked rapidly. 'No, but I'm not working this morning. He's ... that is, we're going to visit some old friends of his who've moved to Swansea Bay.'

'But I thought it was forbidden to use a car for pleasure purposes?'

She hadn't seen her mother's cheeks redden for a very

long time, but Ruby looked even more flustered than before.

'This is a business meeting, even if Mr Mapstone's dealings are with a friend. He knows his way round the rules and regulations, don't you fear.'

Anna never doubted that for one moment. 'So why are you going too? You're his housekeeper, not his secretary.'

Her mother looked down at her rose-patterned cup and circled its rim with a fingertip before speaking. 'Frank wants to introduce me to these friends of his and he decided this was the perfect opportunity. I wasn't sure whether I should say anything to you or not. I know I haven't been widowed for very long, but –'

Anna shook her head. She'd been worrying her mother was still mourning and in need of something to cheer her up, yet here she was, already planning the new future her daughter was agonising over.

'You don't need to explain anything. I can't say I'm surprised and it certainly stops me worrying about you.'

'Anna, nothing's decided. It's much too soon after …'

'After my father died, do you mean? It's all right, Mam, you don't need to worry about upsetting me.'

Ruby's eyelids fluttered and she was twisting her lace-edged handkerchief between her fingers. Anna hadn't seen her do that in a while.

'You sound so disapproving. You think I don't miss your father? You can't possibly understand what it's like to lose the man you love. I idolised Viktor.' Her eyes were bright, but whether with tears or anger, Anna didn't know.

'Don't realise I know you wish you'd had more time to get to know one another? All those months when your pappa was at sea – and now I'm left with just memories. And you with no father to give you away when the time comes.'

'We've got each other, Mam.' Anna spoke softly.

'Yes, love. I didn't mean you weren't important to me. You're part of him and part of me, after all. The way you spoke reminded me of the kind of reaction I have to expect from outsiders – it's how people are in a small town. But I must fend for myself now, and I don't have your confidence.' She leaned across the table. 'I'm asking you to keep this information to yourself. And that includes not saying anything to your grandmother.'

'I won't say a word, but knowing Nana, she'll have guessed anyway. It's not that I disapprove, but I wish you'd confided in me sooner. I'm not a child.' Anna glanced at the carriage clock on the mantelpiece. 'I must finish getting ready.'

'I'll clear the breakfast things. I hope you get on well today, love. Remember how proud of you I am.'

Anna's imagination took her many different ways as she walked to work. Her mind occupied with what the future might bring, she didn't realise the sleek motor car pulling up just ahead was stopping on her account. She drew level as its driver wound down the passenger window.

'Miss Christensen, isn't it? May I offer you a lift? I take it we're both heading for the same destination?' The attractive officer she'd recently encountered was opening the nearside door. *The door to some unknown destination?*

Anna tried to look as though she wasn't that keen about accepting. 'The SRD Offices, yes, but are you sure I'm not putting you out?'

'I'm sure.' He eased himself from the car and came around to see her into the vehicle. She sat on the leather bucket seat, swinging both legs inside as gracefully as she could. He closed the door and was alongside her in moments.

'This is most kind of you, sir.' She still wasn't sure of his rank.

'Charles is fine, while we're off duty, or Charlie if you prefer, but Captain Milburn for when we need to keep things formal … Miss Christensen.'

He almost whispered her name as they were pulling away from the kerb. Anna glanced sideways in time to see a little smile tweak his lips. Her pulse pounded in more than one region of her anatomy, producing a muzzy feeling and she was afraid to say anything else in case her vocal cords had ceased functioning. He was steering the car around the roundabout, taking the tunnel leading to the docks road. Soon he'd be turning into the area reserved for officers' vehicles and she'd failed to utter even one intelligent remark.

'Apologies for my bare head,' he said. 'But I've been for an early dip and I was letting my hair dry.'

'I hadn't noticed it was damp.'

'I'm not sure whether to be pleased or disappointed.' A quick glance. A mischievous smile.

Anna sucked in her breath. She still wasn't as adept at the art of flirtation as she liked to think. This man embodied everything she admired in the film stars she watched with Margaret or Biddy at the cinema – Cary Grant ... Gregory Peck ... David Niven. Such words as suave and debonair would come to mind if she were asked to describe Captain Milburn.

They'd arrived. He switched off the engine and turned to face her. 'You'll have a few extra minutes, now.'

She didn't want to get out of the car, but was he telling her to go? She reached for the door handle with one hand, gripped her handbag with the other. And hesitated.

'It doesn't seem right for you to call me Miss Christensen if you're inviting me to call you Charles. My name is Anna.'

He smiled lazily. Reached out and stroked his forefinger down the back of her right hand, from the tip of her thumb to her wrist. Senses heightened, she shivered, realising he must have felt the tingling ripple through her body.

'You have a delightful name. Tell me, Anna Christensen, which frozen fairyland did you grace with your birth?'

She swallowed. 'My father is ... was born in Norway,

but my mother was born here in Wales, as I was.'

'That is surely one hell of a combination.' He pushed down his door handle and leapt from the vehicle. She waited for him to open the passenger door, managing to swing both legs out together, as she recalled her mother's instructions on how a lady should enter and leave a motor car.

Captain Milburn kept his gaze on her face while she stood up. 'It's been a pleasure to meet you properly, Snow Maiden.'

Her cheeks didn't match the glamorous nickname. 'You too, Charles, and thanks again for the lift.'

She hurried towards the building, hoping he'd call after her, maybe ask if she'd like to meet him for a drink after work, but at the same time hoped he didn't. Charles Milburn did something to her equilibrium. Something disquieting. Something she sensed spelled danger.

Once inside, she took a deep breath before walking towards the typing pool, relieved to find the door already unlocked. Beyond the glass panelling of the inner office, she could see her supervisor, head bent over paperwork, and decided to collect her notebook and pencil case before ensuring Miss Napier knew she was on time. But the supervisor looked up and beckoned and for the first time, Anna noticed the gold ring on the middle finger of her left hand, its central diamond tiny but brilliant, and saw her for the first time not as an office disciplinarian, rather as a kindred soul, albeit years older, but a woman with her own history. Her own desires and experiences. Hopes and regrets.

'Good morning, Miss Christensen.' Miss Napier held out a brass key, dangling from a string with a handwritten brown label attached. 'It's very remiss of me to have forgotten to give you the spare key to the CO's office. He hasn't arrived yet so it would be advantageous if you were to check his Out tray for any filing or mail needing attention. I see you've collected your notebook and pencils.'

A nod of approval. Anna smiled. 'Thank you for your support, Miss Napier. I'll try my best not to let you down.'

'I have faith in you, my dear and see no need to wish you good luck.' A gleam of humour lightened her expression. 'Now, I must get on, as must you.'

Luckily, the supervisor returned to scrutinising her paperwork, so missed the look of sheer shock upon her protégée's face. Already, Anna had the feeling of stepping to another level, filling her with determination to prove herself worthy.

Finding keys to the metal cabinets in the top drawer of the secretary's desk enabled Anna to navigate the filing system. She would be working in a cubbyhole of an office, adjoining that of the commanding officer. She had left his outer door ajar, not shut, in case he tried to unlock it with his own key, and she heard Richard Gresham walk into the room while she filed documents in the bottom cabinet drawer.

He looked surprised as she stood up.

'My goodness, I'd temporarily forgotten Miss Morgan was under the weather.' He removed his cap, and to Anna's amusement, almost clicked his heels as he stood there, beaming and looking embarrassed at the same time.

'I'm Anna Christensen, sir. I hope I can be of assistance to you while your secretary's away.'

He dumped a bulging briefcase on his desk and strode across, extending his right hand. 'Colonel Richard Gresham – probably best you call me Colonel. How d'you do, Miss Christensen.'

Anna almost curtseyed as he grasped her hand with a firm grip. He was so tall, his uniform immaculate, Sam Brown belt polished to perfection, shoes a credit to his batman. She couldn't help but think his greying hair had never known the onslaught of an Army barber's scissors.

'May I fetch you some tea, Colonel?' Anna clasped her hands in front of her, striving to look earnest and helpful.

'My word, that'd be very welcome, then maybe you could run along to the mailroom and see what's in store for us today?'

'Of course.'

On her return, his tea duly sweetened by the woman in the canteen, who assured Anna she knew all the CO's likes and dislikes, he was speaking on the telephone.

Anna placed the cup and saucer upon his desk blotter and left the office to visit the mailroom. Back in her temporary quarters, she sorted the envelopes, placing the ones marked Private and Confidential in a pile and glancing at the internal memoranda, hoping to acquaint herself with the subject matter. The writer of the last communication was Captain Milburn, the subject being the forthcoming dance, news of which had already leaked to all personnel. Captain Milburn hoped the colonel would approve his proposed schedule although he still needed to speak to the female vocalist he had in mind.

Trying not to imagine how it would feel to glide around the dance floor in Charles's arms, Anna jumped at the sound of the intercom buzzing. She leaned towards the squawk box. 'Yes, Colonel?'

'Do you have the mail, Ann– ah, that is, Miss Christensen?'

'I'll bring it in at once, Colonel.'

'Good show.'

She got to her feet, scooped envelopes and flimsy papers into a pile and was heading for the door when she remembered her former tutor's words … *An efficient secretary keeps her notebook and pencil to hand at all times.*

Anna tapped on the CO's door and entered.

'Splendid,' he said. 'Take a seat, please. I see you have your notebook with you. Top hole! Let's try and get shot of this lot before I have to go into my meeting.'

She nodded, pencil poised over notebook, wishing she'd remembered to check his diary before he arrived, but determined to rifle through it in his absence.

He dictated slowly at first but must have realised she needed no spoon-feeding and kept up a cracking pace, never mumbling or getting up and turning his back on her; perils of the job Miss Ring had warned of when initiating her students into the mysterious ways of male bosses.

'That's it.' He smiled as Anna glanced up. 'You even looked as though you were enjoying your work. I'm impressed.'

'I hope my transcription won't change your opinion.' She smiled back at him. 'If there's nothing else, I'll start on these at once.'

'Excellent.' He glanced at his watch. 'I probably won't see you until this afternoon as we've a lot on the agenda, but that first memo and the next two letters are the most urgent.'

'I understand.'

'Perhaps you could inform the switchboard I'm unavailable this morning? Ask them to put any calls through to you, so you can take a message.'

A command rather than a question and back in her office, Anna wasted no time in obeying his instruction before feeding paper into the typewriter. She prayed her fingers would find the right keys, as wasting office stationery was practically a hanging offence, according to Biddy, who'd felt the rough edge of Miss Napier's tongue once or twice.

The telephone didn't ring until after she'd completed

the urgent letters and was looking forward to her mid-morning break. She knew a tray would be brought to her office while she was temporarily higher up the pecking order, but Anna felt a pang at the prospect of missing her usual mid-morning gossip with Biddy.

She picked up the receiver. 'Good morning. Colonel Gresham's office.'

'Is the CO there, Miss Morgan?'

'I'm standing in for Miss Morgan and I'm afraid the colonel's in a meeting. Who's calling, please?'

'Please tell him the bearded man wishes to speak to him. Urgently.'

Anna's stomach lurched. 'I'm afraid my instructions are to take messages this morning, sir.'

'Are they indeed? But those instructions don't apply to me, my dear. Now run along the corridor and fetch the colonel, please. I take full responsibility for requiring you to disobey orders, so don't worry. And on no account mention my codename to anyone else but Colonel Gresham.'

Anna thought quickly. A codename? If the bearded man was as eminent as he seemed and she refused to do his bidding, she could lose her job. But the thought of interrupting an important meeting, after being told she shouldn't do so, sent her pulse rate rocketing. Why hadn't Colonel Gresham briefed her properly? She had no idea what to do, except to go with her instincts.

'I'll be as fast as I can, sir.' She hurried down the corridor, high heels clicking against the linoleum, to arrive, a little breathless, outside the door to the conference room. From inside, the rumble of a voice, speaking rapidly, caused a moment's panic as she wondered what consequences her sudden tap on the door might trigger.

She wasn't prepared for the door to open so promptly. Nor had she thought for even one moment that Captain Milburn might be behind it.

Charles's brown eyes widened at sight of her. Frowning, he stepped from the room, pulling the door closed behind him.

'Hell's bells! Why are you here, Anna?'

Surely he didn't think she'd interrupted because she wanted to speak to him? She felt resentment, but stood her ground. 'Because someone has telephoned, insisting he must speak to Colonel Gresham, so please will you inform him I'm here with a message?'

'And you're certain this isn't something that can be dealt with by anyone else?'

She lifted her chin. 'I'm certain.' Anna stood there, willing herself not to tremble, while Charles narrowed his eyes before stepping back inside. Moments later, the commanding officer stood before her.

'What is it, Miss Christensen?'

Fortunately, his eyes were kindly and his tone far from the suspicious bark she'd been dreading.

She stood on tiptoe to whisper her message. 'The bearded man needs to speak to you, Colonel.'

His eyes widened. 'I'm on my way!'

Anna watched him break into a trot as he headed along the corridor. 'Pick it up in my office,' she called after him.

Charles reappeared. 'I take it the CO's left the meeting? Anything I can help with?' His eyes were curious.

'Nothing, thank you, Captain Milburn. I'd better return to my desk now.'

Those brown eyes narrowed again and she got the distinct impression he was none too pleased with her lack of explanation.

She set off, her senses on high alert. She'd made the right decision. And if Charles Milburn imagined she was the kind of girl to blab out information just because a handsome officer thought he could charm her into indiscretion, he'd chosen the wrong person.

She found the colonel sitting at her desk, telephone receiver jammed against one ear while he jotted something down in her notebook. He looked up, beckoning as he noticed her.

'One moment, Stanley – my secretary's back now.' He paused. 'Yes, I know I am. Very fortunate indeed. Just a tick.' He handed Anna her notebook and she grabbed a pencil from the jam jar on the desk.

'Take this down, please.' He rose and indicated she should be seated.

She scrambled into her seat and as he began listening to the bearded man then dictating, Anna concentrated on creating the strokes, loops and dots so mystifying to the uninitiated, so captivating to the shorthand writer.

'That's it, thank you, Miss Christensen. Type up these notes as soon as possible, would you?' He smiled at her, handing over the telephone receiver. 'Now, please be so kind as to put this call through to my office. You're doing extremely well on your first morning. Jolly good show.'

She could hear the phone ringing while she waited for the CO to reach his desk and pick up his receiver. 'Putting you through now, sir,' she advised the caller.

'Thank you,' the bearded man replied. 'I've told your boss he's a lucky man to have such a competent and charming secretary.'

'I was shaking in my shoes,' Anna said later, while carrying her lunch tray over to the girls' favourite table.

'I'd have probably had hysterics on the spot.' Biddy pulled out a chair. 'But you made the right decision. I know you mustn't tell me what it was all about, but I'm pleased you didn't get a wigging.'

'So am I! And I've no idea what it was all about either.' Anna peered at the food on her plate. 'Spam fritters and carrots – we're lucky, having a cooked meal when we're on duty. Suddenly I'm ravenous, even for canned meat.'

'Meat? More like an apology for it, I'd say, but yes, we are lucky.' Biddy hesitated. Lowering her voice, she said, 'Don't look now, but someone's giving you the glad eye.'

Anna made a face. 'Are you sure? You're the one facing in that direction.'

'Maybe, but it's obvious he's not interested in me.'

'Who is it?'

'How should I know? He's an officer, but why does he seem familiar … I've got it! Remember those two who barged through the door and nearly knocked us flying?'

'Um …' Anna popped a piece of carrot in her mouth.

'Yes, you do! He's the one that doesn't look like David Niven. He's still a good-looking fellow though, and he's obviously got his eye on you.' She heaved a sigh. 'Trust me to pick the prettiest girl in the typing pool to be friends with.'

'Let's eat up. I have loads to do.'

'You need to take a proper lunch break. Miss Morgan always does.'

'But she's an experienced secretary. This is my first day in the job and I don't want to let anyone down. I couldn't hold my head up again if she came back to find everything in a mess.'

'I doubt very much that'll happen.' Biddy looked towards the counter. 'They've just brought in another tray of pudding. I'll go and collect two portions – it'll save you some time.'

'Biddy, you're a saint.'

'My ma named me after Saint Brigid of Kildare but that's as far as being saintly goes!' She weaved her way through the tables towards the counter queue.

Anna continued eating, her mind still playing with the disjointed names and phrases inscribed in her notebook.

They made no particular sense to her but they were obviously significant. This was all about provisioning and on a large scale. Something was up. She was convinced of it. And she felt proud to be playing a tiny part in whatever it might be.

She looked up, sensing someone hovering.

'Hello Miss Christensen. Might I introduce myself properly? My name's Geoffrey Chandler and I'm sorry to interrupt your lunch, but I saw you were on your own, so I thought I'd take the opportunity to ask you something.'

Anna looked up at the man who, according to her friend, had his eye on her. How did he expect her to respond?

'If I may, that is?' He sounded diffident and suddenly her heart went out to him. But she wanted and needed to sound confident.

'That would depend.' She picked up her water glass and sipped from it, hoping her hand remained steady.

'Upon what?'

'Upon whether I can answer your question or not.' She met his gaze. He had kind grey eyes. His nearness didn't cause butterflies to flutter in her tummy, nor did he cause her bones to turn to water. But she enjoyed male attention and if he was about to ask her out, it was only polite to listen.

'I'd very much like to take you out to tea some time, or for a walk, maybe. Or, both?'

'That sounds very pleasant. I'd like that too. Both, I

mean. Or, either … oh dear …' *He'll think I'm desperate!*

'Really? Gosh! That's wonderful, Miss Christensen.'

'Please call me Anna.'

'Thank you, Anna, and you must call me Geoffrey, or Geoff if you prefer.' He pulled out Biddy's chair and perched on it. 'I feel conspicuous, standing there, but I'll leave you in peace now, to finish your meal. Shall we say Sunday afternoon at three o'clock? On the town square? Is that all right?'

'That'll suit me well.'

He rose, smiled down at her and nodded. 'I'll look forward to it and whether it's raining or not, by hook or by crook, I'll borrow a car.'

He made her smile and she watched him while he headed for the door, stopping at one point for a quick word with another officer. She wondered about his higher-ranked friend. Would Geoffrey tell the captain he'd asked her out? Would Charles care two hoots whether he did or not? Anna laid her cutlery neatly on the plate as Biddy approached, carrying two bowls.

'There's even custard today.' Biddy placed two dishes of pudding on the table. 'Was that who I think it was, speaking to you just now?'

'Geoffrey Chandler was here, if that's who you mean.'

Biddy tucked herself into her seat. 'Did he ask you out?'

Anna smiled at her friend. 'Yes.'

'This is like getting blood from a stone. Did you

accept?'

'I did. He seems really nice.'

Biddy was finishing her main course. 'Really nice, or merely nice enough to practise on?'

Anna winced. She'd made that same remark to Margaret, about Davy, but pushed the memory away. 'If I decide to go out with him it doesn't mean I'm planning to seduce him.' She ended on a whisper.

'Huh! So, what exactly do you think you need to practise? More kissing? You better be careful, putting yourself about with these officers. You wouldn't want to get yourself a reputation.'

'It's only one officer and we're going for a walk on Sunday afternoon, if it's fine. Maybe go for tea somewhere. That's what he suggested. I expect you're relieved it won't be dark so I can't perform a striptease then have my wicked way with him in a doorway.'

Biddy stared back, open-mouthed, Anna wondering if she contemplated crossing herself.

'Honestly, Biddy, do I look like Mata Hari?'

Biddy looked blank. 'Matter who?'

'The glamorous woman who was a spy in the last war?'

Biddy pushed aside her dinner plate and reached for her pudding. 'I've no idea but I do know you can't help but attract attention with looks like yours. Now, eat up.'

'It'd help if you didn't keep interrogating me. You're worse than the Spanish Inquisition. What's up?'

But Biddy shook her head. 'Nothing. I just don't want you to get into any scrapes, that's all.'

CHAPTER 9

Charles Milburn was in two minds whether to ask Geoffrey to accompany him that evening. But if Marcia, the vocalist who'd caught his eye when he made his first visit to the Welsh capital, happened to be around, who knew where the evening might end? He might find Geoffrey an encumbrance.

The nightclub he intended visiting was in the basement of a large hotel close to the city centre. Charles rang the doorbell and stood, inspecting his immaculate fingernails. He felt gratified when the club's manager opened the door, at once recognising him.

'Captain Milburn, it's good to see you again, sir.' He stood back to let Charles through. 'On your own tonight?'

'Afraid so, Denis. Many in?'

'So, so – not too bad considering it's early yet. I believe there's a table waiting just for you.'

Charles followed as the manager led the way to a table near the stage. The lights were low and the glamorous vocalist was just closing a song. Charles knew, while acknowledging her applause, she was aware of his arrival.

Denis clicked his fingers at the nearest waiter. The chap limped forward, smiling. They were either too young to be called up or like this man, beyond the crucial age or ability barrier. 'Arthur ... a drink on the house for Captain Milburn.'

'That's very civil of you,' Charles said. 'A Scotch and soda would go down well, thank you.'

Left alone in the semi-darkness, he settled on the crimson banquette and focused his attention upon the small stage. He decided the singer's slinky black lace dress with its plunging neckline, could make a bishop kick his way through a stained-glass window. The gown suited Marcia's dark, exotic looks and he mentally undressed her as she began a new song. *Blues in the Night.* Hearing the bittersweet words, he couldn't help wondering whether she saw him as a two-faced, sweet-talking man? The night was young. No one knew how many more nights lay ahead. At that moment, Charles's mind was on anything but planning the forthcoming dance. As the waiter placed a cocktail mat on the table and set his drink before him, he glanced up.

'Arthur, when convenient, would you be so good as to ask madam to drop by my table after her set?'

Anna glanced at the clock moments before she heard her mother's key in the lock. She'd returned to the house two hours before and changed from her office clothes into a pair of navy-blue slacks, and a pink and white striped cotton blouse, even though her mother would never allow her to step outside the house while wearing trousers.

'How did it go today?' Ruby stood in the living room doorway, her hat, Anna noticed, slightly askew, and her cheeks a deeper pink than she'd ever dare rouge them.

'It went very well, thanks. You look as though you've had a good time, Mam. There's soup left if you want it.'

Her mother's eyelids fluttered. 'We stopped for a meal on our way back. Such a pretty little hotel near Porthcawl, and before you ask, I've had two glasses of sherry.' She flopped down on the old sofa and kicked off her high-heeled shoes. 'So, was the colonel pleased with you?'

'I think so, considering it was only my first day. I hope I don't make some awful blunder while I'm standing in for his secretary, but it's so interesting, working for him.'

'I wish your father could be here to see what a lovely young woman you've become. You've far more confidence than I've ever had.'

Anna curled her legs beneath her in the armchair. 'I know you miss Pappa, but he wouldn't want you to marry again just for security, Mam. I can help a bit now, can't I? We'll manage.'

'I'd rather you put your money in your National Savings account while things are still all right. And you have a new life now, Anna. You won't always want to live with me. Who knows what'll happen after the war's over?'

'I still think I should help.'

'It's good to know you have my best interests in mind, but I'm not about to do anything rash. Yes, Frank has asked me to be his wife, and he says there'll always be a home for you with us.'

Anna stared back at her. 'I thought it wouldn't take long for him to propose.'

'Anna! I can assure you, Frank's behaviour towards me has always been beyond reproach. Wars cause people's attitudes to change, and I'm sure your father would be pleased we have a kind man to look after us.'

'Whatever you say, Mam, but I … I'm not sure I could live with you and your new husband. Ever.'

Ruby sighed. 'You'll get used to the idea. I told you before, it'll be a while before anything happens.'

'He's been a widower for years, Mam. He won't want to wait too long to make you his wife and I need to think where I'll go when the time comes. Please don't take this the wrong way, but I don't want to feel the odd one out.' She stopped herself from saying *again*, even if she had eventually become reconciled to her father's arrivals and departures in Ruby's and her lives. In contrast, Frank Mapstone spent most of his time in his own home and Anna didn't relish the thought of conforming to his rules.

'You'll have a beautiful room, love. You could have a wireless up there and there are plenty of books in the house. With your own door key, you could come and go as you please. Once the war's over, Frank wants us to do a bit of travelling.'

Anna huffed out her breath. 'I'm pleased for you, Mam, but I still don't see me fitting in.'

Seeing her mother's face, she rose and went over to sit beside her, reaching for her hand. 'I'll be eighteen soon. If I didn't have this job, I'd have to join up and be posted who knows where. At least we'll still be in the same town.'

'Really, Anna, where do you think you'd live? We can't expect Frank to let you stay here for free, when he has a beautiful home with room to spare and he can find a paying tenant for this house?'

'I don't need Frank's help, anyway, Mam. I thought I'd have a word with Nana. She and I get along well and Grampy's in his own little world most of the time.' She squeezed her mother's hand, but Ruby's expression remained wary.

'You'll find your grandma a lot less tolerant than me when it comes to boyfriends and getting home late at night.'

Anna thought of Geoffrey. 'I haven't asked to bring anyone home yet, so how do I know what you're like?'

'You have an answer for everything. I can't help thinking one of those fellows down in the docks' offices will be asking you out before much longer. You must realise what a beautiful girl you are? The Casanova types out there will always try and sweet-talk you, especially now, with a war on and so many people ending up far from their homes and their usual lives. I'm talking about older men, Anna. Not lads stealing a kiss outside the chip shop or having larks down on the prom.'

'Between you and Biddy, I should be well prepared how to cope, if someone makes a pass at me. As it happens, one of the officers has asked me out on Sunday afternoon, but I don't think he's a wolf. He seems quite shy, actually.'

Her mother sat up straight. 'Are you going?'

'Yes. His name's Geoffrey.' She hesitated. 'He's probably in his late twenties but I can't see that's a problem.' *Charles must be even older than Geoff.* 'Anyway, I can look after myself.'

'How many girls have said that, I wonder?' Ruby pursed her lips.

'Did you, Mam? I've never thought to ask how you and Dad met.'

Her mother jumped to her feet and stood facing Anna; her fists clenched. 'All right, all right! If you must know, we had to get married in a hurry. We had an excellent excuse, because Vik was due to go on a long voyage. Your grandparents accepted that and the wedding was arranged quickly. As it happens, you were born a couple of weeks later than I anticipated, so everyone thought you were a honeymoon baby. Your father was still at sea when you made your arrival and he didn't hold you in his arms until you were six months old.'

Could that have accounted for the feeling of being distanced? Anna got up and put her arms around her mother. 'Thanks for telling me. I didn't mean to upset you and of course I won't tell anyone.'

'The best thing you can do for me is to agree to move in with us when the time comes. Think of the money you'll be able to put by. Remember, you'll be Frank's stepdaughter after he and I are married.'

'So I shall …'

'Please, Anna, will you at least think about it? I want my daughter with me while I still can. Time enough to wander further afield when you've no other option.'

'No other option?'

'Marriage is something that might mean moving away with your husband, especially when this war's over. That's all I meant. But until then, you'll be better off with us, biding your time and saving your pennies.'

Charles knew better than to offer Marcia a drink between sets. He got to his feet the moment he saw her approach, revelling in the glances, whether envious or admiring, as men at nearby tables realised where the sophisticated vocalist was heading.

'You look even more beautiful than I remember.' Charles hastily stubbed out his cigarette and kissed her on the cheek.

She settled herself on the banquette, her sensuous perfume drifting into his nostrils and invading his senses. The first time they met, he'd asked what her scent was called, then chuckled and told her *Shocking* was the perfect name for something so capable of hitting him for six. Now he cursed himself for not even thinking of obtaining a bottle of her favourite fragrance, resolving to put that right before the dance took place. He was positive she'd consent to sing at the event, also confident about ending the evening in a most satisfactory way.

Marcia was married, her Canadian husband in a different time zone, making her the ideal remedy for his current love life dilemma. She desired nothing more than a few stolen hours of pleasure from their still-new relationship and, unlike Janice, didn't appear to recognise the word guilt. She accepted sex with him as happily as she accepted a drink or a compliment. He and Marcia matched one another well. He should have visited her before now.

The waiter brought Charles another double whiskey, and for Marcia a small pot of coffee with cup, saucer and silver spoon on a silver tray. No sugar. No milk. Charles took note. He had also spotted the built-up shoe on the man's left foot and his less than speedy gait, underlining his unsuitability for active service. Marcia smiled up at the waiter and Charles could tell from his face how much he worshipped her, poor sod.

'How's Elsie, Arthur?' Marcia looked as though no one else in the world mattered to her at that moment.

Arthur's careworn face split into a wide smile. 'Bearing up, madam, thank you. The wife's pleased as punch with that blouse you sent. Says to say thanks ever so much.'

'Bless her! Do give her my best regards.'

The waiter nodded and left. Marcia turned to Charles.

'I wake up this morning wishing my husband there to pleasure me, but then you turn up tonight, Captain Milburn.' Her hand rested lightly on his knee.

'So, I'm a consolation prize, am I?'

'I thought we decided we didn't need to analyse our relationship?' She took a sip of coffee.

'Touché. Do we both want the same thing tonight?'

'Oh, I think so, chéri. It's been a while.'

'Excellent. I've taken a room at *The Falcon*. I'm temporarily without digs and they gave me a decent rate for a few nights. The manager's a good egg.'

She raised her eyebrows. 'He'll turn a blind eye, you mean. I suppose hotels have to, these days. Doesn't the Army provide you with somewhere to rest your weary head?'

He laughed. 'I could hardly take you back to camp. I try to avoid the tents wherever possible, but my previous arrangement fell through and I'm considering my options at the moment.' Charles leaned across the table to light Marcia's cigarette. He watched her draw on it and sit back in her chair.

'It is good to see you again, Charles. Does this visit mean you've missed me, chéri?'

She could play him like a violin. Already his libido was going into overdrive. A minx of the first order, the singer was fiery and unpredictable and he'd no more marry a woman like her than he'd set his sights on becoming consort to the beautiful young Princess Elizabeth. He knew how to play the game though. And he suspected Marcia's birthplace was Pimlico, not Paris.

He reached for her hand and kissed it, gazing into her eyes. 'You know very well I've missed you, you beautiful seductress.'

Laughing, she threw back her head, letting her lustrous black hair settle behind her, kissing her shoulders. 'Not so much David Niven as Clark Gable this evening, darling!'

'We aim to please.' He leaned closer. 'I have a proposition for you. Totally legal and one you might class as war work.'

'How intriguing! Tell me more.'

Charles saw what happened next in a series of snapshots: Marcia's husky tones echoing in his ears. Her beringed hand reaching for her coffee cup. The manager's voice yelling above the sound of the musicians still playing Glen Miller's *In the Mood*. Someone was knocking the blazes out of the door at the top of the stairway. An air raid siren began wailing, the sound strident, even in that basement.

People were jumping to their feet. People were shouting. And before he could drag Marcia beneath the table and shield her with his body, the explosion ripped across the room, opening the portals of hell. Through the smoke and the mayhem, the screams and the anguished moans, the last thing Charles saw was the singer's lovely mouth opening and closing. Opening. Closing. With no sound emerging as Marcia crumpled and slumped across the space where their table had stood.

He woke in a strange bed, his head pounding when he tried to raise it from the pillow, his mouth dry and his throat sore. He breathed in the hospital smell and reality punched him like an express train exploding from a tunnel. Where was she? He had to find out what happened to her.

'It's good to see you awake, Captain Milburn. You're a very lucky man.'

Charles was looking at the world as though blindfolded with a gauzy scarf. But despite blurred vision, he could make out a good-looking fellow dressed like the typical motion picture hospital doctor.

'Where am I?' he rasped.

'In the city hospital where you'll stay put until we decide you're fit for discharge. You arrived wearing almost all your uniform, and with your ID intact, so we were able to contact your commanding officer. Someone will telephone and let him know you've regained consciousness.'

'The explosion ... did it kill many people?'

'Too many, I'm afraid. It's thought the German bomber went slightly off target and their gunner dropped the bomb on the big hotel whose nightclub you were in, rather than over the docks.' He hesitated. 'Were you at the club with companions?'

Charles thought as quickly as his bewildered wits would allow. 'I went there alone, but I was sitting with Marcia – with the vocalist – when it happened.'

The doctor nodded. 'If you give me her full name, I'll see if it matches anyone admitted to hospital. Or, taken elsewhere.'

He won't say the word but he means the morgue. Please don't let her be at the morgue.

'Her name's Marcia Dubois. She's married to a French-Canadian pilot whose name is, I think, Etienne. I'm afraid I don't know his rank.' Charles felt shame flood him. He'd been on the verge of taking her to his hotel so she could commit adultery. While Marcia's husband was back in his homeland, helping train young recruits to become pilots. Training young airmen so they could kill other young airmen, let alone civilians. There must be many other girls like Marcia working the clubs, painting their faces, singing and wiggling their hips as a means of scraping a living. Many of them sleeping with arrogant arses like him.

The doctor's reflexes were lightning fast. He grabbed a basin from the bedside cabinet, shoving it beneath Charles's chin as he vomited, and calling for a nurse to attend to his patient.

He patted Charles on the shoulder. 'Delayed reaction, that's all, Captain. I'll see you next time I do my rounds.'

The nurse's hands were cool against Charles's face as she wiped his forehead with a damp cloth. Her smile was sympathetic when she plumped his pillows up behind, so he could sit upright. She looked about fourteen. He felt like death. What a bloody stupid, pointless expression that was. How could anyone know what death felt like whilst they were still living their earthly life?

He couldn't stop seeing Marcia's mouth working as though a puppeteer pulled her strings, working to produce words no one heard her say.

Anna stood in front of the town hall steps, trying to look relaxed. How she hated being the first to arrive. But the clock barely commenced striking the hour when Geoffrey appeared round the corner, beaming as he loped across the square. He was in uniform and she was glad she'd chosen to wear a simple pink and white polka dot dress and white bolero jacket.

'How pretty you look,' he said, holding out his hand.

'Thank you. It's good to wear something not so formal when I'm not working.'

He nodded. 'I'm parked round the corner. How about we drive to the pebble beach and take a stroll, maybe call at that nice hotel near the station for tea on the way back?'

'That sounds lovely.' She wasn't sure whether to link her hand through his arm but decided against it in case he thought she was being pushy.

'Are you looking after Captain Milburn's car then?' she asked, noticing the eye-catching Vauxhall ahead of them. 'Colonel Gresham said you'd collected the key when you visited Charles in hospital.'

'Yes, he's entrusted his favourite lady to me.' Geoffrey opened the passenger door. 'He asked me to give her a run while he's still laid up and even though it's not raining, he told me you deserved a little spoiling. I gather the CO has been singing your praises.'

Anna felt warmth flood her cheeks, unsure whether this was caused by the colonel's compliments or the fact that Charles was thinking of her. Hastily she arranged her skirts while Geoff closed the passenger door. The tang of the leather and the way the bucket seat welcomed her took her straight back to that first time Charles stopped to offer her a lift. She dragged herself back to the present. Geoffrey was starting the engine.

'I'm doing my best. I'm sorry Miss Morgan's still unwell but I want to make a success of this job.'

'You're certainly going the right way about it.' He drove away while Anna smiled to herself. Women weren't the only ones to enjoy a little gossip. But she wondered how Miss Morgan might react when she returned to work and discovered a chit of a girl from the typing pool had been making her mark.

'How is Captain Milburn? I wondered about writing to him. He lost a friend that awful night, didn't he?'

'I don't know if she was a long-term friend, but yes, the club's resident vocalist lost her life, poor woman. I can tell Charlie's pretty cut up about it. Would you like me to pass your message on to him? Unless of course, you'd prefer to drop him a line?'

'I hardly know him. What if he thinks I'm being too familiar?'

He chuckled. 'Not if I know Charlie! If you wish, I could deliver your letter next time I visit.'

'That's very kind of you. I'll leave it on your desk tomorrow.' Anna didn't know why she felt it important to include him in this course of action but felt it might be diplomatic. She was out with the captain's friend, being chauffeured in his car, so surely, to insist on sending her letter through the post, might appear a little clumsy? These days, she was fast learning that trusting her own judgement appeared to be the best option. So far, anyway.

Once Geoffrey had parked the car close to the beach, he asked whether Anna wanted to walk down to the stretch of sand yawning between the pebbly slope and the shoreline.

'The sea looks like a sheet of blue satin today. Are you all right to clamber down the pebbles?'

'I think my sandals are strong enough to cope.'

He offered his arm. 'We'll stagger down together, shall we?'

She was too polite to remind him beaches were very much her natural playgrounds as a child. He wanted to know whether she had brothers and sisters. Asked whether her father was involved in the war effort. Anna hesitated, not wanting to make him feel awkward, but she explained the sad ending of what had been a good career and kaleidoscoped Viktor's marriage to her mother and how he'd have liked her to have a younger sister or brother. She found Geoff extraordinarily easy to talk to.

'Your mother's still young then?'

They were walking along the sand, arm in arm now.

'She is. She was nineteen when I was born. My father was at sea and he didn't set eyes on me for another six months.'

'He must have been thrilled to bits. You'd have brought him a lot of joy, Anna. It's sad that his life was cut short, but always remember how much he must have loved you.'

Strangely, Anna felt a surge of emotion, strangely absent throughout the time her mother had travelled to Scotland and returned, sadness clinging to her like mist.

'Forgive me. I spoke out of turn. Let's head back and find that afternoon tea, shall we?'

Geoff insisted upon driving her home after their visit to the hotel.

'You're on my way, Anna. Why would I let you walk?'

'You might think I'd be better walking off those cakes we ate!'

He glanced sideways and smiled. 'Rest assured, you've no worries at all in that direction. We're fortunate these catering establishments can provide reasonable fare.'

'We do pretty well in the canteen too ... considering.'

Geoffrey slowed down as he approached the roundabout marking the junction of several roads. On his way to meet Anna, he'd stopped for petrol at the garage on the corner.

'Straight across,' Anna reminded him.

'Thanks. You know, the Officers' Mess isn't the same without Charlie. He told me he almost invited me to join him the night he went to see that vocalist, but decided to go alone in the end.'

'Would you have gone?'

He hesitated. 'Yes, probably. He's the kind of bloke who likes to live life to the full and sometimes I envy him, other times I think he throws caution to the winds. But something stopped him from asking me along that night.'

'You were lucky then. And he was lucky to have survived.' Anna spoke softly. 'As for what you just told me, maybe there's a lot of truth in that old saying. The one about your number being up?'

'Maybe.' They drove on in silence until they were almost at Anna's turning. 'You said the third road on the right after the roundabout?'

'Yes, we live at the top of Wynd Street. Ours is the last house on the right.'

He slowed, changed gear, and the motor car lapped up the gradient. 'It's no wonder you stay so slim. You must get plenty of exercise climbing this slope.'

'Over the years, I must have walked up and down it countless times, but you're not doing so badly on the exercise front. Didn't you say you and Charles played tennis a while back?'

He chuckled. 'To be honest, I think Charlie wanted to make new contacts among the tennis club ladies. It would be awful to have a shortage of partners for the men to dance with.'

She wanted to ask whether he and Charles had found suitable ladies to invite to the coming function but decided against it.

'Were you thinking of attending the dance, Anna?'

'I hadn't given it much thought, actually. What with my new temporary role and, you know …'

'Well, it would be splendid if you'd allow me to escort you. I should warn you my efforts would never make Fred Astaire jealous, but if you dare risk it, I'll be a very happy man.'

Why not? He's kind. I feel safe with him. 'All right. Thanks, Geoff. I'd like to come with you.' But her thoughts returned to Charles, even though she suspected she'd be as safe with him as a toddler with a box of matches. 'Will Charles be fit enough to attend, d'you think? You said you'd been checking on details so you can reassure him.'

Geoffrey turned into the side street beside Anna's house and applied the handbrake. She reached for the door handle just as he cut the engine.

'Let me see you out. As for Charlie, I'll be able to report on his progress after I visit him tomorrow evening. I'll bring you up to speed then, if you like.'

'I'll write a note tonight and bring it to work.' She hesitated. 'I'd ask you to come in, but my mother has a lot on her mind at the moment.'

'Good lord, I quite understand.' He jumped out and hurried round to her side. 'I expect she can do with a quiet life for now at least. It sounds a strange thing to say, given the times we live in, but you know what I mean.'

'I do. Thanks for a lovely afternoon, Geoff.'

'I've enjoyed it too, Anna. Um, I'll see you tomorrow then.'

She hesitated, unsure as to whether he was angling for a kiss, but moved towards her front door before either of them became embarrassed.

Anna let herself into a silent house. Her mother had left a note propped against the clock on the mantelpiece.

Frank's called to take me out, Anna. We're going to that hotel where he took us for dinner all that time ago. Isn't that nice of him? I hope you had a lovely time with your lieutenant. Mam x

Anna folded the note and threw it in the wastepaper basket. If she'd brought Geoff inside to find they were unchaperoned, how might he have reacted? She pulled off her sandals and flopped down on the couch. She had absolutely no doubt he would have behaved like the gentleman he was. On the other hand, if it had been Charles placed in the same position, she suspected he'd have grasped the opportunity to steal a kiss. And possibly more …

Her cheeks were burning at the thought. Her chest felt tight. Why did merely thinking about the captain steal her wits away? She knew he was the wrong man for her, in so many ways. But that didn't prevent her imagining how his lips would feel upon hers.

CHAPTER 10

Charles was feeling pleased with himself. He'd rung Mary, the leggy brunette from the tennis club, to check whether she planned to attend the dance, and ended up acquiring a rather cosy little billet with her aunt and uncle who lived on the outskirts of nearby Penarth. He hadn't made a date with Mary, who knew he was still not up to dancing, let alone chasing tennis balls, but she confirmed she'd be at the dance, along with three other young ladies, including the demon backhand specialist, Sylvia.

He'd also been surprised and touched to receive a short note of condolence from Anna Christensen. Geoffrey was obviously besotted with the girl, yet he'd acted as go-between and brought the letter to him. Anna, far too young and undoubtedly naïve for the kind of dalliances Charles indulged in, would be far better off with Chandler, although he still thought the younger man shouldn't get himself too involved with any girl just then. Wartime emotions could run high. People often rushed into making promises they later found impossible to keep. If indeed they still remained alive.

Charles's "lucky escape" still kept him awake at nights and the whole pointlessness of this bloody war rankled, much as he realised the futility of raging about something far beyond his control. His commanding officer had personally driven him to a small, luxurious hotel further down the Vale of Glamorgan, and Charles was spending several nights there before returning to his new digs and to work.

He looked at his watch. Geoffrey was driving the Vauxhall to the hotel that afternoon. This was a social visit but they could discuss the dance, about which Charles was now feeling oddly ambivalent. No cheek-to-cheek opportunities for him, until his balance and coordination were fully restored. But he'd set the whole caboodle in motion even if Geoffrey now occupied the driving seat. Charles wouldn't let anyone down. And as he was no admirer of fruit punch, he planned on taking along his trusty hip flask as well as a full cigarette case.

Anna sat beside Geoff as the car purred along, eating up the miles until he turned off the main road and they saw the sea glittering in the distance. Already the leaves were turning, the hedgerow aflame with reds, coppers and yellows. Ahead of them lay the secluded hotel where it was rumoured many a secret liaison had taken place, according to Ruby who commented when Anna told her mother where she was off to.

'Geoff needs to visit Captain Milburn, Mam, and he's asked me along for the ride. I don't think I'm in any danger of being corrupted!' Anna had laughed at her mother's expression.

'Are you becoming fond of this young man?'

She'd pondered her reply. 'Fond? Yes, I suppose I am. But I'm not in love with him.'

Now, as Geoff steered the car through the hotel gateway, she wondered how she'd feel when she met Charles. She'd felt something stir in her when Geoff issued his invitation and her conscience told her this wasn't how a well-brought up girl should feel when keeping company with a nice young officer who obviously liked her.

But Charles, dashing Captain Milburn, with his debonair looks and list of romantic conquests rivalling that of the former Prince of Wales, would probably laugh his elegant head off if he knew how much effect he had upon the girl he'd nicknamed Snow Maiden.

'It must cost a bob or two to stay here for the night,' Geoff commented and to her amusement, promptly realised his remark might be misconstrued. 'N ... not that I'm contemplating it, of course.'

'Shall we go inside? I can't wait to see what it's like. My mother's fiancé brought her here for lunch a few weeks ago. I never thought I'd have the opportunity to visit.'

'Nor me!' Geoff took her elbow, guiding her up the steps. 'I imagine Charlie would rather be back in harness, but if he has to recuperate somewhere, this can't be too bad a billet.'

In the wood-panelled reception area, Geoff was about to ring the small brass bell on the front desk when a woman, dressed in a smart grey costume, her dark brown hair beautifully waved, emerged from the office beyond. She greeted them, and Anna, discreetly sniffing, also having trawled the beauty counters of Cardiff's department stores, decided the hotelier's rich woody perfume must be *Mitsouko*.

'Good afternoon,' Geoff smiled at the woman. 'We're here to see Captain Milburn, if that's convenient.'

'Of course. I know he's looking forward to your visit, sir. I'll take you both through to the sun lounge.'

She led the way across the foyer, through a spacious residents' room where several people were reading papers and taking tea. Anna followed the woman through an elegant archway to a smaller yet welcoming space, with wicker lounge chairs sporting lacy antimacassars, and occasional tables positioned around the perimeter. Charles reclining at the far end, on spotting them, raised a hand in greeting.

'I'll send the waitress through to take your order, Captain,' said the woman.

'Thank you, Arlene.' Charles flashed her a smile.

Geoff mock-frowned at his friend as she hurried away. 'Arlene?'

'Good afternoon, Anna, and please take no notice

of this reprobate. Mrs Arlene Cooper runs the hotel and she's an extremely capable lady for whom I have a deal of respect. Now, do sit down, both of you. We'll order tea when the waitress arrives, unless you'd care for something stronger?'

'Not for me, Charlie. Um, is tea all right for you too, Anna?'

'Lovely, thanks.' Anna chose an upright chair. 'What a glorious view! You can see right over to the other side today.'

'Is that Somerset?'

'Probably Minehead or Porlock, Geoff, if my geography's correct.'

'It's very comfortable here, but I can't wait to be fully up and running again.' Charles gave their order to the young waitress who'd appeared, before settling back in his seat.

'Any idea when they'll let you leave?' Geoffrey asked.

Charles shrugged. 'I have another medical examination mid-week. Should find out a bit more then.'

Anna sat quietly, her gaze focused on the view as the two men talked, Charles speaking briefly about the sadness of the nightclub bombing, as well as how his second-in-command's workload was shaping up. She was trying to recall which English coastal town she'd visited as a child that time her father had taken her mother and her on the steamer, deciding it was probably Weston-Super-Mare, when she heard her name mentioned.

'Actually, Anna has been a tower of strength,' Geoff said. 'She's helped me a lot with the last-minute stuff.'

'I'm not surprised.' Charles's brown eyes twinkled. 'Miss Christensen is a very capable young lady. Ah, here comes our pretty waitress.'

Anna watched the young woman's cheeks turn rosy as the captain complimented her on her speedy service and her gorgeous smile. Did he have a similar effect on every woman he met, she wondered? How would it feel to be engaged, or even married, to such a charmer? Would you ever fully trust him when he was away from you? The men were still discussing the coming dance.

'We should have a good turnout,' Geoff said. 'Shall I be mother?' He winked at Anna.

'As long as you have a steady hand, old chap.' Charles said.

'The memorial hall's a good place to hold a dance,' Anna said. 'My mother says the acoustics are excellent.'

'Who's acting as MC, Geoffrey?'

'The trumpeter. Says he's done it before.'

'Good show.'

Anna caught the expression in Charles's eyes. Saw a flash of anger laced with sadness. She wanted to say something but daren't. She barely knew this man, after all, but realised he must still be haunted by his nightmare experience.

'I'm forgetting my manners,' Charles said. 'Anna, many thanks for your note of condolence. My apologies for not mentioning it before. You have a gift for words, my dear. No wonder our esteemed commanding officer is half in love with you.'

Anna felt the oncoming blush before her cheeks revealed her loss of composure. Both men laughed, but in a kindly way. Geoff handed her a cup of tea. Charles leaned forward and picked up the silver cake stand, moving it closer to her. She caught her breath as his knuckles brushed her hand.

'The service here is excellent!' She selected a sandwich.

'I should take something else, before this chap demolishes the lot. I'll swear he has hollow legs!'

Anna accepted another sandwich and added a fairy cake to her plate while the two men were bantering. That remark about Colonel Gresham had been embarrassing but she realised Charles meant it as a compliment. To her relief, he asked if she'd seen any good films lately. This was far safer ground and even if she didn't totally keep up to date with the latest cinema offerings, her mother, with her insatiable demand for movie magazines, could always be relied upon.

Once tea was over, Geoff excused himself and left the table.

Charles rose and offered Anna his arm. 'How about we take a little stroll?' He laughed as he saw her expression. 'I only mean us to walk through the French windows and on to the lawn. Your dashing hero will be back soon.'

'To be accurate, we're friends, that's all.' Anna tucked

her hand through the crook of Charles's elbow.

He waited until they were outside before speaking. 'So, are you playing the field, Anna?'

'That, Captain Milburn, is a rather impertinent question.'

'I know it is, but I love seeing your eyes spark when something displeases you. Fire and Ice! Such a potent combination in a woman.'

She'd forgotten how mesmeric he was. Already she had a muzzy feeling. A dangerous feeling. She turned her head but there was no sign of Geoff.

'I rarely apologise,' Charles said, 'but find myself saying sorry to you for the second time this afternoon.'

'There's no need. I know things must be difficult for you.'

He stopped walking. Turned to face her. 'Don't, please don't feel sorry for me. I don't need your pity. We live in an ugly world and I have to take the flak the same as anyone else. Geoffrey and I realise how lucky we are here in South Wales, compared to many other military men.'

He was looking at her mouth. 'My God, but your lips look so extremely kissable. How many fellows have told you that, I wonder?' He began walking again.

She was struggling for an answer when Geoff joined them.

'I've received my marching orders. Your friend Arlene tells me it's time you took a rest.'

Charles bowed his head. 'The lady's word is my

command. Anything that'll help get me back to doing something useful is all right by me.'

'It's been lovely to see you, Charles,' Anna said. 'Thank you very much for tea.'

'Ditto! You're looking in very good shape, old boy,' Geoff said. 'I'm on standby to drive your motor car over here whenever you say the word.'

'Good to hear.' Charles pointed towards the shrubbery. 'You can go through the gate there and access the driveway. I take it the car's parked there?'

'That's right. We'll say cheerio then.'

Geoffrey reached for Anna's hand. She made no move to deter him and wondered whether this was for Charles's benefit or was purely a friendly gesture.

CHAPTER 11

'What about that dress your grandmother made?' Ruby watched Anna discard yet another pretty frock.

'I'm not sure it's what I had in mind. It's fine for daytime but not quite dressy enough for evening.' Anna took out a dark blue, crepe, longer length gown and held it against her before the cheval mirror in her bedroom.

'But it's not like you're off to a grand ball. If you want my opinion, the blue's perfect. And you haven't worn it since Frank took us out to dinner to celebrate our engagement.'

'It was a shame Geoff couldn't come with us.' Anna hadn't particularly enjoyed being the odd one out again.

'We're at war, Anna. Though it's easy to be lulled into a false sense of security, living somewhere like this.'

'We have plenty of air raid warnings, Mam.'

'I'm not disputing that. But there'll be another chance for us to meet your young man, love. And the fact that he hasn't seen you in this dress is another point in its favour.'

Anna shrugged. 'I'll try it on. The only other one is the

silver grey.'

'You need a cocktail frock really. I've had so much on my mind, I hadn't thought. If you're really stuck, you could look through my wardrobe.'

Anna wriggled her way into the blue crepe. 'I'm several inches taller than you, Mam. Anyway, I wouldn't dream of wearing any of your trousseau before you've even gone on your honeymoon.'

Ruby regarded her critically before rising and adjusting the dress across her shoulders. 'I think that's better now. You should always adjust from the very top so the fabric hangs as it should. If you twirl round, we can see how it'll look when you're dancing.'

'The trouble is, I used to dance with so many girls in those classes at school, I shall probably freeze completely when I take to the floor with Geoff.'

There was a bang on the front door. Mother and daughter looked at one another.

'Are you expecting Frank to call?'

Ruby shook her head. 'He's spending the afternoon in the garden. Someone's helping him create a little bower for me. It'll be lovely for next Summer.'

Anna made no comment as Ruby went downstairs. She heard the low tone of a male voice but thought nothing of it, twirling this way and that, inspecting her image in the mirror. Yes, this dress was her best option.

'Anna?' Her mother's voice percolated up the stairwell. 'You have a visitor. He's waiting in the drawing room.'

'Coming!' *Surely, it's not Charles? Why on earth would it be Charles, you stupid girl?* Anna descended the stairs, wondering. *Could it possibly be Charles?*

Ruby stood in the hallway. Anna mouthed 'Who is it?' but her mother pursed her lips and went into the living room, closing the door behind her.

Inside the drawing room, the mantelpiece clock, her father's pride and joy, ticked as it always did. Her visitor however, appeared mesmerised by the bearskin rug, a souvenir which had alternatively terrified and delighted Anna as a child and which now was evidently affecting this young man in the same way. The animal's head was still attached, something that either fascinated or repelled visitors viewing it for the first time.

The young man glanced up as she stood in the doorway. For moments she looked blankly at him before it dawned on her how hours of marching, training, fresh air and regular meals, added to the twelvemonth since they last met, had transformed the gangly Davy into a muscular, handsome soldier.

He twisted his uniform cap between his fingers and smiled shyly. 'Anna. I ... who's the lucky fellow?'

She moved towards him and they clasped one another in an awkward hug, Anna giggling when she bumped her left foot against the bear's head, for probably the hundredth time since her days as a toddler and young child.

He steadied her. 'Whoa – that's some rug! Did ... did your father bring it back from his travels?'

'Of course. I used to sit on Teddy's head when I was little. Goodness, Davy, you've changed so much since I last saw you.'

He smiled. 'If the cap fits, Anna ...'

'I doubt I've changed as much as you have, though you can't call me shrimp nowadays!'

He gave a growl of laughter.

She stopped staring at his broad shoulders. 'Would you like something to drink? We can go into the kitchen with Mam.'

His expression became wry. 'You're thinking the drawing room should only be used for visits by the doctor and the vicar and for entertaining the relations on Christmas Day? If your family's anything like my lot, it is.' He shuffled his feet. 'I'd rather we stayed here to talk.'

'Well, sit down then. Stop making the place look untidy.'

He perched on the chaise longue. 'All right here?'

She sat in an armchair close by. 'Of course. How long are you home for, anyway?'

'Just a seven day leave before our battalion's off again.'

She nodded. 'I know better than to ask where. Did you know I've been working at the SRD since my business training?'

'So Ma said. I guess you're typing and taking dictation? Working with Army officers, I hear.' His eyes questioned her.

'I've been lucky to get a good position. I can walk to

work and of course, because of the nature of our duties, they don't call us up at eighteen.'

'I forgot to thank you for your letter. To tell the truth, I didn't expect an answer.'

'I didn't want you to think I didn't care about you, but I didn't want to make you think you and I ...'

He shook his head. 'Don't worry. I could tell from the way you wrote that I didn't stand a chance.'

'Oh, Davy. I'm sorry. Is that why you didn't write back?'

'Would you have replied if I had?'

She thought for a moment. 'I'm not sure. Probably.'

'Lots of the lads have sweethearts back home writing to them.'

'I'm sure they do.' Anna didn't meet his gaze, trying to think of something to say that would neither wound nor encourage him.

'Earlier on, I asked you who the lucky fellow was. I can't imagine there isn't someone.'

'Why do you say that?'

He chortled. 'You've grown into a beauty, is why. What's more, you still blush, like you used to.' He swallowed and she watched his Adam's apple jump beneath the pale skin of his throat. 'In some ways, I wish we could turn the clock back to your fourteenth birthday when you cut me a slice of cake.'

Viktor had still been alive then. 'You told me once you couldn't wait to fight for your country.'

'That was the kid talking. I know more about it now, see?'

The clock on the mantelpiece struck the hour. Four chimes.

'I'd best go and leave you in peace.' He got to his feet.

Anna gazed up at him. 'Are we still friends?'

He didn't answer at first.

'Davy?'

'One walk with you! One walk to the beach and back, is what I'd like. Something to dream about after my leave ends.'

She stood up. He was a bit taller than Geoff. Probably similar to Charles in height. His background would make it difficult for him to compete with either officer if it came to a man of the world contest. That indefinable assurance each had gained from their upbringing and education was absent in Davy, though his bearing and physique would put him ahead in terms of fitness.

'There's a dance at the Memorial Hall tomorrow night. It's organised for the soldiers stationed outside town and you'd be very welcome to come along. Don't worry, there'll be plenty of girls there.'

He raised his eyebrows. 'Are you going?'

'Yes. Someone has asked me to go with him. But it'll be a very friendly gathering. We can have a dance or two. Only if you want to, of course.' She looked away, seeing the longing in his eyes.

She'd forgotten about those little tics of his when he

was thinking. How he pushed down his lower lip with his forefinger.

'You have a solder boyfriend?'

'A friend who's a soldier, yes. Not a boyfriend in the way you mean.' How could she stand there, seeing the way hope flared in his eyes?

'So, you're not spoken for, then?'

'No. No, of course I'm not spoken for. Geoff's very nice, but ...'

'You better not lead him on, Anna. Wartime's not the time to do that. Not when a fellow doesn't know if he'll make it to the end of the year ... end of the month ... end of the bleedin' night.'

She put her arms around him and he pressed his mouth to her hair. She could smell *Brylcreem*, mixed with a whiff of stale tobacco and medicated soap. Not unpleasant though. It made her think of Viktor. And then Davy pulled her even closer. His arms felt strong, made her feel protected. Anna lifted her face towards his and he bent to meet her, their mouths touching in a butterfly kiss. Then as if he truly did wonder whether he'd still be around to see the dawn of a new day, he kissed her with a passion and an urgency that almost rocked her off her feet.

She closed her eyes, kissing him back, dizzy with longing at the feel of his lips against hers. What was she doing? What if her mother walked through the door? But there was a recklessness springing inside Anna, a sensation that Geoff, for all his kindness and sweet nature, could not kindle. And that longing which Charles had first awakened was dangerously alive and hungry now.

Davy released her, though reluctantly. 'Would you come out with me on Sunday? I can't bear to watch you dancing in some other bloke's arms tomorrow night. Sorry and all that.'

She shrugged. 'If that's how you feel, we could walk to the beach like we did that first time.'

'I'll collect you. How about two o'clock?'

'I can meet you in town, if you prefer.'

'No, I'll come here. It'll give us extra time together. God, I wish I had a car!'

'Don't be silly.'

He tucked a strand of her blonde hair behind one ear. She'd seen her father perform that same action upon her mother. A shiver rippled through her, but at once Davy's expression, so packed with joy and anticipation, sliced through her like a blade. She must not – would not promise something she couldn't honour.

She thought of the old photographs her mother kept in a brown leather album. How furious Ruby had been the time she caught her three-year-old daughter scribbling inside the front cover with a green crayon. How relieved her mother was to find the photographs untouched by childish scrawls. This memory had remained with Anna, just as the crayon marks remained distinct. When her father had been around, her mother's face used to bear the same expression as Davy's just did.

In one photograph, Viktor, blond and clean-shaven, skated on an ice-covered lake back in his homeland, his blades carving swirls into the ice. His carefree image remained frozen in time against a backdrop of tall fir trees and dark mountains. How strange such a faraway moment, depicting a period when the skater was yet to meet his future wife, should generate such a wave of emotion in his daughter.

CHAPTER 12

Frank drove Anna to the Memorial Hall as Geoff was scheduled to spend an hour's duty on the door and couldn't collect her. She left her coat in the cloakroom and obtained a ticket stub. An intoxicating cocktail of face powder and scent hung in the air as chattering girls crowded around the only mirror to catch a glimpse of themselves. She contented herself with a head twist as she bent to make sure her stocking seams were straight before returning to the foyer and joining the queue of young men and women waiting to enter the ballroom.

'Anna! I'm so glad you came.'

'Didn't I promise?' She handed Geoff her dance ticket which he tore in two.

'Pop this half in your bag and hand it over when refreshments are served.'

'Thank you. I'll see you later.'

'You bet! Have fun. I'll come and find you, the moment I'm free.'

Why can't I fall in love with him? Or maybe I should

be pleased I'm not in love with him? Because I don't want to become a stay-at-home wife, living for my husband's return and looking forward to taking off my pinafore. I want a proper career, something to provide security in years to come. I don't ever want to end up like my mother, afraid to live life without a man to provide for her.

'Anna!' Biddy was beckoning from her seat in the line of chairs near the musicians.

Anna walked towards her and, laughing, pulled her friend to her feet. 'Don't sit there like a wallflower! That pretty yellow frock deserves to be shown off.'

'I don't know any of the other girls as well as I know you. I'd have felt an eejit standing up on my own.' Biddy glanced around and whispered to Anna. 'See those two soldiers eyeing us up? They look nice. I wish girls could ask men to dance.'

'You'll need to wait for a *Paul Jones*, I think. Unless ... are you feeling daring?'

'What, brave enough to ask a man to dance?'

'Why not? They can only say no.'

'But what'll people think?'

'There's only one way to find out.' Anna grabbed her friend's bag and pushed it with hers beneath a chair. Taking her time, she sauntered towards the two soldiers her friend had noticed. At once each stood to attention. Biddy hovered slightly behind her as the band began playing "*Let Me Call You Sweetheart.*"

'Not dancing, boys?' Anna looked enquiringly at first

one young man then the other.

The taller soldier clicked his heels and held out his hand. 'Corporal Miller, Miss. May I have the honour of this dance?'

'I'd be delighted. Can you waltz, Corporal Miller?'

'Case of having to when you have three sisters, Miss.' He took her hand and led her on to the floor where a few brave couples were swaying to the music.

Anna fixed Biddy with a meaningful look as she waltzed away with her partner. Biddy must have taken confidence from her friend's approach because Anna saw her say something to the other soldier, who, although his pale complexion promptly took on a beetroot hue, gallantly took her by the hand so they too joined the dancers.

More people were arriving now and Anna exchanged smiles with several girls from the typing pool. The waltz finished and Anna and her partner stood, waiting to hear which dance would follow.

'A quickstep? Are you feeling brave, Miss Christensen?' The corporal smiled down at her.

'Why not? You're an excellent dancer.' She felt relaxed with this young man. He'd regaled her with tales of his sweetheart in Bristol and how they planned to marry once the war was over. Anna felt a pang, wishing with all her heart that Corporal Miller and the girl he loved would be spared and able to set off on a new journey together. She noticed Geoff standing in the doorway and saw him glance her way once or twice, but next time she looked, he'd vanished.

Charles was out in public for the first time since the Cardiff bombing. He'd bumped into his tennis club chums, Mary and Sylvia, both of whom seemed delighted to see him. He'd complimented each of them on her dress and apologised profusely for being unable to partner them that evening.

'I was one of the lucky ones,' was all he'd say when the girls expressed their concern, having heard of his injuries from Geoff.

'Did I say how everyone's missing you at the club?' Mary said the moment Sylvia wandered off, probably going in search of Geoff.

'Kind of you to say so, my dear. Hopefully I'll be back to playing before the end of summer. I apologise for not getting in touch, Mary, but … it's taken a while to get my bearings. No complaints about the digs. I'm truly grateful to you for the tip off.'

'Aunty Doris is pleased to help. Uncle Gordon wasn't sure about letting a room at first, but you've won him over.' Mary's eyes met his. 'Something tells me that's a speciality of yours.'

Charles shrugged. 'My father's military career was similar to that of your uncle. I can be a good listener when necessary.' He winked at her and beckoned to a young man standing on his own.

'Mary, allow me to introduce Second Lieutenant

Richard Curtis. Richard, this delightful young lady is Miss Mary Whitchurch. To my intense annoyance, I'm not yet fit for dancing, so you're going to have to help me out. I know she's longing to glide around the floor with an upstanding chap like you.'

The young officer looked as though he'd been promoted. 'My pleasure, sir. Would you do me the honour of partnering me, Miss Whitchurch? I promise not to tread on your toes. Well, not all of them at once, anyway!'

She inclined her head gracefully and Charles watched the pair melt into the throng. Already she was laughing. Mary would get on well with young Curtis. And Charles needed space to think.

He also needed a drink. Badly. Needed to give his face time off from smiling before his mouth set in a rictus grin for evermore. The musicians were pleasing the crowd, that was for sure. For moments, he pictured Marcia standing on the small stage as she would have been. Should have been. Marcia in a gown painted on her curves, probably something sparkly. Glamorous, gorgeous Marcia. It was so bloody unfair.

He turned and went into the foyer then round the blackout screen protecting the entrance, sidling outside where he reached inside his uniform jacket to find his hip flask. He knocked back a swig of Scotch and stared into the darkness. No visions now. Just nothingness.

'Charles?'

He knew who it was at once. Turned around slowly, trying to ignore the surge of excitement gripping him at the sound of her voice.

'Why aren't you foxtrotting with young Lochinvar? Or has Sylvia collared him at last? And no, you're not sharing my whiskey. It's purely medicinal.'

Her laugh was husky. Her perfume reminded him of days in the sunshine spent frolicking with a beautiful woman: the prelude to a night of passion. He wished he could woo her, but knew he'd be doing her no favours. She deserved better than him, but fleetingly he hated Geoffrey for being Geoffrey.

'Geoff's on the dance floor, but I've no idea if he's with the girl you mentioned.'

Charles drank another mouthful from his flask. 'Smallish person, a bit on the plump side, curly brown hair. A tad eager?'

'I'd say she fits that description. Why am I not surprised that you know so many girls?'

'In my defence, she's a member of the tennis club to which I belong. Geoffrey came along as my guest one evening before the ... Sylvia may well have designs on young Lochinvar, but I know his heart belongs to another.'

Anna laughed again. 'You're incorrigible, Captain.'

'I'm sure you've said that to me before.' He put away his flask and felt for the slim gold case he always carried, turning away to shield the flare of his lighter as he lit a cigarette. 'Filthy habit,' he said. 'You're very wise to abstain. Now, why are you out here? Aren't you having a good time?' *If he stretched out an arm, he could pull her to him.*

'I'm enjoying myself, thank you. I expect Geoff will miss me in a minute.'

'Are you by any chance trying to make him jealous, Miss Christensen?'

'I don't play games, Captain Milburn.'

He took another pull at his cigarette. The single malt and the nicotine were softening the edges now. 'I believe you. I also suspect that in some ways, you and I are two of a kind.'

He waited for a response. Smiling into the darkness. Moonlight was no friend of inappropriate assignations. And somehow, picturing that delicious mouth of hers was even more erotic than gazing at the real thing.

'Should I feel flattered or concerned?'

'If you can read my mind at this moment, my dear Anna, then you probably should feel somewhat alarmed.'

He knew she was struggling. Gave her a little time as he dropped his cigarette on the concrete footpath and ground it beneath his shoe. Heard a rustle of petticoat as she moved a step closer. No way did he intend making a move. Any contact between them had to be her decision. But, by God, he wasn't sure how much longer he could resist temptation …

He caught a drift of jasmine. Roses maybe. However sweet, this was a torture no man should be expected to endure. Charles cursed softly beneath his breath as someone slipped through the blackout curtaining behind them.

'I don't know what you must both think of me! Requesting the pleasure of a young lady's company at the dance, then abandoning her. Thank you, Charlie, for keeping Anna company.'

'My pleasure, old boy. But you really should take better care of her, you know. I couldn't help noticing how that young corporal was whirling her round the dance floor.'

'I'm quite capable of looking after myself, thanks very much.' Anna raised her eyebrows.

'We realise that. Although thoroughly modern young women like you still appreciate a touch of old-fashioned courtesy, I think. Don't you agree?'

'Well, yes I do, though I refuse to apologise for asking that corporal to dance.' She sounded triumphant. 'Would you believe his friend hasn't left Biddy's side since their first waltz? She's looking pretty pleased about it too.'

'I happened to see you taking the initiative. As did almost every other man in the place, I imagine.'

Anna bit her lip. *Rebuke or compliment?* She couldn't always get Charles's measure.

'Actually, I came to suggest we all go in for a spot of supper.'

'Excellent suggestion, Geoffrey. High time I showed my face again. I did promise the colonel I'd make an appearance, given he felt he might put a dampener on the occasion if he turned up.'

'He's very thoughtful. For a man.' Anna ducked behind the blackout curtain.

Both men burst out laughing.

Charles led the way. 'There you have it, my friend,' he said. 'Miss Christensen's opinion of the male gender summed up in a nutshell.'

The three of them stood in the space beyond the function room where trestle tables held plates of sandwiches, savoury patties and cakes. Men and women were queuing in goodhearted fashion and carrying their refreshments away, to sit or stand in pairs or small groups; girls in colourful frocks bright butterflies against the sea of khaki.

Charles was surveying the scene. 'Taking a dekko at this lot, if it weren't for the uniforms, you could almost believe there wasn't a war on.'

'One day, everything will be back to normal. You'll see,' Anna said.

'It can't come soon enough.' Charles cleared his throat. 'I'll leave you both to it, I think. Do a tour round then get back to my digs so my long-suffering driver can finish for the night. You happy with that, Geoffrey?' He hesitated. 'It's just occurred to me, how are you getting home, Anna? Surely not on the bus?'

'No, Charlie,' Geoff butted in. 'The CO allocated a staff car, so I can drive Anna home as soon as all's in order here.'

'Then I'll see you both at the office on Monday, all being well.' He turned to Anna, raised her right hand to his lips and kissed her fingers.

She watched him begin his walkabout.

'Anna? Shall I fetch you some refreshments or will you queue with me?'

'I'll come with you.'

Suddenly he put his arm around her waist and guided her towards the now short line of men and women. 'I know I can't compete. I'm not an idiot.'

'Geoff! I never thought for one minute you ...'

'I need to say this one thing to you. Men like Charles Milburn are like birds of paradise set amongst a flock of pigeons. Charlie's a good soldier and he's brilliant company into the bargain. The CO thinks he walks on water and I've a hunch you might well feel the same way.'

Anna waited for him to finish. Geoff passed her a plate and she helped herself to two sandwiches and a slice of currant cake.

'I just can't bear to see you hurt,' he said. 'That's important to me. Maybe I shouldn't say any more but I needed to get this off my chest.'

'Two teas, sir?' The attendant asked.

'Anna?'

'Yes, please. Not much milk.'

Geoff nodded at the orderly. 'Thank you.'

They carried their cups and plates across the room.

Geoff found a table where two couples were leaving. Anna noticed how the soldiers scooped up their crockery and cutlery to pile neatly on a nearby trolley. Geoff thanked them and pulled out a chair for her.

Across the room, Charles was speaking to the girl she'd seen dancing with Geoff earlier. Sylvia – that was her name. And an attractive girl with dark hair was seated next to a young officer Anna hadn't noticed before. The girl was chatting with her beau while watching Sylvia with some amusement. Maybe Sylvia yearned for Charles? Or was it the dark-haired girl who had her eye on the charming Army captain? She watched as Charles kissed Sylvia's cheek and appeared to be bidding the group farewell. As Sylvia's gaze travelled towards Geoff, Anna felt a pang as she realised who it was the young woman really yearned for.

'It probably wasn't the best idea I've ever had – asking you to be my partner this evening when I needed to be on duty.'

'Geoff, don't say that. You know I enjoy being with you.'

'Please don't patronise me, Anna. If you prefer not to see me anymore, out of the office, I mean, then I'd prefer to know now, rather than later.'

Why did men become so intense so soon? 'Honestly, Geoff, I don't want to enter into a relationship with anyone at the moment. I've seen too many folk disappointed. We live in such troubled times.'

He gave a short bark of mirth. 'Hell's teeth, but you sound like Charlie! That's his mantra. His excuse for loving 'em and leaving 'em, to be brutally honest.'

I suspect that in some ways, you and I are two of a kind. Was that really what Charles thought? Should she be concerned at the way he perceived her? For the second time that evening, Anna found herself at a loss for words.

'I won't beg you, but I wish you'd see me simply as a man who has fallen in love for the first time and not blame the conflict for being an unsuitable time to begin a relationship. We can't bottle up our feelings simply because there's a war on, you know.' He glared at his sandwich as though he couldn't understand what it was doing there.

Anna reached out and rested her hand on his.

He sighed. 'Who am I to tell you what to do? I'm sorry for being a complete fool, especially when I've just told you I'm not an idiot!'

They locked gazes. Burst out laughing at the same time.

'We'd better eat up,' she said gently. 'Can we not go back to how we were? I do truly enjoy being with you. Please don't turn your back on me because I'm not ready for the kind of commitment you're looking for.'

'Turn my back on you? I enjoy being with you too much to do that. And if you, as a modern young woman, decide you'd like to spend time with me one of these evenings, I shall be delighted to co-operate.'

But the tenderness in his eyes reminded her of Davy's expression. Her mother would be horrified at the thought of Anna going for a walk with the young soldier. She'd be thrilled to bits with Second Lieutenant Geoffrey Chandler though. And as for Captain Milburn ... he was an entirely different matter. Charles spelled danger and should be treated with extreme caution.

Anyway, she was much too young to interest Charles. Wasn't she?

CHAPTER 13

Captain Milburn was counting his blessings. He'd had many a lucky escape in the past. Some involving last minute dashes away from the current lady love's residence – one necessitating a hasty exit through a window, as if he was a blasted commando. While driving towards his lodgings, he reminded himself of the most significant escape of them all. He hadn't wanted to recuperate at his parents' home after his release from hospital and had given them and his fiancée the excuse that he wasn't fit enough to travel. In fact, he'd needed time to think.

But it wasn't a huge distance to Lower Coombe. And that was where he intended going as soon as he'd arranged the necessary documentation, and provided Eleanor still agreed to a quiet wedding. She'd originally decided they should get married the following Spring with as many trappings as this time of austerity allowed. But Charles, although he usually kept his views secret, suspected things were ramping up in this god-awful war. He'd been playing the field long enough. And when Eleanor had written to run some arrangements by him, it hit him, though not with panic, that it was time he reassessed his situation. After all, they were engaged, even if he didn't always behave like a man on the verge of plighting his troth.

He'd been shocked by his feelings about fatherhood, especially the thought of guiding a son along the journey to manhood. His own father, poor sod, had tried his best with him, but Charles, the only son after two daughters, had been packed off to public school as soon as his prep school spat him out and into the jungle that Seton Towers proved to be.

He'd known Eleanor since he'd spotted her at her elder sister's twenty first birthday party. She was nineteen and fell into his hands like a ripe peach slipping from the branch. She'd given herself willingly to him after their engagement took place and he knew how much that must have meant to her. But for the time being, he didn't want to tell anyone about his proposed change of status.

He could drive to her house, fix a date and take her out for an hour to remind her of what attracted her to him in the first place. Fleetingly he thought of Anna. Eleanor wasn't that much older than the Snow Maiden, but probably much better in bed. The lord only knew what some of those boarding school girls had got up to after lights out in the dormitory. His fiancée kept some rather delicious little tricks up her sleeve, as well as possessing a cut-glass accent that would slice carrots. Eleanor's father owned half the county and luckily for Charles, had taken a liking to him, meaning his prospective mother-in-law didn't take long to change her mind about the age gap between her younger daughter and Charles.

All, so far, was highly satisfactory. He'd been enjoying the best of two worlds: his Army commission, coupled with plenty of high jinks with the fair sex, balanced against a future that looked not half bad. A wedding and a baby would cheer everyone up. As long as he could stay out of trouble. As long as he could stay alive.

'Why don't you invite your lieutenant to lunch next Sunday?'

Mother and daughter were both still in their housecoats, each drinking a leisurely cup of tea while Ruby read aloud snippets from *The People*. Anna noticed her mother was wearing a new dressing-gown, a chic little number in silver grey satin, but declined to comment, knowing it must have been a gift from her fiancé. The sleeves were wide and the fabric fell in shimmering folds from her shoulders. Anna felt a pang as she wondered what it was like for her mother to have another man adoring her after years of being married to Viktor, whose desire to have Ruby to himself had often irritated his young daughter.

'It's a nice thought, but he isn't my lieutenant and I don't want him to get too serious.'

Ruby rustled the paper. 'I don't understand. I thought you liked him?'

'I do! But Geoff's looking for romance.' Briefly, Anna

closed her eyes. 'It's the same with Davy. Why must men try to hurry things?'

'There's no comparison between your officer friend and Davy Griffiths. As you know, I wasn't too pleased when that lad turned up. I don't know what your grandmother would say.'

'My choice of friends isn't Nana's business.' Anna almost added '*Or yours*,' but thought better of it. If she slipped out early enough, her mother wouldn't know who she was meeting.

'Well, Davy will be off again soon, whereas Geoff is based locally. With so many young men away fighting, the pool of eligible males isn't that big, Anna. You're fortunate to have a decent job and a nice young man to squire you, even if I've never met him.'

'Mother, I realise how lucky I am, thank you. But I don't intend rushing into something just for the sake of having a steady boyfriend. And please remember we've only been out together twice. You can't really count the dance.' She shivered as she recalled those stolen moments outside with Charles. *Am I relieved he didn't kiss me, or do I wish he had?*

'Before you do anything reckless, you need to consider the likelihood of an engagement to a suitable young man in a year or so.'

'Really?' Anna examined her fingernails. 'I wonder why? That's the very thing I'm hoping to avoid.'

Ruby was shaking her head. 'I'd hate to think you

might end up an old maid if you insist on staying on your high horse. This business of women needing to be independent – I wonder what all those poor war widows from World War One would make of you? Women like Miss Ring, your business tutor – let alone those single lady teachers at the Grammar School, all in the same boat because their sweethearts and fiancés lost their lives.'

'I hate to say this, Mother, but you married young and that didn't stop you from …' She bit her lip. She shouldn't have raised the subject of Ruby's own widowhood.

'Your father and I had a happy marriage, Anna, even if I endured many months without him. If I hadn't married Vik, you wouldn't be where you are today, my girl. You'd do well to remember that and to accept you and your generation of women should be prepared to have children and repair the damage this horrible war will have done by the time it finishes.' Ruby's eyes shone with unshed tears.

Anna got up and put her arms around her. 'I'm sorry. I didn't mean to upset you, but can we declare a truce now, Mam?'

Ruby fished out a tiny lace handkerchief and dabbed her eyes. 'Have you ever noticed how you call me Mother when you're finding fault? Then it's back to Mam again when you realise you might have gone too far.'

Anna chuckled. 'Oh dear, I hadn't actually. All right, I'll try not to climb onto my high horse too often. And if it'll make you happy, I'll ask Geoff if he'd like to come to

Sunday lunch sometime soon. Mr Mapstone might like to come too, as long as you tell him I've made my feelings about marriage very clear to my boy-friend.'

Her mother raised her perfectly-plucked dark eyebrows. 'With any luck, that'll make Geoff keener than ever to win your heart.'

Anna left the house well before two o'clock. Her mother was still seated at the lunch table, sipping her cup of tea and listening to a request show on the wireless. Anna, obliged to tell a white lie when Ruby asked why she was in such a hurry to go for a walk, told her Biddy's mother had visitors for tea, so her friend needed to be home in time to help entertain them.

She saw Davy turn the corner and start loping up the hill as she stepped onto the pavement. He didn't immediately see her so she continued walking down, conscious of her mother's strict views on calling out in the street.

He broke into a gallop to arrive in front of her. 'I must've been far away,' he said. 'Didn't realise you were walking towards me.'

He took her hand. Anna didn't protest as they walked down the hill and along the main road towards the town. 'Shall we get a bus?' Davy broke the silence.

'Maybe to come back? I'm quite used to walking to the beach from home.'

'At least it's a fine day and not too hot. I hope your mother's well. And that you had a good time last night,

140

of course.'

Anna giggled. 'You sound so polite! The dance was OK, thanks. But tell me how you got on with your training? Have you made any special mates? Did you go to any dances? What was the food like? That sort of thing.'

'I didn't enjoy all that square bashing. Some of the lads in my hut could snore for the Olympics but I've palled up with a couple of lads, one from Pembrokeshire and one from Cardiff, funnily enough. The food was about as good as I expected and as for going to dances, we went along to a Saturday night hop and I danced with a few nice girls but ...'

'But what?'

'It doesn't matter what. There's only one girl I want to write to when I get across to France.'

'Davy, you know my views. But you sound as though you're coping well with your new life.'

He squeezed her fingers gently. 'Your nana told me you were doing well in your job. We've had a chat over the garden wall now and then, the pair of us.'

So much for Mam's comment about Nana being shocked if she knew Davy had called on me...

'I'm sorry for thinking your family were stuck up. And I apologise for talking about your ma having gentlemen friends that time. You were only a kid back then and I should've known better.'

'I was quite the little innocent, wasn't I? Did you know

my mother is engaged to her one and only gentleman caller? To my knowledge, he was the only one she was seeing, anyway. Difficult not to when Mr Mapstone was our landlord and friendly with both my parents. Mam was working as his housekeeper, of course.'

Noticing his cheeks colouring up, she felt a whoosh of guilt. Her mother's words reached to her over the years. '*I think your ears have been flapping and I need to put you straight on a couple of things.*'

This time she squeezed his hand. 'Davy, it's my turn to apologise. Being an only child, I was around the grown-ups a lot and often overheard things I shouldn't have. That was a strange time for our family – for us all in fact – and I hadn't really got the hang of relationships.'

'And you have now?' His tone was teasing.

'Yes, if deciding not to get too close to anyone is the secret to a quiet life.'

'You should be so lucky! Anna, have you any idea how attractive you are to men? Don't you never look in the mirror? That officer who took you to the dance – I bet he's asked you out again.'

'He hasn't, actually. I've made it clear I don't want to become too involved.'

'I'd almost feel sorry for the poor devil if I didn't hate him so much.'

She couldn't help laughing. 'Geoff's mother probably already has her eye on a likely bride for her son. She wouldn't see me as good officer's wife material – I'd be just another little typist in her eyes – not that I'm likely to meet her, of course.'

'If you ask me, any bloke who'd let his ma come between you and him wouldn't deserve you anyway.'

'That's nice of you. But I'm only guessing. Mrs Chandler might be very different from how I imagine her.'

They walked on in silence, past the town square and down the main street. Anna stopped to look in a shoe shop window, admired a pair of ankle strap green suede shoes but didn't linger.

'Penny for 'em?' Davy asked as they began walking again.

'My thoughts are probably not even worth a halfpenny. I was just thinking how strange wartime is. All the comings and goings … women doing men's jobs … kids being evacuated …'

'I try not to think too hard about the future. I'm just a humble squaddie so what do I know?'

She stopped walking again. 'How dare you say that? Don't you ever run yourself down again, David Griffiths! Nana told me your boss thinks the world of you – says he's still sorry at having to lose you to the Army. So there!' She reached for his hand. 'Let's go and have an ice cream and talk about anything you like except war.'

CHAPTER 14

'Can we go Dutch?'

'Nah! I invited you out, so this is my treat.' Davy pushed open the door to the ice cream parlour. He pulled off his cap and made a mock bow. 'Mademoiselle!'

'Thank you, kind sir. Well, if you insist on paying, you must let me treat you next time you get leave.' *Why say that? I'm trying not to raise his hopes, aren't I?*

He ignored her comment. 'You choose a table. What sort of ice cream would you like?'

'A North Pole, please. With raspberry sauce.'

'Are you sure you wouldn't like a Knickerbocker Glory?'

'Positive, thanks.'

'Coffee?'

'Ooh, that'd be nice. They make a lovely brew here. Thank you.'

She headed for a window table. Davy followed as soon as the dark-eyed proprietor produced two North Poles and two cups of coffee.

'Come on then,' she said as he unloaded the tray. 'Which movie star do you have a crush on?'

'Will you tell me yours if I tell you mine?' He sat down opposite her.

'There are so many, but I know who I'm going to say.'

'Veronica Lake for me.'

'Oh yes, she's beautiful. I'm going to choose Alan Ladd.'

'He's a bit short for you. And does that mean you prefer older men?'

'Veronica's older than both of us, so does that mean you prefer older women?' She shot him a mischievous glance. 'Alan's height doesn't matter as I'm never likely to meet him.'

'Well, I suppose I'm tall, but that's about all I have over him.'

'We only see the celluloid image,' Anna said thoughtfully. 'It strikes me these stars have more marriage break ups than anyone I know in real life.'

'Maybe they have too much too soon? They get to the point where they're always looking for the next new thing – the latest car – the pretty young starlet …'

'Who is probably several years younger than their current wife.' Anna added. 'That's very discerning – very shrewd of you.'

'You see? I'm not just a pretty face!'

She looked at him smiling at her across the table and thought again how much better he looked since joining the Army. But what his new life might bring for him and for his fellow soldiers was beyond her imaginings. She knew she could never fall in love with Davy, but the thought of him being snuffed out in what she saw as pointless waste was beyond sad.

She determined to banish such dark thoughts. 'I expect your mam and dad are pleased to have you home.'

He shrugged. 'Ma's probably pleased even if she don't always show it. Pa's had me working in the garden. Reckons his joints are too stiff for him to do much digging these days.' He grinned. 'That's his excuse anyway. But they're not bad folks. I could've had worse ones.'

'I cringe sometimes when I remember what I was like as a child,' Anna said.

'Spoilt, weren't you?'

She stirred raspberry sauce into her last scoop of vanilla ice cream. 'Not as much as you might think. Sheltered, yes, and I was lucky to have had nice clothes and treats, but Mam had to be careful with money even though my father used to say she over-indulged me while he wasn't around. I think my parents were quite strict.'

'I bet your dad made a fuss of you when he came home on leave.' Davy crunched his last piece of wafer biscuit.

'To be honest, I always knew it was my mother who really lit up Pappa's life.'

Davy frowned. 'What did you call your dad?'

'Pappa. It's Norwegian. Each time he came back, it was like an invisible shield went up around the two of them. And there were times when I knew they'd much prefer to be alone. That feeling of being the odd one out was something that stayed with me, even though I loved him and wished he could be at home more.'

He regarded her thoughtfully. 'It's not all milk and honey being the eldest of three, you know. As soon as I was old enough, Pa gave me the job of emptying the bucket from the privy.' He grimaced. 'Still does, now I'm back on leave.' He sat back. 'Ah, well, it's the least I can do for the old feller.'

'Your dad's not that old, surely?'

'Too old for active service, but he's joined the Home Guard and he don't half rise to it if I tease him. You know what they say – Look, duck and vanish!' He checked his watch. 'Do you have to be back at a certain time?'

'Not really, but I probably should go home soon and get my clothes ready for the morning.'

He wrinkled his nose. 'Women! Do you fancy a little stroll through the gardens? Then we could get a bus back to town and I'll walk you the last bit home.'

'OK. Mam used to take me to the gardens some afternoons but I haven't been there for years.'

They left the café, both of them calling goodbye to the owner's elder son. He saluted Davy, blew a kiss to Anna, then asked her to remember him to her mother. She'd been enjoying the family's lovingly made ice cream since she was a little girl and the café was part of her life, part of the town's fabric. As she grew older, Anna suspected him of having an eye for her mother, but Ruby's life had revolved around Viktor and she'd never responded to Nick's outrageous flirting, apart from favouring him with a smile and an occasional blush.

Davy took her hand again as they crossed to the promenade and walked until they turned off into the gardens. He led her purposefully to a bench at the far side, the seat half-concealed by the sweeping fronds of a weeping willow.

They settled themselves, each gazing out at the white horses ruffling the restless waters of the Bristol Channel. Anna shrugged her shoulders into the pale blue angora bolero she'd been carrying.

'Cold? Might a humble soldier be allowed to put his arms around you?'

She was torn between agreement and refusal, but while she hesitated, he leaned towards her, hugging her close. Their lips met almost immediately, whisking Anna back in time to the moment Davy kissed her while they clung to each other beneath her dripping umbrella. This second kiss was equally pleasant and almost without realising, she was responding. The kissing became more urgent. Davy's hands stroked her back and the warmth she'd been seeking filled her body. She felt his fingers touch her left breast, a butterfly touch so gentle, she didn't protest. Far from pulling away and reprimanding him, she lost herself in this new sensation. Now his hand touched her left knee, his fingers gently stroking her leg through her nylon stocking. Moving upwards to the bare flesh above her suspender.

'Anna, you're so beautiful. Can I ... please... will you let me?' He sounded breathless.

'We mustn't,' she heard herself say.

Davy groaned. 'Hey, you were enjoying it!' He put his arm around her shoulders. 'Before I go back to barracks, could we ... could we possibly meet again? I'll find somewhere for us to go and ...'

'Davy, no! You know I can't ... daren't.'

'I promise to take care of you. You don't need to worry. They even gave us a lecture and handed out ...'

She moved away from him. 'We mustn't do anything we might regret. I'm sorry, but I shouldn't have let this happen.'

'You liked it though, didn't you? Have you done it before? Let a bloke go this far? That officer who fancies you ...?'

She stood up, straightening her blouse, her cheeks flushed. 'What do you take me for? I've never let anyone else do what you did.' She sat down again and took out her powder compact to check her appearance in the mirror, one hand smoothing her blonde locks into place.

'Have you any idea how that makes me feel? Have you, Anna? Over the moon is how I feel, so please don't spoil it for me or for yourself, sweetheart. You must like me just a little? I'll be gone from your life soon, but please don't send me away, feeling like I do.'

She shivered, despite the sunlight. 'A girl should be a virgin on her wedding night.'

His laugh was hollow. 'Sez you! Nowadays, girls live for the moment and I think you know why that is. I can borrow a car. Let me collect you tomorrow evening. Please?'

'There you are, one bowl of mutton stew for her ladyship!' Biddy laughed as Anna pulled a face. 'You ungrateful wretch. Sit down and be thankful I don't make you say Grace ten times as a penance.'

Anna flopped into her seat at their favourite window table. 'Thanks, Biddy, it was kind of you to get my meal. What a morning!'

'I shan't ask. There'd be no point, now would there?'

Anna peered into her bowl. 'What? Oh, right. I can't talk about work but I need to talk to you about something else.'

Biddy was coping with a chewy piece of mutton. She swallowed and put down her cutlery. 'Talk about strong elastic! Now, might this concern your love life, by any chance?'

Anna sighed. 'How did you guess? I'm afraid I've got myself in a pickle.'

Biddy dropped her knife with a clatter.

'Holy Mother of God, you're not telling me you're …'

'No, you goose. I haven't got myself into trouble in the way you mean.'

'That's something to be thankful for, I suppose. So,

what's bothering you? Surely not Geoff Chandler? He always seems such a gentleman.'

'That's because he is. No, it's Davy, the boy next door to my nana's. I promised myself I wouldn't lead him on and guess what?'

Biddy leaned forward. 'Tell me.'

Anna rested her chin on one hand to shield her face while she whispered brief details of the previous afternoon's outing. 'Then I felt as though he was almost blackmailing me into – well, you know what I mean.'

'I can't believe you agreed to go out with him again. What are you playing at, girl? Stand him up! He deserves it for trying to lead you astray.'

Anna groaned. 'The thing is, I didn't take much leading. I don't know why I let him near me, but it was as if that first kiss lit a flame.'

'Very poetic, but no reason to jump into the fire with him tonight. When does he return to his regiment?'

'Um, tomorrow or the next day. Can't remember.'

'Can't you get a message to him? Tell him you're under the weather and worried you won't be fit for work tomorrow.'

Anna pulled a face. 'I feel really bad about this. I'm half to blame, after all.'

'Use your head. You can't totally trust him to be careful and you don't want to marry him, so why risk meeting him again! Why not write a note to say you can't see him after all, stick it in an envelope and give it to me?

I'll go to his house and push it through the letterbox. That way, you won't need to see him and if you make it clear you think it best not to meet, he'll know not to come knocking on your door before he goes back.'

'Are you sure you don't mind? It's taking you out of your way.'

'I wouldn't offer if I minded. Anyway, you'd do the same for me, wouldn't you?'

'You know I would. Except you're nowhere near as likely to mess things up as I am.'

Biddy shrugged. 'Eddie's very sweet and I sometimes think he doesn't know what to make of me and my daft comments. But he's growing on me.' She reached for her dessert. 'Marmalade sponge pudding and custard. The perfect thing to send me to sleep at my desk.'

'I doubt Miss Napier would let you get away with that. You know, suddenly I'm hungry. I'm so glad I told you about Davy, even if I feel like a coward, letting you do my dirty work.'

'It's hardly dirty work, and us girls have to stick together in these troubled times. By the way, when's your ma marrying that rich fiancé of hers?'

'Not until Christmas or New Year. She's being a bit vague about it. Probably feeling disloyal to my father, if I know Mam.'

'And what about you? Will you move in with the newlyweds like they want, or will you go to your grandma's?'

Anna bit her lip. 'I'm not quite so keen as I was about moving in with Nana. I mean, because of Davy's family living next door.'

'He'll be away for ages now, won't he? It's not like he's in a reserved occupation and out in the garden every evening hoping to see you.' She lowered her voice. 'Don't turn round, but guess who's just come in.'

Anna put down her spoonful of pudding. 'Are we late? I hope it's not Miss Napier come to chivvy us?'

'David Niven's turned up with Geoff in tow.'

'I hope they're not coming this way. Is my nose shining?'

Biddy giggled. 'Like a beacon! No, you eejit, the nose is fine and they're talking so hard, I don't think they've noticed us. Just as well, with you having so much to think about at the moment.'

'Probably.' Anna knew a quiet life was just what was needed. But the feeling of shifting sands stayed with her. She felt relieved when she and Biddy made their way out, while the two officers queued at the counter, chatting to the serving ladies.

Two attractive males: *Why, oh why can't I fall for the one I know would never let me down?* 'Maybe I'd be better off entering a nunnery,' Anna muttered as she and her friend headed for the ladies' room. Once inside, the pair of them burst out laughing.

'Becoming a postulant might be a little drastic,' Biddy said while they were washing their hands. 'How about trying not to juggle two men at a time?'

'It seems to me even one at a time can prove tricky.' Anna pulled a face at herself in the mirror. 'I wish I knew whether it's fair to see Geoff again. I really do like him, you know.'

'So, how's the love life going, Geoffrey?' Charles's gaze took in a nearby table where a vivacious brunette was holding forth to two other young women. He caught her eye. At once she looked away, then moments later, looked back again. Charles winked at her, succeeding in making her blush before he decided to pay attention to what his companion was saying.

'I have to report it's at a standstill, I'm afraid.' Geoff grimaced.

'I was under the impression you had something going with the Snow Maiden?'

'Me too! Until she read my cards and brought me crashing down to earth. Crikey, is that really what you call Anna?' He shot a suspicious glance at his companion.

'Only because of her name and heritage, old boy. No other reason, I can assure you. Since that awful night when Marcia's number came up, I'm finding it difficult to return to old habits. Some might say that's a good thing, given I have a fiancée who apparently still thinks the world of me.'

'Hell's bells, it must have been brutal for you, Charlie.' Geoff hesitated. 'You hardly ever talk about your fiancée. You could have gone home to convalesce – I'd have driven you there and caught a train back.'

'You're one of the good 'uns, Geoffrey. Many thanks, but while I did contemplate the notion, my brain wasn't totally in top gear so I opted not to go rattling cages for the time being.'

'What's the young lady's name?'

'My betrothed's name is Eleanor. As in Eleanor of Aquitaine.'

'Knowing you, she's probably equally as beautiful.'

Charles pushed away his plate. 'God, I hate what this war has done to all our lives. The canteen ladies do their best but ...' He swallowed the rest of his tea. 'As for my fiancée, she's an extremely delightful young lady and far too good for me. Her mother had the local doctor lined up as a potential son-in-law until he joined the Army and then I came along anyway.' He frowned. 'Or was it a young clergyman? Anyway, Eleanor and I met at some dreary party when I was home on leave last Spring and we got on well, though I think I must have proposed in a mad moment.' He grinned.

'A mad moment? You regret becoming engaged?' Geoff put down his cup.

Charles got to his feet. 'Of course not. We shared a romantic weekend before I came here. Eleanor had to meet me in secret and tell her parents she was staying with an old school friend. She writes me wonderful letters to which I try to reply when I can.' He grimaced. 'She wanted to visit me when I was recuperating, but I couldn't face it. How could I have told her I was with another woman the night of the air raid, Geoffrey? How could I have made light conversation?'

He gripped the back of his chair. 'You know what?' His voice was low and husky with emotion. 'I really wish I could stand face to face with Marcia's French- Canadian husband. I really wish I could tell him how much she loved him and missed him. Every day. Every hour. And if he suspected I'd bedded her and he thumped me for it, I'd damned well have taken my punishment, then helped him get drunk.'

Geoff glanced round. Fortunately, nobody nearby appeared to be taking any notice of Charles. 'I know you would. Shall we get back to the office now?'

Charles straightened his shoulders and walked ahead, holding open the canteen door. 'Duty calls.'

Geoff followed him down the corridor. He sensed an innate restlessness in Charles Milburn that didn't bode well for the future.

CHAPTER 15

Anna finished work later than usual. She'd scribbled a hasty note to Davy and dropped it on her friend's desk when she next visited the typing pool. She would have walked part of the way home with Biddy, but expecting her friend to wait around for half an hour then go out of her way to deliver the note seemed unfair.

She walked through the main entrance, fretting over the possibility of Davy not noticing an envelope pushed through the letter box long after any postal deliveries would have been made. She consoled herself, knowing the geography of those houses and realising anyone descending the stairs would have full view of the front door and notice the note on the mat. Having him turn up, expecting to find her waiting for him was too awful to contemplate.

She was quickening her pace when a familiar vehicle came to a halt a yard or two ahead. Her heartbeat quickened. *What excuse could I give for not accepting a lift?*

Charles leaned across to open the passenger door. 'Hello, you. May I offer the Snow Maiden a lift?'

She frowned. 'I thought you were staying in Penarth now?'

'Correct, ma'am. But Fate directed me this way this evening. Why don't we drive down to the beach?'

Anna chuckled. 'I'm not dressed for the beach, Charles. But don't let me stop you.'

'Then how about a quiet drink instead? I'm going back to the Mess for dinner so I can drop you off at your house, wherever that may be. Come on, live dangerously!' He hopped out of the car and came round to her side.

She got in. 'All right. One drink, then.'

'Good girl.'

Why did she feel so jittery? So acutely aware of his nearness as they drove through the town. Aware in a way she hadn't experienced with Geoff in the driving seat. The feeling was unnerving – unsettling and yet, exhilarating. Neither spoke and somehow their silence was even more arousing than if Charles had complimented her on her perfume. She wondered what was happening. Told herself she knew what was happening and she couldn't do a thing about it.

He reached out his left hand and squeezed her elbow. 'Penny for 'em?'

She felt the rush of heat to her cheeks and turned her head, hoping he wouldn't notice. Trying to think of something witty and sparkling to say and failing dismally.

'Not easy, is it, sweet girl?'

'It's not, but I'm doing my utmost to please Colonel Gresham and not leave the office in a muddle for Miss Morgan to find when she returns.'

Charles chuckled. A deep, rich chuckle that dried her throat and caused a sweet yearning she fought to ignore. Despite her reply, she realised exactly what he meant and she also knew he was aware of it. The comment had nothing to do with her secretarial capabilities.

'Our man at the top has nothing but praise for you, Miss Christensen.'

Anna seized on the remark with relief. 'Well, Miss Morgan's efficiency is enviable. It's made it easier for me to take up the reins.'

She knew she sounded prim. Stilted. This was a man accustomed to mixing with sophisticated people. Geoff had told her something about the chain of conquests Charles Millburn trailed like clouds of glory. She had no doubt these women were all beautiful and sophisticated, their conversation sparkling. She would find herself out of her depth in their company. As for his fiancée …

The Vauxhall's engine purred as its driver took the hill in low gear. Everything about Charles's movements was smooth and unhurried. Her mother had once told her, in a rare unguarded moment after drinking two glasses of Amontillado, the way a man drove his motor car reflected the way he made love. Anna had felt intrigued and a little embarrassed, but now she remembered Ruby's words.

And wondered.

'I know where we'll go. There won't be many evenings like this now we're heading into autumn.'

'But …'

He glanced sideways. 'It's not a problem, is it?'

'No, no of course not. My mother knows I sometimes need to work late.'

That chuckle again. 'I hope the colonel doesn't make a habit of keeping you at your bench, my dear. But this won't be a late night. Just a quiet drink while we forget the war for an hour or so.'

He asked her about her mother's wedding preparations. Anna couldn't recall telling him about the forthcoming nuptials but felt relieved to have something to talk about, though she feared she was gabbling and probably boring him.

She recognised the hotel gateway. When he pulled into the driveway, he found a convenient parking place and switched off the engine. She waited, wondering if he'd kiss her before they went inside. But he was out of the car and round to open the door, offering his arm as they walked to the entrance. It seemed a long way to bring her just to have a drink, but she made no comment.

Anna walked into the foyer and recognised the woman behind the reception desk.

'Well, look who's here!'

Charles strode forward and the hotelier held out her hand. He promptly took it in his own, kissing rather than shaking it.

'Always Sir Galahad, Captain Milburn.' She turned to Anna. 'And your friend too. How lovely to see you again, my dear.'

'It's good to see you too, Mrs Cooper.'

Charles, very gently, slipped his arm around Anna's waist. She shivered with pleasure, suspecting Arlene Cooper hadn't missed her reaction.

'We'll go through to the cocktail lounge, Arlene, if that's all right.'

'Of course, Charlie. I've taken on a new waiter since you were here last. A young man who's returned home because of health problems. But Cyril's fit for hotel duties and I'm training him personally.'

'I bet you are …'

Anna caught the frisson between the two. She wouldn't be at all surprised if Arlene Cooper was yet another of Charles Milburn's fair ladies. She further reflected on what could only be a girlish fancy – imagining he might consider someone as unsophisticated as herself, as another conquest.

The front door was opening as he guided Anna towards the lounge. They could hear the rumble of voices and Arlene greeting a small group of RAF officers, presumably from the base a few miles along the coast.

'Let's get ahead of the flyboys.'

He steered her to a table for two in the furthest corner where sunshine still beamed through the windows.

Charles pulled out a chair for her and as she sat down, the waiter came to greet them. Anna thought he looked vaguely familiar but couldn't think why.

'Good evening, sir … madam. My name is Cyril. What might I tempt you with this evening?' He swished a small cloth lightly across their table's already well-polished surface.

'I think something gin-based and fruity for the lady, please, Cyril. And a whisky sour for me.'

'Certainly sir. Do you have a tab?'

'I do indeed. Captain Charles Milburn. I'm a friend of your employer. Bad luck on your demob, by the way. Were you in my lot?'

'I was indeed, sir. Got a few chunks taken out of me one way or the other. Could've been worse.' He glanced at Anna. 'I beg your pardon, madam. I'll prepare your drinks straightaway.'

Anna noticed Charles's eyes narrow as he watched the young man move away.

'He looks familiar to me, though I can't think why,' she said.

Charles shrugged. 'Poor devil's lost half of one finger and his gait suggests he might have lost a toe on his left foot. He also has a cavity behind his right ear, though that could have been caused by mastitis when he was a child.'

Something stirred in Anna's memory. 'Goodness, I remember now. There was a boy in my class at the school

I first attended and he had a definite hollow at the back of, I think, his right ear. He sat across the aisle from me and I used to sneak glances at his head – dreadful child that I was.'

'I can't imagine you being anything less than a well-behaved little girl.' He reached into his pocket and withdrew his cigarette case.

How have I not noticed before that he's left-handed? 'I always wanted to impress the grown-ups.' She was watching his hands. Wondering how they would feel as he removed her underwear and cupped her breasts.

He looked up at her. 'Only child?'

'Yes. How about you?'

'I have two older sisters. I spent several years at boarding school. My father always wanted me to join the Army and I didn't want to disappoint him. Funny to think I'd have ended up in the mob anyway.'

'I imagine your father must be pleased you're an officer.'

'I suppose so, though you'd never know it. Anna, I'm sorry, I've never seen you smoking, but would you like a cigarette too?'

She shook her head. 'No, thanks. I don't enjoy smoking and I certainly won't smoke to look sophisticated, as some girls do.'

He put his cigarette case on the table. 'One of the things I like about you, young lady, is how you see things. It strikes me you've decided to make your own way in life. You also have a certain quality that demands respect. Why do you think Maud Napier hauled you from the typing pool?'

Nonplussed, Anna didn't quite know how to respond. She gained thinking time when Cyril appeared with their drinks. He placed Anna's cocktail before her and she thanked him, only then noticing the half finger.

Charles nodded his thanks as Cyril put down his whiskey sour. 'So where do you call home, old chap?'

'I was born in Barry, back along the coast, but I have a room here at the hotel. Mrs Cooper has been extraordinarily kind.' He stepped back. 'Enjoy your drinks.'

Charles raised his eyebrows at Anna as the waiter left. 'He could well be your old schoolmate then. If I were to bribe him to rack his brains, how many deadly secrets would he reveal about you, I wonder?'

She laughed and reached for her glass. 'I was a little shrimp of a child so he won't have the least idea who I am, though he might well remember my name. I did stand out amongst the children called Davis, Williams, and so on. Some had English surnames of course, but I was the only pupil with a foreign-sounding name.'

'Ah ... singled out for stardom right from the beginning.' He lifted his glass. 'I drink to the future of Anna Christensen – Snow Maiden.'

She acknowledged his toast with a wry smile and sipped her cocktail. 'That's delicious. Does your choice of nickname mean you think I'm cold and hard-hearted?'

'I don't know, do I? Yet.'

CHAPTER 16

He held her gaze, making her sizzle with something she could only define as electricity. But Charles was an accomplished seducer and scoundrel. Geoff had made her only too aware of those dubious credentials. And yet, here she was, enjoying a drink with the only man she ever fantasised about. She raised her glass to her lips again, trying to appear unflustered.

'What happens when Miss Morgan returns to her post? Have you thought about it?'

'There's no need. I shall return to the typing pool and go on doing what they pay me to do.'

'What a waste. No thoughts of looking for a better position elsewhere?'

'Only if a post on the top floor became vacant. If I left, I'd be called up. In some ways that would be exciting, but I think I'll wait and see how things work out.'

He nodded. 'Of course. I'd temporarily forgotten you were in a reserved occupation.' He hesitated. 'What would bring more excitement to your life, I wonder?

Presupposing the CO's secretary returns from sick leave, of course.'

'I hope she does recover. I wouldn't wish ill health on her, or anyone.' She thought of her father when he was hospitalised hundreds of miles from his family and never recovered his health.

'A shadow passed over your face then. Dare I ask why?'

'My father died earlier this year. He became very ill whilst at sea.'

'I'm sorry. How very sad for you and your mother.'

'She was lost without Pappa, but she has a new life to look forward to now.'

'You'll have a stepfather. Will you remain at home?'

'At Frank's home, yes. Well, that's the plan. Mam's not keen for me to find lodgings. Says it's more sensible to save up for the future.'

'Excellent advice. I'd like to meet your mother one of these days.'

Anna felt her cheeks heat. Ruby would have forty fits if she knew her daughter was spending time with a man ten or twelve years her senior and engaged to be married at that.

'Though maybe that's not such a good idea. Not when I'm about to pose you another kind of question.'

Anna, wondering what Charles could possibly want to ask her, was temporarily diverted as three RAF officers entered the lounge. The young men congregated at the bar, each of them having called a greeting to Charles who acknowledged them cheerfully before draining his glass. Anna wasn't sure whether to finish her drink quickly or not.

'Another? Or shall we make a move?'

'Maybe make a move?' She drank the remainder of her cocktail.

'Come on then. Perhaps you'd like to inspect the ladies' room before we set off?'

Anna felt pleased he'd saved her from mentioning this. He pointed out the door and set off on his own errand. Before she returned to the foyer, she took out her powder compact and freshened her make-up, applying another coat of bright red lipstick then rubbing some off with her forefinger. Finally, she dabbed a little scent on each wrist, hesitated then applied some behind each ear.

She found Charles leaning on the desk, chatting to Arlene Cooper. The hotelier broke off her conversation and gave Anna what her grandma would call "a once over," before greeting her.

Again, Charles placed his arm lightly around Anna's waist. 'We'd best be on our way. I'll see you before too long, Arlene.'

'I look forward to it, Captain.'

Outside, streaks of orange, crimson and gold tinted the sky. Charles saw Anna into the car and settled himself behind the wheel. Before he started the ignition, he turned to her. 'How reliable is that lipstick?'

'I beg your pardon?'

'If someone kissed you, how well would it stay on?'

'I'm sure a man as experienced as yourself in the ways of women must know the answer to that. Is this the question you mentioned earlier?'

The engine purred into life, its throaty sound encouraging Anna to relax into the comfortable bucket seat. She glanced sideways and saw he was smiling.

'Touché. I'm sure you realise, it wasn't. Let's get going.'

He drove for a couple of miles then turned off the main road.

Anna frowned and looked at him.

He reached out a hand and patted hers. 'Fear not, beautiful lady. There's a quiet spot not far along where we can park and talk while we watch the sun sink into the sea. I believe it's time to address something that's bothering both of us, don't you?'

Anna shifted in her seat. It was no use pretending she didn't understand, but a feeling of panic enveloped her. *What do I say if he wants …?*

'It's all right, you needn't say anything yet. But you do need to think hard about your answer.'

A couple of minutes later, Charles steered the Vauxhall down a narrow lane, turning it round by a padlocked gateway before switching off the engine. In the distance, across the field, she could see the sea.

'I love this view. I come here when I want to escape from it all. There's a path down to the shore but we won't tackle that this evening.'

Anna waited.

'Tell me – why did you accept my offer of a lift?'

'I thought it was very kind of you.'

'Piffle! Do you enjoy my company?'

'Of course, especially now I've got to know you a little better.'

'And do you enjoy Geoffrey's company?'

'Yes. He's a lovely man.'

'A lovely man who worships the ground you walk upon. But you don't feel the same, do you? I'll answer my own question. You obviously don't, because you didn't mention him once this evening until I introduced him into our conversation.'

She hesitated, knowing whatever she said would surely incriminate her.

'Anna, be honest with me. Are you in love with Geoffrey?'

She looked down at her hands. 'I'm very fond of him, but I know it's not love. I may be inexperienced, but I'm sure there needs to be something more than just friendship.'

'That's a shame. He's a charming young man and highly suitable boyfriend material. You'll always be safe with him. Geoffrey Chandler will never cheat on you and break your heart. Young Sylvia with the whiplash backhand would walk across hot coals if it meant becoming his girlfriend. You do realise that, don't you?'

'Yes,' she whispered. 'I know you're right.'

He was looking at her mouth. 'I wouldn't ask you this if I didn't think you wanted it, but maybe you'll prove me wrong. I hope not, because I don't think I can bear it any longer if I don't kiss you. May I, Anna?'

She turned her head to gaze at the rapidly changing sky. Purples and mauves, shot with dark blue and gunmetal, swam before her eyes as she turned back to face him, placing her hands on his shoulders.

Charles groaned and bent his head, his lips meeting hers, his hands caressing the tops of her arms. Their kiss deepened. Sweetened. Anna had wondered time and time again how this would feel. And now she knew. And she was lost, her doubts and concerns melting away more swiftly than the setting sun sank into the darkening sea.

He drew back. 'I can tell how we shall be together. But first you need to acknowledge your nature. I have a feeling you're of a passionate disposition, but you maybe don't realise it yet.'

She remembered Davy's caresses and how much she'd enjoyed his touch before she felt too frightened to allow him another chance.

'What are you saying, Charlie?'

'I'm asking you to acknowledge I'm right. If you were an ordinary sort of girl, set on marrying a decent young man and having a family, you'd be delighted to have Geoffrey mooning over you and you know it.'

'He doesn't moon over me and obviously I'm not

leading him on, because he knows my views. Not that it's any of your business, Charles Milburn.'

'I knew it! We're kindred spirits, you and me.' He reached out again and kissed her, his fingers gentle on her breasts, stroking and teasing through her blouse until she was breathless and wanting more. Much more.

'Dear God, I'd better get you home,' he said at last, keeping his arms around her.

'Charles … when will I see you again?'

'That's up to you, my dear.' He smoothed a tendril of hair away from her face. 'I know I don't deserve to have you in my life, yet there's something between us that draws me in and frankly scares me out of my wits. I shan't rush you into doing something you might regret. You have to come to me. And you must remember I'm a lot older than you and engaged to another woman. Do you understand what I'm saying?'

'Yes, of course. I'm not a child. I don't care how old you are, but this is a big step for me, even if it's just another affair for you.'

'Don't say that, my darling. But I shan't lie to you. I've had affairs with many ladies – mostly married ones – I imagine Geoffrey must have marked your card?'

'I make my own decisions, Charles. I will come to you.'

He whistled – a long, low note. 'If you only knew how often I've dreamed of hearing you say that. Dare I hope you might come away with me at the weekend?'

Her heart bump-bumped. She took a deep breath. 'I'll make some excuse. Pretend Biddy's asked me to stay with her.'

'We're at war, darling. You'd need to take your ration book to stop your mother from being suspicious. Why not say the department's carrying out an exercise on Friday afternoon through until Saturday afternoon? Practising evacuation and survival techniques, including night time.' He grinned. 'Such manoeuvres have been known. Then you can bring an overnight bag to work and Bob's your uncle.'

'But I wouldn't have an overnight bag with me at the Dock Offices in a real emergency situation.'

He kissed her nose and withdrew his arms from around her. 'True, but if you're asked, you can say your supervisor suggested it. On Friday morning, I'll pick you up. You can tell me exactly where, when I drop you off this evening. Your bag can stay in my car so nobody will question you about it. Will that be acceptable to madam?'

CHAPTER 17

Anna's mother became more and more engrossed with wedding preparations. The couple planned a church ceremony for the few family members and close friends they possessed. Frank's son, an RAF Flight Lieutenant, had put in for leave in late December and was to be best man, while Anna would be Ruby's maid of honour. She privately thought there was rather too much time and attention devoted to the bride's trousseau, but didn't blame her mother for making the most of this second time around marriage.

She realised Ruby and Viktor wouldn't have had much time to plan their 1924 wedding, given they needed to fit in the ceremony before Viktor set off on another voyage. It would have been a case of make do and mend and no doubt her grandmother pursed her lips and sighed over it, but Ruby and Viktor had been very much in love. So when Anna arrived the following year, nobody ever suspected their daughter was anything but a honeymoon baby.

Anna still recalled that sense of exclusion urging her

to impress her father at times, especially during early adolescence. Viktor had been the kind of man people describe as "larger than life" but to her knowledge, he was a faithful and loving husband. She wondered how Charles Milburn viewed the husbands of the ladies he'd charmed over the years. She suddenly remembered him mentioning his fiancée back home. *How can I contemplate going to bed with a man who obviously has no respect for marriage and all it stands for?*

Why didn't she give him the brush off and get to know Geoff better? But it was no good. The craving inside her could only be cured in one way.

Anna didn't tell Biddy about her clandestine trip. If her friend knew nothing, and someone noticed Anna driving off in Charles's car on Friday afternoon, Biddy would have nothing to say other than Captain Milburn sometimes gave Anna a lift home. If interfering people decided that was inappropriate use of his petrol allocation, then it was too bad.

She washed her hair on the Thursday evening and spent time drying it in front of the gas fire Ruby had lit as the evenings were chillier now. Feeling at the same time the sensations of excitement and trepidation, she told herself it wasn't too late to cancel this rendezvous as she'd done when deciding she'd be better off not meeting Davy. She still felt a certain amount of guilt at having fobbed him off with a note of apology, rather than meeting him and making her feelings crystal clear.

Was she really in love with Charles? Or was she in love with the thought of Charles? He was as different from Davy as caviar from bread and dripping – not that she'd ever sampled the former. Davy wanted – needed – a girl who'd giggle and let him take liberties. He wanted a sweetheart who'd write him letters sealed with a loving kiss. Charles wanted – and got – more women than probably any other officer in the camp. As for Geoff, she knew, of the three men, he was the only one who might possibly love her for the right reasons.

She saw how his face lit up when she was near him. He'd made it plain he understood her feelings about Charles. But how could that be, when she herself didn't feel sure? Yet here she was, about to go away on what people would condemn as "a dirty weekend."

Anna was deep in thought when Ruby chose that moment to come in from the kitchen. 'I hope they're going to feed you on this exercise or whatever it is.'

'Pardon? Oh, sorry, Mam, I was miles away. They're bound to feed us, but I think I'd better take my ration book. Just in case …'

'I can't think why.' Her mother crossed to the sideboard. Their ration books were kept in the top drawer and Ruby selected Anna's and handed it to her. 'Be sure to take good care of it. We don't want all the palaver of applying for a replacement – you'd probably have to answer all kinds of questions as to how you managed to lose it.'

Anna, still kneeling in front of the fire, hoped Ruby would decide heat from the flames was causing her daughter's flushed cheeks. She drew back and rose, hairbrush in hand. 'Almost dry now.'

'Wouldn't it have been better to wait until you came back from your work thing? If you have to crawl down corridors and jump out of windows, you'll probably need a bath as well as a shampoo!'

'Um, I don't think it'll be as bad as all that. I think it's more about paying attention to detail, answering phones promptly and keeping an eye open for anything suspicious.'

'But surely that's the kind of thing you do normally?'

Desperate to change the subject, Anna spotted her mother's film magazine. 'I see you bought *Picturegoer* today. Anyone interesting in there?'

Ruby passed her the magazine. 'Have a flip through.' She settled herself on the couch, her gaze on her daughter.

Anna began babbling about the beautiful gown Rita Hayworth was pictured in and how handsome her escort, Clark Gable, was. 'I wonder what it's like to be a film star,' she said, looking up.

'I doubt it's as glamorous as people imagine. And some of them have so many love affairs …'

Anna fanned her hot cheeks with the magazine before handing it back. 'Goodness, I must've been too close to the fire.' She scrambled up and sat in an armchair, smoothing back her hair.

'Anna, about your lieutenant coming to lunch on Sunday. It is still on, I suppose? Frank said he'd get us a joint of beef from his farming pal and your granddad has plenty of vegetables.'

Anna swallowed hard. She'd temporarily forgotten all about Sunday lunch. It was a good job Charles planned to deliver her home on Saturday morning. In any case, it wasn't worth explaining Geoff's rank.

'Geoff and I are friends, Mam. We're not courting and as for Sunday dinner, we're not that short of money, are we? I can give you a bit more, you know.'

'You're a good girl, but it's all right. You know your granddad grows more vegetables than we can eat, so I'll be making lots of stews again this winter, but the beef will be a godsend for Sunday and there should be some left afterwards. As for pudding, I'm wondering about jam roll and custard. That should fill us all up.'

'I'm sure it'll be lovely. I can help you on Sunday morning.'

'It might be useful if you could collect some vegetables from Pa on Saturday afternoon – carrots, parsnips … whatever's going. I hope your people won't keep you hanging around too long once they give you all your breakfasts.'

Anna was in agonies, convinced her mother guessed something was up and that something involved her daughter getting up to no good. She told herself not to worry so. Her mother liked things to be just right, and anyway, why should Ruby doubt her word?

Next morning as usual, her mother tapped on Anna's door on her way downstairs. 'Are you awake?'

'Nearly,' Anna called.

'Well, don't go back to sleep.'

Anna stretched her arms above her head and yawned. Sleep hadn't come easily the night before. Her mind kept projecting images of Charles which she found difficult to erase. By the time she drifted off, she'd convinced herself to say she was unable to join him. But this morning, she felt nothing but excitement. This was, after all, the kind of life she wanted, wasn't it? She had no desire for domestication, even if came with a gold band on her ring finger. Life was much more fun for single women, even if all most of them cared about was finding a husband.

She had concerns about protecting herself and decided, now she was a woman of the world, or almost, she would inform Charles he must take charge of that side of things. Anna couldn't imagine him not being equipped to do so and was determined not to show embarrassment or to feel guilty at being unable to deal with this herself.

Her first problem was what to wear. She didn't want Ruby to pass comment, nor Biddy and possibly Miss Napier, though she could fob her off much more easily than she could the other two. She opted for her smartest two-piece costume with a white blouse beneath and she'd packed a green crepe cocktail dress and black suede high-heeled shoes to wear to dinner at the hotel. When she slipped a string of pearls, wrapped in chamois leather, inside one of her smart shoes, she thought of her father. The pearls once belonged to his mother, who'd died not long after his father. What would Viktor think of his only daughter, if he was still alive today?

And yet, he hadn't behaved responsibly when he got Ruby pregnant. Although it appeared those two had been so besotted with one another, Anna's grandparents hadn't been surprised when the young couple wanted to marry before Viktor sailed away again.

Anna didn't want the same fate. She might feel differently one day, but for the foreseeable future, there were other items on her agenda.

She reached the bottom of the hill, clutching her overnight case, with her shoulder bag bumping against her side as she walked. She crossed the road and before long, heard a car engine. Turning her head, she recognised Charles's Vauxhall, with its distinctive silver lady mascot on the bonnet, pulling up beside her. He applied the handbrake, left the engine ticking over and jumped from the driver's seat to grab her case.

Anna hopped onto the running board and slid into the passenger seat. As Charles selected first gear, she squeezed his hand with hers.

'Good morning, Snow Maiden,' he said, shooting her a grin. 'Not a bad day for it!'

'At least we co-ordinated our arrival times. Did you drive past then turn round in a side road?'

She sensed him bristle. Did he think she was curious as to which direction he'd come from? Where he'd spent the previous night?

'That's right.' He glanced sideways at her again. 'No problems at home, I hope.'

'A bit tricky last night. But I think I handled it OK, even if my mother thinks our bosses are very inconsiderate.'

'Anna, we can talk properly later, but I'm very much aware how privileged I am to have this chance to spend time with you, even if for only one night. I'll do my absolute best to make sure you enjoy yourself.'

'You will look after me, Charles? I'm sure I don't need to explain what I mean.'

They were driving into the dockyard now. He waited until he was parked in his usual spot and cut the engine. 'Don't worry, lovely girl. Don't worry about a thing.'

She opened her door. 'It's probably best if we ignore each other for the rest of today, don't you think?'

He shrugged. 'Act as normal, my darling. I'll be my usual self, paying outrageous compliments to the Canteen ladies and any other unsuspecting female who comes my way.'

'You're such a dreadful flirt.'

'I know, but from the time we leave here until I bring you home, I am yours. Absolutely and utterly at your command, my darling.'

She walked into the building, smiling. Yes, he was incorrigible, but he was such fun. Anna had hardly settled at her desk when Miss Napier rang, asking to see her. She set off for the typing pool and tapped on the supervisor's door. Miss Napier was seated at her desk.

'Miss Christensen – Anna – I've just taken a telephone call from Miss Morgan's mother. I'm afraid we shan't see Rita back at work until after Christmas and even that's not a certainty.'

'I'm so sorry,' Anna said. 'That must be difficult for her and the family.' Her thoughts were racing. Did they want her to continue as the CO's secretary, or did they have someone else in mind? After all, there were other secretaries, more senior than herself, in other departments. But she hoped this wouldn't mean a transfer.

As if reading her mind, Miss Napier clarified the situation. 'Colonel Gresham has indicated he's happy for you to remain as stand in secretary. I take it you agree?'

'I'd be honoured to continue, Miss Napier. I'm enjoying the work and the opportunity to gain more experience.'

'That's pleasing to hear. Needless to say, we hope Miss Morgan's health continues to improve so she may return in the New Year. I fear you may not be so happy to return to the typing pool though.' She raised her eyebrows, but Anna made no comment, though she bit her lip.

'You've impressed us by coping so well with the demands of this post.'

'Thank you.'

'I'd like to assure you, should a suitable position fall vacant elsewhere, Mr Taylor, who you met at your interview, and myself have decided you should be in the running. Is that agreeable to you?'

'Very much so. I'm delighted you're pleased with my work.' She paused. 'If I may, I'd like to thank you and Mr Taylor for giving me this chance in the first place.'

'Between you and me and the gatepost, the secretary to the Personnel Manager is leaving early next year, as she's ... ahem...expecting a happy event. I can tell you Mr Taylor would be happy for you to be short-listed for the position, and I know I can trust you not to mention this to anyone.'

'Of course. Thank you for telling me.'

'Now, I'd better let you go. Unless there's anything you wish to discuss with me?'

Why was there a quizzical expression upon the supervisor's face? Anna's stomach churned. Surely, Miss Napier couldn't have heard any rumours about Charles and herself? That would be a nightmare: all Anna's efforts towards advancing her career vanishing because of a few idle words.

'Nothing I can think of, Miss Napier,' she said, sitting ramrod straight. 'Colonel Gresham's a most considerate gentleman and I'm very happy to continue working for him.'

In the staff canteen at lunchtime, Biddy arrived while Anna stood in the queue for food.

'Sorry I'm late,' she said. 'I had to finish typing a memo for Second Lieutenant Chandler. I usually panic when I have to hurry but thank goodness the angels were with me today.'

'Geoff's always so patient, isn't he? Are you having the fish?'

'A good Catholic girl like me?' Biddy smiled at the aproned lady. 'That's two of the cod, please, Jean.'

Anna was collecting two portions of Plum Charlotte and two cups of tea. She scooped up the cutlery and headed for the nearest vacant table, but as she unloaded the tray, she spotted Charles and Geoff at a nearby table. Charles had his back to her and Geoff was holding forth about something or other and hadn't noticed her. She chose the seat where she'd face away from them, as Biddy arrived.

'Any plans for this weekend?' Biddy was settling herself.

'Well, as it happens, I've invited Geoff to Sunday dinner.' Anna hoped Biddy wouldn't ask about her Saturday plans.

'Good for you! He's accepted, I take it?'

'Yes, and much to Mam's relief, my stepfather-to-be has wangled a joint of beef from somewhere.'

'So, your mum and Mr Mapstone and you and Geoff. Cosy!' Biddy giggled. 'Could this be a sign of things to come?'

'Eat your fish and don't pry!' Although Anna was smiling, she felt a little uncomfortable with the situation. Having her prospective lover sitting with the young man who was visiting her home on Sunday, suddenly seemed bizarre. But events had conspired to make this happen and she'd no intention of backing out of either date.

'Goodness!' She rested her cutlery. 'I haven't thanked you properly for taking that note round to Davy's house. This is the first time our lunchbreaks have coincided since then, isn't it?'

'It's been very busy, but I prefer it like that, now I'm more confident.'

'I'm pleased for you.' Anna hesitated. 'I wondered … did you see any of the family when you got to the house?'

'I was coming back down the path when a young lad opened the front door. For a moment I was afraid it would be Davy.'

'Oh no! I'm so sorry – that must have been his brother.'

'He looked about twelve or thirteen and he was very polite – asked me if I wanted him to call someone and I told him no thanks, because I'd delivered a note for Davy.'

'Phew!' Anna resumed her meal. 'I can't help feeling ashamed about the whole business. I got myself in too deep, but Davy was so persuasive.'

'You need to toughen up,' Biddy said. 'Don't ever let any man persuade you into doing anything you don't want to do.'

Anna remembered the sensations he'd produced in her and felt even more ashamed. Now she was hours away from her assignation, she reflected upon what Charles might expect and whether she could live up to these expectations. But she daren't say anything to Biddy about this. She knew what her friend's reaction would be and Anna feared being accused of being called a floozy – or worse – losing Biddy's friendship.

But Biddy noticed the two officers Anna was trying to avoid and leaned forward. 'I don't think those two have seen us. Do you want me to wave?'

'No, thanks very much. We haven't had a chance to chat for a few days. Tell me how things are with you and Eddie.'

Biddy's eyes sparkled. 'He's lovely, Anna. I'm trying to pluck up courage to ask Ma if he can come to Sunday tea soon. She'd blow a gasket at the thought of an extra one for dinner when there's already five of us.'

'Does Eddie have brothers and sisters?'

'Only one younger brother, so he might find us a bit overwhelming.'

'He'll probably enjoy it. Does this mean you're officially courting?'

Biddy's creamy complexion pinkened. 'I suppose it does.'

'I'm so glad I'm not the only one round here who blushes.'

Almost as though she'd sensed it, Anna glanced sideways and realised Geoff was gazing at her. She mouthed 'Hello' then gave him a smile which he returned.

Biddy had been watching the little pantomime with

interest. 'So, Geoff's noticed you? Do you think they'll come over now?'

'As I said, I hope not.'

'But you're looking forward to Sunday?'

Was she? Yes, she rather thought she was. The big hurdle facing her would be behind her then. But the thought of being dropped once the lure of the chase was over didn't appeal. Yet, what else did she expect?

That afternoon, Anna thought her boss appeared somewhat pre-occupied. He spent considerable time on the telephone, before calling her into his office, saying he needed to dictate a couple more things.

'The first memorandum is to Captain Milburn, with a copy to Second Lieutenant Chandler. Mark it Strictly Confidential, please.' Colonel Gresham got up and strolled across to the window, standing with his back to the dockyard.

Anna waited; pencil poised. What he began dictating caused tingles to race down her spine. If the project saw life, she knew it would have a huge effect upon military proceedings. She concentrated hard on getting every word down.

'I'd like that one typed as a matter of urgency, Anna, but after I sign, keep the top two and the file copy in a folder and put it on my desk, please.' He hesitated. 'This is all about being prepared, should the occasion arise, and I don't need to tell you we're talking top security here. This isn't a warning – I have no doubts regarding your integrity.'

Anna nodded. 'Thank you, Colonel.'

The CO also dictated a few other things before dismissing her. Back in her office, she started on the most important task and was finished and halfway through the rest of the dictation when she noticed it was almost time for her boss's refreshment break.

She sped off to the cafeteria and found, as usual, his tray prepared and only lacking the boiled water being poured into the pot. As she waited, she chatted with one of the assistants, an old schoolfriend of her mother's. This lady was always very interested to hear about Anna's progress in the romance stakes and Anna did her best to quash queries without appearing rude, even though, inwardly seething.

Charles came clattering down a flight of stairs while she carried the tea tray to her boss's office. The building was something of a warren and Anna hadn't visited half of it and saw no reason to explore. Charles looked oddly nonplussed to see her and swiftly straightened his tie and smoothed one hand over his hair.

'Hello, Miss Christensen. May I carry that tray for you?'

'No thanks, Captain Milburn. It's really not heavy.'

'Toodle pip, then.' He winked, looking round him before gently touching one finger to her lips and going on his way.

She stared after him. Had she imagined that smudge

on his left cheek? It looked suspiciously like lipstick. Was someone else playing kissing games with him? If so, which of the many females employed at the Dock Offices, used a shade so dark it reminded Anna of the deep purple Deadly Nightshade flower?

The hands of the clock flew round the dial and Anna now had mixed feelings. Should she ask Charles whether that had been lipstick on his cheek? Some start to a romantic rendezvous that would be! But this assignation owed nothing to romance, did it? There was no point in getting starry-eyed over an engaged man. After ignoring Geoff's warnings, and with her overnight things locked in Charles's car, suddenly the situation seemed sordid.

She took her time leaving. She visited the lavatory, washed her hands and touched up her make-up, just enough to keep her nose from shining. She left her hair tied back from her face and dabbed a little perfume on her pulse spots. Anna wished she could afford a more extravagant scent than her everyday one, but maybe the time would come when that became possible.

Leaving the ladies' room and deciding the corridors were almost empty of office staff, she walked towards the main entrance. There was no sign of Charles or of his car, as she stood, waiting and wondering. But almost immediately, she saw him beckoning from across the car park so didn't hesitate to follow him around the corner of the big stone building.

'I thought it prudent to move the car at lunchtime.

And you did the right thing in taking your time to leave. There's hardly anyone about now.'

His smile would melt the stoniest of hearts, and how could she let her suspicions cloud their trip? 'I see you've wiped off the lipstick,' she said, following up with a mischievous smile.

Charles unlocked the passenger door. Anna stood waiting for his reply.

'Aha! Haven't I told you about the bit of sparring going on between Captain Carstairs and me? We have an ongoing arm-wrestling competition and when I won today, he produced a lipstick from somewhere – probably his wife's or his secretary's – and daubed some on my left cheek. I thought I'd got shot of it, but when I visited the washroom just now, I realised you must have wondered what was going on. When I next see Geoffrey, I'll kill him for not marking my card!'

His explanation sounded plausible. And according to every woman she had consulted, including her mother, men often behaved like schoolboys. Anna got into the car.

Charles closed her door and walked round to climb behind the wheel. Before he started the engine, he glanced at her.

'I've been wanting to kiss you all day, but now's not the time. Windows might have eyes ...'

'I can wait.'

He burst out laughing. 'You know, when we first met,

you weren't sure about me, were you? You were wary and quite rightly so. But now, you're perfectly capable of putting me in my place and coping with my ridiculous banter. The girl is becoming a sophisticated, mature young lady. In my turn, I'm helpless as a … helpless as a lovesick student.'

'Pull the other one, Charles.'

The engine was ticking over. He drove out of the carpark. 'In case you're wondering, we're heading east. Away from the coast and into the countryside. I know it's almost October, but I have no doubt we can keep one another warm – as long as the gin fizz is cold.'

CHAPTER 18

'What the hell?' Geoff had enjoyed a few beers in what passed for the officers' mess the night before, but surely, he hadn't ordered an early wake-up call?

Colonel Gresham's batman, solely responsible for the disturbance, saluted the moment his victim stirred. He aimed the torch light discreetly away from the officer and coughed. 'Begging your pardon, sir, but Colonel Gresham requires your attendance in his office at the double.'

Geoff rubbed his eyes. 'He does, does he? What's up, Corporal?'

'Not for me to say, sir, but my guess is those that burn the midnight oil at Westminster have set something in motion.'

'All right, Corporal Clark. I'll be as quick as I can.'

'I'll light the hurricane lamp for you, sir. I'll be waiting in the jeep when you're ready.'

Geoffrey scrambled into his uniform, cursing when he couldn't find his socks, but twenty minutes later, he arrived in the CO's office.

'Geoffrey, where the hell has Charles got to?'

'Good morning, sir.' Geoff sought a credible response. 'I haven't seen him since yesterday afternoon at close of play, but if he's not in camp, he might be taking a twenty-four hour ...'

'Sod it!' Colonel Gresham looked up as his orderly arrived, bearing a tray. 'Excellent, Corporal. Just leave it would you? I take it you checked to see whether Captain Milburn's car was parked anywhere around?

'Affirmative, sir. No sign of it, I'm afraid.'

Geoff waited while the corporal left the room, closing the door quietly behind him.

'If I might make a suggestion, sir ...?'

'Go on, my boy.'

'Captain Milburn has taken digs in Penarth. It's highly likely he's there.'

'Why the hell didn't you say so, then?'

Geoff hesitated.

'I'm well-aware of my officers' peccadilloes and I shan't haul him over the coals for not being in camp. But there's something big coming off and I need both Charles and you here. Do you have a telephone number for him?'

'I do. He gave it to me when he moved in after his convalescence.'

'Then kindly ring it.'

'Sir!' Geoffrey took out his wallet, extracted a slip of paper and headed for the telephone. The number was ringing out, and, to his surprise, someone picked up the receiver quickly.

'Penarth 642.'

He recognised that voice, but why was its owner staying with her aunt and uncle? For one moment, he wondered if Charles could be the reason, but knew that was highly unlikely.

'Is that you, Mary?'

'It is. I'm sorry, who is this?'

'Geoff Chandler. I apologise for disturbing you, but dare I ask how you were so swift to answer? I hope all's well?'

'Hello, Geoff. I'm afraid my uncle's poorly, so Ma and I decided I should stay here in case my aunt needs a hand.'

'I'm sorry to hear that, Mary, but I need to get hold of Charles – urgently. Is he at home, d'you know?'

'No, he said yesterday he wouldn't be back until late this afternoon. He has a key – comes and goes like a fox in the night, apparently.'

I bet he does, Geoff thought. 'Thanks, Mary. Well, apologies again for the disturbance. If he should turn up, please ask him to contact Colonel Gresham as soon as possible. Better still, get in the car and drive to the office.'

'Will do. I'll write a message and leave it on his pillow.'

'Excellent. I hope your uncle gets well soon.'

Anna woke in the night. At first, she couldn't think where she was. Then it dawned on her she was in bed with Charles Milburn. By the sound of his regular breathing, he was fast asleep and although the last thing she recalled was snuggling against him with his arm around her, the two of them now lay beside each other, but separately. She had no idea of the time and with the blackout in operation, could see nothing at all.

She turned over cautiously, hoping not to disturb Charles's slumber and wondering why she felt no particular emotion. But why should she? She hadn't expected a declaration of love or a marriage proposal so wasn't disappointed by not receiving either. He'd wined and dined her, making sure she drank enough to wave goodbye to any last-minute misgivings, but not allowing her to drink to excess. He was excellent company, considerate over the awkwardness of undressing, and treated her as though she'd break in two, until realising she was actually enjoying herself.

Now she was no longer a virgin. But this was wartime and many girls were flouting convention for many different reasons. Anna smiled at the darkness, closed her eyes and wondered whether to startle him by taking the initiative next morning. Something told her he'd probably enjoy that very much indeed.

Geoffrey Chandler had one thing on his mind and that was to track down Charles Milburn. As he drove the jeep from the carpark, he felt neither apprehensive nor confident about what he was about to do. He did, however, feel wretched about having to back out of his appointment for Sunday lunch next day. Somehow, he must find a way of sending flowers to Mrs Christensen, by way of apology. Or maybe he'd find an opportunity to nip into town and buy some, so he could deliver them personally.

Prioritise, man! Such a nicety could only happen after this shindig was done and dusted. Geoff drove up the hill, turning into the side street to park. The CO had been tetchy enough when Geoff told him he needed to ask someone close to Charles if they knew of the captain's whereabouts.

'No telephone? Well, off you go then, but don't take all day about it!' Colonel Gresham had barked. Normally a placid kind of fellow, the current development, compounded by Charles's inexplicable absence, was testing his patience to a high degree.

Why the heck hadn't Charlie left a contact telephone number? He wasn't officially on duty, but this was wartime, for God's sake. Geoff scrambled from the jeep and walked back to the house, jumping over the low wall surrounding the neat square of black and white tiles between where an iron gate should have been and the front door. The brass knocker gleamed even on such a dull day and its rat-a-tat-tat caused a surprisingly fat tabby cat lurking on the pavement to hiss its displeasure before swishing its tail and disappearing round the corner.

It wasn't long before he heard sounds from inside as someone opened the door a few inches.

Geoff was in uniform so automatically saluted. 'Mrs Christensen?'

'Yes.'

Making a swift assessment as the attractive dark-haired woman opened the door wider, Geoff decided she probably wasn't even forty.

'What's this about? Is my daughter all right?'

He raised his hand. 'Whoa there, I didn't mean to alarm you. I'm Second- Lieutenant Chandler and I'm afraid I have no idea where Anna is. I take it she's not at home?'

'But surely …? My goodness, you'd better come in, Lieutenant.'

'Please call me Geoffrey – or Geoff.' He wasn't about to explain the commissioned officers' rankings system.

He followed her inside and she pushed open the first door on the right. 'I'm dreadfully confused. Surely Anna's at work? And I assume I'm speaking to our Sunday lunch guest?'

'Well, yes, but I'm afraid something unexpected has come up and that's the reason I'm barging in on you like this. I'm so sorry – I truly don't know where Anna is, but it occurred to me she might know Captain Milburn's whereabouts.'

'Please have a seat.'

Geoff wondered if he should offer to make her a hot drink but she seemed more composed now. The room was obviously the one used for more formal visitors but his gaze focused on an extraordinary bearskin rug stretched out before the fireplace. Its dark fur was still glossy and two dark brown glass eyes gleamed in its massive head. Geoff took an instant dislike to the beast, while still feeling sorry for it.

'You're looking at Teddy?' Ruby smiled for the first time. 'People always do. My late husband brought him back from one of his trips. He's not to everyone's taste, but he's certainly a conversation piece.' She seated herself at the other end of the settee. 'Tell me this. If my daughter has been at the office since yesterday morning, why haven't you asked her if she knows your friend's whereabouts?'

He frowned. 'I beg your pardon, Mrs Christensen, but Anna isn't at work today. She's not in her office and only a very few of the admin staff are in the building. I don't understand …'

Yet suddenly he did. Everything slotted into place and he felt at once devastated, embarrassed and angry. Bloody Charles Milburn! And now he, Geoff, had kicked over a hornets' nest and dropped both Anna and her lover into trouble. Not that Charlie didn't deserve it.

Anna left with her overnight bag yesterday morning, having told me the whole department would be involved in an exercise geared to practising emergency procedures. She isn't due back until this afternoon. Are you insinuating there's something going on between my daughter and your Captain Milburn?'

He shook his head, very slowly. 'I don't know for sure they're together, but I do know they're friendly, hence this visit.'

'Ha! But you didn't think they were that friendly? I'm so sorry. I was under the impression you were fond of my daughter.'

'I am fond of her, but now I worry she'll end up hurt. I'm sorry if I'm speaking out of turn.' He needed to get back. Colonel Gresham would be pacing his office like an expectant father.

'How old is this man?'

'Early thirties, I believe.'

'Lord help us! One more question, then I must let you get back. Is he married?'

'No.' Geoff prayed she wouldn't ask if there was a fiancée waiting in the wings.

'Something to be thankful for then.' Her smile was bleak as she got to her feet.

Almost as fast, Geoff rose and held out his hand. 'I'm so sorry our first meeting has had to be like this.'

'I'm sorry too, Geoffrey. And now I've met you, I'm even sorrier that you won't be coming to lunch tomorrow. I imagine you'll be up to your eyes in whatever it is that's the problem?'

'I'm afraid so.' He was twisting his cap between his fingers. 'I ... please don't be too hard on her. The captain is an extremely charming man and ...'

Ruby's smile was wistful. 'I'm afraid your news makes me feel very anxious, even if I've known something like this might happen sometime, I suppose. And if Anna gets her heart broken, she won't be the first girl to do so. Or the last.' She touched his arm. 'I'm so sorry.'

Geoffrey drove back to the dockyard, trying to reject murderous thoughts. He hadn't known what more to say to Anna's mother. Obviously, the pair must have gone off together, else why would Anna lie like that? But the pain he felt, knowing she'd finally succumbed to Charles's charms, wasn't as devastating as realising his brother officer could ignore Geoff's feelings and steal the girl he'd admired since first setting eyes on her. Or should he feel sorrier for Charles's fiancée than for himself?

On the way to the CO's office other officers acknowledged his presence, some with grim expressions upon their faces, others looking excited at the prospect of real action. Soon he stood in front of the colonel's open door, shaking his head as his superior raised his eyebrows.

'Geoffrey, you are from now on my second in command for this operation.' The CO rose and came from behind his desk. 'We have men and vehicles and kit to move. Are you up to it?'

Geoff straightened his shoulders. 'Yes, sir. I'll do my very best, sir.'

Colonel Gresham nodded. 'Then get yourself some breakfast and decide who you want as your second string.' He looked at the wall clock. 'I'll brief all commissioned officers at eleven o'clock in my office. The majority of this company is being posted to Italy – to a seaport called Bari.' He noticed Geoff's expression. 'Yes, I know. From Barry to Bari, but from now on everyone refers to Code name

200

Humming Bird. All we have to do is follow instructions.'

'Yes, sir.' Geoff hesitated. 'Might I ask whether you're moving out too, Colonel?'

'Negative. I'm to remain here for the foreseeable future. Another Commanding Officer and a skeleton staff are on their way to Italy already.'

Geoff nodded. 'What about me, sir?'

'You'll take over from Captain Milburn, with a well-deserved promotion to Lieutenant. There's plenty of life in this blasted war yet, I'm sorry to say.'

Anna gazed through the car window at the passing countryside. Their early morning lovemaking had been joyful. After breakfast, Charles asked if she wanted to stop anywhere in particular on the way back, but she asked him to decide. Already she felt uneasy about returning, especially with Geoff arriving for Sunday dinner next day. With the momentous event behind her, Anna now realised she shouldn't see Charles any more, and also bitterly regretted telling her mother such a blatant lie.

'All right, my sweet,' Charles had replied. 'We can stop for a little refreshment somewhere along the road and I'll drop you off at home, then I have business to deal with.'

'I have some errands to do this afternoon,' she'd said, thinking of vegetables for the next day's meal. Wondering what Geoff would think if he could see her now.

Charles had lifted her off her feet then, swinging her round until she was helpless with laughter and breathlessness.

'You're an enchantress,' he'd whispered, putting her gently down again. 'And I adore being under your spell.'

Now he was singing as he drove. Fortunately, he had a pretty good voice and the song he'd chosen was one called *Our Love Affair* and what was more, he knew most of the words. This caused Anna another twinge of discomfort as he sang about a happy couple's love affair being such fun and how they'd be the envy of everyone. Maybe he was thinking of his fiancée?

They stopped for coffee a few miles outside the village of Caerleon. Charles pulled a face when he tasted his, but managed to drain his cup. Anna contemplated tackling him on the thorny subject of his romantic life but scolded herself for her stupidity. She knew of his engagement, so why did she even think about questioning him?

They drove in silence until she realised Charles had said something and dragged herself back to the moment. 'I beg your pardon?'

'I asked whether you knew where you were now?'

'You can't really miss those battlements, can you?'

He patted her knee 'It would be appalling if Cardiff Castle took a hit.'

'Goodness, yes. I say prayers every night, asking for this war to end.'

He glanced sideways at her as they drove past the imposing landmark. 'Do you now? Well, let's hope your prayers are answered before too much longer.'

She suspected that particular wish might take a while

to be granted, but said nothing.

He turned to her again. 'I think I should deliver you to your door. I'd like to meet your mother.'

She frowned at him. 'You can't mean that.'

'Oh, but I do, my angel. I'm intrigued to meet the woman who produced such a beautiful daughter.' He reached for Anna's right hand, raised it to his lips and kissed her fingers.

'Charles, what if she suspects we've been away together?'

'There's no reason she should. I shall say I offered you a lift home as I was coming this way anyway. What's the matter? Are you ashamed of me for some reason?'

She turned to face him. 'Don't be silly. I just think it's better if you drop me off somewhere nearby.'

'Remind me which turning to take when we get close, then.' He began to sing the opening lines of *Let's Face the Music and Dance* and despite her feelings, she couldn't help laughing.

'Let's hope there isn't trouble ahead for us,' she said.

'My sweet, life never comes without a dollop of problems.'

Charles parked outside her house and Anna knew there was no dissuading him. But surely, her mother wouldn't take one look at them and guess they were lovers?

Charles went round to the boot and took out Anna's case before opening the passenger door. 'Back to reality,' he whispered. 'And we really must do this again soon.'

She held her tongue. Her mother was opening the front door. And for whatever reason, her expression made Anna's throat constrict.

'Mam?' she called. 'What's happened?'

'I think you need to tell me that, don't you?' Ruby's gaze fell upon Charles. 'I suppose you're Captain Milburn?'

'At your service, ma'am. I happened to be coming this way, so gave your daughter a lift.' He placed Anna's luggage on the doorstep and stood back.

'You need to go straight to your office, Captain.'

'I beg your pardon?' Charles frowned.

'I've no idea what's going on, but the lieutenant was here earlier, looking for you.'

'Geoff was here? Looking for Charles? Am I needed at the office too?' Anna spoke without thinking.

Ruby glared at her. 'The lieutenant was looking for you, to see whether you knew where he might find Captain Milburn. I, of course, told him all I knew was that you were involved in some kind of exercise and due home later this morning.'

'Which we are,' Charles soothed. 'However, I must confess to coaxing Anna to accompany me on a visit to a brother officer and his wife, who live in Gloucestershire. We enjoyed a pleasant evening and I kipped on a camp bed while Anna was given the guest room. We had a delightful time and I was able to enjoy the chance to talk to my friend before his regiment leaves for Burma next week.'

Ruby stared at him. 'Really? Well, Captain, it seems

your commanding officer wants to see you immediately, so you'd best be on your way, hadn't you?'

Charles held out his hand. She shook it, reluctantly.

'I hope we meet again soon and under less stressful circumstances.' He released her and turned to her daughter. 'Thank you for your company, Anna. You helped me out of an awkward situation and your charming conversation cheered up my chum's wife enormously.'

Anna conjured up the best smile she could. By now, she was almost believing his story herself.

Her mother was looking from Charles to her and back again when he called goodbye and hastened back to his car.

'We need to talk.' Ruby picked up Anna's case and drew her into the narrow passageway. 'I wasn't born yesterday, nor would I trust that man further than I could throw him.'

'Enter! And not before time.' Colonel Gresham folded his arms as Charles walked through the open door. 'I've had Geoffrey running round like a blue-arsed fly, trying to locate you. Sit down, man, while I explain the situation.'

Charles saluted and took a seat. 'I can only say how sorry I am, sir. It truly didn't occur to me to leave my old friend's telephone number. It was something of a mercy dash. He and I went through military college together and he's off to Burma next week, so wanted a reunion before he left. I got his letter yesterday and left straight after work.'

'Luckily, everything's progressing smoothly, thanks to Geoffrey. I've made him my second-in-command by the way.'

Charles raised his eyebrows. 'I see. Well, I'll do my best to support him once you tell me what all this is about, sir.'

'You're off to Italy, my boy. On Monday at sparrow fart. That's why people were dragged out of bed this morning before dawn. We'll know more by this evening.'

Charles gulped. 'What's brought this on, Colonel, if I may make so bold?'

'As Bari is situated north of Naples and further south than Rome, the powers-that-be have decided these factors pinpoint the city as a major supply centre for the Allies. You've been selected because of your expertise and you'll be instrumental in keeping the pot boiling. There's a small unit gone ahead, but you'll be sailing from an as yet undisclosed port with the bulk of the kit we need out there.'

'Will I have office staff?'

'Affirmative. There'll be someone to help you deal with the inevitable bumf. And you've fallen on your feet regarding accommodation. The department's based in an hotel and you'll be allocated quarters, with a batman to attend to your needs.'

Charles nodded, his spirits rising. 'Thank you, sir. If that's all for now, I must go and relieve Second-Lieutenant Chandler.' He rose and saluted. 'I'm on my way.'

'It's Lieutenant Chandler now, Captain.'

'Sir!' Charles saluted again and went in search of his fellow officer.

He found him supervising the sorting of important records. The younger man looked up as Charles entered the office and immediately got to his feet. At once, Charles sensed his anger. He didn't want to fall out with him because Geoffrey was a good chap, but he'd no intention of grovelling.

Charles spread his hands. 'What can I say? I was pushed for time and it didn't dawn on me I should've left a contact number.'

Geoff nodded.

'And, as we both know, we weren't expecting anything of this magnitude to kick off at this time. Shows how wrong one can be.'

'Look, Charles, I know I put my foot in it, calling at Anna's house. It seemed like a good idea at the time.'

'Really? Why, precisely?'

Geoff's eyes narrowed. 'It's obvious you've been moving in on her, ever since I stupidly confessed my feelings. I can only assume the pool of married ladies has dwindled.'

'Ouch! Geoffrey ... come on now. Anna's a grown woman. She makes her own choices. I'm sorry, but you know how I am with the fair sex. Agreed, I don't usually touch the Annas of this world with a bargepole, but there's something special about her. I don't need to tell you that.'

'So now you're about to break her heart. That's a statement, not a question. Captain Milburn.'

Charles shrugged and saw Geoffrey ball his fists at his sides. He knew he was riling the younger officer, but he still smarted at being caught on the back foot. 'We're at war. You and I are soldiers. We're moved around like chessmen. I'm that much older and in Miss Christensen's eyes, probably more glamorous, if you'll forgive me for saying so. You're much more suitable as husband material, old chap. And mark my words, now I'm leaving, the field will be clear for you to woo the lady to your heart's content.'

'You bastard! It's love 'em and leave 'em with you, isn't it?'

'You shouldn't be so serious, Geoffrey. I did warn you. And you could have had a good time with that cuddly little bird ... you know – Mary's mate from the tennis club? She's obviously head over heels ...'

Geoff snapped at him. 'What is it about women that makes you not respect them, Charlie? I'd really like to know.'

Charles smiled. 'I should feel insulted, but rest assured, I handle my women with the greatest of respect. When I'm with them, they receive my full attention and I treat them like royalty. Believe me.'

'And now you'll say goodbye to your latest conquest and be on the lookout for the next one. Isn't that how it works? D'you know, the person I feel most sorry for is that unfortunate fiancée of yours.'

'Go and get some food, Geoffrey. I don't want to fall out with you, but let me remind you we are at war. None of us knows whether we'll get through it in one piece. Take my advice. Live each day at a time and if you really want to win Anna's heart, you need to stop behaving so much like a bloody gentleman!'

Geoff turned on his heel and left the room, knowing if he stayed, he'd punch Charlie in the jaw. There was hardly anyone in the canteen, but one of the assistants called in to cover this unexpected event, hurried over to greet him. 'I can find you some sausage and mash, sir. Is that all right?'

He summoned up a smile. 'You're a jewel, Maisie. That'd be perfect with a pot of tea, please.'

The woman beamed. 'Caught us all on the hop, didn't they? Outside of here, we don't say nothing, but I hope you're not on the list of them that's going overseas, sir?'

'That'd be telling.' But he was smiling as she prepared his meal. At least it seemed he was someone's pin-up.

Geoff carried his order over to a window table. A couple of young women – departmental heads' secretaries – were sitting nearby. The one facing him caught his eye as he settled himself. She gave him a shy smile and he smiled back, before beginning on his food. Maybe that was what he needed? A date with someone pretty and smiling and not besotted with Charlie? But his rebellious libido catapulted an image of Anna into his consciousness.

However, he definitely needed to get over her. He'd been looking forward to the Sunday lunch at her home, but since she'd invited him, events had moved on with a vengeance. Including, where she was concerned, in the romance department. Romantic for her maybe, but for Charles? Geoff knew the answer to that.

CHAPTER 19

'Have I taught you nothing at all?' Ruby stood in front of the sitting room fireplace.

Anna walked towards her mother, determined not to be treated like a child. 'You've taught me lots of things. What precisely are you referring to?'

Ruby stared back. 'Don't get clever with me, miss. You know very well what – or whom – I'm referring to. Captain Milburn is nothing but a lounge lizard!'

Anna laughed out loud. 'Hardly.'

'Believe me, I can tell his sort from yards away. He probably has a string of lady friends. What on earth were you thinking of, accepting an invitation to go away with him?'

'He's fun to be with and he treats me as if I'm special. I can't see what the problem is.'

Ruby drew herself up to her full height which was still several inches below her daughter's. 'My problem is that you lied to me, Anna. You told me there was some kind of office exercise going on which involved night-time

211

activities. In fact, I don't doubt that at all, except they didn't take place in the office.' She folded her arms. 'I'm not only angry because you told a lie. I'm worried that man took advantage of you.'

Anna sighed. 'He didn't take advantage of me. Charles would never force me to do anything I didn't want to do.'

'What kind of answer is that? Oh, Anna, please tell me you didn't sleep with him!'

'I'm not going to discuss this any longer. You have no right to interrogate me.'

'Really? When it's a question of your well-being and your … your morals? You're under the age of twenty-one and I think, as your mother, I have every right to expect an honest answer.'

'I'm eighteen and already holding down a responsible job, yet still you lecture me as if I was twelve years old! Did Nana lecture you, Mam? Weren't you expecting me when you were my age?'

Ruby's cheeks reddened. 'I might have known you'd dig that up. Believe me, your father was a very different calibre man from Captain Milburn. We were in love and Vik had already spoken about marriage.'

Anna had no intention of dwelling upon her mother's sexual awakening. 'How
do you know what kind of man Charlie is, Mam? How can you say the things you did after spending only two minutes in his company?'

'I can sum that man up very easily, by looking at

him and hearing him trot out such a glib explanation. He must take me for an idiot if he thinks I believe one word of that nonsense. He manufactured a convenient excuse for you to give me, so you could stay away for a night – now tell me I'm not right. Having a reunion with a brother officer, indeed. Taking you along to keep the wife company! If that had really been the case, why was it necessary for you to give me that rigmarole about needing to stay overnight at the office? Oh, how I wish I'd taken more notice and stopped you from going.'

Anna sat down. She stared at her hands. Looked up to meet her mother's gaze. 'You couldn't have. Stopped me from going, I mean. It's what I wanted.'

'He took you to a hotel?'

'Yes.'

Ruby sat down beside her daughter. Straight as a ramrod and keeping her distance. 'Did he protect you?'

'Of course. I can't believe we're having this conversation. Charlie's a man of the world.'

'That's just what bothers me. He's so wrong for you. Goodness only knows why you can't be happy with the lieutenant. He was devastated when he learnt you'd gone away. It's my belief he realised who you were with, my girl.' Ruby's face crumpled. 'Ha! Now you've got me sounding just like my own mother.'

Anna couldn't help laughing. Nor could she stop herself from cuddling up to her mam either.

Ruby stiffened at first then put both arms around her.

'I wish you'd waited, love. Surely you can see this man isn't the marrying kind?'

'Mam! I wish you'd acknowledge it isn't every girl who longs to walk down the aisle wearing white frills.'

'You'll change your mind before long; you wait and see.' Ruby smoothed Anna's hair back from her face. 'Meanwhile, I hope you'll bide your time and wait for the right man to come along. Someone you can love and who'll love you back. Please don't cheapen yourself, sweet girl.'

Later that afternoon, Anna answered a knock at the door. Her mother was lying down, making her daughter cross with herself for feeling guilty at causing Ruby's apparent emotional turmoil.

A lad, bicycle propped by the wall, stood on the front step, holding out a bouquet of flowers. Anna blinked, for moments wondering if Charles had sent them and half-hoping this wasn't the case. Her mother would probably refuse to allow them in the house.

'Delivery for Mrs and Miss Christensen.' The boy held out the mass of yellow, white and bronze chrysanthemums for Anna to take.

'These are beautiful. Who sent them, please?'

The lad dug into his pocket. 'Sorry miss – here you are.'

Anna took the envelope. 'One moment …' She went into the front room where her mother always kept a store of small change in a china pot. She took out a sixpenny piece to hand to the lad, who muttered his thanks, before grabbing his bicycle.

Anna took the flowers through to the kitchen, her nose buried in the petals, breathing in their earthy, herby scent. She placed them carefully on the draining board, but before finding something to show them off in, she ripped open the envelope.

Dear Mrs Christensen and Anna,

This is to say I'm very sorry for any inconvenience I have caused you. I was very much looking forward to joining you for lunch tomorrow, but it seems the war has other ideas. Please accept my apologies and I trust you'll enjoy the flowers.

Yours sincerely,

Geoffrey Chandler

Anna read the brief note through again. How very tactful he was. He'd managed to apologise twice, yet without referring to the way he turned up at the house that morning. No doubt her mother would be impressed and it occurred to Anna, had Charlie sent a floral gift, Ruby would doubtless have complained about it being ingratiating and only to be expected from such a man.

As Anna found a vase and arranged the blooms, she smiled at the splash of colour they made and decided to put them on the living room table, so her mother saw them as soon as she came downstairs. She placed Geoff's note beside them and realised she'd had nothing to eat since early breakfast. Her heartbeat quickened the moment she recalled Charlie suggesting they must get together again soon. But how could she do this? She wasn't in the least lovesick – just as well, considering what she knew of the captain's track record. But deep down, she enjoyed how their relationship had progressed beyond flirtation and stolen kisses.

Softly, softly catchee monkey had been one of her father's expressions. How strange that should pop into her head so suddenly. But she thought it suited her current situation. She must allow her mother time to accept this was wartime and young people were seizing opportunities wherever they could, whether love affairs, employment, or the obtaining of much-missed foods.

She ate her frugal sandwich thoughtfully. Would she see Charlie on Monday? Or would he have been sent off somewhere in the course of duty? She wanted it to be the former, but if he were to be posted elsewhere, she probably wouldn't ever see him again. Meanwhile, once she'd taken her mother's tea upstairs, she'd walk round to her grandparents' house to collect whatever vegetables were available, even if Geoff couldn't come for his dinner.

Next morning, Geoffrey was eating breakfast when he spotted Charles approaching the canteen counter. Having done his best to keep conversation strictly business-like the previous day, he turned his attention to the items upon his plate but before long, saw the captain heading towards him.

'G'morning, Geoffrey. As I shan't be around the place much longer, how about we call a truce and enjoy one another's company today?'

Geoff put down his cutlery. 'You're welcome to sit where you please, Captain.'

Charlie grimaced. 'I realise I'm not one of your favourite people, but amongst other things, I want to congratulate you on your promotion.' He pulled out a chair and sat down.

'Thank you. Are you looking forward to your new role?'

Charlie shrugged. 'Yes and no. I relish the opportunity to try something different, even if it means leaving the delights of South Wales. But I'll carry with me some happy memories, although ... the bomb taking out so many people that night in Cardiff, including Marcia, is not something I can easily forget, no matter where I'm sent. No point in becoming mawkish though.'

Geoff picked up his cutlery again and stuck his fork into a chunk of congealed scrambled egg. 'Wonder if they'll cook fresh eggs for you in Italy?'

Charlie chuckled. 'You never fail to amaze me, Geoffrey.'

Despite his feelings, Geoff raised his eyebrows. 'Why is that?'

'You're so adept at changing the subject. They should recruit you for the diplomatic corps, because you must wish you could beat the hell out of me for stealing your girl, yet ...'

'Anna's not my girl.'

Charlie poured his tea. 'You saw her first. I behaved like a Class A jerk, to quote our American friends.'

'All's fair in love and war, so they say.'

Charlie stroked his chin. 'Hmm ... didn't give myself the best of shaves this morning. And do you really believe that twaddle, old boy?'

'I'm not sure whether I do or not, to be honest. Yet, once we lose our moral compass, where do we go from there?'

Charlie cut into a bacon rasher. 'That's a good question. I take it you still feel you've been wronged?'

'I feel that the friendship I thought we'd established, obviously means sod all to you, Captain Milburn.'

'Look, Geoffrey, I'm sorry if you feel like that, but how was I to know you felt so strongly about the girl? She's a tempting morsel, but – before you smash your plate in my face, remember I leave here later today, and the day after tomorrow I'll be on my way to southern Italy. Miss Christensen will probably miss the attention, but a girl like that's never going to be short of a boyfriend.'

'Does Anna really mean so little to you that you can dismiss her with a snap of the fingers, now you've got what you wanted?'

'Dear me, this egg is beyond a joke, or should I say a yolk? Ah, sorry old chap, I'm being crass, aren't I? Anna's a terrific girl. She deserves someone much nicer – someone much more suitable than yours truly in her life. You can console her, man! I must confess I would have liked a couple more months in which to enjoy her company, but for goodness' sake, don't go and mess this up by letting some other fellow get ahead of you.'

'I'll bear your advice in mind, but believe me, I shan't try and railroad her into anything.'

'You might find she comes to you.' Charlie waved his fork at him. 'I had that philosophy in mind when I first got to know her and realised how special she was. There are certain women who like to make the running and I do believe she's one of them. Take heed of one who knows. Play hard to get. Make a date with young what's her name from Penarth, or that brunette I've seen eyeing you up and mention it to Anna, or her pretty Irish mate. I'll leave Mary's phone number on my desk – or rather, your desk now.'

Sunday afternoon, after an excellent lunch, Anna insisted upon clearing up the kitchen while Frank drove his fiancée the short distance to his house in order to listen to a Home Service concert. Apparently, Ruby's old wireless wasn't up to the job. Anna was happy to have the place to herself and to write a letter to Margaret, c/o the Nurses' Home, explaining her dilemma. Her friend had been busy with her training for a while now and Anna hoped she'd be sympathetic. She told herself this had nothing to do with Charles. She liked the thought of being able to take control and not rely on the man should she find herself in a similar situation to that of Friday night.

She'd dried the dishes and tidied everything away when she heard a ring at the doorbell. She had no idea who it could be. Her mother wouldn't be back until later and she had her key with her anyway. Anna removed her apron and stopped to check her reflection in the hallway mirror before opening the door.

'Goodness, this is a surprise!'

'Hello, Anna.' Charles, uniformed, stood before her. 'Apologies for barging in like this, but I wonder if I can persuade you to come for a short drive? Or even to sit in the car with me while I give you my news?'

'My mother's not in, so you can sit by the fire with me, if you like.'

'That sounds delightful, my angel. If you're quite sure I shan't contaminate either you or your surroundings?'

'You're such a wicked man. Remember, it can't be easy being my mother.'

'I couldn't possibly comment.'

Anna held open the door. Her heart gave a little flutter as she wondered why he looked so serious. For one wild moment she wondered if he'd broken off his engagement, then dreaded learning he had.

She led him to the living room. 'It's warmer than the parlour.'

Charles waited for her to sit down before sinking into the plum velvet couch. His gaze took in the gorgeous chrysanthemums on the sideboard and he nodded in their direction.

'I'm betting those are from either your mother's intended or, could they be from a certain Geoffrey Chandler?'

'I don't know why you'd think that.' Anna felt disinclined to outline the reason why Geoff had seen fit to send flowers.

'My guess is I'm right and, Anna, this is what I'm trying to get through to you. That young man is the very essence of politeness, good taste and thoughtfulness. I am in awe of him.' Suddenly he bent his head towards hers. 'Are you aware how sublime you smell?'

'I probably smell of roast beef and boiled cabbage, with an undertone of *Palmolive*.' She turned to face him, reaching out with her left hand and placing her palm flat against his chest. 'Now, what's this all about?'

He took her hand in both of his and kissed the back of it before kissing her fingers. Anna shivered, desire already stirring. She had little knowledge of drugs but wondered if she was becoming reliant on Charlie's presence. Telling herself to concentrate, she sat up straight, trying to ignore the way that presence bombarded her senses.

He continued to hold her hand but didn't meet her eyes. 'There's no easy way to say this. I've received a new posting.'

She caught her breath. Suddenly seeing everything around her as if from a long way away.

'They're sending me to southern Italy. I don't think any of us guessed what lay ahead, but I shall soon be on my way, and I'm here because I didn't want you to turn up for work and find out from your boss – or one of the canteen ladies.' He smiled wryly.

'Thank you.'

'Timing's not good for you and me, of course. What began between us is exciting, but the Army's a hard taskmaster and doesn't understand the meaning of emotion. God, Anna, I couldn't be sorrier that you and I have had such a brief relationship.'

She felt as though someone had socked her in the midriff. This man, her first lover, was going away and soon would be a mere memory. Now he was putting one arm around her shoulders and drawing her close. She shut her eyes, breathing in his zesty aftershave, one she knew he purchased from *Harrods* of London. Unlike her, with her working girl's scent and a bar of no-nonsense soap for every day.

'Will I ever see you again?'

She waited for what seemed like ages. Then he put one finger beneath her chin and tilted her face upward. His eyes looked slumberous and Anna caught her breath, closing her own again as he touched his lips to hers, a butterfly touch, soon exploding into passion. With his free hand he reached beneath her pale blue angora jumper, groaning as his fingers found their targets then moving swiftly downwards to unclip her suspenders and roll down her stockings. Oh, so carefully. She gasped as he moved his attention, gently stroking her and sending tingles through her veins. Into her bones. Through to the very core of her body.

He stroked the top of one of her thighs then broke away, his breathing irregular. 'Anna ... let me leave you with another happy memory. Please, my angel ...'

'But Charlie ...'

His mouth fastened upon hers again. Purposefully. Claiming her. Impossible to resist.

They clawed at one another's clothes, standing up and wrenching off the garments until they stood stark naked before the coal fire. He knelt in front of her and she curled her fingers in his hair, closing her eyes in ecstasy as his fingers and mouth worked their magic. *How could this be wrong when he and she so obviously longed for one another?*

He guided her gently down to the rug and straddled her, his hands warm and firm upon her skin.

'God, you are so beautiful. I have to have you, Anna. Now!'

She was in no state to refuse. Reaching for him. Guiding him. Anna lost all thought of practicalities. Lost the ability to think straight as her body reacted to his lovemaking as a rosebud opens its petals to the sun. His hands stroked and caressed while she soared, reaching a plateau from which there was only one way to fall. She heard herself cry out as if from a long way away, then lay beside, leaving her floating in a bath of warm honey.

At last, he kissed her forehead and she closed her eyes while he made himself presentable, before kneeling beside her. 'I'm so sorry, darling girl. I have to go now. Better this way than a long, drawn-out farewell, don't you think? Look after yourself, Snow Maiden, and be happy, won't you?'

'But Charlie, this is dreadful. I shall miss you so much!'

'It's called war, my darling.'

'Will you write? Please say you'll write! Let me know how you're getting on? I …'

He bent over and kissed her one more time. 'I'll see myself out. Remember my advice …'

She scrambled to her feet, hearing him groan as his gaze roamed her body. She knew her hair was tousled, her desire satiated, yet her emotions jangled like the notes of a badly-tuned old piano.

From the doorway he blew her a kiss. And then he was gone, leaving behind him a faint trace of his favourite cologne. Anna waited until she heard the front door close then began pulling on her underwear, replacing the layers of clothing, while the tears trickled down her cheeks. She'd given him her body and her heart and it seemed neither meant anything to him.

She was in bed before her mother returned at around seven pm. Pleading a headache. Longing to be left alone, reliving those stolen moments before he'd turned his back on her for ever.

Next morning, she walked to work, chiding herself when she turned around, not once but twice, hearing what she imagined was the sound of Charles's car engine. Colonel Gresham was already in his office and she hardly had time to think before he buzzed for her to take down a long memorandum, detailing the events leading to the departure of certain key personnel. Charles's name came up more than once, making her long for something startling to happen: maybe some mistake in communication, necessitating his immediate return to Wales.

But she knew that was a vain hope and applied herself to her work, shutting out all thoughts and emotions in a way that later she was to marvel at. The empty feeling inside her owed nothing to the fact she'd temporarily lost her appetite for food and she wondered whether the shock of losing Charles had caused this phenomenon. It was a relief when lunchtime came and she met Biddy inside the canteen.

'Are you not having anything at all to eat? Just a cup of tea? Anna, what's happened? You look so pale' She lowered her voice. 'Is it the wrong time of the month?'

'No, but I didn't get much sleep last night.' Anna surveyed the food containers. 'Maybe I'll try one of those plain scones.'

They carried their trays to their favourite table. Anna deliberately didn't allow her gaze to wander, but kept her attention on her snack and her friend, although Biddy's curiosity required the answering of several questions.

'I'm sorry, Biddy, but that's all I know,' Anna said at last. 'Charlie came round yesterday afternoon to say goodbye. Geoff has taken his place and I imagine another officer will be appointed as his assistant.'

Biddy gave a low whistle, then turned her head to grimace at Anna. 'Dirty looks from one or two men over there who don't approve of women whistling. You'd think they could find other things to vent their feelings on – like all the folk suffering in this dreadful war for one thing.' She forked up a slice of suet dumpling and glared at it. 'Not to mention atrocities like this piece of nastiness!'

Despite her gloom, Anna laughed.

'Thank goodness you still have a sense of humour, girl. I know you must feel desperate sad, but you can write to him, can't you? Let him know you care about him. You do care, don't you?'

Anna swallowed hard. 'I probably care more than I realised.' She sipped her drink. 'But I've thought a lot about it and decided it's not my place to write him letters. After all, he has a fiancée somewhere in England. And before you ask, yes, I did know about her.'

'Do you think he might break his engagement?'

'Because of me? That would be highly unlikely.'

'You never know. He might miss you so much he'll decide you're the one for him after all.'

'He goes where he's ordered. He'll hardly have time to waste on personal matters. He's no longer in my life, Biddy.'

Anna's attention was taken by Geoff coming through the door. He didn't notice her at first, but while waiting for his order, he turned his head to survey the room and the two of them locked gazes. Anna returned his smile, determined to hold her head high and not reveal any of the feelings haunting her.

Biddy, with her back to the food counter, turned round to see who'd come in. 'I imagine a certain someone's more than willing to console you.'

'I don't think so.'

'Still, I bet he chooses a table near ours, see if he doesn't.'

'I need to get back to the office. See you tomorrow.' Anna rose, carried her tray to the used crockery counter, and headed for the door. Out of the corner of her eye she noticed Geoff sitting down opposite a pretty, dark-haired girl at a nearby table. When Anna saw her next, Biddy would probably declare the girl had looked desperate pleased to see him. Anna couldn't help thinking he hadn't taken long to seek out another potential girlfriend. But she felt relieved at not having to endure his feeling sorry for her just yet. Though courtesy demanded she write a short thank you letter for his beautiful flowers.

CHAPTER 20

That afternoon, Colonel Gresham put his head round the door of Anna's office and informed her Miss Napier wished to see her.

'I hope I've done nothing wrong,' Anna blurted.

'Far from it. It's all about matters going through the right channels. Maybe you could bring my tea after you see her? I'd appreciate a word with you too.'

Full of curiosity and some misgivings, Anna picked up her notebook and pencil and headed for the supervisor's office. Miss Napier spotted her walking through the typing pool and rose to welcome her. Anna noticed Biddy glance at her before looking away again. Whatever she was about to hear would probably be their conversation topic at lunch next day and anything that took her mind off Charlie was welcome.

'Come in, Miss Christensen. Take a seat.' Miss Napier closed the door behind Anna and headed back to her desk.

Anna, experiencing a flash of panic, wondered whether

this could possibly have something to do with Charlie.

'I shan't beat about the bush. This news is sad, but you may not be too surprised to hear that our Miss Morgan has handed in her notice.'

'Oh dear. Does this mean her condition has worsened?'

'I'm afraid so, but she and her mother have decided to move to Gloucestershire, where they have relations. I tell you this, Anna, because it means I can offer you a permanent position as the Commanding Officer's secretary. You may take a little while to think about it if you wish, my dear.'

Anna, still shell-shocked at this news, felt even more startled at hearing the supervisor address her so informally. 'Forgive me for asking, Miss Napier, but does this meet with Colonel Gresham's approval?'

The supervisor's eyes crinkled. 'That comment, my dear, is indicative of the way you calmly and logically analyse situations, whether significant or mundane. So, it is for this reason, as well as for your secretarial skills, that your promotion is the logical thing to happen. And Colonel Gresham, while saddened to hear of Rita's decision, will be delighted if you accept. Do I hear a "Yes?"'

'Yes, Miss Napier. Oh, yes, please.'

The supervisor sat back in her chair and beamed at her protégée. 'I shall authorise your salary rise as a matter of urgency. Well done, Anna. Your business tutor will be very proud when she hears.'

Anna blinked hard. 'Should I write to Miss Ring, do you think?'

'That is entirely up to you, but I'll be delighted to tell her of your appointment when I see her next. If you decide to write, you're welcome to give the letter to me to hand to her.' Her eyes shone. 'Emily is my oldest and greatest friend. Each of us lost a fiancé in the Great War and having met through belonging to the same church, we've spent much time in each other's company over the years. Indeed, so much that I sometimes feel we should set up house together, but I suppose that's a decision we should make once this wretched war is done with. However, I mustn't keep you from your duties any longer. Congratulations on what you've achieved in your career so far, my dear.'

Anna walked back to her office in thoughtful mode. She still felt bruised by Charles's abrupt farewell and the cool way he'd blanked her suggestion about keeping in touch. That hurt, even if she knew it shouldn't. It also proved her mother had been right. And Geoff had been right. And she was left looking foolish. But what was that, compared to losing the man who'd blazed into her life and taken her to the point of no return?

Each of the two women who had tutored her and guided her into a business career knew the sadness of separation, followed by the extreme agony of knowing the life they'd dreamed of and anticipated could never be.

She'd never wondered about Miss Ring's personal

circumstances. She'd been a strict teacher and besides instructing her students in the ways of the business world she'd pushed them hard into practising their shorthand squiggles and typing in time to music, the keyboards of their machines shielded, so forcing them to touch type almost without realising. Anna had nothing but respect for her former tutor and felt it was no wonder these two women were friends. Each had been destined never to become a wife and mother, so maybe their students and fledgling shorthand typists became substitutes for the children they would never nurture. Something told her the close friendship between the two might well extend into a scenario she knew little about. Yet, far from being shocked, she now began to think 'why not?'

If they found solace in each other's company and if that included physical affection, she could totally understand. She was so immersed in these thoughts that she almost forgot the CO's afternoon tea and had to turn around and scamper to the canteen.

But carrying the tray back, Anna felt as though she'd finally grown up. After several years of being impatient to leave childhood behind, she'd experienced passion with Charles, even fancied they were in love, but now she finally realised how wrong she'd been. Why hadn't she seen it at the time? Because, she'd closed her mind to criticism and warnings and happily enjoyed his attentions, surrendering herself to this man, duped by the skills of an accomplished seducer.

Geoff, though younger than Charlie, was so much more mature, so much more likely to make her happy. But she'd thrown away any chance of a relationship with him. He probably didn't even like her now. And that made her very sad indeed.

'Go on then! What else did Colonel Gresham say? I'm so pleased for you. But I'm surprised you didn't tell me the moment you came through the door.' After their evening meal, Ruby and her daughter were relaxing in the living room.

'He said some very kind things about my work and how impressed he was by the way I'd handled some quite tricky situations.' Anna felt a pang as she remembered her first day in the job and how she'd needed to interrupt that important meeting where Charlie was amongst those present.

'Colonel Gresham also said he'd told Miss Napier there was no need to interview any other applicants, provided I accepted the position.'

'That must have given you a boost.'

'Well, yes, but the other side of the coin is that Miss Morgan's very poorly and it's only because of her illness that I was given this chance in the first place. I wouldn't want to go around crowing about it.'

'I realise that, but don't sell yourself short. You wouldn't have been offered a permanent position if you weren't up to scratch. I'm so proud of you and so would your father be if he was still with us. I know Frank will be, once he hears.'

Anna still felt as though she was acting out scenes, rather than living in the real world. Why was that? *Because Charles has left you!* She winced as a little voice whispered the words in her head. Yes, that probably accounted for her state of mind. But the promotion meant a positive step up in her career. Thinking of her predecessor, she resolved to ask Miss Napier for Miss Morgan's address so she could write and offer her best wishes for the future.

Her mother was strangely silent now. Anna turned to her. 'Are you OK, Mam? You seem very thoughtful.'

Ruby surprised Anna by squeezing her arm. She wasn't usually demonstrative. 'Frank booked the church today. Our marriage will take place at eleven o'clock on Friday the thirty first of December.' She stared into the fire.

'Oh, that's good. I was beginning to wonder whether you'd postpone the wedding until next year.'

'No, Frank's son should be home on leave by then so that spurred him on. I have my trousseau ready and Mrs Evans has made an excellent job of my pale blue costume so I shall wear that to go away in. I'll show you later. It's hanging in my wardrobe.'

'And I know you have your hat and all the other things. I'd forgotten about Frank's son. I don't think you've met him?'

'I've only ever seen photographs, but there's no mistaking who his father is.' She turned to face Anna.

'Just as you are so very like Viktor.'

Anna swallowed hard. 'Tell me, Mam, how do you ... how can a person be sure whether or not they love another person?'

It took Ruby a few moments before she spoke. 'I suppose this is about that officer?'

'No, it's not. Anyway, no doubt you'll be pleased to hear Charles has been posted. He left on Sunday afternoon.' She was struggling to keep her voice steady. To keep her emotions under wraps.

'I understand you'll miss him, but some things aren't meant to be. As for your question, I think it's easy to mistake infatuation for love. Intense feelings for someone can blind you and affect your judgement. But loving someone is different. Loving someone is a much better feeling than all that giddy stuff which can make you believe you're in love. You need to love someone for reasons far beyond the cocktails and dinner dates – look beyond the whirlwind romance before deciding to spend the rest of your life with them.'

Anna bit her lip.

Ruby spoke softly. 'But even at the beginning of a love affair, if one person feels more strongly than the other person, and is then left behind or rejected in favour of someone else, he or she can still experience a broken heart.'

'Oh, Mam, I can't bear it!' Anna burst into tears and her mother took her in her arms and rocked her gently, somehow managing to extricate a clean handkerchief from her pocket. Anna took it, mopping up tears while her sobs slowly faded.

'I know it hurts. It will go on hurting, but one day you'll suddenly realise you haven't thought of him for hours. And you will love again. It may seem impossible now, but I don't believe it's your destiny to become an old maid. Oh, I do so hate that stupid expression!'

She hugged Anna again. 'In our school yard,' Ruby said, 'we used to play a game of chase where the person who lost was called the old maid. Even though it was all nonsense, each one of us dreaded earning that title. Marriage was every girl's goal – or nearly every girl's – and we never thought beyond that. Not in my group of friends anyway.'

'Things haven't changed much, have they?' Anna smoothed back her hair. 'Unless they want to study medicine or become a teacher or something else involving long training, girls want to find a steady boyfriend. They don't want to seem over-eager in case they frighten him away, and they certainly don't want a string of boyfriends, in case people think they're flighty. I think I'm happy to stay single for several years yet.'

'Fair enough. But if the right man comes along – which he will,

one of these days – you might change your mind.'

'I can't imagine it. Not at the moment, anyway.'

'I don't think you need to be physically attracted on

first meeting. Yes, it's nice if a man's good-looking, but he doesn't have to be Cary Grant or Clark Gable.'

Anna immediately thought of Charlie's resemblance to the film star David Niven. She knew it hadn't only been good looks that first attracted her. They'd been like two planets spinning on a collision course. Too late now for regrets.

'I'm going to pour us each a small glass of sherry,' Ruby said. 'To celebrate your success and to drink a toast to your career.'

Anna felt relieved. 'Even though it may not involve marriage for some while yet?'

Her mother nodded. 'I won't deny I'd like to see you settled down before too many years go by. But you're still young, love. You've time to work hard at your career first.'

CHAPTER 21

Charles straightened his tie, standing to attention to check his appearance in the mirror. His father tapped on the door before entering the room.

'All well, my boy? We should be on our way soon.'

Charles nodded. 'Better get it over with.'

'I'd say you're a lucky man, marrying Eleanor. She's been a patient and faithful fiancée and it's high time you tied the knot, especially as you're off to the Adriatic.'

'It's a rum thing, Pa, getting married then having to head off to Liverpool.'

'With your bride beside you, and willing to drive your car back tomorrow morning. Didn't I say you were a lucky man?'

Charles had to admit Eleanor was the kind of young woman who'd jump to it when the occasion arose. 'At least we'll spend our wedding night in a smart hotel.' Charles picked up his cap. 'Where's my best man?'

'He nipped outside for a cigarette. Your ma didn't want the least trace of smoke on her wedding outfit.'

'No, I suppose not. Well, after you, sir.' He followed his father from the room. His kitbag was already in the Vauxhall, together with Eleanor's overnight case. Another suitcase – another woman. And so soon too. But all that with Anna was behind him now. Janice had literally given him his marching orders the last time he'd visited, declaring, after he bedded her, she was from that time on, back on the straight and narrow, with her husband due leave. As for Marcia, he still thought of her sometimes and wondered how her husband was getting on, poor devil.

Charles was about to plight his troth in the village church where he was baptised, as Eleanor had been, and where each of his two elder sisters were married. Did he regret any of his amorous adventures? He didn't think so. Though he felt a sense of shame about the way he'd left the Snow Maiden. She wasn't married and seeking a bit on the side like Janice. She wasn't sophisticated and missing her conjugal rights, like Marcia, God rest her soul. Having laid down the law to Geoffrey about giving virgins a wide berth, Charles had totally disregarded his own advice and enjoyed deflowering Anna. But she'd get over him. Once Geoffrey beat his chest and realised what a peach she was, in bed and out, they'd be as happy as Larry. Whoever Larry was.

Charles's cousin returned from his quiet smoke and adjusted Charles's tie, despite the groom's protests.

Brigadier Milburn poured measures of Amontillado

into crystal glasses and they all drank a toast to the ending of hostilities. Soon it was time to leave.

Inside the church, with the organist playing quietly, Charles watched close family and friends take their places. 'Are you sure you've got the ring?' he asked his best man, suddenly beset by a fit of nerves, one half of him longing to escape and get on his way to Italy, the other half determined to do the right thing by Eleanor.

She'd particularly wanted to make her entrance to the tune of *Mendelssohn's Wedding March* and now Charles heard the first chords. This was the moment when the uncertainty within him and the cowardice he tried to cover up, battled for supremacy.

His cousin nudged him. 'Need to get to your feet, Charlie.'

Charles rose and turned to watch his bride take the first step towards her groom. She was on the arm of her father, who looked so proud, and beamed so lovingly as he glanced down at his youngest daughter, that Charles took a deep breath and cast all his demons away. He could not, would not, break her heart. Somehow, he must make this work.

Unfailingly susceptible to the scent of a beautiful woman, he sucked in his breath as the bride's veil was carefully drawn back, revealing Eleanor's smooth complexion and the elegant sweep of her neck. She wore her raven dark hair pulled into a chignon and her perfume seemed more reminiscent of the harem than an English country garden. Charles made it his business to familiarise himself with expensive scents and he swallowed hard on recognising Eleanor's. *Shocking* encapsulated precisely how he liked his women. Sweet as the scent of jasmine and roses, but with a touch of sharpness spiking the rich sandalwood and heady incense. Unfortunately, it also catapulted him to his final and tragic meeting with the vocalist, Marcia.

He hadn't seen his bride for far too long. He'd already taken her virginity soon after they became engaged, and now it was time to claim his beautiful wife.

After the signing of the register, the bridal procession progressed down the aisle, both bride and groom smiling at familiar faces amongst the small congregation, Charles almost causing Eleanor to laugh out loud as he commented sotto voce, 'Good Lord! Who brought your Great-Aunt Myrtle out of mothballs?'

Eleanor was almost as tall as her groom, slim, long-legged and with an easy assurance to match his own. Would she be a faithful wife whilst he was away from her? She'd better bloody be! And at that moment, he decided he needed to be a dutiful husband, even though his new wife would never know if he wasn't. He was saying farewell to those carefree bachelor days and in a way, felt rather relieved.

One of Eleanor's cousins took photographs but bride and groom were conscious of time running out and the party moved on to Eleanor's home for a simple spread.

Charles marvelled at the modest yet surprisingly edible wedding cake. He chatted to the aunts and the vicar, always keeping close to his bride and earning more than one approving look and admiring comment. This brief hiatus between wedding and next morning's departure must, he determined, be a time they would always remember. And as he wondered if he could make Eleanor pregnant in the process, he reckoned that would be a most satisfactory state of affairs.

'You were a dream come true last night, my darling.' Charles put his arm around his wife as they stood beside the Vauxhall, close to the quay from which he would depart. She raised her face so their lips met in a long kiss.

'Spare my blushes, Charlie! You'd best go quickly before I decide to stow away!' she teased.

'Darling, you may be able to visit me once I've settled in and certain things are in order. It won't be the best time of year to make the voyage, but unless I'm granted leave, which I doubt, it'll be the only way we can be together for some considerable time.'

'I don't care if the seas are rough, as long as you're waiting for me at the end of the voyage.'

He kissed her again. 'I love you, Eleanor. Remember that when we're apart.'

'And I love you too, Charlie. More than you'll ever know.' She broke away. 'I'm going now, husband. I'll take good care of your beloved Vauxhall and I'll write as soon as I know your address.' She gasped. 'Gosh, don't go before giving me the car key!'

He fumbled in his pocket, winked at her and handed the key over. She turned on her heel and hurried towards the car, but he pursued her and flung his arms around her, kissing her and holding her so close, he could see she was breathless once he let go, kissing her hand before walking back to collect his kitbag.

To his intense amazement, he felt bereft at leaving her. But this was fitting, surely, as it signalled an end to his "love 'em and leave 'em" ways? His recent dalliances were memories now he faced far greater challenges than he ever had before.

Anna saw Geoff come round the corner while she headed for her office.

'Good morning,' he called.

'Goodness, Geoff, you're full of beans for a Friday.'

'It must be because I'm about to become the proud owner of a second-hand car. It's a little extravagant, I admit, but it's a bargain and it'll make life more interesting.'

'I suppose so. Your girlfriend will be pleased, I'm sure.' Anna tried to sound enthusiastic.

'My girlfriend? Who might she be, I wonder?'

His eyes told her something she hesitated to acknowledge, even though she knew she was being stubborn and doing herself no favours. Her two closest chums were always occupied when she was at a loose end. Margaret, having become friendly with a young male student doctor, wanted to spend as much time as possible with him. As for Biddy, though she and Anna still lunched together, in the evenings she either helped her mother with her younger siblings, or knitted socks and wrote letters to the young corporal she'd been walking out with before his posting.

'I'm sorry. It's only that some of the typists are gossiping about you and that pretty dark-haired girl whose name I don't know.'

'They probably mean Muriel Evans. She and I have shared a table in the canteen a few times, that's all. For your information and for Biddy's and the rest of the typing pool's benefit, Muriel has a boyfriend stationed overseas. I won't poach another man's sweetheart, no matter how attractive and charming she might be.'

He held the door open for her. He was referring to Charles, but she couldn't help feeling a little annoyed. It wasn't as though she and Geoff had been going out regularly together. Yet Charles must have known Geoff would be upset if he made a play for her. And how she'd responded! She'd fallen for Charlie almost without knowing what was happening and at times wondered how she could bear to carry on as normal when she felt numb inside, now he was no longer in her life.

'I apologise, Anna. That was unfair of me.' They stood close together, an island, with faceless employees passing either side of them on their way to or from the canteen.

'It doesn't matter.'

'I imagine it very much does and I wish I could help you through this, though I'm not sure I can ever forgive him, you know. He's treated you appallingly.'

She swallowed hard. 'I should go. One thing I seem to get right is my timekeeping, so I'd better not blot my copybook.'

He grimaced. 'Anna, may we talk soon? Properly talk, I mean. As friends of course. I promise I won't expect anything from you that you're unable to give.'

'I'd like that.'

'Are you free this weekend?'

'My calendar's empty, apart from my mother's wedding day, but that's not until New Year's Eve.'

'Then what say I pick you up on Sunday afternoon at two o'clock? We could go for a short drive, find some tea, and still have some daylight left.'

He was waiting for her response. Was she being foolish, expecting him to be content with her friendship rather than her love? Because she still felt raw. Too exposed to analyse exactly what her feelings for Geoff were.

'That sounds nice.' She hesitated. 'I'd suggest you came to lunch first, but ...'

'Don't worry. And do wrap up well. I'm afraid this car isn't a deluxe model. Maybe I should get hold of a rug.'

She laughed. 'My turn to say don't worry. I'll take your advice and wrap up well.'

She set off down the corridor, aware he still stood, watching her walk away. She couldn't help thinking she and Geoff were like two lost souls. It was Charles who linked them and Charles who divided them.

CHAPTER 22

Bari, Italy - November 1943

Charles Milburn stood at his office window, studying the scene below. His voyage from Liverpool had not been uneventful, but given the stage the war had reached, it was no surprise when their ship narrowly escaped being torpedoed by an enemy submarine.

The Allies' successes in Italy were achieved despite a background of overstrained resources and shortages of ammunition, back-up and shipping. Charles knew he must remain optimistic, but found it difficult to summon his usual nonchalant approach to life.

He still felt short-changed by the whole speediness of his posting, his decision to marry Eleanor and his transit to Italy. Yes, his new quarters were sumptuous compared to his former lot. Yes, he felt sure marrying Eleanor was the right decision. But he still felt he lacked something in his life, though he found it hard to define precisely what that something might be. Perhaps, once fully settled in, he'd gain satisfaction from putting his all into an important job.

His bird's eye view gave him a partial view of the harbour in the distance. Although not near enough to discern movements of dock workers and military personnel, he could easily visualise the activities taking place. Closer, the tall spire of a church dominated the landscape. Apart from on his wedding day, he couldn't remember the last time he'd stepped inside a place of worship. Maybe he should visit the church he saw in the distance? If he had to state his religion, he'd consider himself to be, like his father, an Anglican. But surely the Church of Rome wouldn't disintegrate if he should walk into a Catholic sanctuary in search of something to calm his feeling of displacement? This sensation of a slice of his life left incomplete?

Anna noticed the flimsy envelope on the doormat as she let herself into the house. Her mother must have gone out. All the better, should the letter be from Charles. She closed the front door and telling herself not to be ridiculous, turned the envelope over and felt puzzled by the unfamiliar hand-writing.

Inside the living room, a small fire still glowed and Ruby had left a note on the dining table, to say there was boiled ham in the larder. Anna put her letter on the arm of the couch and, kneeling before the hearth, shovelled pieces of coal on top of the embers, watching the hiss and flare as the fire reacted.

The letter must be from Davy. Anna felt neither elated nor irritated. Dully, she thought it would have been a miracle to hear from Charles, given the way he'd slipped away as though he couldn't wait to escape. She still felt numb, tired by her busy day at work, and, if she was honest, missing the buzz he used to generate.

She got to her feet and crossed over to the sideboard, reaching for the sherry bottle and glass. The stimulant might buck her up before she ate her supper. Ruby wouldn't be long, but having lunched with Frank, wouldn't need much to eat, according to her note.

The letter revealed nothing of Davy's whereabouts, of course, but he'd written down his rank and BFPO address. Anna scanned the sloping script, noting the errors, then feeling ashamed of her criticism.

Dear Anna,

I hope you and your mam are keeping well. I expect shes got married by now anyway give her my best wishes and the same to your gran and grandpa. I miss my little chats over the fence with the old feller. I hope his allotments still going strong.

Your probably dreading me asking you to write back. Well, guess what I've found myself a girlfriend. Who'd have thought it, ay? We met at a dance in a village hall and my mate dragged me on the floor when they announced a Paul Jones. Betty was the second girl I danced with.

When the band leader anounced the next dance I walked up to her and asked if I might have the pleasure. She was a better dancer than yours truly but very patient with my clodhopping so patient I began to hope she might like me a little bit.

In the interval I asked for us to keep in touch and she wrote down her adress on the back of a letter I had in my battledress pocket. Now I keep Bettys letters in the same safe place as I keep my mothers. And the first one my girl wrote to me is the one I keep next my heart.

Betty is a land girl in Kent. She lives on a farm with three of them billeted in an attic but she seems happy and glad not to be stuck in a Munitions Factory.

By the time you get this letter I shall be up and away to parts foreign. Maybe you and me will see each other again one day. Maybe both of us will be married by then. Who knows? If I'm spared, I'd like to get back to the old town and one day, set up my own garage business. Betty knows about my dream and I'm glad to say she hopes to be part of it.

Your friend
Davy

He sounded cheerful enough, but goodness knows where he might be now. She really should write to wish him well and thank him for thinking of her. He'd shown consideration in not mentioning the way she'd let him down and Anna knew she'd been selfish. Knew she'd blown hot and cold and deserved that awful name men had for women who led them on, before rejecting them.

Lost in thought, Anna jumped at the sound of the front door closing. Ruby didn't call out a greeting but came into the room still wearing hat and gloves.

'My goodness, it's cold out there. I've always hated November. The fire looks good, love. How did your day go?' Ruby pulled off her gloves and stood before the mirror over the sideboard, carefully removing two pearl-studded hatpins from her dark-green velvet turban, before settling beside her daughter on the old couch.

'I've been busy as usual.'

'And drinking on your own, I see.'

'Well, you're here now. Shall I pour one for you?'

Her mother hesitated. 'All right then. How many have you had, by the way?'

'This is my first glass. I hardly ever take alcohol these days.' Anna half-expected a snide comment about Charles, but Ruby remained silent.

Anna got up, dropping Davy's letter on to her mother's lap. 'You can read that if you like. You get a mention.'

'Really?' Ruby picked up the letter. 'Who's it from?'

'Remember Davy, next door to Nana and Grampy's?'

Anna found a glass and poured the sherry.

'That lad always had his eye on you, didn't he?' Ruby began scanning the lines. 'Oh dear – he's made several mistakes.'

Anna placed her mother's glass before her. 'I thought he made a good job of the letter, considering he left school as soon as he could. Don't forget he's a very good motor mechanic – the Army must be pleased with him.'

'And you must be pleased he's found himself a girlfriend.' Ruby handed back the letter and picked up her glass. 'Kind of the lad to think of us, I suppose.' She raised her glass to Anna. 'Here's to the future, love.'

'I'll drink to that, even if I wonder what it'll bring.'

'Without a crystal ball, I daren't even guess. Peace, I hope. Peace for far longer than we had between the Great War and this one. And one day, I want to see my daughter happily settled with some nice young man who'll cherish her as her father cherished me.'

Anna swallowed hard and wished for the umpteenth time that her mother wouldn't keep returning to the same subject. No doubt she'd be heartened when she knew "that nice lieutenant" was still in the picture. Anna would probably be reprimanded for not inviting him to Sunday dinner but she suspected she and Geoff shared the same view on that particular subject.

'The weather could be worse, but we'll probably be glad of our raincoats.' Geoff glanced across at Anna. 'You look very smart, as usual.'

'Thank you, kind sir.' Her little blue costume was an old favourite and, remembering to wrap up well, she wore a thick white jumper and woollen scarf.

'I thought we'd head for Penarth,' Geoff said. 'Is that all right with you?'

'I love Penarth. Are you pleased with your car?'

'So far, fingers crossed and all that. We could walk along the pier, if it's open that is? Is it right they used to hold dances there?'

'That would've been in the Marina Ballroom. It used to be very popular, but it closed after war was declared so you'll probably have a long wait for it to reopen.'

Again, that sideways glance and wry smile. 'It's not really my style.'

'You seemed to be doing a fair impersonation of Fred Astaire at that dance we all turned out for!'

Geoff laughed out loud. 'You're very kind, but I doubt it. Anyway, Charles was still suffering from the effects of that terrible nightclub bombing. He'd have had my guts for garters if I hadn't tripped the light fantastic with as many young ladies as possible.'

They drove in silence for a while. Anna thought back to that evening. How she'd found Charlie outside and how, as they talked, she sensed their mutual attraction heightening until it almost shimmered in the air. Now she waited as long as she could before turning her head towards Geoff.

'Have you heard from him?'

Geoff was slowing down as he drove through the town. 'Um, only that they all arrived safe and sound.'

She glanced sideways, noticing the tension in his jaw. 'I gather it's not the easiest of postings.'

'Not like here, you mean?'

'Geoff, I know all of you have to go wherever the powers-that-be decide to send you. I wasn't ... I didn't mean to detract from ...'

He interrupted her while pulling up on a quiet road. 'We're all in it together, of course, but some postings aren't always the ones we might wish for. I'd like to get in on the action, I really would.'

'Don't say that! Your work here's as important as anyone else's and none of us can guarantee our safety. You just made me think of that poor singer who lost her life that night in Cardiff.'

He glanced at her. 'I shall never forget how I might have been in that nightclub had Charles invited me along. He had a lucky escape, but I bet he'll never forget it – never take his safety for granted. Now, let's stretch our legs, shall we?'

He moved round to open the passenger door and took her raincoat, holding it out for her. As they walked down to the promenade, she automatically took his arm and they fell into step.

'On a more cheerful note,' he said, 'I'd really appreciate your help with the New Year's Eve dance. How would you feel about that?'

'We didn't make too bad a team for the last one, did we?'

'I should say not. Does that mean you'll give me a hand?'

'Of course. The wedding shenanigans should all be finished by then.'

'I'd temporarily forgotten your mother's big day. As long as you're sure you're not too busy helping with the preparations?'

'She has everything under control. Anyway, it's not a big affair – just close family and friends and a reception at the Cliff Hotel.' Anna hesitated. 'This is a bit of a cheek, as you'd have to request time off, but you'd be doing me a very big favour if you agreed to attend, as my escort. I'm my mother's maid of honour so I wouldn't be sitting with you in the church, but it would be lovely to have your company at the reception. It'll all be over by four o'clock.'

He remained silent and she squeezed his arm.

'I'm sorry. I have a nerve, asking you after all that's happened. Please forget I said anything. It's me being selfish as usual.'

'I told you I valued your friendship and that holds true. I'd be honoured to attend your mother's wedding as your escort, duties permitting, of course.'

Anna looked at him and saw the tenderness in his eyes. Her own were brimming with tears and she let go of Geoff's arm and fumbled in her handbag for a handkerchief.

'That's a lovely thing to say although I don't deserve it.' She turned her head and mopped up the tears.

'I wish you wouldn't blame yourself for what happened.'

'I behaved outrageously and I can't ever forget that. I think I must have been deranged!'

'Hey, I thought we were going to talk about cheerful things.'

And I mustn't let Charlie spoil my relationship with Geoff, Anna told herself.

Geoff glanced at the rain clouds clustering above and squeezed her arm. 'Judging by that sky, we'd better get a move on if we want to blow away the cobwebs.'

On New Year's Eve 1943 at two minutes past eleven, Anna walked up the aisle behind her mother.

Ruby wore a dark chocolate brown lace dress with a saucy little mink stole, a gift from her doting husband-to-be. Ruby's high-heeled suede shoes matched her dress and her still-lustrous dark hair was coiled at the back of her head beneath a cream satin pillbox hat with a spider's web veil. Anna's friend Biddy had managed to seek out a neighbour who cultivated hyacinths to flower at Christmas, so the bride carried a small spray of sweet-smelling white blooms and fresh greenery tied with white ribbon.

The bride's father had declined to walk his daughter up the aisle a second time, deeming it bad luck. Nobody protested and Ruby's brother was roped in to carry out the duty. On entering the church, Anna saw Geoff seated in a rear pew and smiled at him as she passed. He looked well-groomed in his uniform and obviously taking seriously his role as maid of honour's escort. She'd never imagined herself attending her mother on Ruby's second wedding day, but here she was, dressed in a high-necked turquoise velvet frock, her golden hair secured by Frank's gift: a pearl-studded silver slide. She carried a simple spray of baby's breath and green foliage.

But she found it difficult to concentrate. In her mind's eye, she pictured herself, dressed in blue, standing at the altar beside the man who'd broken her heart and left her disillusioned. Would she never learn? How many love letters must his fiancée have written to him by now? Anna gazed at the jewel colours of the stained-glass window above the altar where a robed figure held out his arms in supplication.

'I now pronounce you man and wife.' The vicar beamed. 'You may kiss the bride.'

Anna briefly closed her eyes and swayed slightly. Briefly she thought of Jane Austen characters swooning, but was relieved to recover her equilibrium ready to join the best man for the signing of the register.

Soon they were walking back down the aisle, behind the happy couple. Outside the church, a handful of neighbours waited in the churchyard, ready to call congratulations to the former Mrs Christensen, now Mrs Mapstone. Anna looked round gratefully as Geoff reached for her hand and squeezed it.

'The bride looks beautiful. But you, Anna ... well, I don't have the right words. I understand how you must be feeling and I won't make trite comments, but remember you have your life ahead of you. What I am sure about is that your father would have been very proud of you.'

Anna looked at Geoff and gave a hardly visible shake of the head.

Geoff, still holding her hand, raised it to his lips and kissed her fingers. 'You may not believe me now, but the time will come when you will, my love.'

She bit her lip as he whispered the endearment though she knew very well this must be as difficult for him as it was for her. She held his hand tightly while, once again, that slightly dizzy sensation overcame her. She'd eaten very little for breakfast, which must be the reason for this light-headedness. The last thing she wanted was to come down with influenza and have to stay home from work.

Anna shivered as a playful breeze ripped its way through the waiting wedding guests. The photographer did his best to record the occasion and not before time, in Anna's opinion. She and Geoff were bringing up the rear as family members and guests followed Mr and Mrs Mapstone to the cars.

'Could I come with you, Geoff? Please ... I won't have to make polite conversation then.'

He chuckled. 'It's probably not etiquette, Miss Christensen. What if we set tongues wagging?'

'I don't care about that. Anyway, you're my escort.'

Without a doubt, Ruby was happy with Anna's decision to invite her young lieutenant to attend the wedding. The second-time bride radiated delight on her wartime wedding day, and on their return from honeymoon, when the photographs were developed and printed, that joy would shine out from the black and white images delivered to the newly-weds.

'You must be exhausted after the last few weeks,' Geoff whispered to Anna when at last the cake was cut, the toasts were made, and the happy couple left the reception to prepare for their drive to Tenby. The groom had arranged for them to spend their week's honeymoon in one of the coastal town's best hotels.

Anna daren't tell Geoff she was in no mood to attend the dance that evening, but she was determined not to let him down, after all the kindness he'd displayed.

'There's plenty of time to rest before I need to get ready to go out again.'

'How are you getting there?'

Anna gasped. 'Goodness, I hadn't given it a thought. Anyway, I can get a bus – the church hall's not far from the stop.'

'Or you can let me drive you and bring you home afterwards.' He shot her a quizzical look. 'Unless you capture the heart of one of the dashing young officers who've recently joined us while they await their next posting.'

'Very funny.' She lowered her voice. 'I think I'm best keeping out of the line of fire, Geoffrey, old chap.'

It was obvious who she was imitating. Geoff burst out laughing. 'I like your sense of humour. Got him to a T!'

'I'm sorry to say I think about Charles quite a lot, though I wish I didn't.'

'No need to apologise. I miss him too, despite those times when all I wanted to do was punch him. You wouldn't be human if you could switch off your feelings with one click of your fingers.'

'Oh, wouldn't it be good if we could?'

He drank the last of his coffee and put down his cup. 'I don't agree. We have emotions and we need to deal with them in the best way we can. Ruby, for example, will never stop loving your late father. Even though she's no longer a widow, it doesn't mean she should banish Viktor from her memory. Anyway, she has you as a constant reminder.'

Anna, touched by his remark, swallowed hard and took a while to reply. 'Had my father not been taken ill like that, I believe he and my mother would have stayed together for many years. Like swans. Don't they mate for life?'

'I believe so. Now, let's get you home and I'll return at half-past six. That'll give us time for a last-minute check before the bun fight starts, though come to think of it, if we've forgotten something important, I guess there's nothing we can do about it.'

It was a relief to kick off her shoes and put the kettle on. Anna climbed the stairs to her bedroom and carefully removed her velvet dress before snuggling into her woollen dressing-gown and warm slippers. Downstairs again, catching the kettle as it began to sing, she drew the curtains while waiting for the tea to brew. As an afterthought she visited the pantry, feeling relieved to find a small jug of still-fresh milk on the marble slab. After she'd read a few items in the newspaper, it seemed a good idea to top up the kettle and fill a hot water bottle to take upstairs.

Anna felt too tired to clean off her makeup so, although she heard her mother's voice in her head scolding her for her lack of fastidiousness, she settled herself beneath the old pink eiderdown. A new bed and bedding awaited her in a much bigger room in Frank's house, but she preferred to remain in the only home she'd ever known, until he and Ruby returned to begin their new life together.

She closed her eyes, allowing the day's events to play through her mind in slow motion. Her mother had looked beautiful, so beautiful, Anna experienced a poignant moment as she thought how sudden and simple Ruby's first wedding would have been. Her mother had stood before the altar with the love of her life on that faraway day, only she and Viktor knowing the real reason behind their impulsive wish to marry. That secret had been the baby they conceived together and Anna now felt this second marriage signalled the closure of her own formative years.

Everything had fallen into place today, including the wedding breakfast which owed a lot to her stepfather's mysterious and anonymous contacts, but that was no concern of hers. She tried to push away thoughts of Charles and concentrated instead on how kind and understanding Geoff had been. One day he would find the right person to love him in the way he deserved. One day ...

Anna awoke to the sound of someone banging on the front door. The bedroom was in semi-darkness, lit only by the light filtering through the curtains from the streetlamp. She had no idea what the time was, but realised she'd slept for far longer than intended. Yet as fast as she threw back the bedclothes and jumped from beneath the covers, she promptly sat back down again. Rocked by a wave of nausea, Anna pressed the back of one hand to her lips.

Surely the shrimp starter couldn't be the culprit? And the chicken had been delicious even if her appetite hadn't quite been up to the mark. Anna couldn't even think about the Peach Melba without swallowing hard. She got to her feet again, this time gingerly, before putting on her slippers and making her way on to the landing and downstairs.

'Anna! What's happened? Are you ill?'

She shook her head and realised that was a mistake. It took all her will power to retain her equilibrium and answer his question. 'I'm afraid it's possible something I ate has disagreed with me, but … oh dear, Geoff, I don't think I can face coming out this evening.'

'You poor thing. What rotten luck! May I come in?'

She stood back. 'I'm forgetting my manners, yes of course you can. I doubt whatever's wrong with me is catching.'

Geoff secured the door and put his arm around her shoulders, to escort her to the sitting room. 'Let me light the gas fire. It's probably not worth making the coal fire up now – or should you go back to bed?'

She sank on to the couch and huddled into her dressing gown. 'I think I've slept enough for now but I can't tell you how sorry I am to let you down.'

He made sure the fire was burning steadily before getting to his feet. 'Anna, you've helped tremendously with all the arrangements and you've had a taxing time lately. I don't like leaving you here like this, though.' He sat down beside her and reached for her hand.

'I expect I'll be right as rain by morning.'

'Well, with your permission, I'd like to call and make sure you are. Is there a neighbour you trust to come in later and check you're OK?'

She shook her head. 'I don't need anyone, Geoff. Truly I don't. But if you want to visit me tomorrow morning, I shan't say no. Though it baffles me as to how you put up with me.'

'I'll ignore that.' He glanced at the clock. 'I'd better

be on my way, but you look after yourself, do you hear?'

'Yes, sir. I hear you loud and clear.'

'Oh, Anna. I wish …'

'I'm sure everyone will have a marvellous time. I'll see you in the morning.'

'It'll be later on, probably around eleven after I've done a final check of the church hall.'

'Thanks, Geoff.' Much as she was fond of him, she needed to be on her own now.

'Be sure to lock the door once I've gone. I shan't walk back to the car until I hear you do so.'

CHAPTER 23

Once alone, Anna switched on the wireless, not caring what she listened to, but needing something to help gather her thoughts, while perversely wishing Geoff could still be with her. Curled up on the couch, she counted backwards to the afternoon Charlie made love to her in the firelight. Gnawing her thumb, she walked into the kitchen to consult the calendar hanging beside the gas cooker. She'd need to tear off the page tomorrow and hang up the new calendar waiting in the drawer. She didn't want to think what the coming year might bring, but counting backwards through the weeks only confirmed her worst fear.

Yet the nauseous feeling was passing, although she didn't feel at all hungry. Maybe she was worrying unnecessarily after all. Maybe she'd picked up some kind of ailment from work though she couldn't think of anyone displaying ominous symptoms or being absent from the typing pool.

It occurred to her, whenever she heard the girls in the

canteen discussing pregnancy symptoms, sickness was always mentioned as a sure sign of someone "being in the family way" or "in the club." Yet, she'd felt fine when she woke up that morning and all through the rest of the day until coming home.

And wasn't it true that wartime rationing was held responsible for people not receiving the right diet? Maybe she was anaemic, as she knew her mother had been when she was fourteen or fifteen. Perhaps she'd inherited that tendency and it was finally making an appearance because of the food restrictions?

She decided there was nothing she could do about it for the time being. The thought of visiting her grandmother and confiding in her sent shivers down her spine. Nana, who was the unofficial midwife for the street she lived in, would doubtless question her and Anna dreaded to think what certain of those questions might be.

But what on earth would she do if she was expecting Charles's baby? It didn't bear thinking about, but she hugged her arms around herself, imagining how she might compose the letter she'd write. His departure had been so abrupt, after their brief but passionate lovemaking, but that was understandable, surely? He would have had so much on his mind and as he said, long, drawn-out farewells could only prolong the agony of parting. Except she doubted he'd been agonising over leaving her.

She decided to carry on as normal but there was someone who she hadn't spoken to in a while. Her old friend Margaret had dropped her a line, giving some advice on birth control, but expressing concern for her friend's welfare. *It's not as if you're even engaged* was the comment which stood out, but surely Margaret wouldn't refuse to help her now? Anna decided to telephone her next morning, around ten o'clock so she'd be back in time for Geoff's visit. She could wish her friend a Happy New Year and see if she was free to meet up with her. If Margaret was at the hospital, she'd have to write to her.

After a surprisingly sound sleep, Anna woke at eight o'clock, blinking as memories of the previous day's events percolated into her head. This was the first day of the New Year and when, she wondered, would she next find an opportunity to wear her turquoise blue frock?

Downstairs, filling the kettle to make tea, she felt a sense of relief to realise she felt fine. Maybe Geoff was right when he reminded her how much she'd had to contend with, both at work and with Ruby's wedding looming, not to mention her help in organising the dance.

Did she even need to bother Margaret? Yes, she must. But if her friend happened to be at home, maybe she wouldn't mention what prompted her to get in touch. It wasn't the easiest of topics to raise, even with a dear friend, but it would be lovely to see her again. They'd been best friends for years, though the differing hours they worked prevented them from meeting regularly.

The nearest telephone box wasn't far away. Anna arrived to find someone just leaving, so slipped inside, coins at the ready. It wasn't long before she heard a woman's voice and pressed Button A to make herself known.

'Hello, is that Mrs Griffiths?'

'This is she. Is that you, Anna?'

Anna smiled down the phone. 'I'm amazed you still recognise my voice. How are you?'

'We're all well, thanks. I gather your dear mother has remarried? Are you living with her still?'

'I will be, sometime after she and Frank return from honeymoon.'

'That's nice. Now, let me give Margaret a call.'

'Oh, thank you.' Now it had come to it, Anna was experiencing decidedly cold feet. She licked her dry lips and gazed through the glass panes at two small boys kicking a football around on the other side of the road. One looked across at her and pulled a face as she stared back, unseeing.

Then the sound of feet hurrying down the stairs. Moments later a familiar voice in her ear. 'Hullo stranger! How lovely to hear from you, just as I was thinking about you. How did the wedding go?'

'Very well, thanks. Listen, could we meet up some time soon? It's ages since we saw one another.'

'When did you have in mind? Are you still working in the docks office?'

'Yes, I'm free in the evenings and at weekends.'

'Are you indeed? Whatever happened to that chap you

were keen on?'

Anna's mind's eye provided a smiling Charles Milburn. 'It's a long story.'

'I can't wait! Can you come round at about two, this afternoon? My parents will be out so we'll be on our own. I'm due back on the ward at five, but we could have a good chat before I need to get ready.'

Anna felt shaky with relief. 'Thanks, Marg. I'll be there at two.'

Margaret chuckled. 'My goodness, no one's called me by my pet name for ages!'

'See you later.' Anna replaced the receiver and pushed against the heavy door. It would be so good to see her old friend, but even better if any advice forthcoming proved unnecessary.

She got back with time to spare before she heard someone banging on the brass knocker. She hurried to let Geoff in, smiling as she held the door wide.

'Well, you're a sight for sore eyes. Did you get a good night's sleep?' He bent his head and kissed her cheek.

'I did and I feel much better this morning, thanks.' She closed the door behind him. 'I'm afraid we'll have to make do with the gas fire but there's a pot of coffee brewing.'

He raised his eyebrows. 'Real coffee? Or shouldn't I ask?'

'I never ask. I'm always grateful and I trust my stepfather to keep on the straight and narrow – well, mostly. Come on through and tell me how everything went.'

He followed her into the sitting room, rubbing his hands together. 'This room's very welcoming. Won't you miss living here?'

'To be honest, I'd prefer to stay put, but I really can't afford the rent on my own and I can't expect Frank to let me live here when he could let it to someone else.'

'If I was a female, I'd ask if I could share with you.'

Anna burst out laughing. 'Well, there's a thought. But I doubt any of the girls in the typing pool would be interested in going halves. I'll be all right once I get used to the situation. Let me bring the tray through.'

But he beat her to it. 'Why don't I do that, as you've gone to the trouble of brewing coffee. I must say it smells delicious.'

Anna settled herself at the dining table. 'Come on then. How did it go last night?'

'Better than I'd imagined, I'm pleased to say. We had a good turnout and the boys in the band came up trumps again. No vocalist, but we had a very pleasant evening. I missed you though.'

'Did Sylvia and Mary and their chums turn up?'

'In full force, bless 'em.' He picked up his cup. 'This is a pretty coffee set.'

'My father brought back many treasures from his travels, but don't change the subject. Did you make a date with Sylvia at last?'

'Um, no, Anna, sorry to disappoint you, but I didn't.'

Anna sat back and folded her arms. 'Why are you smirking?'

'Because she made a big hit with one of the young officers. He hasn't been with us long and he's known for being on the quiet side, but Henry didn't waste any time once he spotted Sylvia – the milkmaid, as Charlie dubbed her.'

Anna unfolded her arms and picked up her cup. 'Well, good for Henry. And typical of Charlie to find Sylvia a nickname.' A pang shot through her as she wondered whether she'd ever again hear him call her his snow maiden.

'And what about Mary?' she asked. 'Charles had a nickname for her, of course. The tennis club's Hedy Lamarr, he called her. I imagine she must be missing Richard Curtis?'

'We had a couple of dances and she spoke of very little else but Richard. It was Charlie who played Cupid there, in case you didn't realise.'

Anna smiled. 'Of course! That was after Biddy and I asked a couple of soldiers to dance with us.'

'I wonder which one of you two bright sparks came up with that idea?' Geoff stroked his chin as though mystified.

'I wonder! It worked brilliantly for Biddy. She's still writing to her nice corporal, though obviously she has no idea where he is.'

Geoff looked serious. 'Curtis, of course, is out in Italy with Charlie. He's a career soldier, is Richard. Wouldn't be surprised if he reached a high-ranking position one day. Presuming he comes through this hellish war, of course. Thank the lord none of our lot were affected by that atrocity in early December.'

Anna didn't meet his eye. She'd cried herself to sleep after hearing the news of the Bari bombing and the devastation caused in and around the dockyard.

'I'm sorry. Me and my big mouth! We know it was horrific for everyone.' He grimaced and glanced at the coffee pot.

'Do help yourself. And you should know by now, I'm not the type to swoon at the mention of something Miss Napier would describe as "not nice." Whether we're over here or over there, not one of us knows whether we'll survive. I know we're all supposed to keep on hoping for right to prevail.'

'I only wish I could do more to help you.'

Anna sighed. 'You already do plenty, but I wish you could find someone nice enough to deserve you, I really do.'

He scowled. 'You're as bad as my mother. But, as you already said, we're at war, which means romance doesn't always arrive when people wish it would. In any case, why would I want to find a girlfriend when I … when I …'

'Geoff, if it's helpful to you and it means keeping your friendship, I'm happy for you to tell your mother I'm

your girlfriend. After all, I am a girl and I count myself
as your friend.'

His smile was wistful. 'Thank you, dear Anna, but
that's not necessary. I can cope with my mother and as
for our friendship, you need have no fears on that score.'

The house seemed empty after Geoff left around noon.
Suddenly ravenous, Anna toasted two slices of bread,
grimaced at the thought of margarine and spread them
with some of her grandma's very passable homemade
plum jam. There was still vegetable soup in the larder –
allotment soup as she and her mother called it – which
would do well for her evening meal.

It was a good forty five minutes' walk to her friend's
house. Dr Griffiths and his family lived in a large,
detached property overlooking the park at the other end
of the town, but Anna was never bothered about walking.
Determined not to arrive early, she slowed her pace as
she neared their road, and arrived on the doorstep as the
clock on All Saints' Church tower chimed twice.

Margaret must have seen her walk up the path because
she flung open the door and gave Anna a big hug while
they stood on the doorstep. 'Happy New Year! Now,
come in and get warm. Ma and Pa have gone to visit my
aunty and uncle, but they send their love and it means
we have the house to ourselves so we can sit by the fire
and gossip.' She reached out to take Anna's navy-blue
overcoat and velour hat. 'Your cheeks are nice and rosy.
You look well, Anna.'

Anna laid her gloves and scarf on the hall table, smiling as Margaret babbled away, only slowing down to let her friend get a word in once both girls sat beside the sitting room hearth. Anna looked around her, recognising paintings and furniture she hadn't seen since schooldays. 'I remember the first time I came to your house,' she said. 'It was just after the summer term ended and we hadn't been friends very long.'

'I remember that too, though I've no idea what Ma gave us to eat.'

Anna chuckled. 'I was a bit finicky over my food back then, but I recall she'd made a jam sponge cake with icing on the top and I had two pieces.'

Margaret exclaimed. 'Silly me! My manners are dreadful. Would you like some tea? It's no trouble.'

Anna shook her head. 'Not for me, thanks. Now tell me how your training's going.'

Margaret flopped back down on the settee and rolled her eyes. 'Contrary to Pa's dire predictions, I'm enjoying most of it. Not all of it, but I know I can cope with seeing things many people wouldn't wish to and according to Sister Tutor, that's a good sign.'

'Well done, that's excellent news. Are the other student nurses easy to get on with?'

'Most of them, yes. I share a room with a girl called Lizzie from Cardiff and we get on very well.'

'Oh, Marg, how dim of me! I didn't think to invite you to the New Year's Eve dance. It's good to have plenty of girls to dance with the soldiers. I'm friendly with the officer who was organising it, but it coincided with my mother's wedding day and there was a lot to think about.'

'I'm afraid I dipped out of the dance some of the others went to last night. My feet were killing me so I didn't feel very sociable. Besides, Dan was working …'

'Is he the trainee doctor you mentioned in your letter?'

Margaret's cheeks turned a delicate shade of pink. 'Yes, we met one day last October in the hospital canteen.'

'How lovely.' Anna thought back to that first encounter with Charles and Geoff as she and Biddy collided with them while leaving the canteen.

'Yes. Dan's very special to me. He's not what you'd call handsome, but he has lovely fair hair and beautiful hands and he seems to have taken a fancy to me.'

'As you have to him, judging by the way your eyes shine when you describe him. Believe me, Margaret, it's usually the most handsome ones who cause the greatest heartache for we women!'

'Oh dear, I've touched a nerve, haven't I? Is this the officer you mentioned you're friendly with? A trouble shared is a trouble halved and all that …'

Anna sat up straight and gazed at the fire. 'No, that's my friend, Geoff. You remember when I wrote to you a while back?'

'Of course. I don't think I was much help though. We all have it dinned into us that we should keep ourselves intact until our wedding night and I truly didn't like the idea of you …well, you know what I'm saying. For someone who's training to be a nurse, I'm pretty useless when it comes to my best friend's welfare.'

Anna felt touched that Margaret still thought of her so affectionately. 'You were a bit, well, direct, I suppose, but you explained a couple of things.'

'Are you still seeing this man?'

Anna, staring at the fire, watched a flame lick a sizzling log and spark a fleeting patch of sapphire. 'No. He, Charles that is, has been posted overseas.'

'I don't suppose that surprised you, but you must miss him? Is he good at letter writing?'

Anna shook her head. 'He won't contact me. Things moved fast after he received his new orders.'

Margaret rubbed her chin. 'So, you didn't have time for a proper goodbye? I'm so sorry …'

'Oh, he made sure he said goodbye to me in a most intimate way, if you understand my meaning.' She couldn't stop the words from tumbling out and realised how bitter she sounded.

'I hope you were prepared – or that he was?'

'I'm afraid not. I'm also afraid I did nothing to stop him.'

'And you're worried now that you may be …'

'Exactly. But I've been so busy lately, what with one thing and another, that I hadn't realised until this weekend that I've missed.'

'I see. Well, there are other reasons for missing, so you

could be worrying for nothing. Whatever you do, please don't try any old wives' tricks. You could endanger your health.'

'I can't help hearing the girls at the office talking about their friends or their sisters who have boyfriends in the services and some of the so-called remedies are, well, quite worrying. I think I'd be too frightened to muck around like that.'

'I'm glad to hear it. But this man, Charles – how could he treat you like that? He sounds irresponsible to say the least.'

'I trusted him the first time. He knew what he was doing, but when he called to say goodbye, he wasn't prepared. Neither of us intended what happened to happen.'

'All you can do now is bide your time and try not to worry. I know that's easy for me to say and I'm not judging you. We live in such peculiar times.'

Anna stared into the fire. 'The same thing happened to my mother, though in her case, my father asked permission to marry her because they were madly in love and he was due to sail away. Luckily, they were married and everyone assumed I was a honeymoon baby.'

'Would you like to marry your Charles?'

Anna took a while to answer. 'He's not the kind of man a woman could ever expect to remain faithful. I realise that now. Anyway, marriage isn't an option as he has a fiancée tucked away somewhere.'

'Oh, Anna. When did you find out? I'm sorry to say it, but he sounds like a cad.'

Even to herself, Anna's laugh grated. 'Geoff warned me Charles was engaged to be married, because he genuinely didn't want me to be hurt.' She sighed. 'And a fat lot of notice I took, didn't I?'

CHAPTER 24

On Monday morning, Anna awoke, feeling more energetic than she had for a while. Was this a hopeful sign or might it be the result of two very early nights and more sleep than usual? Yesterday after Margaret insisted on driving her home, she'd stretched out on the couch and taken a nap. But that left her with a peculiar taste in her mouth and even thinking of another cup of tea prompted the nausea. Yet, the prospect of consulting the family doctor, as her friend advised, filled her with dismay, though luckily, theirs wasn't Margaret's father.

She needed to get ready for work. If what she suspected proved true, there would be decisions to make. Dare she wait and see whether her monthly visitor turned up, or should she pluck up courage and seek advice sooner rather than later? Anna sighed at the thought of breaking unwelcome news to her mother.

While Anna's boss visited London, meeting with Whitehall top brass, she concentrated on filing and checking everything was shipshape. Around eleven o'clock, when Miss Napier rang, she wondered whether the typing pool was short-staffed and might need to borrow her. She gave the switchboard her whereabouts and on arriving, the supervisor beckoned her to enter the glass-partitioned office.

She closed the door behind Anna. 'Do sit down.' Miss Napier's high-heels clicked against the linoleum as she moved back to her desk and raised her eyebrows at her protégée. 'So, did things go well at the weekend?'

'How kind of you to ask. All went very well, thanks, Miss Napier. No hiccoughs, fortunately, and a surprisingly delicious wedding cake, given the restrictions.'

'Excellent. When are the happy couple due back?'

'Saturday, early afternoon.'

'And you're enjoying being alone in the house?'

Anna wondered what this might be about. 'It doesn't bother me. After the excitement of the wedding, I caught up with my sleep, and I visited an old school friend.'

'How lovely for you both.' Miss Napier picked up a pen and twirled it between her fingers. 'Miss Ring was asking after you when I saw her at church yesterday.'

'I hope she's keeping well.'

'She is indeed. And she has a full complement of students on her register.'

'That's good. Please give her my very best wishes next time you meet.'

'That's why I wanted to see you. Miss Ring ... Emily ... would like you to join us both for afternoon tea on

Sunday, at her house. Would you be free? Or will your mother need you?'

Anna felt surprised but she owed much to these two women and her social diary was hardly brimming over. 'I'm sure it'll be all right. Goodness, it seems an age since I last saw Miss Ring.'

'She has always followed your progress, my dear.' Miss Napier picked up a piece of paper and pushed it across the desk. 'Here's the address. I think she's written the time on there too.'

'Yes, thanks. Four o'clock on Sunday. What a lovely road to live in. So close to the beach.'

'Yes, Emily inherited the property from her parents.'

'I never knew where she lived. I thought maybe she had a flat above the college premises in Gladstone Road.'

Miss Napier laughed and leaned forward. 'Being a student is very different from becoming a valued colleague. At your age, I too would never have dreamed of asking my tutor anything remotely connected with her personal life.'

Anna nodded. There was something going on here, she felt certain. But what it might be, evaded her.

Back in her office, she took her personal diary and wrote the appointment on the following Sunday's page before tucking the address and telephone number inside the diary. She flicked the pages backwards to the entry for Wednesday evening. All being well, she and Geoff were off to the cinema, to see a film based on Monica Dickens's book, *One Pair of Feet*. Two social engagements only days apart – one she'd temporarily forgotten and one a total surprise. She looked up as someone tapped on her door and she saw the man himself peering at her through the glass panel. She pulled a face at him and he grinned back.

'Come in, Lieutenant.'

He closed the door behind him and saluted.

'Ah, so this is an official visit?'

'What else?' He loped across and sat down. 'I tried ringing earlier but you were apparently unavailable, Miss Christensen.'

'I was in an important meeting with Miss Napier.' Her lips twitched. 'Anyway, what can I do for you?'

'The CO's been on the phone.' He raised his hand. 'Don't panic! He wasn't trying to get hold of you, but he wanted to tell me that a project I've been working on needs actioning as soon as possible and in decent English rather than gibberish. And in his absence, he feels you're the right person for the job.'

'Does he indeed?'

'Oh dear, that sounds ominous. By the way, Anna, you look very much better than you did on Saturday.'

'You really do know how to compliment a girl!'

Geoff looked panic-stricken before realising her eyes were shining with merriment. 'Well, yes, sometimes words come out differently from how one would have wanted. Seriously, this is high priority confidential stuff and I rather loaded the dice in your direction when your boss mentioned you as the best candidate for the job. It's no reflection on the typing pool ladies, of course. Between you and me I think he's afraid you might get bored without him to run around after.'

'How considerate of him. Well, I enjoy a challenge, though your handwriting's only marginally better than Captain Milburn's atrocious scrawl!'

'That's me put in my place. And you feel better now, after a rest?'

'Yes, thanks. You can bring your notes to me whenever you're ready. Or did you want to dictate them to test my capabilities?'

She met his gaze. What was she doing? What if he thought she was deliberately flirting? Some light-hearted banter was permissible, but she daren't go further, even with Geoff.

'Shall we see how you get on? I'll read through the first section again and bring it through to you. Does that sound all right?' He got to his feet.

'That'll be fine.'

'Still on for Wednesday evening?'

'Oh, gosh, yes thank you. I'm looking forward to it.'

'Excellent.' He winked and made his exit.

Anna caught her breath. What if she confided her suspicions to Geoff on Wednesday? As her friend, would he suggest contacting Charles to gauge his reaction? She longed to confide in him, but what if she was panicking for nothing?

The evening Geoff drove Anna to the cinema, on reaching their seats, she refused to remove her coat or gloves, much to his amusement.

'If you dare make a snow maiden comment, I'll kill you,' Anna whispered as they took their seats.

The supporting feature was just beginning so Geoff swallowed his mirth. 'I promise not to, but I think you're right about keeping our coats on.'

They left the cinema, arm in arm and when Geoff drove Anna back home, she

offered to make cocoa.

'It's not very glamorous, but it'll warm us up.'

'Suits me! I'm not a glamorous sort of chap.'

'I'm very pleased you're not.'

Anna's remark sounded so heartfelt Geoff gave her an enquiring look as he lit the gas fire.

'Has something happened?'

She was watching the jets splutter and steady. 'Nothing at all.'

'And you were hoping to hear from Charlie.'

'I notice you didn't mean that as a question. I'll make our drinks now.'

He followed her into the kitchen where she busied herself with cups and saucepan.

'I forgot to ask how you're getting on in your Penarth digs.' She reached for the cocoa tin.

'Very well, thanks. Nice people. Apparently, I'm there much more than my predecessor used to be. That's no surprise though, is it?' He hesitated. 'Anna, there's something I need to tell you.'

She sighed. Poured milk into a pan and added a cupful of water. 'You've received a new posting.'

'I suppose the old man told you?'

'He warned me, in confidence of course, that it was on the cards. When did you hear?'

'On the phone this afternoon. I didn't want to say anything earlier – thought we needed a bit of escapism with the doctors and nurses.'

'It was fun. Stewart Granger's one of my favourites.' Anna smiled as she measured cocoa powder into the cups and dribbled a little cold milk into each. 'If you open that tin with the roses on, you can help yourself to a piece of wedding cake.'

'Really? I don't want to be greedy … are you having some?'

'No, thanks. You go ahead.'

Geoff sat beside Anna on the couch after they carried their drinks through.

'So, when do you leave? I suppose Charlie requested you as his right-hand man? You two always worked well together.'

Geoffrey shrugged, recalling Charles's remark about leaving him to pursue Anna. 'We always felt slightly uncomfortable to have landed such a good posting, compared to others. I imagine it's chaotic out there now, after the horrific bombing raids in early December.'

'I shall miss you. What will you do about your car?'

'Why? Do you want it?'

Anna laughed. 'No thanks.'

'Someone will buy it from me. And it goes without saying I'll miss you more than you'd ever suspect. Also, I'd be highly honoured if you could drop me a line from time to time.'

'Yes, of course I will. And you can give my best regards to Charlie when you see him, can't you?' She knew she sounded sarcastic, but couldn't help herself.

'Did he ... did he say anything about the future before he went? Did he say he'd write?'

'He skilfully avoided the subject. Anyway, I knew his fiancée would be sending letters. He made a touching little speech about disliking long, drawn-out farewells. I almost applauded.'

'Anna, you knew he was engaged. I marked your card, even if he didn't have the guts to tell you himself.'

'I know! I know! I'm the most stupid, the most idiotic girl in the whole world because I didn't listen, did I? Even when he did eventually mention his fiancée.' She tried to hide her sniffle with a cough.

'You fell for him, hook, line and sinker. Nor would you have been the first.' He wrapped his arms around her.

Mostly he concentrated on cuddling her, smoothing her hair and rocking her gently until her sobs subsided and she took a huge shuddering breath and patted his cheek. 'I must look a fright. Mam keeps brandy over there in the top drawer. I think we deserve a drop in our cocoa.'

She gave Geoff a lopsided grin after he doctored the hot drinks.

He stood, cradling his own cup in his hands, his face thoughtful. 'I'm so sorry you've had to put up with all this.'

'It's a mess, isn't it? In different circumstances, I could write this whole business off as being down to experience. But that's not so easy now.'

'Why? What are you trying to say?'

She shook her head. 'I know I don't need to ask you to keep this to yourself, Geoff, but it's possible I'm expecting a baby.'

It sounded strange, hearing those words leave her mouth. All at once she felt as though she and Geoff were actors in a play, a drama where the heroine, having become involved with a charming scoundrel, finds herself poised to scandalise her family and friends. More than ever, she felt sure her suspicions were correct. She was in trouble, as no doubt her grandmother would declare, once she heard the spectacularly unwelcome news.

She sipped her cocoa and replaced the cup. 'I imagine you're not surprised.'

'I'm bloody furious, if you'll pardon my French. He's not some carefree youth! He had no right to behave so irresponsibly – no right at all. How soon will you know for sure?'

She shrugged and reached for his hand. 'I suppose I'll have to find the courage to visit the doctor. Maybe next week …'

'Will you tell your mother?' He squeezed Anna's hand and raised it to his lips, kissing the fingers so tenderly she needed to steel herself in case the tears flowed once more.

'I shan't say anything until it's confirmed.'

'That sounds sensible. Ach, this is such bad timing. I'm off to Italy sometime in the next few days.' He turned to face her, cupping his hands around her face. 'I shan't be around to offer you any support, but what I shall do is speak to Charles and make him aware of what he's done. He shouldn't be allowed to get away with this.'

Anna had said goodnight to Geoff with mixed feelings. It was so hard, having this worry nagging at her. Now she had told her friend, Margaret, and almost without meaning to, Geoffrey as well. She'd begged him to say nothing to Charlie until she received her doctor's verdict.

'But I'll be gone by then!' He'd frowned and shaken his head.

'This is my muddle. I appreciate your thoughtfulness, but I shall write to Charlie only if I have to. And quite honestly, if the worst comes to the worst, I really don't know what he can do about it. I don't want to think about that at the moment.'

Once she'd locked the door behind him, Anna prepared for bed in front of the gas fire, switched it off and dashed upstairs, having placed a stone hot water bottle in her bed. She lay there, hugging herself, imagining a possible scenario where Charlie applied for compassionate leave and went home to end his engagement, thus allowing him to marry Anna.

Such a possibility was too comical for words. Such a possibility frightened the daylights out of her. Anyway, she knew it could never happen. He'd be a disaster as a husband, yet fear of scandalising her family and friends haunted her.

A postcard from Ruby arrived next day. Anna found it on the doormat on arriving home from work and sank down on the couch to read her mother's message, written on the back of a view of Tenby's North Beach, which their hotel overlooked.

Darling Anna, I'm so pleased the Carfax is one of the hotels not requisitioned for the Yanks. Frank has known the owner for years and we have a lovely room, with a sea view. I know some might wonder why we're honeymooning beside the beach, when we live in a seaside town, but being here's nothing like being at home. Hope all's well. See you on Saturday. Love, Mam xx

One more day at work before the weekend and her mother's return. Ruby and Frank would go straight to his house. Most of her mother's stuff was already there. Some of Anna's was too, but there were still items she needed to take with her. Her current dilemma had occupied her mind and now she resolved to sneak in a few favourite pieces, just in case Frank had any protests over how much his stepdaughter wanted to hoard in his home. Or, their home, as he insisted on her regarding it.

CHAPTER 25

The following morning, when Geoff came into her office, she greeted him with a big smile. 'Just the man I wanted to see.'

'What have I done?' He perched on the end of her desk. 'Or, should I say what haven't I done?'

She shook her head. 'It's nothing to do with work. It's just dawned on me that my mother and Frank are due home tomorrow afternoon and I'd rather like to move a few items into the house while they're not looking.'

'Fair enough. Barring emergencies, I can call round in the morning and help you. If I can't get away, I'll send someone.'

'Thank you. Is ten o'clock all right?'

'It is.' He was gazing at her. 'How are you? I must say, you look really well, Anna.'

'That's what Margaret said, Miss Napier too, though I can't see it.'

He shook his head. 'You never fail to amaze me. The way you stay so calm and collected – no wonder the old man sings your praises. And his former secretary was an absolute paragon.' Suddenly his expression darkened. 'God, Anna, I shouldn't ask, but have you made an appointment with your doctor yet?'

'I have. I shall work through my lunch hour next Wednesday and leave the office early.'

He nodded and removed himself from the desk. 'But you shouldn't skip meals.'

'One won't hurt.'

'When's Himself back, d'you know?'

'Monday morning.'

'Excellent. I want a word with our CO.'

Anna sucked in her breath. 'This isn't about me and Charlie … it's not about my situation, is it?'

Geoff turned to face her, his hand on the doorknob. 'Of course not! It's a personal matter. I'm off now to liaise with the town's mayor – the usual sort of stuff, you know.'

'Tea and a bun?'

'If I'm lucky. Now, if I don't see you later, I'll see you in the morning.'

After her treasures were safely delivered to her room at Frank's, Anna spent the rest of Saturday tidying the house she'd always lived in. She was conscious of a sense of change in the air, a feeling of not knowing quite what lay ahead. But this was wartime. She was also leaving her family home, so what else should she expect? So many tears and so much laughter throughout her journey from child to adult were imprinted in the atmosphere. She still missed her father. *What would Viktor have made of all this?*

Ruby arrived mid-afternoon, eager to know how her daughter was getting on and chatting about the places she and Frank had visited and how he took her to visit friends of his whom she already knew and liked.

To Anna's relief, her mother didn't push her regarding moving out, merely reminding her to let them know so they could arrange to transport her bedroom bits and pieces. Anna didn't mention how Geoff had helped her move most of it and she avoided Sunday dinner with the newlyweds by explaining about her afternoon invitation. Ruby hugged her daughter before returning to her new home in Gladstone Road, leaving behind a trail of *Chanel*.

On Sunday morning, Anna washed her hair as usual and ironed a periwinkle blue blouse and skirt she planned to wear with a misty green angora cardigan her grandmother had knitted. Luckily the day dawned fine, if cloudy and chilly. Anna tied a headscarf over her hair and set off in good time, arriving at the house a couple of minutes after the hour.

Miss Ring opened the door almost immediately. 'Anna, it's so good to see you after all this time. Do come in, my dear. Did you walk?'

'Oh, yes. I enjoy walking. And it's lovely to see you again, Miss Ring. I owe you so much.'

'Oh, fiddlesticks! And I think we can dispense with the formalities, so why don't you call me Emily? Now, let me take your things then we can join Maud in the drawing-room. I purposely lit the fire early in there.'

Anna took off her coat, her eye caught by a large, rather gloomy oil painting of distant hills. But an ornate mirror hanging nearby deserved a mention and she received an approving nod from Emily. She'd brought slippers to change into and that also proved a good decision, as did a pot of Nana's homemade plum chutney.

'What a considerate young woman you are,' her hostess declared. Anna decided it would be difficult, remembering to call her former tutor by her forename while in her house. But she appreciated being treated as an equal, rather than a former student.

Emily bustled ahead, pushing the drawing room door wider and calling, 'Our visitor has arrived, Maud. You can take your nose out of that newspaper now.'

Maud Napier closed the Sunday paper and rose, holding out her hand to their guest. 'You look very charming in your blue and green.'

'Thank you very much. Blue and green – seldom seen – according to my grandmother.' She looked around her. 'This is a lovely room. Those little wild flower water colours are exquisite.'

Emily, Anna thought, suddenly looked ten years younger. 'My sister's the artist. They are rather delightful, aren't they? Are you interested in art?'

'I don't know much about it, but I like to see what other people's tastes are.' She didn't say there was very little in the way of it at home, though her stepfather owned several oil paintings.

'Sit down, do.' Maud patted the space beside her on the chaise longue. 'Or do you prefer to be closer to the fire?'

'Here's fine, thanks.'

'I'll go through and make the tea now.' Emily beamed at Anna and Maud. 'It's delightful to have you both here. We can enjoy a good catch up.'

'May I help?' Anna asked.

'I'll call if I need you. How's that?' Emily closed the door behind her.

Anna tried to think of something intelligent to say. Anything at all. But Miss Napier, or rather Maud, beat her to it.

'Isn't this room beautiful? Of course, having that view helps, but Emily has superb taste. I'm afraid my house is rather a hotch-potch of styles, mostly nineteen twenties stuff and earlier as well.'

'My mother adores art deco. She can indulge her tastes now she has more money available.'

Maud shot her a shrewd look. 'Forgive me if I'm speaking out of turn, but are you all right with your home situation now? I take it you'll be moving in with your mother and stepfather soon.'

Anna shrugged. 'I can't say I'm over the moon about it, but I need to do what they want me to do. I expect we'll get on all right.'

To her surprise, Maud pulled a face. 'You don't sound too enthusiastic, but let's wait until Emily's back. We have a suggestion for you.'

After Emily gave a shout, Anna carried the tray carefully from the kitchen to the drawing room, her hostess following with a silver cake stand upon the top layer of which reposed a modest selection of sandwiches. A whole Victoria jam sponge dominated the bottom layer. Anna noticed the delicate sprinkle of icing sugar topping the cake and thought of her grandmother. Nana too would somehow keep producing little surprises to cheer up people. She'd be wondering why Anna hadn't visited lately. Anna pushed this thought away. All in good time …

Maud took pristine white table napkins from the sideboard, peered at the tray, frowned and left the room, reappearing with three silver dessert forks.

'There.' Emily placed the cake stand on the table. 'The tea needs longer to brew, but do help yourself to sandwiches, both of you. I've made cheese and there are some fish paste as well.' She made a wry face at Maud. 'I hope my cake isn't too awful! I so rarely bake these days.'

'It looks delicious.' Anna unfolded her napkin. 'I don't bake much either. My grandmother's a better cook than I am or my mother is, for that matter.'

She prayed she'd manage to drink her tea without mishap. Perhaps a sandwich would help. She nibbled then swallowed hard, aware of her hostess's gaze focused on her. 'This is all so lovely. Thank you very much.'

'It's a pleasure to see you here,' Maud said. 'But we have a confession to make. We do have an ulterior motive for inviting you.'

Anna accepted a cup and took a sip. Then another. Her spirits rose. Maybe she'd worked herself up into a turmoil because of worry? She needed to concentrate upon what the two women were saying.

'You know Emily and I have remained close friends for many years now, Anna?'

'I imagine you have lots in common?'

The two friends glanced at one another and Maud chuckled. 'Two old spinsters? Yes, I suppose we have.'

'Oh gosh, I didn't mean anything like that.' Anna thought quickly. 'I don't believe we women should all be expected to find husbands. Why should that be?'

'It's the expected thing to do, I suppose,' Maud said. 'In the view of most people, anyway. Emily and I had our sweethearts killed in action during the Great War. It's a tragedy that there are already plenty of war widows this time around too.'

'Yes, I know, and it's so, so sad. It must have happened to so many women, but that doesn't stop it from being painful. Yet look at how you've turned your lives around since.' She turned to her former tutor. 'Emily, I understand every place at the college is filled. And, Miss Napier – sorry, Maud – you should know Colonel Gresham says the Supply Reserve Depot would disintegrate into chaos without you in charge!'

Emily chuckled. Maud looked surprised. 'Does Richard really say that? Gosh, I'm tickled pink.'

'As well you should be, you goose!' Emily reached out her hand and stroked her friend's cheek. 'Now, will you ask her, or shall I?'

Anna looked from one to the other. Emily's tender gesture, accompanied by that loving glance, intrigued Anna and hinted at a deep affection. Or was she imagining things? What did they want to ask her? Did they suspect something? Did she look as though she was expecting? Her heart pumped a little faster and she sucked in air while reaching for her cup as though she hadn't a care in the world.

'Emily and I have found our close friendship developing into something much more significant, if I may use that word. We understand you may find this confession embarrassing or distasteful, but we've talked about our situation for so long that we now feel it's time to follow our hearts, no matter what others may think.'

Anna put down her cup. Until moments ago, she hadn't seen this coming, and why should they bother to tell her? Unless … perhaps there was a burning need to tell someone about their relationship and they considered her broad-minded enough to understand.

'Are you very shocked?' Emily patted her mouth with her napkin.

'Goodness, no! Why should I be? It would make me a

terrible hypocrite if I was.'

The two friends exchanged glances. 'I'm sorry, Anna. I don't understand,' Maud said.

'I'm trying to say, the way I've behaved over a certain officer has shocked my mother and caused ...' Anna gulped. The words wouldn't come.

Maud got up and stood behind Anna, placing one hand upon each of her shoulders. 'You don't need to say anything, my dear, but if you wish to talk, you can be certain what you say will go no further.'

'Thank you. I'd expect nothing less of either of you. Unfortunately, I have to confess to behaving irresponsibly. I think that sums it up.'

'I think being at war can prompt us to make quick judgements, right or wrong decisions are made quickly, and people often end up separated, though they mightn't wish to be. Dare I ask whether the man in question is married?'

'He's engaged and he's also out of the country now. I was made aware he had a fiancée, but I'm afraid I didn't let that stop me from accepting his – well, his advances.'

Maud sat down beside Anna again. 'I think I know who you're speaking about, don't I?'

Anna nodded. 'If you mean Charles Milburn, then yes, you do.'

Maud sighed. 'The dashing captain ... a heartbreaker, if ever I saw one. Even a woman of my age presents a challenge ... an opportunity to make a conquest, even if never carried through to fulfilment.'

Emily stopped cutting slices of sponge cake and waved her knife in the air. 'Anna, you couldn't have been expected to know this chap had a fiancée when he first made advances.'

Anna sighed. 'No, but after I heard of his engagement, I went on seeing him. I imagine I don't need to go into details, but I'm ashamed to say I'm no better than he is.'

If she'd been expecting protests about her stupidity, she was proved wrong. Maud was blinking hard and Anna could see tears glistening as she turned her head to gaze through the window. Unusually, the sitting room was upstairs, its bay window allowing a fantastic view of the pebble beach. Stormy grey today. Wind whipping the waves into white horses.

Emily bowed her head, as though withdrawing from the conversation, and it was Maud, the woman who'd guided Anna through her typing pool days and into Colonel Gresham's secretary's chair, who spoke first.

'I take it Captain Milburn broke things off before he left?'

Anna nodded. 'I didn't beg.' She hesitated. 'Yes, I did. I begged him to write and let me know how he was. He'd no intention of doing so. I shouldn't really be telling anyone about this, but I think you two will understand.'

Maud nodded. 'It's quite a thing to keep secret, isn't it? When you're scared people might suspect something, yet you long to pour your heart out?'

Anna waited for her to add that was how she imagined someone in that position must be feeling, but once again she was proved wrong.

'I was left in the same situation when I wasn't much older than you. Robert, my fiancé, was twenty one and I was nearly nineteen when he left for the Front. Neither of us had any idea I might be in the family way.'

Anna sucked in her breath.

'Looking back,' Maud said, 'I suppose we were caught up in the momentum of war, the partings, the emotions ...'

'It could have been me as well.' Emily said. 'Byron and I jumped the gun, as the saying goes, as soon as he knew he was off to France. In some ways, I wish I'd been left carrying his child, but that's easy to say, with hindsight.' She walked over to the settee and stood behind Maud and Anna, resting one hand lightly upon each one's shoulder. 'I know what my dearest friend went through, so if you're terrified as to whether you might be expecting a baby, we can both imagine something of how you feel.'

Anna didn't like to question Maud about her experience. But she didn't have long to wait.

'The matter was taken out of my hands, once my mother discovered my unfortunate secret. I was packed off to a widowed aunt living on the outskirts of London. She was well off and her companion had left without giving notice, so I became the replacement. It was the perfect cover for a girl in my position. My mother told everyone I was living with my aunt as her companion, which was true. Aunt Lucinda gave me a gold wedding ring, which had apparently belonged to my grandmother, so I wore that. When the time came, my aunt paid for her private physician to deliver my baby. Someone took my daughter away within hours of the birth and I never saw her again.'

'I'm so sorry.' Anna blinked away tears. 'I didn't mean to bring back unhappy memories for you both.'

'That's what friends are for. To share experiences too painful, too beautiful, too precious to be shared with any old person!' Maud chuckled. 'It's about time you brought out the sherry, isn't it, Em?'

'Shouldn't we explain our idea first? Just let me hand round the cake.'

'Ah, thank you.' Maud eyed her slice appreciatively. 'My goodness, we got carried away by our reminiscences. But now I have a suggestion for you, Anna. I realise you may not wish to make a rapid decision, but I'm wondering whether you'd like to move into my house after I move in here with Emily?' She bit into her cake.

Anna couldn't believe what she was hearing and for moments, struggled to reply. Her future teetered, depending on what the doctor said. If her worst fears were confirmed, might she be sent away to one of those homes for unmarried mothers?

'Of course, you may have other plans if what you suspect is true,' Emily said. 'But I know I speak for Maud too, when I say we'd like to help and support you, whatever you decide.'

'Of course.' Maud nodded. 'I'm not keen to let my property to strangers, so you'd be doing me a great favour. And let's say the rent would be a peppercorn one.'

Anna needed to swallow hard, but as she opened her mouth to speak, a familiar, ear-splitting wail began its eerie onslaught.

'Air raid warning! Come on.' Emily grabbed a small basket from the sideboard and began bundling leftover food into it. 'Pick up all our coats, Maud! Anna, bring your gas mask and follow me. With any luck it'll be a false alarm, but if the enemy's heading for Cardiff, we daren't take chances.'

Anna, drowsy after two glasses of sherry, had drifted easily into slumber. Now she woke to the sound of voices murmuring. Opening her eyes, she pushed away the blanket covering her and dragged herself to a sitting position on the bench.

'Hello.' Emily beamed. 'We just heard the All Clear and it's barely eight o'clock, so Maud says she'll drive you home. We can all get some sleep in our own beds before the working day begins.' She used her torch to see her way over to the light switch. The overhead bulb gave off a dim but welcome glow.

Anna nodded. 'Thank you.' She still felt taken aback by Maud's kind offer. The thought of having her own accommodation had appealed to her, once Ruby decided to marry Frank. But financial considerations, as her mother kept reminding her, obliged Anna to move in with the couple. She'd wanted to ask questions before the air raid warning intervened. She appreciated Emily's house was well-equipped for sheltering, but she desperately wanted to go home to bed now and disguised a yawn while she gathered her wits.

'You two get going as soon as you're ready,' Emily said. 'I shall go straight upstairs once I've locked up again.'

She opened the cellar door and stood back so the other two could climb the short flight of steps. 'Maud, you take the torch and I'll follow you and see you both out. We all have work to go to in the morning, but I've enjoyed our get together and I'm sure we'll all meet again soon.'

CHAPTER 26

Supply Branch HQ, Bari, Italy. 10 January 1944

Charles Milburn was reading through the letter he'd just finished writing to his wife.

Darling Eleanor,

I think about you every day and imagine you're with me when I'm in bed, trying to go to sleep. But no amount of dreaming can bring you to me. I know I told you it might be possible for you to visit but the situation out here is too unstable at the moment and we must possess ourselves in patience.

After our wedding, you teased me about my former girlfriends and I reminded you of the many beaux lining up for you when I was fortunate enough to meet you at that tedious Hunt Ball. Somehow, I beat off the opposition. There are times when I can't help wondering if my beautiful bride is only a dream, but keeping your letters beneath my pillow and your photograph on my dressing table, remind me our marriage is very real. Once we're together again, I can hold you in my arms and tell you just how much I love you.

You sound busy, with all that knitting and helping your mother with those bun fights. As for your voluntary work with the wounded officers in the manor house, I try not to be jealous – knowing the suffering they've endured, that would be stupid and selfish. But in the past, I'm afraid that's how I've often behaved. I hope that is all behind me now and pray this war won't go on too long, so that we may be reunited.

You asked how I was getting on with my secretary. Well, Hilda is a very pleasant lady and knows her stuff, so I count myself fortunate. She has a good knowledge of Italian too. My former aide, Geoffrey Chandler, is due out here soon so that'll take a lot of the pressure off.

Well, darling Eleanor, I'll call a halt now so this letter can go out tomorrow with the rest of the mail. I'm pleased to hear things are quiet where you are and long may that continue. Please send *your parents best regards from their son-in-law.*

All my love,
Charlie xx

He smiled to himself as he sealed the flimsy blue sheet inside the envelope. He suspected Eleanor's mother still doubted he'd make a good husband, but if he came out of this shindig in one piece, Eleanor's pa would help him find suitable employment, unless of course he decided to remain in the Army.

He glanced at the clock on his bedside cabinet. Nine forty-five and all seemed well. He reached for his overcoat and shrugged it on over his uniform. He checked he had his wallet in his inside breast pocket, picked up his cigarette case and taking out a cigarette, flicked his gold lighter into life.

He ran down the wide staircase, called a greeting to the soldier on duty at the entrance and went out into a starry night. Crossing the square by the light of the moon, he slipped down an alley, frowning at shadows, picking his way along the narrow pavement. On reaching his destination, he knocked three times, paused then rapped twice more.

The door opened a little. 'It's only me,' Charles murmured.

The door revealed a little subdued light. He smiled at the slim young woman, her dark silky hair framing her oval face. 'Are you going to let me in, Gina?'

'Maybe.' She beckoned to him and he stepped inside. He smelt garlic and wax polish. A gas mantle sputtered, giving off a faint glow. Gina bolted the door and turned to him. 'You back here, then?'

'Didn't I say I would be?' He tipped her chin upwards and bent to kiss her. She wound her arms around his neck and whispered in his ear.

Charles chuckled. 'Naughty girl. I can't wait! Are you alone? Apart from the baby, of course.'

'*Si. La bambino sta dormendo.*'

'He's asleep? Good show.'

She turned, walked to the staircase at the end of the corridor and ran lightly up it while he followed. On the next floor, she opened the first door and beckoned. Charles unfastened his overcoat and shucked off both officer's cap and greatcoat. Gina sat on the edge of the bed, rolled down her stockings and stepped out of them. Standing up again, she pulled her thick woollen jumper over her head. Charlie's breath snagged at sight of the delicate lace camisole outlining her firm, young breasts. Then she stepped out of her slacks, revealing matching pale grey French knickers. As she jumped beneath the bed covers, she called, '*Sbrigati*, Charlie!'

She'd no need to tell him to hurry. The room was chilly and Gina's lush, warm body awaited his attentions. She'd been recommended to him by his commanding officer and at that moment, no other woman existed for the British Army Captain.

Anna awoke in her familiar room, and thought at once of her mother, who would be waking up in her new home, alongside her new husband. For all Anna's protestations about marriage not being the be all and end all of a woman's existence, what wouldn't she give to be someone's wife now she found herself in this thankless position? Except, in that case, she'd doubtless have been praying for a positive verdict from her doctor. Instead, Anna put her hands together in prayer, fervently hoping her fears would be banished once the doctor confirmed her own diagnosis as incorrect.

She began her morning ritual. Stepping into her navy-blue skirt and pulling it over her hips, she couldn't help noticing a little difficulty in fastening the button at her waist. Telling herself to stop worrying and concentrate on her job, she was able to drink a cup of tea and eat two slices of dry toast with a boiled egg. Anna was checking all was safe in the kitchen before leaving for work, when she heard a knock on the front door.

Might this be her mother? And if so, what could be wrong? She hurried to find out, but the silhouette outlined through the opaque glass panes was far too tall to be Ruby's.

'Aha, I hoped I'd catch you!'

'What's wrong, Geoff?'

'Would you like a lift?'

She peered round him at the damp, dismal morning. 'I'd love a lift. Are you going to tell me something I don't want to hear?'

He stepped inside, closing the door as she headed back to the sitting room. 'I wanted to tell you in private. We're off soon, Anna. I can't find the words to say how sorry I am about everything.'

She said nothing as he helped her on with her raincoat. Even as she reached for her handbag, she didn't meet his gaze. 'I'll collect my umbrella on the way out. Don't let me walk past it.'

He grabbed her spare hand. 'Look at me! You know I wish I didn't have to leave you. Keep in touch. Promise me you'll keep in touch. And when … if you say the word, I swear I shall tackle Charles.'

'I can't talk now. I can't concentrate on anything but hanging on to my job. I'll miss you, Geoff, I hope you realise that. I've been such an idiot!'

'God, Anna, if only things had been different.'

She shooed him down the front passageway, picked up her umbrella and poked his rear playfully. 'Let's go. If any of the neighbours notice me leaving with you without having seen you arrive, then that's just too bad.'

'Come in,' the CO called. 'Well, everything's in apple pie order, and while I think of it, Anna, you made an excellent job of that task I landed you with last week.' He beamed up at her as she approached his desk. 'My word, I was dreading having to get used to a new secretary when poor Miss Morgan became ill. Downright selfish of me, of course, but I needn't have worried.'

'Thank you, sir. Lieutenant Chandler is here when you're ready.'

'Give me two minutes, please. And perhaps you could organise a brew for the pair of us?'

'Of course.'

Anna closed the adjoining door to her office. Geoff stood in front of the window, gazing at who knew what?

'Two minutes, he says. I'm off to fetch you both some tea.'

He turned to her. 'Do you ever get fed up with tasks like that?'

'I don't have to make it.'

'I know, but why don't I scoot down to the canteen and chat up the tea lady?'

'You'd make her day, but I doubt Colonel Gresham would appreciate it. Thanks for thinking of it though. Not all men are as enlightened.'

'Maybe one day you'll be a company chairman or chairwoman – something like that, anyway. Scaring the life out of some spotty little office boy who has a pash on you.'

'I'm going.' Anna pointed at the clock on the wall. 'Knock on his door exactly one and a half minutes from now.' She opened the outer door. 'See you later. And don't you dare leave without saying goodbye.'

She didn't wait for an answer.

Left alone, Geoff looked around Anna's domain. She'd charmed her boss, there was no doubt about it, but although some of his fellow officers had dubbed her "the blonde bombshell," as Charles did originally, he doubted whether many of them possessed Miss Christensen's intelligence. And she was discreet. Even if facing interrogation by some snarling Gestapo officer, he'd bet his gold watch on Anna turning the tables.

He hated having to leave the country before knowing how she fared at her doctor's. He may have got his wish now, ordered to take on a far more challenging role, but how much better if he could be around when Anna found out the worst. At least she had some extra support from a surprising source. In the car, she'd told him how sympathetic her old tutor and her supervisor had been when she confided in them.

Her mother would get a shock if her daughter's fears were realised. And he knew someone else who'd receive an even bigger shock, should he have to break the unwelcome news to Charles.

But it still might be some kind of blip. And Anna just might, one day, change her attitude to the man she called her best friend.

Time was up. Geoff adjusted his tie, picked up his cap and tapped on the CO's door.

CHAPTER 27

Bari, Italy

Geoff couldn't help smiling when the transport dropped him at his destination. *Hotel Romeo*? An imposing building which now accommodated an older English version of Shakespeare's iconic character. He made himself known at the desk then waited; standing on an expanse of black and white tiled flooring, gazing at the paintings adorning the walls and temporarily forgetting everything bar the magnificence of the art. The Holy Mother and Child. Mist-swathed mountains. Swarthy fishermen hoisting paniers of glistening sardines. He snapped to attention at the sound of heels tapping as someone walked towards him.

Hilda Barnes introduced herself without delay. 'You must be Lieutenant Chandler.'

She held out a well-manicured hand for him to shake. Her clasp was firm, that of a woman confident she was doing a good job. Fleetingly he thought of Anna. Her work persona exuded confidence. Yet, Anna with her guard down … he dragged himself back to the present.

'That's correct,' he said, saluting. 'I'm pleased to meet you, Mrs Barnes. I imagine Captain Milburn's expecting me?'

She inclined her head. 'I'm afraid he's taking a telephone call at the moment, Lieutenant, so he's sent me instead. If you'd like to accompany me, I'm sure he'll be free before long. But we must get your bags left with the porter so they can be delivered to your quarters. You're on the top floor, at the rear of the building.'

Geoff kept his attaché case with him but duly dropped off his kitbag and greatcoat at the porter's desk. He managed to greet the man with a cheerful *Buona Sera* though he wasn't sure if that was appropriate as it was only three o'clock in the afternoon. The porter beamed at him anyway, addressed him as sir and wrote down the room number Mrs Barnes supplied.

Geoff, making small talk while walking beside her up the stairs, noted with no small sense of relief that Charles's secretary was probably in her mid-forties. She was in uniform and wore her coppery hair in a tight bun. Behind her schoolmarm spectacles, however, a pair of brown eyes snapped with amusement as he asked whether she was enjoying her posting.

'That's an intriguing question. As postings go, it could be very much worse, but sometimes I feel being here is rather like watching a pot of water and wondering when it will boil over.'

Geoff glanced sideways. Her expression remained impassive. 'You're anticipating another bomb strike? The one you endured on December third must have been horrifying.'

'It was, and as you know, we can never be certain when the enemy will attack. However, the current situation might continue as it is. How were things in Wales?'

'Generally quiet in our neck of the woods. Isolated hits when a German pilot sashayed off course and mistook us for bigger prey. Fortunately, that didn't often happen, but the capital city has suffered. And further along the coast, poor old Swansea has taken an awful beating.'

His mind's eye flashed to black and white newsreel images of smoke and rubble and grim crump holes where houses once stood. Women wandering around, clutching clothing bundles and wailing children. Families split asunder. Families wiped out. Yet despite the mayhem, here and there a Victory sign and a cheery grin, making him marvel at the Welsh spirit.

They'd reached the first floor. 'Our offices are to the right,' Hilda said. 'I'll take you round and introduce you to everyone after you've caught up with Captain Milburn. Meanwhile, I'll rustle up the inevitable tea.'

'And very welcome too. Thank you.'

'Come and wait in my office. Captain Milburn thinks very highly of you, Lieutenant.'

'Kind of him to say so. Yes, we worked well together in Wales.' Geoff wondered whether Charles had changed his ways now he held a more responsible position. Could a leopard ever change its spots? Especially a big cat possessing what appeared to have been an insatiable appetite for beautiful women.

Hilda picked up a telephone and ordered tea. So, no running to the canteen in this well-organised citadel. He must tell Anna that.

Then the connecting door opened and Charles breezed in. 'Geoffrey! I'm delighted to see your ugly mug again, old boy!' He clasped Geoff's right hand in both his own, eyes twinkling, face creased in a genuinely welcoming smile.

Geoff could do nothing else but greet him in similar fashion. 'It's good to be here.'

'Liar! Now, come on through and we can catch up.' He looked at his secretary. 'And is there honey still for tea?'

She licked her lips. Geoff couldn't believe the woman actually licked her lips.

'You read the poem!'

'Right through to the final line.'

She cleared her throat. 'Tea is on its way.'

Charles grinned at Geoffrey. 'Our Mrs Barnes is invaluable to an ignoramus like me.'

He timed the comment so his secretary heard it on her way out and Geoff saw her lips twitch. No, Charles certainly hadn't lost his touch, but it was a surprise to find him taking an interest in the great English poets.

'I'll introduce you to the CO a little later. He's a good sort but he's in a meeting with a couple of the local bigwigs at the moment. Now, sit yourself down Geoffrey, and tell me how things have been back in Wales.'

Geoff hesitated. Anna came straight to mind, but he'd no idea how her doctor's appointment had gone and though he disapproved of Charlie's behaviour, it seemed pointless to raise what might be an unnecessary alarm. Time enough for that if Anna relayed bad news. He put her from his mind. Tea arrived, together with slices of Sicilian lemon cake, making Geoff raise his eyebrows. The office canteen seemed a world away.

Charlie shot him an amused glance. 'I know, old chap – a totally different way of life. But we're right in the thick of things here. The port is extremely busy and a vast quantity of petroleum spirit passes through. I'm sure I don't need to explain the devastation of the dockyard bombing in December. We're still coming to terms with the consequences and I know you won't make the mistake of thinking Bari is as cushy a number as Barry was.'

Later, dinner provided the opportunity to meet other personnel based in the spacious building. Geoff enjoyed meeting Richard Curtis again and the pair were discussing the dubious joys of living in a tented camp compared to *Hotel Romeo*, when he noticed Charles leave his seat and make a quiet exit. Contrary to what Geoff expected, the captain didn't return, so obviously wasn't responding to a call of nature.

Richard must have noticed his companion's interest, because he leaned closer and murmured. 'Doubtful he'll be back before we shoot off to our beds.'

Geoff's antennae were twitching and he had a rough idea of what might be coming next. 'Um, well, Captain Milburn always did prefer to vary his routines.'

Even as he spoke, he realised the fresh-faced young man seated opposite was grinning like the proverbial Cheshire Cat.

'The word is, he's found himself a lady friend.' Richard paused as a steward glided forward and collected their glasses, offering a refill.

Richard raised his eyebrows at Geoff. 'One for the road?'

'I don't see why not. Then I must get some shut-eye.' Geoff needed time to absorb this news but didn't want to seem rude.

Richard looked up at the steward. '*Grazi,* Luigi.' He followed this with something that baffled Geoff.

He'd need to ask Hilda whether she had an Italian phrase book he could borrow. 'Let me get these,' he said.

'Another time. I've asked for them to be put on my bar account.'

'Thanks. I'll set up an account tomorrow.' Geoff leaned forward, determined to change the subject away from rumours about Charles. 'I have to tell you, Richard, that I danced with your young lady on New Year's Eve and she told me how much she's missing you.'

The young officer sat up straight. 'Did she indeed? Well, I feel the same way about her. In fact, if I ever get back to Blighty, I've a mind to pop the question.'

Geoff felt relieved their conversation had changed direction. As the latest arrival in Bari, he would try to avoid exchanges concerning his immediate superior. This young blood should know better.

'Mary Whitchurch is a charming young lady, Richard. She had no shortage of dance partners on New Year's Eve, but I saw her and three of her chums into her car well before the witching hour. She's obviously saving herself for you, old chap.'

Richard looked thoughtful.

Geoff made up his mind. 'Far be it from me to advise you, but if you really feel like that – and I'm convinced Mary's of the same mind – why not propose by letter? Or better still, book a telephone call and pop the question.'

Richard nodded. 'You're right. And I'm glad you gave me a nudge. It would be good to have some certainty in my life and I don't think Mary, once she accepted a chap, would mess him around.' He glanced up. 'Here come our whiskies.'

'Then let's drink to your success when you request the lady's hand in marriage.'

Anna was almost home before she realised it. This gave her the strangest of feelings. How could a person walk almost a mile without realising where she was? After an initial numbness, she'd plunged into a black hole of despair on leaving the doctor's surgery. *What if?* and w*hy did this have to happen to me?* – these weren't easy questions to answer. And worst of all, both Charles and Geoff were hundreds and hundreds of miles away, in an Italian warzone. She walked the last few yards towards her house, wishing things could return to how they were before her involvement with Charles.

She hadn't faced shock or disapproval. Her doctor had advised her to contact the baby's father straightaway as it was only fair for the fellow to know while there remained enough time to sort things out. He obviously assumed a speedy marriage would be the right course for Anna, whose family history he knew as well as she did, but she felt so numb, she couldn't face explanations. She'd been relieved at having to return to the office and concentrate on her work.

Oddly, now, walking home, it was Geoff she felt most need of, though if Charles knew of her predicament, wouldn't he see reason? He'd taken her by surprise on that last visit, neglected to take precautions and vanished from her life – it was surely up to him to do the right thing?

Should she write to him next day? She could bring home some airmail stationery, compose her letter and post it next morning. Mail sent to serving military personnel didn't need postage stamps. Anna reached inside her handbag and took out her door key as she reached the front gate. Except, of course, the iron gate itself was long gone, requisitioned for the war effort.

As she let herself in. As she closed the door behind her. As she drew the same faded velvet curtain she remembered always being there, she felt she wasn't alone. Anna held her breath. Listening. A dull thump echoed from above. She heard the sound of a drawer closing. And with the next breath she took, she knew who'd entered ahead of her. Her mother's perfume whispered her presence and Anna steadied herself, placing one hand against the wall, fighting a wave of dizziness.

'Anna? It's only me.' Ruby's voice percolated down the stairwell. 'I'm sorting through some final bits and pieces, love. I'll be down soon if you want to make us a pot of tea. I thought it was time we fixed your moving in date.'

Anna's fist went straight to her mouth, stifling a sob. Pushing back a howl of despair. *Why now, Mam? Why, when I'm still reeling after discovering my worst nightmare is coming true? How can I act as though I haven't a care in the world, when all I want is to creep under my eiderdown and wake up to find everything's fine?*

'Okay,' she managed to croak before rushing to the lavatory, dry heaving and praying the spasm would pass before she faced her mother. She wasn't ready for confrontation. Not yet. And she knew now which of the two men she would write to.

Geoff found himself kept busy. The wheels of war continued grinding and he knew he mustn't waste time regretting having not asked Anna to marry him, when there was so much else to think about. His feelings went far beyond caring whether she was pregnant or not.

Uncertainty around that matter changed the evening he left his room to join his colleagues for dinner and picked up an airmail letter at the reception desk. He glanced at the handwriting and realising who'd sent it, tucked it inside his jacket pocket, deciding to open it when he returned to his room. If Charles noticed him reading a flimsy blue sheet of notepaper, he'd be certain to tease him about his love life – or his lack of one, as Geoff perceived it. He still felt anger towards his superior for his past reckless behaviour, but if Anna's doctor had confirmed her misgivings were wrong, she must try to forget what went before. And Charles of course would forever remain in a state of blissful ignorance. Geoff found a quiet corner and slit open the envelope.

Wynd Street,
Barry
21 January 1944

My dear Geoff,
I hope you're keeping well. Thank you for the picture postcard which arrived safe and sound. Bari looks interesting, though I imagine it's very different in wartime.

You asked me to let you know how I got on with my doctor's appointment. I think I've always known my fears would be confirmed, but it was still a shock to be told. My doctor seemed convinced the father would do the right thing and marry me. I've no idea how he got that impression. Maybe he was just trying to be kind.

So far, apart from you of course, I've confided in Emily Ring and Maud Napier. You've heard me mention Emily before, and both she and Maud have been very kind and I know I can trust them. In fact, they have a secret of their own which I won't discuss in detail, and again I know you won't say anything. Emily and Maud both agree society isn't ready yet to accept relationships such as theirs.

Maud has invited me to live in her house. My mother and Frank think I should move in with them by the end of the month, however, I've decided that living in Maud's house would suit me better. She says I'll be doing her a favour because she can stop worrying about it while she's staying with Emily. If things don't work out as they hope and Maud returns to live in her own home, she says I can remain there as long as I need. Isn't that kind? My brain whirls with questions more than answers, but most of all, I mustn't let my mother, or anyone else, bully me into going into a home for unmarried mothers. I know they're the salvation of many a girl, but now he or she is on *the way, I'm determined to keep my baby.*

I'll be visiting Maud this weekend as she wants me to see her house before deciding, though I doubt I'll find anything to complain about. She tells me a coal-fired boiler has recently been installed, so it's a warmer house than this one, though I shall feel a wrench when I leave here, as you know.

Please forgive me for asking how you feel about tackling Charles on my behalf. Might he actually be pleased to learn he has fathered a child? I understand he's still engaged, but strange things happen during wartime and common sense tells me he's a man with a habit of changing his affections. Of course, I don't want to make trouble, but I agree with my doctor when he says the baby's father should be told, so decisions can be made.

Deep down, I know it's unrealistic even to contemplate Charlie might marry me. It might seem like the end of all my worries, but how can I expect him to give up the woman he obviously loves and marry me to please convention? Especially as I realise what I felt for him owed nothing to do with love.

Here, Geoff groaned in frustration. She was admitting she didn't love Charles! She must realise becoming his wife would be far from a bed of roses? Yet … he read on.

I hope to keep my secret for as long as possible. I'll decide how to deal with my mother and Frank after I've had a good think and after, perhaps, I've heard from you or from Charles. I don't know how much longer I can continue to work, but will trust in Maud's judgement. I'm sorry to land this on you, Geoff, but you've been such a good friend to me all along, though I'm well aware Charles (and yours truly) haven't always given you the consideration you deserve.

Oh dear, reading this through, I realise how self-centred it is. I'm sorry to bother you with my problems, and I suspect Charlie will receive my news with nothing but irritation. Yet, he must be told.

Sending warm wishes and hoping you all keep safe and well out there.

Love,
Anna xx

PS: I really do have a nerve, asking you like this. I hope, and pray, one day I can make it up to you.

After dinner, most of the officers drifted through to the bar as usual, some opting for a game of cards or chess, others preferring conversation, lubricated by liquor. Charles was talking to Richard Curtis, but Geoff opted not to join them. As the weather was cold, though not as frigid as a British January, he went upstairs, took out his letter and read it through twice before putting on his outer garments and returning downstairs, ready for a short walk. He wasn't looking for company. He wanted to think Anna's situation through, so he could approach Charles armed with all the facts. That might have to wait until the morning.

But as he walked, keeping to the main area, Geoff noticed a man ahead of him, hurrying along on the other side of the road. Tall. Slim build. Walking as if the world owed him a living – it didn't take long to recognise Charles. But instinct made Geoff hold his tongue and he slowed his pace before crossing the road in time to see the captain turn down what looked like an alley leading off the main concourse.

Intrigued, Geoff followed Charles's example, still keeping a safe distance behind. Charles upped his pace, but stopped beside a door, and knocked on it. Geoff hesitated, flattening himself against the wall, his lips twitching as he imagined himself as actor George Sanders in his latest spy film.

Before long, hearing the murmur of voices, Geoff moved away from the wall and saw Charles enter the house without a backward glance. Whoever opened the door to him was a woman, that was for sure. The sound of her tantalising laugh rippled through the air before the door shut out the night.

CHAPTER 28

Charles Milburn bounded up the front steps and arrived, slightly breathless, in the foyer of the *Hotel Romeo*. To his surprise, as he pulled off his cap, Geoff rose from an armchair close to the bar entrance, and beckoned.

'Geoffrey! Fancy a nightcap, old chap?'

'Drinks are on me, Charlie. We need to talk.'

Charles frowned. 'Is that so? Can't it wait until morning? It's been a long day.'

'I think this is something you need to hear. It's a personal matter and nothing to do with work.'

'More and more mysterious! Well, if you insist.'

Geoff approached the desk. 'May I order two large Scotches, and could you have them sent to the dining room, please? We need privacy.'

The duty man nodded. 'Drinks to be charged to your account, sir?'

Geoff nodded. 'Please.' He turned to Charles. 'Let's go.'

Ignoring small groups of chattering personnel, Geoff

led the way across the checkerboard tiled floor and opened the dining room door, allowing Charles to enter ahead of him. Across the room, a couple of employees were placing gleaming cutlery into wicker holders, but the women, chatting in their own language, ignored the two officers.

Charles pulled out a couple of chairs at a table near the door. 'This suit you?'

'Very well. I doubt those two ladies have sufficient English to understand what we say.' He waited for the other man to sit down.

Charles stretched his long legs in front of him. 'What's all this about, old boy? It's not like you to be so mysterious.'

'This news isn't for common knowledge, Charlie. As you will hear.'

The moment he mentioned Anna, Geoff knew the captain had guessed why he had buttonholed him. His face revealed his feelings.

'You took advantage of her,' Geoff said. 'You neglected to protect her.'

'Heat of the moment and all that and with so much on my mind – man to man, seeing her there, naked and sumptuous in the firelight, even you would have done what I did!'

'I'll ignore that. Anna's doctor has confirmed she's expecting a baby. She hasn't told her mother yet, but she's grown closer to her former tutor at the business college, also, would you believe the redoubtable Miss Napier? Both of them are aware of her predicament and Anna may well move into Maud Napier's house as Maud is, um, planning to stay with a friend. Before the doctor confirmed Anna's condition, she confided her concerns to both these ladies.'

'Jesus Christ.'

'Maybe him as well. Who knows?'

But Charles didn't laugh. He stared at his friend. 'And why are you telling me this?'

'Your drinks, gentlemen ...'

Swiftly Geoff signed the chit and the barman glided away.

Geoff picked up his glass, cradling it in both hands. 'You ask me why? Because Anna assures me you're the father. Decisions need to be made. The girl's worried, Charlie. Fretting about gossip, anxious about her mother's reaction and scared of losing her job. Please don't tell me you're denying what you know to be true.'

'I don't deny sleeping with her on two or three occasions.' Charles shook his head slowly. 'But the girl's a minx, Geoffrey. I wouldn't mind betting I wasn't the only one enjoying her favours.'

Geoff narrowed his eyes. 'Again, I'll pretend you didn't say that. It was obvious how besotted she was, so please don't deny responsibility.'

'And what about you?' Charles gulped his whisky. 'You were hanging around her as well. Remember what I said when my posting came through? How I'd be coming out here, leaving the coast clear for you to make a move?'

Geoff didn't rise to the bait. 'You know very well Anna isn't that kind of girl. If only you'd abided by your own rule. After all you'd said about not getting involved with girls who were …'

'I believe virgins is the word you're seeking, old chap.'

Geoff ignored him. 'You know I took her out, called to see her on a friendly

basis, but as for anything more – bloody hell, Charlie, what kind of a man do you think I am? More to the point, what kind of a man are you? Surely you have to rethink your plans now?'

Charles sat back in his chair and looked his friend in the eye. 'Before you marry me off, I too have news. My status is no longer that of a bachelor because Eleanor and I tied the knot the day before I sailed from Liverpool.'

Geoff stared back at him. 'Are you serious?'

Charles grunted. 'Never more serious in my life. I'd been leading her a dance, as you're well aware, but suddenly, knowing I was being sent out here, I decided it was time to do the right thing. Thanks to my old man and Eleanor's father, we got the church booked and the marriage licence granted. I'm sorry you weren't invited, old chap. But it being a wartime wedding, we kept everything low-key and it seemed rather pointless to go around spreading the news with so little time left before we made our vows.'

'Yet, before you left Wales, you managed to find time to call on Anna and leave her a gift she couldn't return. You're despicable.'

Charles looked down at his glass of Scotch. 'You're understandably bitter, and I realise – the lord only knows how much I realise – you've every right to be.' He sipped his drink and met Geoffrey's gaze again. 'I'm sorry I sounded off about her. Of course, she must be devastated, poor girl, and obviously I'll help financially.'

'And your wife? Will Mrs Milburn be made aware of the situation?'

Charles shook his head. 'I see no reason for that. What happened between Anna and me was over while I was still single.'

'What, like a farewell to your bachelor days, d'you mean? You never did do things by halves, did you?'

'Those last few days in Wales were extremely chaotic. And Anna, as I recollect, was as eager as I was to say goodbye in the most personal way possible. It wasn't as though I forced her into doing something that would make her unhappy.' Realising what he'd said, he made a helpless gesture. 'Look, I can't just leave here and sail back to Blighty, can I? I can't do anything to help the situation except offer financial help. In any case, even if I was still single, do you really think I'd contact her and ask her to make wedding preparations? At least that's one disaster that's not going to happen. Surely you must realise that?'

Geoffrey shook his head. 'Well, whatever else happens, it's obvious that becoming your wife isn't on the cards for her. Some might say "lucky escape!"' He drained his glass.

Charles rose. 'Same again?'

'That sounds like an excellent idea.'

He returned moments later. 'You see me as an out and out reprobate, don't you?'

Geoff shrugged. 'You know how I feel about Anna – how I hoped things might pan out between the two of us.'

'I also remember saying how I thought she'd been attracted to me only because I was older, maybe more of a challenge, also because I didn't automatically make a move in her direction.'

'You still behaved recklessly. You took her away that weekend. You encouraged her to lie to her mother.'

'If only I'd let things rest there. That little outing was, shall we say, a planned seduction.' He looked up. 'Drinks are coming.'

'You really are a heartless bastard. And now the poor girl is left to deal with your mess. There's no other way of putting it, is there?'

'I suppose not.' Charles raised his glass to his friend. 'I'm not as unfeeling as you might think, Geoffrey. And, as I'm not in a position to do the right thing by the lady, how about you step in? It really does make sense, you know. How many times have I told you what excellent husband material you are?'

Geoffrey lay awake for what seemed most of the starless Italian night. He'd been shocked by Charlie's suggestion – a flash of anger inflaming him at first. But now, thinking of it logically, recalling Charlie saying he and Anna made the perfect couple, he realised what he most wanted in the world. It was to take care of her. Shield her from wagging tongues and the inevitable sneers about getting into trouble or deserving all she got because she'd slept with a soldier. A soldier who, being a commissioned officer and on the verge of marriage, should have known better.

But long-term, would that worry him? Bringing up another man's child? And Charlie's at that. How would Anna react? She could well be appalled at the idea. Anyway, what was to stop her wearing a wedding ring and telling anyone curious enough to enquire, that she and her new husband had married as soon as he received his Italy posting, not wanting to upset family and friends who would have expected at least a modest celebration? Sadly, there were already too many young women made widows by war. A husband who never existed in the first place, could easily be reported as killed in action and "mourned" by his devastated young bride.

Geoff turned on his other side and thumped his pillow. Anna's description of the support offered by her two friends was heart-warming and she seemed much happier with the idea of moving into Maud's house than with living with Ruby and Frank. Even if he and Anna were to wed, they would be unable to set up home together in the foreseeable future. At least, from what he'd learnt, she would have a comfortable place to live while awaiting the birth of her baby.

Tomorrow, he'd respond to her letter. Break the news about Charles and let the dust settle. Give her a chance to become used to the idea that the father of her baby was unlikely to figure in the lives of his child or herself, except for financial assistance. After a suitable interval, he'd write again.

'You don't look too grand, if I may say so.'

Anna placed her tray on the table opposite her friend and sat down. 'Well, thanks for nothing, Biddy.'

Her friend pulled a face. 'Aw, Anna, you know I speak my mind. You look tired is all I meant. Burning the midnight oil with another beau, is it?' She inspected the contents of her dinner plate with an air of resignation.

'Hardly! I've spent hours packing my stuff and tidying up our house ready for my moving day. No time for boyfriends – not that I'm interested.'

Biddy was chewing, though not with enjoyment. 'Any news from Geoff?'

'He's not my boyfriend.'

'Well, you know my views on that.'

'The last thing I need at the moment is a man telling me what I should or shouldn't do.'

Biddy put down her cutlery and leaned forward. 'Look, Anna, I'm not stupid. Something's bothering you.

Is it that you don't want to live with the newly-weds? You're thinking your stepfather might be too strict? Am I right?'

Anna nodded. 'In a way. I don't want to upset my mother but I have another option. I'll tell you about is as soon as I can, but I can't imagine Frank caring one way or the other.'

'You don't know that. From what you've said, it sounds like he's a kind man. Anyway, once the war's over, you might be able to move into your own place. Or marry Lieutenant Chandler when he returns victorious!'

'Will you stop going on about Geoff and marriage? You're as bad as my mother – if not worse.' Anna jabbed her fork into a potato.

Biddy sighed. 'I can imagine you miss kicking up your heels now and then. But we're so lucky compared to many other folks.'

Anna drank a mouthful of water. 'If you say so.'

Her friend put down her cutlery and leaned forward again. 'Don't tell me it's the poor man's David Niven you're pining for!'

Anna stared back at her. She bit her lip and shook her head. 'I had a letter from Geoff this morning. He told me Charles got married before embarking for Italy. It came as a shock, but whether or not I miss him makes no difference now.'

Biddy's eyes widened. 'You weren't hoping to marry him, surely? Not with his reputation – and after all you've said about not wanting to be some man's slave?'

Anna looked around her and reached across to clutch Biddy's hand. 'I'm in a difficult position. Please don't say a word to anybody because I'm telling only a very few people who I totally trust to keep my secret.'

Biddy's eyes were solemn. 'Oh, dear God Almighty,' she whispered. 'Are you saying what I think you're saying?'

'There's no doubt about it, I'm afraid. Having all that packing up to do is a great excuse for tiredness, but the truth is, I'm expecting a baby in August.' She suddenly realised she must be looking as distraught as her friend was. The last thing she needed was to cause people to wonder what serious matter the two were discussing. 'No!' Anna withdrew her hand. 'I didn't think the film would end the way it did either.'

Biddy cottoned on quickly. 'Yes, crazy, wasn't it?' She lowered her voice. 'Has, um, has your ma seen that film yet?'

'Not yet. I can't imagine her liking it anyway.' Anna also lowered her voice. 'I need to decide where I live, because I do have a choice and it's come from someone unexpected.'

'I shan't ask,' Biddy murmured. 'Will you keep working? Or would you need to move away if you chose this unexpected offer? I'd hate to lose you.'

'I wouldn't need to move away and I want to keep working as long as possible, for obvious reasons.' Anna pushed her knife and fork together. Biddy passed her a dish of rice pudding with a small dollop of red jam a bull's eye in the middle.

'I'd lie through my teeth, so I would,' Biddy said, lowering her voice. 'I'd invent a grand husband for myself and stay indoors all one weekend then come back to work on the Monday, showing off my wedding ring. I'd say my feller had a weekend pass so we got married, but he's on his way to France or wherever else you fancy sending him. Do it, Anna. You'll stop people gossiping and surely your mother can't say anything when eventually she's going to become a grandmother!'

'But Ruby knows all about Charlie and me.' Anna smiled as if thrilled about it. 'It's too complicated to explain properly, but he drove me home one Saturday and she didn't take long to twig what was going on. She's well aware Captain Milburn's engaged to another woman.'

'So, what if you have someone who's loyal and so fond of you that he'll let you use him as cover? I like the sound of that!'

Anna ate a spoonful of pudding. How could she sit here, bantering about a life-changing event while eating a dessert needing much more than a blob of jam to render it palatable? But she supposed she should be eating for two. And despite everything, she felt perfectly calm. 'I suppose we're back to Geoff now? Wouldn't that be a rotten trick to play? When he's the one I went out with in the first place, before I lost my wits along with you know what else!'

Biddy said nothing, but her face showed her sympathy.

And Anna, for all her remarks about not needing a man to look after her, suddenly and inexplicably longed for Geoff to walk into the room. He was so easy to be with, so kind, not only to her, but to others. The canteen ladies used to giggle over Charlie's extravagant compliments and saucy jokes, but it was Geoff who made their faces light up. Especially Maisie's. She reckoned he was the son she'd never been granted. All of a sudden, he and Italy seemed a lifetime away.

Anna returned to her desk to find a note awaiting her. It simply invited her to drop by the supervisor's office when convenient. Anna checked Colonel Gresham didn't need her at that moment and asked if she might visit Miss Napier. He seemed a little distraught but she knew better than to probe further. There would, of course, given it was wartime, always be something nagging at his thoughts. She promised him an extra cup of tea and won a wide smile before he returned to whatever he was writing and which would doubtless soon appear on her desk for typing.

She discovered Maud studying a handwritten list, but the supervisor looked up and beckoned when Anna knocked upon the office door.

'Take a seat, my dear. Thank you for coming to see me so promptly.'

'I think Colonel Gresham's about to give me one of his lengthy screeds to type up but luckily I've learnt to decipher his handwriting more quickly than I used to.'

'Indeed.' Maud placed both elbows on her desk and rested her chin on her interlocked fingers. 'Tell me, have you thought any more about my proposition? I don't want you to feel rushed, so if you need more time to think, that's perfectly in order. And I speak for Emily too, of course.'

Anna nodded. 'I still haven't told my mother anything. I know she'll be distressed, probably angry and disappointed, but I can cope with that because it's how I expect her to react.' She hesitated, fingers plucking at a pleat in her skirt. 'As it happens, a close friend has suggested a solution which I know Ruby will have trouble in accepting, but it would stop gossip and thanks to you and Emily, I won't have to contemplate living with the nuns, as I might have to do in different circumstances.'

Maud smiled. 'I shouldn't find the thought of you living with the nuns so amusing, but somehow I do. Here's another alternative. You could be posted somewhere miles away, and it would be explained that you've been promoted and sent to the War Office to work for the duration. Emily and I would help you financially and you'd return, of course, with everything over and done with, but I can see by your face how much that idea displeases you.'

Anna closed her eyes briefly. 'I very much appreciate

your generosity, but while I felt differently when I first suspected what was happening, I know now how much I want to keep my baby.'

'That's a brave decision and I'm proud of you.' Maud nodded her head so vigorously, she needed to re-anchor a hairpin. 'Will any financial support be forthcoming from the … um … father?'

'I believe so. I may not want to, but I'll accept his help, in case my mother decides to have nothing to do with me. It's so unfair, Miss Napier. Ruby was still single when she found out I was on the way, but she and my father married quickly and things worked out well for them. Yet I can't help feeling she'll have no sympathy for me, although she could have been left in the same position had my father returned to sea before they married.'

'Then surely, she should be sympathetic? I very much hope so, because a young woman needs her mother's support when she's in your position. Now, why not tell me about this plan your friend suggests and if I may, I'll tell you what I think.'

Anna explained quickly, saying, 'I think I prefer the idea of an unknown soldier rather than asking Lieutenant Chandler to come to my rescue. After all, why should he? There's a saying my father used to recite. It was something about tangled webs and deception.'

A slow smile spread across Maud Napier's face. '*Oh, what a tangled web we weave, when first we practise to deceive.* There's a lot of truth in that expression so I'll not comment further. You know where I am if you want me, but I think you've already decided it's time to confide in your mother.'

After Sunday dinner at Ruby and Frank's house, Anna and her mother washed up together. Frank was in the parlour, reading the paper, or, as Ruby whispered to her daughter, more likely catching a crafty forty winks. Anna hadn't missed an occasional appraising glance from her mother and was panicking slightly, uncertain whether to confess her plight or wait and see.

'It's good to hear work is still going well.' Ruby lifted the last piece of cutlery from the sink and pulled out the plug. Anna dried the last dessert spoon, held it up to inspect for smears and placed it in the tray.

'Always busy, but I enjoy it.'

'You're pregnant, aren't you?'

Anna froze. She put out a hand to steady herself at the kitchen table. 'How did you know?'

Ruby pulled out two chairs. 'Don't be silly. Shall we sit down while we talk?'

Anna hung up the tea towel while her mother took a seat and waited for Anna to join her.

Ruby placed both hands palm down on the table. 'I want to know what your plans are.'

Anna bit back tears. Her mother didn't sound angry, but might be working up to it. 'I was about to break the news. There's quite a lot to talk about, including where I live.'

Ruby reached for her daughter's hand and held on to it while she listened to Anna's account; very watered down, but nonetheless honest about the way she'd succumbed to Charles's advances.

'I knew that man spelled trouble, the moment I saw him. Is he going to do the right thing by you?'

'Mam, what you consider the right thing really wouldn't be, honestly it wouldn't. In any case, Charlie married his fiancée the weekend he left for Italy.'

Ruby's face looked drawn. Suddenly Anna could picture her mother in years to come. Contrite, she got up and put her arms around her, hugging her tight. 'I'm so sorry. I must have been blind, but I trusted him, and he let me down just as I've let you down.'

'Never mind that. He can't be allowed to get away with this. After all, he's ruined your life!'

Anna winced. 'He's offered financial support.'

'I should think so too. We'll need to ask Frank's advice. He and his solicitor will make sure your precious captain doesn't talk his way out of his responsibilities.' Ruby gently released herself from her daughter's arms and went across to a tall cupboard, taking out a bottle of brandy and three glasses. 'I think we need a little pick-me-up. Frank can have his once he surfaces.'

'I know I must be practical, but it seems so cold-blooded, talking about money like this.'

'You'll need all the support you can get, now and after the baby arrives. Captain Milburn must be made aware of his obligations. Oh, Anna, when are you going to move in with us?'

'Frank married you because he loves you and values your companionship. He won't want napkins and feeding bottles cluttering up the place. Maud Napier has offered me accommodation after she moves in with her old friend. If I move into her house, I shan't be far away and she'll be in and out. She's already said I can have all the visitors I want and I can stay there indefinitely.'

'She sounds a kindly soul. Especially as she's decided to move in with her old friend to give her companionship.'

Anna gazed out at the backyard. Snowdrops would be showing soon. She crossed her fingers beneath the table. She looked down at the Sunday best white cloth and prayed Maud would never know of the modifications Anna had made to the facts. In fact, neither of the two friends would find it easy to keep a straight face. Ruby had so far remained calm, but Anna wasn't sure her mother was ready to acknowledge Maud and Emily's proposed lifestyle.

'Does Miss Napier have a telephone installed?'

'Yes. She's a single woman with a good career – as Emily Ring is, of course.'

Ruby nodded and sipped her brandy. 'They've both been a great help to you. Maybe I could get to know them …'

Anna coughed as the fiery spirit hit the back of her throat. 'Um, I'm sure that'll happen one day. Remember, they both work full-time, Monday to Friday.'

'Excuse me for interrupting, but have you given any thought to your expenses? I presume you'd pay this lady to stay in her home, Anna?'

The sudden intervention startled both women. They turned to see Frank standing in the doorway.

'I didn't mean to sneak up on you, but the door was ajar and now I see you've put out a third brandy glass. I appreciate I'm butting in, but you're my family now, Anna, and I want to help. I apologise for eavesdropping. I tuned in when I heard you make that kind comment.'

Anna closed her eyes and swallowed hard.

Frank stood behind her and placed his hands on her shoulders, something he'd never done before. 'Let it out,' he said. 'Your mother and I are here to help. Unless you prefer me to go away again?'

'No, please stay,' Anna croaked, while her mother got up and came back with a man's handkerchief. Anna accepted it gratefully. 'It's just that I thought you'd both be so very angry and disappointed.'

'It's wartime, my dear. Strange things happen. People act out of character. As for your baby's father, do you have any idea where he might be at the moment?'

'Charles is stationed in an Italian port called Bari. It's in South East Italy.'

'Where they endured that devastating bomb attack? So many suffered and died from the mustard gas which was released. Yes, I know a little about the area. I imagine you must have contacted him?'

Anna gulped. 'Not directly. I wrote to a mutual friend, Geoff Chandler, who you met on your wedding day. He's billeted in the same hotel as Charlie and he's the one who broke the news.'

'And does Charlie intend to marry you eventually?'

'It seems he already has a wife, Frank.' Ruby pursed her lips.

'I'm afraid I always knew he was engaged, but I only know Charlie got married before leaving for Italy because Geoff told me.' Anna took another sip of brandy and out came another shuddering sigh.

'Would you have married this man, had he been single?'

Anna closed her eyes for moments. 'I used to think so, but I've come to realise what a disaster that would have been. Also, how stupid I've been not to take Geoff more seriously. I was flattered – blinded by Charles's attention – and I'll never forgive myself for that.'

'I take it you plan to keep your baby?'

Despite her confused feelings, Anna felt a surge of love. Her baby! She must do her level best to look after him or her.

'Yes, oh yes. I understand life won't be easy, but it isn't for most people, is it? I'll need to return to work eventually, as long as they'll have me back, of course.'

'I hardly think Miss Napier would wash her hands of you, from what you've told me.'

'I know, Mam, but Colonel Gresham might have something to say about employing a fallen woman.'

'When one of his own officers is to blame for my daughter's predicament? We'll soon see about that!' Ruby glowered. 'Fallen woman indeed!'

Frank chuckled. 'Spoken like a true daughter of Boadicea, my dear. But I fear we're getting ahead of ourselves. I need time to think things through. That is, as long as you'll allow me to offer assistance, Anna?'

'You're very kind,' she murmured. 'I know I haven't always been as welcoming towards you as I should.'

'Nonsense. Your mother and I would prefer you to live with us, but I understand your need for independence. Just be aware you'll always have a home here.'

CHAPTER 29

Geoff sighed while examining a pile of requisition slips, all bearing Charles's signature. Should he query certain items? No, Charlie must know what he was doing. His thoughts slid towards the subject most upon his mind as he wondered whether to send a telegram to Anna, saying he'd be in touch soon with an idea she might like to consider. He'd pushed away such thoughts on and off throughout his working day and now, with late afternoon draining the daylight, knew what he must do.

He couldn't resist a wry smile while accepting his feelings. He might well be shot down in flames, but he was prepared to risk that. He knew little about the workings of the female mind, though realised, if Anna decided to keep her baby, she would somehow achieve that, despite the obvious pitfalls. But if she agreed to marry him …? He'd do his utmost to make her happy. If only this confounded war could be over and done with so he wasn't stuck overseas!

He took his handwritten telegram message to the outer

office and left it with a clerk, telling him he'd appreciate its despatch as a matter of urgency. It would be good if Anna could receive it next morning, which was a Saturday. On his way back, he rapped on Charles's door. No response. He hadn't noticed him leaving so he knocked again and opened the door, glanced at the desk and decided its tidy state must be down to Hilda, who kept a tight rein on her charge, in working hours anyway. Shutting the door behind him, he headed for Mrs Barnes's hideaway.

'Hilda, any idea where Charles is?'

The secretary gazed at him over her spectacles. 'He said he was leaving early, to meet someone at the dockyard, Lieutenant.'

'Right.'

'Would you like to leave a message? Or will you catch him later?'

'Oh, no doubt our paths will cross this evening, thanks. By the way, have you heard how your mother's operation went?'

Her face softened. 'It's so like you to remember, Geoffrey. I had a telephone call from my sister earlier, letting me know Mother is comfortable and there's no reason she shouldn't be moved to a convalescent home soon.'

'I'm pleased to hear that. It must be worrying for you, being away from loved ones and unable to do a thing about it.'

Her gaze took in his expression. 'Indeed. Are you sure

I can't help you?'

'Positive, thanks.' Geoff was about to leave when a thought occurred to him. He turned towards Hilda again, his tone automatically becoming more formal. 'Did Captain Milburn have sight of that last signal that arrived or had he already gone out?'

She removed her spectacles and blinked at him. 'He'd left the office, but he'll be on the alert, surely? He said he was off to visit someone at the dockyard and I know he took his gas mask.'

Geoffrey grimaced. 'Did he say why he was going, Hilda?'

'You know his interest in the asbestos controversy? Apparently, one of the dockyard officials has studied the subject in depth and Charles has been in contact with him.'

'Then I doubt he'd take kindly to me going down there and chivvying him.'

'Bari's still recovering from that appalling bombing. Let's hope we can stay out of trouble for a while anyway.'

'I couldn't agree more.' He closed the office door. He'd hoped for a quiet chat to sound Charles out about one or two details before writing to Anna. But maybe it was too soon for that. No matter how keen he was to establish a plan, the lady herself might have other ideas. And he didn't fancy having to endure Charles pitying him.

Charles hurried along the quayside. The official he was to meet would be waiting on board the *Roma*, a vessel tied up towards the end of the line. Charles was well aware that more than one of his superior officers regarded him as a lightweight and he was determined to prove them wrong. Research into the asbestos argument had given him something to focus on, outside of his normal duties and he'd found a kindred spirit in the Italian.

On his way, he dodged around piles of equipment. Labourers were unloading and loading. Overseers shouting instructions. Charles understood only a few words here and there, but further on he could see a welder at work, a sudden surge of orange sparks fizzing against the mundane scene. Charles was almost level with the welder now and the man called a greeting as he paused to wipe his brow. Charles responded with a smile and walked on, wondering whether this Italian administrator would invite him to stay on board for dinner. But before he could walk any further, he stopped suddenly. Deafened by a roaring sound booming in his ears. Blinded by a bright flash of light. Suddenly his legs gave way beneath him. Charles hit the ground as darkness swallowed him.

It didn't take long for word of the horrific accident to reach Army HQ. Hilda burst through Geoff's door without knocking, as soon as she received a phone call, asking her to advise Captain Milburn of a serious incident involving the deaths of dockyard personnel and possibly visitors.

'This is just so awful, Geoff,' she said, wringing her hands.

'What's happened?' Hilda was normally so calm; Geoff pushed back his chair and rose.

'The CO's secretary rang. She wanted me to advise Captain Milburn of a serious incident down at the docks.'

Geoff guided her to a chair. 'Sit down, Hilda. You're white as a sheet.'

'There's been an explosion. It's thought that a gas bottle must have been left open and a welder working nearby somehow ignited it. A shed was blown to smithereens.' She swallowed. 'Several people have lost their lives. Oh, Geoff, what if Charles is amongst them?'

Geoffrey sat at his desk, staring at the wall, still trying to absorb the news. But even though he felt stunned, he needed to tackle a very sad task. The telegram informing Charles's next-of-kin of his death needed dealing with as a matter of urgency. Their commanding officer would write a letter of condolence to Charles's widow, of course, but Geoffrey knew he must also write. He'd never met Eleanor Milburn, but the poor woman would be devastated to lose her husband so soon after their marriage.

Was Eleanor aware of Charles's brush with death that evening he'd enjoyed himself at the Cardiff nightclub which was so tragically bombed? Geoff would say nothing. As for Anna – the news would break when she got to work next morning. Colonel Gresham would inform everyone. Geoffrey knew Anna would take this badly, though maybe it wouldn't tear her apart as much as it would have done, had Charles still been single.

Damn it! Silently, he rebuked himself for his cynicism. Anna would grieve, of course she would grieve. In effect, Charles Milburn left two widows as well as a forthcoming child who would never now meet his or her father. Eleanor would have no idea of this, as surely, she must be unaware of Anna's existence? Geoff wanted to shield her from any added anguish regarding her late husband's amorous adventures. Including the latest one, which Geoffrey suspected Charles had probably pigeon-holed as "rest and relaxation."

Charles had made his feelings plain regarding his wife's feelings, having told Geoff he saw no need for Eleanor to know about Anna's unborn child. But after the first acute pain of bereavement faded, would Anna have her own view on the matter? He told himself not to think too far ahead. Anna wasn't mercenary. But she was left in an odd position, given Charles, though having verbally agreed to provide financial assistance, wouldn't have had time to arrange the necessary formalities. There were months to go before the baby was due, but what if Anna's mother and stepfather decided Captain Milburn's forthcoming child deserved recognition when his executors dealt with Charles's estate?

There was a subdued atmosphere at dinner that night. Geoff, dining with Richard Curtis, realised the younger man's difficulty in dealing with the situation. Both men had downed a couple of gin and tonics prior to the meal.

'I remember hearing how he almost copped it in Cardiff

that time,' Richard said. 'It's as though the fates had it in for him. Damn, but I feel so guilty knocking back this delicious soup and bread when Charles … when he …'

'That's understandable. But we're still at war, Richard. This may sound harsh, but we don't have the luxury of sitting around mourning Charlie, or indeed any other brother officers. Think what it must be like for the bomber crews. Somehow they must learn to take each day at a time.'

'My pa, when he writes, which isn't often, always says we have to keep on keeping on buggering on.' Richard laid down his soup spoon.

'Your father is spot on. And Charlie would have said the same.'

'Captain Milburn told me he only got married the day before he sailed from Liverpool. That's so tragic. His poor wife, when she hears, well …'

'Mrs Milburn will probably gain some comfort from the fact that they did actually marry, so she bears his name.' He broke off as a young waiter removed their soup bowls while another headed towards them, bringing the main course.

'Good Lord! It's just occurred to me,' Richard leaned forward. 'I wonder if Charles's wife is expecting – you know – in the family way.'

Geoff hadn't considered that possibility, probably because he'd been so wrapped up in Anna's situation. 'Well, it's possible, of course. One of those mixed blessings that life sometimes brings.'

'If so, it's sadder still that he won't be around to meet his son or daughter. Happy in that Mrs Milburn would have something precious to remember her late husband by. What is this we are eating tonight, by the way? Whatever it is, it's scrumptious.'

Geoff couldn't help smiling at Tigger, as Charlie, the king of nicknames, had dubbed Richard. The young officer possessed that eagerness, that ability to bounce back like the AA Milne character. Richard didn't need a pep talk. Maybe it was Geoff himself who needed reassurance? He picked up his fork.

'My guess is it's chicken cacciatore or something similar. Better eat up. I have a feeling more than one of us will get drunk tonight. The CO will make a short speech in the bar after dinner. The ladies will be allowed in so they can listen too, and join in a toast to Charles.'

'I wonder whether Mary will hear what's happened although I will wite and tell her, of course. It's through him that she and I met, you know.'

'The dance. Yes, I remember Mary and her friend Sylvia being there.' *The dance to which he'd invited Anna to attend. Was that when Charles seriously began hankering after her? Hadn't Geoff found them outside, deep in conversation? He hadn't caught them in a clinch but he'd somehow felt he was intruding by interrupting their chat.*

'Tell me, Geoff.' (At this point, Geoff felt sure Charles

was at his elbow, slyly indicating Richard was wearing his Tigger face.) 'Is it fair to ask a girl to marry a chap when there's a war on and the chap can't go down on one knee and propose properly?'

'I take it you're referring to Mary and yourself?'

'I am indeed. I've thought about it on and off after you spoke to me and I don't know why, but now it seems like a very good idea. Getting engaged, I mean. Or, d'you think she'd tell me to get lost? What would you do in my place? I apologise if I'm being impertinent.'

Geoff swallowed a mouthful of savoury chicken. 'You already know my feelings on the matter, but I wouldn't raise the subject just now, Richard. Not when we're all in a state of shock.'

'Crikey, yes – I mean no – I'm an idiot. Best keep my powder dry. Thanks, Geoff.'

'But Richard, a little further down the line, if I were a betting man, I'd wager Mary would be delighted to receive your marriage proposal.'

CHAPTER 30

Colonel Gresham called Anna into his office and asked her to close the door behind her. She could tell by his face he had something of a serious nature to impart and she swallowed hard, wondering whether he'd found out about Charles's baby and felt obliged to ask her to resign her post. Before she could say anything, he rose and came round to her side of his desk.

'Do sit down, Anna. Now, I'm afraid I have very bad news, so please believe me when I say this is the worst thing I've ever had to do.'

That sounded ominous. She waited for him to sit down again; hands loosely clasped in her lap, already intent on shielding the secret she hoped to keep to herself a while longer.

'We received a signal during the night.' The colonel shook his head. 'It concerns Captain Milburn.' He hesitated. 'I'm afraid he has lost his life in a tragic accident.' He paused, watching his secretary's stricken expression. 'I'm so sorry. It appears he was at the dockyard on military business when an explosion occurred. There were several other fatalities and, it's cold comfort, I know, but Charles wouldn't have known anything about it.' The colonel looked down at his desk. 'Best not to know further details, Anna.'

He took out his handkerchief and blew his nose. Anna wondered whether he was shedding a tear or maybe preparing himself for her emotions to overcome her. But she felt nothing but numbness.

'I'm aware you, Charles and Geoffrey were good friends and no doubt Lieutenant Chandler will be in touch with you before long. I've discussed the matter with Miss Napier and she agrees, in view of this, and also because of your impeccable record with us, you should be given the rest of the day off.'

'That's very thoughtful of you and Miss Napier, Colonel, but truly, I think I'll be better off at work.'

He raised his bushy white eyebrows. 'At least go and get yourself something in the canteen while you think about it. You've had a shock, dear girl. I'll ring Miss Napier and ask if she'll join you. I'd prefer you to have someone with you.' He reached for his telephone.

Anna, allowing her emotions to rule her brain, rose from her chair, walked around to his side of the desk and planted a kiss on his cheek before leaving the office.

She glanced back before she left, only to see him dabbing his eyes with that pristine white handkerchief.

'I can't believe how I feel.' Anna stirred a sugar lump

into her tea.

'Numb? Saddened at the futility of it all?'

'I suppose so. But strangely, I also feel cheated, Maud. Things moved so fast towards the end. Yes, I should never have let myself be dazzled by him, but it happened and now I can't even write to him. Geoff Chandler made sure Charlie knew about my condition and that's how he found out about Charlie's marriage. Of course, I feel sad for his wife – I mean widow – but I also feel sad for the baby I'm carrying. A baby who'll never know his or her father.'

'Would you have married Captain Milburn, had that been possible?'

Anna's laugh sounded hollow. 'My mother asked the same question, before we heard about the accident, of course. Maud, you wouldn't believe how often I've wished I could have married Charles. That's so ridiculous, because I've never hankered after a white dress and veil, not like many girls do. The times I've declared I've no intention of becoming a stay-at-home wife. Yet here I am, telling you I feel cheated because I can't become Mrs Milburn and not have to worry about people gossiping.'

'That's understandable. You're also thinking about the child more than about yourself.'

'It's people's attitudes I worry about. What if I'm painted as the town's scarlet woman? It'll break my mother's heart and I daren't even imagine my grandmother's reaction!'

'Don't jump to conclusions. Give yourself time to accustom yourself to this situation. Whatever you or any of us may think about his morals, Charles was one of those larger-than-life characters who people either admire or despise.'

'My mother took an instant dislike to him. She saw Charlie as a philanderer.'

Maud nodded. 'A lady-killer. Perhaps she was right, yet, I had a very soft spot for him.' She smiled and shook her head. 'That time you came to tea at Emily's, I think I told you Charles sometimes flirted with me. He used to make me laugh and … well, he always reminded me of my late fiancé, though my Robert wasn't as flamboyant as our Captain Milburn.'

'I'm so sorry. Here I go, bringing back unhappy memories again.'

'Oh, but happy ones too, and I've learnt to live with both sorts, mainly thanks to Emily. So, thank you for thinking of me, but it's you who must take precedence at this time. Take the rest of today quietly. You may wish to remain at work but change your mind later.' She hesitated. 'Maybe your mother isn't the right person to talk to at this time. Is there anyone else? Your old schoolfriend maybe?'

Anna swallowed a sob. 'I wish Geoff was here! I miss him so much …'

It was almost as though someone else had blurted out the comment. But she meant every word of it.

Maud leaned closer. 'Then doesn't that tell you something, Anna?'

HQ Bari
21 January 1944

My Dear Anna,
This is to tell you how very sorry I am. Even though we know none of us can feel secure during wartime, a sudden death and the devastation wrought to human lives is always shocking and painful.

Charlie's burial took place this morning at a simple ceremony. I was asked to read a short poem which I was pleased to do. Still, I find myself feeling so very angry about his death and keep having to remind myself his number was up and that's something we all have to bear in mind these days. It doesn't help though, and it isn't easy to remain stoical, is it? He and I held directly opposite views about love and faithfulness, but as you know, we got on well as brother officers and friends.

I realise what happened between you and Charlie will come as a shock to his nearest and dearest and will prove very difficult for them to come to terms with. Therefore, I want to assure you that, if you wish, I will liaise on your behalf with whoever is managing his estate. I don't think I've ever told you that my father is a solicitor and I'd begun following in his footsteps when the war put paid to everyone's plans. And painful as it may be for Mrs Milburn, after a suitable time of mourning, I'm prepared to contact her and explain the situation. I've already sent her a brief letter of condolence, but didn't think it a suitable time to mention your situation.

Please let me know your address after you move to your new abode. I imagine that must be soon, and I hope your mother makes sure this letter reaches you, if it arrives after you move.

In the midst of your sadness, my love, please remember the hours I've spent in your company have been among the happiest of my life. I'm sure you don't wish to hear any more than that, but I pray that somehow you might one day find it in your heart to think favourably of me. If that day should ever come, I promise you will never know the pain of rejection. My love for you eclipses any other feeling I've experienced.

Fondest love,
Geoff

On the Saturday afternoon, one week after Anna moved to her new home, she washed up her lunch things and took Geoff's letter with her into the sitting room. Already she felt at ease with her surroundings. She adored the Art Deco style of furniture and appreciated the happy jumble of artefacts behind Maud's delightful decor. How could her friend bear to leave her home? But Anna knew the reason. And Maud was hardly moving any great distance. Anna looked forward to frequent visits, but still rejoiced in being independent whilst remaining an easy distance from Ruby and Frank and becoming closer to these two women who'd become so important to her.

Anna nibbled an oatmeal biscuit from a food parcel her mother and Frank had brought round that morning. Ruby was still fussing about her daughter's plans for the future – or the lack of them – but to Anna's relief, Frank was adept in reassuring her that Anna needed time to make decisions and there was no need to worry about finances with him standing by.

It was still hard to believe Charlie's life had been snuffed out. But she was coming to terms with her situation, despite uncertainty over facing the inevitable onslaught of gossip and criticism awaiting her once her condition became apparent. She picked up Geoff's letter to read a second time.

She wiped away a tear when she reached the last paragraph. In many ways, marrying him would provide the perfect solution. Yet, wouldn't it be unfair on him if she became his wife? Yet, knowing this already, he still seemed prepared to take a chance on her. Anna groaned aloud. It wasn't only Geoff and herself to think about. There was also her baby to consider. She might think it brave and in the spirit of the suffragettes to become an unmarried mother, but was it fair to allow the little one to be born out of wedlock when a loyal, lovely, man stood by, wanting to care for his little family?

And for how much longer could she keep wearing her office skirts and jackets and go to work? If she became a Missus before she reached that point, she'd probably be allowed to continue in her post a while longer. She'd gained a deal of experience since taking over from Miss Morgan and wanted to continue working as long as her superiors allowed.

So, should she follow Biddy's advice and turn up for work next Monday morning with a gold band on her ring finger? What would everyone think? Did she care? Should she care? Her thoughts buzzed like angry wasps. In her heart of hearts, she knew she'd be foolish to banish Geoff from her life. If he wanted to marry her, after the dance she'd led him, she should surely count herself a lucky woman? Yet, she had no idea when he'd be allowed leave and she certainly couldn't travel to Italy. Time wasn't on their side.

She reached for the phone. She needed someone to talk to. To her delight, both Emily and Maud walked round to see her, arriving only half an hour after Emily answered the call.

'We decided we could do with some fresh air,' Maud announced as Anna opened the door.

'That's good, but you should have just let yourselves in,' Anna scolded.

'That's not my style,' Maud said, nose in the air, while

pushing Emily ahead of her through the door. Emily exchanged grins with Anna.

'Anyway, thank you both for coming.' Anna closed the front door. 'It's time I made a decision about my future and before I speak to my mother, I'd appreciate knowing your thoughts.'

Geoffrey was finding it difficult to settle back into his former routine. He'd taken over Charles's office and thanked his lucky stars his late superior, although often deemed irresponsible in his personal life, had always ensured his second-in-command knew how to run the department in his absence. Geoff wouldn't let him down. The atmosphere amongst the staff, having been subdued for several days, was lifting, as though people realised Charles wouldn't have approved of so many long faces. Hilda, who Geoff had wrongly typecast as a brisk, no nonsense equivalent of English actress, Joyce Grenfell, was adept at making life easier for him. So much so, he decided to invite her out to dinner the following Saturday evening.

She was waiting in the foyer, clutching her gas mask and handbag as he arrived downstairs.

'I hope I haven't kept you waiting?'

'Not at all. I came down a couple of minutes early.' She fell into step with him and they headed through the front door.

'Not too chilly an evening but we need our overcoats.'

She chuckled. 'It's difficult, isn't it, Lieutenant? Leaving behind our office personas, I mean.'

'Ha! Yes, Hilda. And just to remind you, it's Geoff or Geoffrey if you prefer.'

'All right. I hope you like the restaurant I've booked.' She gestured to the next turning. '*Osteria Guilio* should be six doors down here on the left, according to the hotel housekeeper.'

'I'd have had no idea where to choose. Always best to ask a local, though.' Geoff felt relieved when they'd counted down the doors and arrived at their destination. At least, he presumed this was the right place, as blackout restrictions were being strictly observed.

Inside, they found a warm, candle-lit room, with several tables occupied and the walls adorned with vibrant paintings of local scenes. Geoff inhaled the tantalising aroma of garlic and herbs and speedily ordered a carafe of a local wine the proprietor recommended as a *vino delizioso*. He and Hilda settled on a platter of antipasto followed by a local fish delicacy and though Geoff decided the romantic atmosphere wasn't what he'd have chosen, none of the other diners appeared to take any notice of the British officer and his lady companion.

After his first glass of wine, Geoff decided to be honest with Hilda, who he knew was as likely to spread gossip as a non-Italian-speaking hermit. He didn't want to mention Charles's part in the ongoing saga of his feelings for Anna Christensen, but sensed Hilda, a mature woman who'd been widowed, might help him unravel his tangled emotions.

'Hilda, I must confess to another reason for inviting you to dinner, apart from wishing to thank you for all the help you give me.'

She raised her well-defined black brows and her lips twitched. 'And here was I thinking you couldn't get enough of my brilliant conversational powers.'

Her remark proved a great icebreaker. Geoff relaxed and discovered Hilda was an excellent listener. He talked his way through their starter then continued during the main course. Once or twice, she stopped him to question something, but she took what he was leading up to very calmly.

'You're asking if you're foolish in wanting to marry a woman who you feel doesn't love you? That's an interesting question, Geoffrey.' Hilda laid down her cutlery. 'I don't think I could eat another morsel. That was delicious.'

'We can finish our wine and it's still early enough to sample a gelato. I've been eyeing other people's, like a greedy schoolboy.'

Hilda sipped her wine then looked him in the eye. 'Why don't you tell me, which would be worse, Geoff? Marrying Anna in the hope that in time she comes to love you, or not marrying her, and never knowing whether she might have come to love you?'

CHAPTER 31

'So that's one option I've been mulling over. I realise this must be horrid for you to hear, Maud, but I really need to sort things out.' Anna patted her stomach. 'People will start noticing soon and life at the office will become difficult. I really am at my wits' end as to what I should do.'

'For a start, don't worry about me.' Maud spoke first. 'My mother found what she considered to be the perfect solution to my problem – well, for my parents anyway. And hindsight is a great thing. Remember, if your mother agrees to this plan you're considering, you'll need to move away, as I was forced to. You're quite right – we can hardly hide you here for the next six months.'

Emily looked from one to the other. 'It's perfectly plausible for a woman approaching her forties to find herself in the family way. Ruby would of course need to wear padding, but you'd all be living a lie. A lie for the rest of your lives. Is that really fair to your child? Or to any of you?'

Anna closed her eyes for moments. 'It would be a huge secret to keep and I can't help thinking about that old proverb we talked about in your office that time, Maud. I mean the one about tangled webs.'

Emily nodded. 'I know the one.'

'Unfortunately, our little lies have a habit of growing into bigger ones,' Maud said. 'But surely you and your mother are the only ones who can make such an important decision?'

'Don't forget Anna's stepfather,' Emily added.

'You're right. Frank might utterly hate the idea and then my mother would feel torn, wouldn't she? Oh, dear, why do I feel so weepy all the time?' She pulled a handkerchief from her pocket. 'I'm fine at the office. I can push the problem away there, thank goodness.'

'Why don't I make us all a cuppa?' Emily rose. 'But please talk about something else while I'm gone. I don't want to miss anything.'

Anna and Maud kept off the subject, as instructed. Anna, having permission to make use of Maud's book collection, had started reading a book by Nevil Shute.

'I'm enjoying *Pied Piper*,' she said. 'I didn't think it was the kind of story I'd like, but he has such an easy way of writing.'

'I enjoy his books too.' Maud inspected her fingernails. 'Anna, I know Emily wants us to keep off the subject, but are you absolutely certain you want to keep your baby?'

'Yes, why do you ask?'

'It's just that, if your mother did agree to go through with this sham pregnancy, you'd have to reconcile yourself to her being the child's mother. She'd be the one the child runs to first. You'd be his or her big sister. Are you prepared to handle that?' She watched Anna's face. 'I'm being cruel to be kind, but I want you to think very carefully.' She rose. 'Now I'll go and tell Emily what I've just said and with any luck, return with our tea.'

Left alone, Anna walked across to the window and stared out at the sea. She never tired of this view, even if it didn't rival the one from Emily's sitting room, but at that moment she didn't see an expanse of grey water. Didn't notice a couple of freighters, one heading towards harbour, the other ocean-bound. She imagined herself watching her own child, toddling towards her mother's open arms and not hers. In her head she heard, '*Mam! Look at me!*' In her mind's eye she saw her little girl or boy scrambling over rocks or walking, arms outstretched along the top of a wall. Tears rolled down Anna's cheeks and, in that moment, she knew her answer.

Maud opened the door so Emily could carry the tray inside. 'Here's the brew that cheers,' she called.

'Anna?' Maud frowned, hurrying towards the girl whose shoulders were heaving as she sobbed, hands clasped against her chin. She took her in her arms. 'My dear, I never meant to make you cry! Where's your handkerchief gone? Oh, dash it, Em, do you have a clean hanky?'

'Don't I always?' Emily placed the tray on the table and reached into her cardigan pocket. 'Here you are, my dear.'

'I'm so sorry.' Anna gulped and mopped her eyes.

'No, it's I who should be sorry for upsetting you.' Maud patted Anna's cheek.

Anna blew her nose and managed a shaky smile. 'It's all right. I'm grateful to you for making me understand what I really want. But I don't want Geoff to think all I want him for is to maintain my respectability and to be a father for my unborn baby. In many ways I think I could cope without a husband, despite the inevitable tittle-tattle.' She sighed. 'But I don't want to put my mother and Frank through all that. I hate the thought of them having to put up with gossip.'

'But you know what? I've gradually become to realise what true love means. I miss Geoff so much and as long as he still wants me, I shall be honoured to become his wife. Then people will gradually find out I'm engaged to be married and I don't care tuppence if they whisper about my expanding waistline, as long as Geoff comes home to me. I've been stupid – blinded by the wrong kind of feelings for the wrong man – I only hope Geoff doesn't turn me away after all. Because, who could blame him if he did?'

'Oh, thank goodness you've come to your senses!' Emily reached for her handkerchief.

Maud winked at her. 'And from what I know of that

young man I'd bet a year's wages against him giving up on Anna.'

Barry, 29 January 1944
My dearest Geoff,

Thank you for writing such a kind letter. I won't pretend I'm not sad about Charlie's death, but it's pointless brooding over things I can't control. Neither of us was in love with the other and I think I always knew that, even if I was stupid enough not to admit it.

Your offer to negotiate with Mrs Milburn's advisers is much appreciated. Thank you for your thoughtfulness. I feel sad for her, especially as she probably hoped for a child of her own one day. I can imagine you being an excellent solicitor and I know you'll represent me very well.

Unless I'm reading your words wrongly, I think you're asking me to consider a future together. Please forgive me if I'm being too presumptuous! I know you'll have thought seriously about taking on not only me, but another man's child. I'm putting it bluntly because I need to be absolutely certain this won't create problems. All I can say is, I've always loved you as a dear friend, but lately I've come to realise how foolish and how blinded I have been.

I don't deserve your love but I know now I can and do love you in return. You pay me a wonderful compliment when you say I'd never know what it was to be rejected by you. If I wasn't certain I could promise the same to you, this letter would be worded very differently.

If you and I become engaged, may I tell people? I am a little plumper than I was when you last saw me. If tongues wag, I'm prepared to tell them my fiancé is overseas and they can think what they like!

Keep safe, my darling Geoff. I can't think what I've done to deserve you in my life but I count myself a very lucky woman. If you still want me, I shall do my utmost to make you happy and to be a loving wife.

With all my love,
Anna xx

Geoffrey spotted the envelope on his desk the moment he walked in the door. He hung his cap and gas mask on the coat stand and picked up the letter Hilda must have placed on top of the official documents awaiting his attention. He swallowed hard as he recognised the writing. Was he about to find his destiny outlined in Anna's words?

Still standing, he slit open the envelope, using the ivory letter opener Charles must have used before him.

He cast his eye down the page to the part he knew would contain Anna's answer. He read the last paragraph and the salutation and sucked in his breath. *If he still wanted her!* Mouth dry, head spinning, Geoffrey Chandler pulled out his chair and sat down to read the letter through properly.

In his head he heard her voice. In his imagination he took her in his arms and kissed her soft lips, inhaling the drift of her perfume and hearing her chuckle before he kissed her once again.

Jumping up, he left his own office and knocked on his secretary's door. 'Could you come in, please, Hilda? No need for your notebook.'

Geoff waited while she rose and followed him. He closed his office door behind him. She was standing by his desk, her expression wary.

'I hope this isn't bad news, Lieutenant.'

'The exact opposite! She's said yes. Anna has agreed to become my wife.' He grabbed his bewildered secretary and lifted her off her feet, despite her protests, whirling her round before putting her down. 'This is all thanks to you. You made me address my feelings and I couldn't be more grateful.' He thrust the letter into her hands. 'Please read it and tell me I'm not dreaming.'

'Are you sure about this?'

'Affirmative.' He grinned at her and ran his hand through his hair.

She skimmed Anna's words quickly. 'She writes a

good letter. And she sounds delightful. Oh, dear!' Hilda reached inside her jacket and took out a handkerchief. 'It's like a scene from a Cary Grant film.' She cleared her throat and dabbed her eyes. 'Congratulations, Geoff. I do hope I'm not starting a cold …'

CHAPTER 32

Anna was taking dictation, seated opposite Colonel Gresham, when the telephone rang. He stopped in midflow and picked up the receiver. Anna was mentally writing her version of what the next part of his sentence would be, when she heard the CO say, 'Is he indeed? Well, my secretary's here with me so it's no wonder she's not answering her phone. Put him through, please Gwen.'

Anna smoothed her skirt and wished she didn't feel so hungry. Her thoughts went to Geoff and how long it would take before she'd hear back from him. The colonel was speaking again now. Whoever it was on the other end had obviously surprised her boss.

'Could you repeat that, my boy?'

What now? Anna prayed this call had nothing to do with the Italian situation.

She blinked as the CO offered her the receiver. 'He'd like a word.'

'Who would, sir?'

But the colonel rose and headed for the door, leaving

Anna extremely puzzled. 'Hello? Who's speaking please?'

'Your fiancé, I hope. Good morning, Anna. It's wonderful to hear your voice.'

She began to tremble. 'Geoff? Is it really you?'

'It is, my love. Is the old man listening?'

'N … no, he's disappeared.'

'Good. Now, Anna, I received your beautiful letter. I'm getting down on one knee here. Will you marry me, darling? Say you'll marry me and make me the happiest man on earth.'

'Yes! Oh, yes please, Geoff. I'll marry you whenever you like.'

'That would be today then, but I doubt we can manage that. I don't know whether you realise, but there is such a thing as a proxy marriage. Would you consider it? It means we can be legally joined in matrimony and if anything happened to me, then as the widow of a serving soldier, you wouldn't be left unprovided for.'

She swallowed hard, wanting to protest about the awfulness of this thought but flooded with love over how much he cared for her. 'I understand, but I'm not sure how a proxy wedding actually works.'

'Nor me, but Hilda, my secretary, will make all the arrangements as long as you let me know when and where you wish our marriage to take place. It's not how either of us would want it, but we can have a proper church ceremony once I get leave, or, when this pesky war ends. I want you to feel secure and I'll ask Hilda to sort out the best way for me to send you money to buy yourself an engagement ring and a wedding band.'

'If it's complicated, I'm sure Frank would lend us the money.'

'He's a grand chap but I'll do it my way if I can. I want to look after you, Anna. You and our baby, so you take good care of yourself. I'd better go now, as I'm tying up a military telephone line and probably the old man's lining up a firing squad as I speak. I'll write soon, Anna. I love you very much.'

She managed to tell him she loved him too and was replacing the receiver when the CO put his head round the door. 'Safe to come in?'

Anna turned to face him, tears streaming down her cheeks. She was trying to say, 'Geoff has asked me to marry him,' but a hiccup turning into a sob, somehow garbled her words.

Colonel Gresham hastened to the phone and lifted the receiver. 'Miss Napier, please, Gwen. At the double!'

Anna took a deep, shuddering breath as moments later she heard the CO say, 'Maud? Come to my office as fast as possible, please.'

He put the phone down and gave her a worried look. 'Miss Napier's on her way. I thought it best to ask her to sit with you for a while as you seem so upset.' He hesitated. 'Unless I misheard, it would appear Chandler has proposed. Is that what's making you cry? He's really not so bad a chap you know!'

Anna sat in her office with her supervisor, drinking a glass of water.

'Colonel Gresham frightened the daylights out of me,' Maud said. 'I truly thought something awful had happened. But this is such lovely news. I'm so pleased for you, and I always felt your heart would help you decide what you should do. If you want my advice, I'd tell all the girls in the typing pool about your engagement. You can say you're expecting a baby and that I've agreed you may continue working for a couple more months, during which time you and Lieutenant Chandler will be getting married by proxy. It's wartime! They'll sympathise and be happy for you, I know they will.'

'Thank you. It'll be a relief not to have to keep worrying about my silhouette. But I'll leave my announcement until tomorrow, if you don't mind. I need to tell my mother and Frank first. And it's a while since I visited my grandmother. To be honest, I've been dreading seeing her because she's always prided herself on knowing when someone's expecting a baby, almost before they know themselves. At least now, I can tell her I'm getting married.'

Maud looked at her watch. 'Well, if you're feeling calmer, I'd better return to my desk.' She hesitated. 'If you'd like the rest of the morning off, I can send Biddy in to deal with the colonel's letters.'

Anna shook her head. 'No thanks, I'd rather carry on as normal. I feel such a sense of relief now and that's very comforting.'

'He'll make you a fine husband, Anna.'

'I know. I hope I can be as good a wife.'

'I see no reason why not. After all, you make an excellent secretary.'

Anna felt herself blushing. 'I'm not sure the roles are that similar. But I'll do my level best.'

There was someone else Anna wanted to speak to ahead of the other staff. She knew Biddy had kept her secret as promised and would be thrilled to hear the joyous news, especially ahead of everyone else.

Anna caught up with her friend as she was nearing the canteen entrance. 'Hello! I got away on time for once.'

'Something's happened, hasn't it? You look different somehow.'

Anna clutched Biddy's arm. 'You don't miss much, do you? I'll explain all once we're sitting down.'

'You better had! I'll try and contain my impatience till then. Looks like cottage pie today – plenty of thatch and precious little cottage.'

'They do their best. And I'm ravenous.'

'You always are these days!'

Anna chuckled. 'I only hope I don't put on too much weight.'

'Not in wartime, you won't.'

They were served with hot meals and each collected a piece of jam tart with a dollop of cold custard. Their favourite table was already occupied, so they found another one at the far end of the room. Anna waited until they were settled before making her announcement.

Biddy gasped. 'But that's grand! What a super bloke he is. You must have done a lot of thinking before you wrote that letter though?'

'I'd had enough of sleepless nights. And after Geoff wrote such a beautiful, loving letter to me, I realised all I was doing was torturing him as well as myself.' She put a forkful of cottage pie – commonly known as hopeful pie – into her mouth.

'I'm so pleased for you. I know you'd never have accepted his proposal unless you felt you could return his feelings.'

'It would have been a terrible thing to do to him.' Anna dug her fork into the mashed potato topping. 'I realise now how stupid I was to insist marriage wasn't for me. Hopefully that youthful dimwit Anna has grown up at last. And you're right, of course, Biddy. I truly do love Geoff.'

'Will you keep your engagement a secret?'

'Gosh, no, I want people to find out before they start wondering and whispering. They're a nice crowd, but my condition would make a tasty bit of gossip for the girls. Miss Napier suggests I come down to the typing pool at two o'clock tomorrow to announce my engagement.'

'I'm glad she's been so kind. Do you remember how she frightened the daylights out of us in the beginning?'

'Only too well. For a start we were both convinced we'd failed the interview. I was so pleased when you turned up that first day.'

'Same here.' Biddy chased a chunk of swede round her plate. 'And you've done a grand job, taking over from Miss Morgan.'

'But not so well by fraternising with one officer too many.'

Biddy crossed herself. 'God rest his soul. He was such a charmer. Can I ask you something?'

'As Miss Napier would say, "You can, Biddy. The question is, may you?"'

Biddy pulled a face and leaned closer. 'Will you tell Charles's widow about the baby?'

'I'd decided to, because my mother and Frank thought I should, as did Geoff. But now I'm going to marry Geoff – by proxy – and he's describing the baby as his, I shan't do anything until we've had a chance to talk it through together.'

'A wedding by proxy? That's such a good idea. I haven't told my folks yet, but Eddie has written, suggesting we do the very same.'

'You're getting married too? And you look pretty pleased about it.'

'I am. But I've no idea how the proxy thing works.'

'Geoff's secretary is going to help us but I have to decide the date and where I want to be married. He thinks we should have a church wedding when he eventually gets home. Meantime, Biddy, would you be my maid of honour?'

'But what about Margaret? Shouldn't you ask her first?'

'With all that's been happening, I forgot to tell you she joined QAIMNS. I think that's right.'

'Queen Alexandra's ...'

'Imperial Military Nursing Service,' Anna continued. 'Margaret's in Kent now. She'll understand the need for urgency and she knows you're a good friend to me.'

'Be sure to give her my love when you write, and tell her I'll do my best not to let the side down.'

Anna reached for her pudding just as Biddy leaned forward again. 'Don't look round, but that dark-haired girl who I used to think had her eye on Geoff is heading for our table.'

'You mean Muriel Evans? She got engaged to someone in the RAF, didn't she?'

Biddy nodded. 'Last I heard.'

Anna looked up as the young woman arrived. 'Hello, Muriel. Would you like to join us?'

'I'd love to, thanks.' She parked her tray and smiled at Biddy. 'I'm so sorry, I can't remember your name.'

'I'm Bridget, commonly known as Biddy. I know I'm terribly nosy but looking at your rings, I'm thinking you're no longer engaged, but married?'

'Biddy would make an excellent detective,' Anna chipped in.

Muriel sat down. 'Well, she's right. I'm Muriel Carter now. My husband managed to get leave and we were married at All Saints' church earlier this month. We probably had one of the shortest honeymoons on record. Benjamin's stationed at Aldershot.' She delved inside her handbag and pulled out a leather wallet. 'Taken on our wedding day.' She unfolded the wallet to display two photographs.

'My, but he's a handsome fellow,' Biddy said. 'As for you, Mrs Carter, don't you look a picture!'

Anna looked at the beautiful brunette bride, smiling up at her handsome groom. 'What lovely photographs. You look so happy. And are these your parents in the second photo?'

'Yes. Ben's mother and father live in Washington so I've yet to meet them. His dad was born in Trinidad and his mum's Irish. Quite a combination?'

Biddy chuckled. 'Your husband's handsome enough to be in the movies. I wonder whereabouts in Ireland your mother-in-law's originally from?'

'All I know is she crossed to America with her parents when she was a tiny child. I'll ask him when I write next. He did tell me, but it's a village with an unpronounceable name.' She put her wallet away. 'I mustn't keep you, but I wondered if you had any news of Geoffrey Chandler, Anna? He was so kind to me at a time when I was fearful about telling my parents I'd fallen in love with a man of mixed race.'

'That's understandable,' Anna said quickly. 'And it's so typical of Geoff. He's always helping people. I'm in touch with him so I'll pass on your good news, if you like.'

'Please do, and wish him well, if you would.' Her smile was wistful. 'Geoff told me he was very much in love with someone unobtainable. Then he told me not to let other people's opinions influence my judgement. Benjamin's a doctor and he's several years older than me. But Geoffrey said if two people are determined to make a go of life together, that's all that matters. Loving each other so much that it hurts is the important thing.'

Anna had a huge lump in her throat and couldn't trust herself to speak.

But Biddy helped her out. 'Geoffrey Chandler will make someone a grand husband one of these days.'

'I hope things work out for him,' Muriel said.

'Anna, we'd better get moving.' Biddy began stacking crockery on her tray.

'We certainly must.' Anna followed suit.

The two girls got up, ready to prepare themselves for the afternoon session, but Anna didn't immediately pick up her tray. 'Muriel, it's been lovely to talk to you. Can I trust you with a secret?' She heard Biddy suck in her breath.

'Of course. I kept Benjamin a secret for long enough.'

'It's not common knowledge yet, but it will be soon. Geoff and I are engaged to be married.'

'My goodness, so you're the one he meant?'

'Yes!' Biddy interrupted, eyes sparkling. 'Anna's the

eejit who almost let the feller go, but fortunately she
came to her senses in time.'

'Well, thank you, Biddy!' But all three of them were
laughing.

CHAPTER 33

'For goodness' sake, will you hold still while I fix this curl in place?'

'Sorry, Biddy.' Anna sighed.

Biddy stood back, surveying her handiwork. 'There, you may look in the mirror now.'

Anna wore a pale blue crepe empire line dress with a matching bolero jacket. She also wore, to her delight, a pair of silk stockings and T-bar low-heeled grey suede shoes. A tiny pillbox hat and a whisper of veil completed her outfit.

Biddy handed her a spray of grape hyacinths and primroses. 'Ah now and don't you look the bees' knees! If only he could see you.'

'Is it obvious I'm … you know?' Anna inspected herself in the mirror. She was marrying from Ruby and Frank's house and she and Biddy were using the guest bedroom.

'Not at all. And you'll be married before you know it. That's the important part.'

'Geoff will be getting ready too, I expect. He told me

Richard Curtis was standing up for him.' She turned to face her friend. 'Oh, Biddy, how I wish he could be here with me.'

'Well, of course you do and he'll be feeling the same. Is there any more news about him getting leave?'

'In his last letter he didn't hold out much hope. But all the arrangements are in place at the local registry for him to become my husband.'

'Maybe you could have a celebration service if he's granted leave. You could still wear your pretty blue outfit. You're hardly showing, Anna. Waste not, want not!'

'I know Geoff would like that, but we'll have to see. What time is it?'

'Not quite time to go yet. Don't forget to visit the lav before we leave.'

'I'll leave it until the last minute.'

Biddy checked her watch. 'It's a miracle your ma hasn't been in here, chivvying us.'

'Two minds think alike. Gosh, I feel nervous. I wonder if Geoff is too. It's going to seem so strange, standing beside my stepfather at the altar. Did I tell you Geoff's secretary is standing in for me? Hilda sounds like a lovely woman – another one widowed young in the Great War, I'm afraid.'

As the girls were making their way downstairs, Anna's mother appeared in the hall.

'You both look beautiful,' Ruby said. 'I daren't give you each a kiss!'

'No Mam, not when you're wearing crimson lipstick.' But Anna could have sworn her mother was shedding tears.

Ruby's eyes were suspiciously bright and she clutched a lace-trimmed handkerchief while Frank stood by, holding her free hand. The pair weren't usually demonstrative among other people, but this was rather an unusual day.

At the other end of the town, Maud Napier was regaling her house guest with World War One stories, though she too had her eye on the clock.

'How long did you say it will take us to walk to the church, Maud?'

'No more than five minutes. If we set off slowly now, we'll still arrive in plenty of time. We're fortunate it's such a beautiful day.'

Geoff Chandler rose as Maud got to her feet. 'You look very smart, if I may say so.'

'You too, Lieutenant.'

'I'm very nervous. I hope Anna doesn't faint with shock when she sees me.'

Maud chuckled. 'Not if I know that fiancée of yours.'

He picked up his cap. Things had moved so fast in the last twenty-four hours. His secretary, the possessor of more contacts than a marriage broker, had discovered a military aircraft due to fly to the air base near Barry, the day before the ceremony. It would return the day after the wedding and Geoff had no inkling of the flight's purpose but was relieved those in authority were agreeable for him to hitch a ride both ways. A telephone call to Frank and Ruby ensured he could spend the night at Maud Napier's house, as Anna would be staying with her mother and stepfather the night before her proxy marriage.

More than a few curious gazes were directed at the middle-aged lady in her smart plum-coloured two piece and the handsome Army Officer walking beside her. On reaching the turning for the church, Maud insisted he wait while she checked the coast was clear. 'I doubt Mr Mapstone will have arrived so early, but you never know.'

Geoff did as he was told and, before long, he and Maud were inside. Greeting them, the vicar shook Geoff's hand vigorously, telling him how delighted he was to be officiating the marriage with both bride and groom in the same place.

To Geoff's surprise, a tiny, bespectacled woman dressed in pale grey, her right leg in a calliper, took her seat at the organ. Before opening up her music, she gave him such a beautiful smile, he felt as though she was blessing him. The woman began to play an exquisite piece he didn't know but which he found relaxing. It was a special moment which he knew he'd always remember.

He took a seat in the front pew and sat, head bent, hands clasped, expressing his gratitude at being alive and well and ready to be joined in holy matrimony to the woman he loved. Soon, he heard footsteps and subdued voices as people entered the church. He didn't turn around. If he had, he still wouldn't have recognised

Anna's grandparents or Emily Ring, though he would have exchanged smiles with Mrs Benjamin Cooper, formerly Muriel Evans, sitting next to his favourite canteen lady, who'd been thrilled to bits when Anna insisted Geoffrey, although marrying in Italy, would be delighted to hear Maisie had been present.

A low buzz of surprise uncoiled as people realised who sat in the front pew. Anna's mother and stepfather arrived next. Frank saw Ruby was seated across the aisle before joining the bridegroom.

'Good morning, Frank. Do you have the ring?'

'I knew I'd forget something!'

Geoff froze, but Frank chuckled and reached into his pocket. 'Never fear – all's well.' He opened the box and Geoff saw the slim gold band. 'Anna wanted both your initials engraved. I think the jeweller did a grand job.'

'He has.' The groom watched Frank put the box back in his pocket as the door at the back of the church was thrust open and Geoff got first sight of his bride.

It was as though electricity flared between the two. Anna, on the arm of her uncle, met her bridegroom's gaze, the joy on her face sending shivers down his spine. He smiled back, needing to force himself not to breach etiquette by racing up the aisle to take her in his arms. Frank nudged him and Geoff moved into the aisle, ready to stand beside his bride.

'Am I dreaming?' she asked him, handing a smiling Biddy her posy.

'If you are, I am too,' he replied.

The vicar welcomed the congregation. Geoff felt as though his heart might burst with love as he sneaked glances at Anna in her stylish blue outfit. Each of them made their responses so clearly and joyfully, more than one woman among the "dearly beloved" reached for her handkerchief. And after the groom kissed his bride, with the register signed, the bridal couple walked down the aisle while the organist was still playing *Romance*, a piece by Johan Svendsen, a Norwegian composer, as a tribute to the bride's late father.

Lunch had been booked at a hotel a few miles away and the whole party drove off in the sunshine, the bridal couple in the back seat of Frank's car.

Ruby turned round to speak to them once they were on their way. 'Anna, you took that surprise very well. I think Geoffrey and I were both worried you might faint with the shock of seeing him.'

Geoff squeezed his wife's left hand. 'Did you have any idea what was going to happen?'

'None at all. I still can't believe you're here but I'm very, very happy.'

He lifted her hand to kiss her wedding ring. 'That makes two of us.'

After the celebration lunch, Frank drove the happy couple back to Maud's house and arranged the time he should pick up Geoffrey next morning to catch his flight back from the airfield to Bari. Maud of course had returned to Emily's and once she was alone with her husband, Anna walked into his arms.

'Is it too early for bed?' Geoff whispered after their first long kiss.

'Of course not.' She took his hand.

Once upstairs, Anna found Ruby had placed a gossamer-thin cream satin nightdress on the pillow. Goodness knows how she'd found the coupons for that! Anna drew the curtains and undressed quickly before putting on her new night attire which slid over her shoulders and glided down her body. The groom was using the spare bedroom as his dressing room and he came to her, wearing a dressing gown. She giggled as he closed the door behind him.

'What's so funny?' He pulled her into his arms and nuzzled the side of her neck.

Anna snuggled against him. 'I was wondering whether Maud borrowed that robe from Frank, or if there's something she hasn't told us!'

He kissed the tip of her nose. 'I shan't waste time wondering.' He held Anna at arm's length and gazed at her. 'Are you certain about this, my darling? Is it safe for you?' He gently caressed her tummy.

She stroked his head, running her fingers through his hair. 'I'm certain. Love me, Geoff. I want to remember this day for the rest of my life.'

Much later, they curled up on the settee beneath a blanket, drinking tea, nibbling cheese and crackers. They went upstairs again as daylight became twilight, lying in one another's arms and talking of the future.

'No ghosts, I hope?' Geoff stroked Anna's hair which she wore loose now.

'Definitely no ghosts.'

'I love you more than I can tell you, Mrs Chandler.'

'And I love you so much, I think I might swoon, as you and my mother anticipated.'

'Don't you dare! I haven't quite finished with you yet.'

Anna stroked his cheek. 'Nor I with you, Lieutenant Chandler. And once you come home to me for good, I shall never, ever, let you go again.'

The End